Cotton

Cotton

CHRISTOPHER WILSON

HARCOURT, INC.
Orlando   Austin   New York
San Diego   Toronto   London

www.HarcourtBooks.com

Library of Congress Cataloging-in-Publication Data
Wilson, Christopher P.
Cotton/Christopher Wilson.—1st ed.
p. cm.
ISBN 0-15-101123-0
1. Racially mixed people—Fiction. 2. Vietnamese Conflict, 1961–1975—Fiction.
3. African American families—Fiction. 4. Victims of violent crimes—Fiction.
5. Civil rights movement—Fiction. 6. Icelandic Americans—Fiction. 7. Interracial
dating—Fiction. 8. Saint Louis (Mo.)—Fiction. 9. Spiritualism—Fiction.
10. Transsexuals—Fiction. 11. Mississippi—Fiction. I. Title.
PR6073.I4395B35 2005
823'.914—dc22 2004023117

Text set in Fournier MT
Designed by Cathy Riggs

Printed in the United States of America

First edition
A C E G I K J H F D B

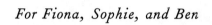

For Fiona, Sophie, and Ben

1

Eureka, Mississippi

When I finally slither out mewling, I've already given Mama hard labor, because she's been cussing and screaming seventeen hours. Then there's a calm until she sees me. Then she starts howling worse. And even though I come by the customary channel, and she feels me struggling out for sure, and we're tied by an umbilical, still she swears I'm not her child and she's not my mother, and what in God's name is going to become of us? On account of my crazy, scary looks, because I just don't present to the eye like a black baby should.

Word spreads round the homestead. Folks gather in huddles, whispering about the strange deliverance. Some say fetch the doctor, and some say the veterinarian's cheaper, but in the end my uncle Nat rouses the Reverend Eugene Spinks for some theology because this baby ain't so much a medical issue as a rude package of life delivered in error to the wrong address, an ugly curse or strange blessing—a secret code written in skin. Besides, doctor is white and charges travel and labor, while the reverend is black and free and always comes willing and wordy whether he's needed or not, with

Christ's answer for anything. After he inspects me all round, top and tail, and lets me suck on his finger, Reverend Spinks confers with my mama. He keeps his questions brisk, blunt, and worldly. He leaves no mattress unturned, he asks plenty personal, and he doesn't spare her modesty. Then he hears enough and he turns on his heels.

"Healthy, normal boy," he booms, bounding down the sprung porch steps beaming. "Eight pounds odd. Sound specimen. Praise the Lord."

"How about his looks?" folks ask.

"Happens. As we sow, so shall we reap"—the Reverend smiles—"and Salmon begat Booz of Rachab; and Booz begat Obed of Ruth; and Obed begat Jesse. This child comes to answer some purpose. Almighty always got his reasons."

"What's this child come to show us?"

"Can't speak for the Lord exactly," concedes the Reverend Spinks. "But never forget He's got himself an Almighty sense of humor."

Eureka, Mississippi, where I got raised, is God's Own Place to grow cotton and stubborn, hardy trees. Clement Creek cradles the tallest cedars in the state. The nearby town of Briar prides itself as the pine capital of the South.

The folk are knotty and resinous too. They sink deep roots. They can handle heat, dust, and drought. Needles fare better than leaves.

Nowadays there's a Eureka community website. The History page says *Eureka has no available history*. The Community Information page announces *The community has no information to share*. The Links page has no links. The Contact Us page gives a box number in Hannibal, Missouri. The Welcome link leads nowhere.

That's Eureka folk. They keep things buttoned up, close to their chests. They can handle progress if it doesn't change things. They welcome any strangers who belong. If you come asking questions, they'll tell as much as they need you to know.

Highway 28 crosses the tracks. To the north are Clement Street and Front Street. They started to build Franklin Boulevard, but it ran out of tarmac and self-belief after thirty yards. To the south is South Clement Street and Back Street. They got most things most people need—a grocery store, three churches (black Baptist, white Baptist, and never-mind-your-color-pass-the-snakes), two diners, a gas station, a sheriff. And if you find yourself in need of a newspaper, tractor tire, haircut, high school, or hospital, you can drive to nearby Briar in less than twenty minutes.

You can see the heat shimmer off the tarmac, hear the rattle of teal, the whining blades at the sawmill, and a bad-transmission Studebaker pickup. You can smell pine resin, sawdust, and hog pens. But the blue sky and cotton horizon look hazy-clear.

Of course they got plenty history—far more than they care to remember or use. Most of it centers round cattle, cotton, and cars. We had some levitations too. Maybe we lie on some fault line of gravity, because we got problems keeping things tidy on the horizon, splitting the ground from the sky. Things sometimes fall upward, and things come down that got no business being up to start. You'll likely think it sounds fanciful. Take it or leave it. You got to experience it firsthand.

But it's the small personal events that stick in the mind. Like the time Lou Carey shoots his Chevy Apache 427 CU automatic outside the Magnolia Diner, once through each headlight, twice through the radiator, and three times through the windshield, and then leaves the corpse to rust and rot by the curbside as a public warning to bad-attitude trucks, which sounds a mean and cranky thing to do, but Eureka folk always got sound reasons, and that's the trouble with history, serving it up cold and stale on the plate, when it needs to be savored fresh and hot.

One month in '57, farmers found their cows gutted or headless in the morning. There'd been buzzing sounds and neon flashes in the night sky. They were awful dazzling lights, of color folks never seen before. Some blamed aliens and some blamed the military. And it was God's own task to recover the loss from the Yankee insurers, who sent down an Italian investigator with an attaché case, homburg hat, horn-rimmed glasses, and a stammer to try get to the bottom of it. But something spooked him into leaving early, after only seven twitchy hours.

There was Elliot Holly, a black kid out of Detroit, who came to stay with kin in Eureka in the summer of '59, but got his neck broke for making repeated personal suggestions to a white girl serving in the grocery store, not knowing the difference between city and small-town manners, black and white.

And it's hard to look at any of the telephone poles down Highway 28 without wondering who's dangled there, besides that boozed-up kid out of Vicksburg who got tossed out of his V-8 Mustang convertible (cherry red, auto, discs, and power hood with pony trim) onto the telephone wires when he drove himself straight into the post of the EUREKA WELCOMES CAREFUL DRIVERS sign at eighty miles an hour.

They got themselves famous sons too—Red McKee, who played tight end for the Dolphins, season '61 through to '63, and Larry Whitters, who played session music in Nashville, backing Patsy Cline, Hank Williams, and sundry other immortals from the Hall of Fame.

And they never forget their famous daughter, Angelina Clement, who just happened to be a close, personal childhood friend of mine.

2

Family and Stuff

I don't come unannounced. I get myself born November 18, 1950, right before it rains bullfrogs on the thirty-acre field and just after Jimmy Cooder's Charolais bull finds itself dangling from a tree, bellowing, rolling its startled chocolate eyes, hanging limp in a cedar, cradled by two branches under its belly, forty feet above the ground, and the *Meridian Star* sends out their headline reporter to see for himself, and a radio crew comes all the way from Jackson and syndicates the footage abroad, far as Houston to Memphis, and even today no one knows how the beef got there, because bulls never show no natural enthusiasm or aptitude for tree climbing, and the veterinarian says it's the most unnatural bull-brained act he'd witnessed in Jones County, and he'd been practicing thirty-seven-odd years, and some folks say it was some left-handed hex that maybe ricocheted off some human target onto farm stock, or that some supernatural hand had lifted the beast into the tree and left him dangling there as a warning, because although God was surely almighty and all knowing, he sometimes speaks round corners, devious obscure, and the bull was sure spooked and ran scared, so he never get to do the natural act with a cow thereafter and had himself ground up for hamburger meat, because he just become a skittish ornament, no other use to beast or man.

They had me baptized Leifur Nils Kristjansson Saint Marie du Cotton, to speak my roots, for my genes were knitted from rainbow yarns. But the Mississippi mouth drawls its way round foreign curlicues, so my name gets rubbed smooth to the stub of plain Lee Cotton, which avoids drawing focus and saves on needless explanation.

I grow up rural with flies, Delta loam, forebodings, a shovel for my callused hands, the scent of wild azaleas and the stench of pigpens, corn bread, chitlins, and stern love.

The Mount Zion Baptist Church burdens me with more sins than I could recall the proper names for, or tell apart the separate guilts. And Mama daily amends Moses with fresh commandments all her own.

Folks forever been telling me I'm odd-looking. But the way I saw it, I wasn't strange, just misplaced. Different Mama, different home, I'd seem natural as Johnson weed, dashed hopes, and broken crockery.

What marked me out in life was real potent, yet pure superficial. It was the happenstance of getting born passable white-looking—with buttermilk skin, azure blue eyes, and straw-blond hair—to a black mother. It's all in the genes. It comes of my racial mix. You got to think *double recessive*.

My mother's mother was Celeste Anastasia Saint Marie du Cotton. She got herself born in Ville Platte, Louisiana, and there was some foreground Cajun and some background Sioux in her pedigree. She called herself mulatto. Those days, people called themselves all sorts of off-white names—quadroon, octoroon, quinteroon—we don't

use now because they confuse race with arithmetic or brag about
being pale.

I only knew her in her faded years—mole blind, twisted up to
a question mark, knotted by arthritis, bony as a starved goat, with
wispy silver hair and a face crackled like alligator skin. But I seen
from photos she was one scary-eyed beauty in her prime when she
worked as a mambo in Baton Rouge. In the pictures, she's never
smiling at the photographer but staring over his left shoulder at
something becharming behind, or through his forehead at something within. Some, she's smoking a cigarette through a holder. Hers
is a spooky gaze—makes you blink, blush, and look away. It's told
she had a rare clairvoyance and a sturdy hindsight—but not a tad
of common foresight.

Daylight hours, she spends the best part of her time tending her
shrines, mixing her herbs, and chatting to whatever dead folk pass
her way. After dusk, she gets entered by spirits and possessed by
gods. So she can hardly call her body or time her own and finds
herself spiked on her spirituality—twitchy, vague, and unworldly.
Though plenty men and money pass through her warm, careless
grasp, she never bothers to attach herself to either because they just
short distractions, to be brief enjoyed and spent quick. Easy come,
easy go.

Celeste has two daughters. The older—Alvenia—dies of a
brain fever before her first birthday. But her younger daughter—
Corinne Arminta—the way it turns out, is fixing to become my
mama, when my time's ready.

Mama comes of Celeste's familiarity with a southern gentleman
author of fictions, known to those who work libraries or read literature. He is some name—though Celeste never discloses it—and
maybe still gets *spoken of* and *written about*. He consults Celeste to
inquire of the spirits of his Dixie forebears. Taking a shine to her,
he overstays his hour's consultation. They draw the blinds and he
books himself in for an extra week.

But his hand ain't available to my grandmother, nor his name to my mother, on account of propriety and prior commitments—which include a wife, sundry children, and some solid reputations.

You got to suppose a woman who communes with gods, and comfit their favorite potions, and gets knocked up by well-known writers knows enough to get an abortion. You got to suppose, then, she elects to go full term and birth her child.

The photos show two happy arrivals. Mother and child ride round in the only six-cylinder, four-door Mercedes sedan in Baton Rouge. Perhaps the father confers some settlement, or else Grandma celebrates her confinement with a long winning streak at the gaming tables.

Album shows the car and daughter gone within a year. Mama gets sent to Eureka, to live with Celeste's half brother, Nat Claiborne, his wife, Hannah, and four children. Don't know about the car, but Celeste moves on to New Orleans.

Thereafter, she sends money monthly. And she comes herself, laden with parcels, bundles, and cases, every year, for the full month of August, so she can spend time with the child and make sure she knows her own mother. She brings clothes for all climates, and toys for all ages, and foods for most every taste but ours.

Then every August the back parlor gets cleared for Celeste's bedroom, and the Claibornes enjoy an early Thanksgiving and Christmas. Things get brought to Eureka that've never been before—including absinthe, ice skates, Chinese wind-dried duck, mah-jongg set, leather-bound works of Baudelaire, quart bottles of cologne (which Uncle Nat mistakes for fancy liquor), lacquered Japanese fans, violin strings, riding crops, Polish sausage, eggplant pickles, ballet shoes, score of *La Traviata*, funny baccy (which Aunt Hannah mistakes for dried marjoram), metronome, seven-string banjo with tortoiseshell inlay, jasmine tea, writing paper with watermarks and Claiborne family crest (which never existed before Celeste commissioned it), microscope, ball python, candied cherries, tins of wild boar pâté, cocktail shaker, anchovy-stuffed olives. And every time she brings hair oil for her brother. And every year she finds he's still bald.

Pity this. A piglet or a bag of seed corn would bring more benefit and save a squander of money. Everyone knows Celeste's spending silly to buy us pleasure. Only some things are best enjoyed in New Orleans—where they've got ice rinks, ballet, cocktails, and orchestra music and foreign languages. It's all a bit rich and Frenchified for Eureka taste. Most in the house prefer pork belly to Chinese duck. And you look just plain overdressed with a rhinestone tiara on your head and silk scarf round your neck when you've got knee holes in your overalls. In addition, there's little enough space in the house already, without we got to open an ethnographic museum. But that's just ungrateful slant.

When she passes sixteen, Mama starts spending the summers with Celeste in New Orleans. She keeps house, learns city ways, takes piano lessons.

After the second summer she skulks back to Eureka looking shamefaced in a black taffeta dress, with a guitar over her shoulder, city dreams in her head, a bloom to her sulky cheeks, and with a copper washer on her wedding finger.

New Orleans is a melting pot. All sorts from all nations pass through. There's enough drinking, freethinking, and easy living to make a country girl giddy. This maybe explains how Mama comes to get herself knocked up and let down by an Icelandic seaman, who's my daddy—Leifur Nils Kristjansson—who I only know through one water-stained, frayed-edge photo. He looks six feet six and two hundred fifty pounds with flax straw hair and an expression that mixes timidity, confusion, and guilty satisfaction. When I hold that photo, I feel him landlocked now. I see him limping along, close by horses and cattle.

It's a five-day romance. They meet on a Tuesday when he docks. Come Saturday, he sails off on his boat. All he leaves is human seed corn. Maybe I got half brothers and sisters spattered all along the Atlantic coast.

A deal gets done. Nat builds a three-room shack as a separate home for Mama and me. He has placed us downhill beyond the duck pond, in sight but out of hearance. Celeste repays by buying him a new green-and-yellow John Deere tractor.

Poor Mama gets to bask a single season in the sun. Then she contracts me. And I ain't just any bawling, messy, contrary, cussed boy. I come with complications.

"Where's my daddy?" I ask.

"He's gone to Reykjavík, Lee."

"That up North, Ma?"

"Another country, Lee. Far north, across the seas."

"How long's he been gone?"

"Seven years, son."

"Guess he got held up."

"Suppose so." She nods regretful.

"Maybe he'll write soon. Say what's keeping him."

"Maybe," says Mama. But you can tell from her voice she isn't imminent expectant.

Suitors come calling on Mama, then quickly melt away. Maybe a high-strung, sulky homegirl with a strong gospel habit and a freaky white kid comes across real tart for most tastes, without the lick of honey. And I guess from some remarks I overhear, Mama never unbuttons quiet and easy. Not a second time. She always comes over particular fastidious about doors, locks, curtains, underclothes, and privacy.

Take Jesus hisself, unzip that banana

"You're a black soul in a white wrapper," she tells me, "but not everyone knows that, because they go by your skin. When you ride the bus, Leaf, you got to keep out of trouble. You got to remember one thing . . ."

"Mama?"

"Black folk go in the back. White folk go up front."

"So I go in the back?"

"Depends . . ." She sucks through her ivory teeth and considers. "You don't want to cause no incident. You don't want to show no disrespect. Anyone knows you knows you're black. But strangers . . . they're going to think you're white. So you don't want to crowd no nice black strangers by sitting down with them. And you don't want to get uppity with no white folks that know you by taking their seats. And, then again, you don't want to offend no black neighbors by sitting apart. But you don't want no white strangers to think you're some ignorant redneck trash by sitting at the back. You understand me, son?"

"Sure, Mama. And what if there's all sorts?"

"Better stand halfway and shuffle a bit." She bites her lip. "And if people start making remarks . . ."

"Yes, Mama?"

"Best get off and walk."

I don't say Mama is plain shamed of me, but when we're in Eureka or Briar, she makes me walk ahead and calls me "Master Lee," like she's just minding me for my white mama.

Lord what a messy, painful thing a child is. You hew them out of your own flesh. They chew your tits off. Then they just hurt you till they leave you

All this comes of the time she gets herself arrested in F. W. Woolworth's for slapping a white child. Police just won't believe she's my mother and entitled to belt the very shit out of me.

"Come here now, Master Lee," she says, "if you please."

"Yes, missy," I say. I learn to obey, because every stroke I escape in public incurs interest and gets charged compound once we reach home.

Anyway, some news of me spreads down a long, tangled grapevine because two plump, pink, sweaty bald men in gray suits, called Molloy and Schwarz, drive down from Tupelo in a green Chevy to proposition Mama. They invite her to call them Al and Benny.

"Yes, sirs," she agrees.

They explain they make cosmetics for black people so they can look more like whites while still staying most parts black. They unpack their tubes and bottles, potions and pastes on the dining table. They explain they sell beauty, freedom, and choice in attractive wrappings and at affordable prices, with reasonable-interest credit for the deserving poor.

There's Liten Up, which makes you pale as a china plate. And there's Straiten Up, which uncurls your hair. Then there's Hi Tone for colored folk that feel the need to turn their black curls ginger.

All the while, they're swatting the air—like we're keeping more than our share of flies—and the damp circles under their arms keep on spreading, and they're giving off this smell of disdain, cologne, and sweaty mules.

"It gets you the vote? It gets you a white job?" asks Mama.

"No," Molloy concedes. "Just makes you look paler."

"Who'd want to look like a spook?" Mama asks. "Like some albino freak?"

They shrug weary.

"Why've you come telling me this?" Mama says. "I ain't buying none."

"Point is, we hear about your boy," says Molloy.

"Might use him as a *model*," says Schwarz. "We need a true picture of how the Negro looks when he's near-enough bleached up."

"Lee," she calls me in from the porch. "Come here, nigger boy. Gentlemen want to meet you, son."

"Hey, that's a white *white* boy," says Schwarz, squinting at me unfriendly, like I'm trying to swindle him with my skin.

"We were looking for a white *black* boy," says Molloy, like we're the dumb ones. "Or even a brownish white boy. We aren't prejudiced."

"You could black him up a tad," says Mama. "How much you paying?"

"We're not paying for no white white boy," says Molloy. "We can buy them for nickels and dimes."

"You could crinkle his hair," offers Mama, "and generally nig-gerfy him some. Don't you make no product for white folk that want to look like blacks? You could use it on him."

"No, we don't," concedes Molloy. He doesn't look directly. You could tell his mind wasn't full on the job.

silky tits like peach skin

"There isn't the demand," Schwarz explains. "Not enough white folk want to black up."

"Got to go," says Molloy, packing his potions back into a leather carryall. "Got another call to make."

warm, wet honey split

"That Gina Mae, suh?" I ask, pleasant enough. It just comes to me. I don't mean no offense. I'm only making small talk. Sometimes things just come to mind. I can taste a shivery, moist pleasure.

"Mind your mouth," hisses Mama.

"Gina Mae?" Molloy asks. "What you know about any Gina Mae?"

It's the first time I've turned a pink man scarlet. I sense some change in the weather indoors. Like when it darkens before thunder. The air's so thick you can chew it. Everyone's staring at me, waiting for an answer.

"Nice, friendly white lady. She works tables. In a diner."

"What else?"

"She's got a husband, Wayne. He's a mechanic with a Lincoln and a temper."

Well, I got a clear picture in mind. And it sure wasn't there till Mr. Molloy comes along. But I'm real young and I been brought up strict Baptist with curtains, so I don't swear I understand it all.

The way I reckon it, Gina Mae's got herself stuck in a sticky position. She's kind of squatting over Mr. Molloy, who's got his trousers slid down to his knees. Her blouse has come unbuttoned, and her panties are tangled round a twitchy ankle. Both parties are jigging and jerking, to and fro, like they can't decide to stick or twist, pull apart or stay together. They got strained, suffering expressions. It's like some crazed puppeteer is twitching their strings.

"She got freckled titties?" I ask. "Orange nipples. And a ginger fuzz below her belly?"

"Stop," hisses Mama. "Don't talk dirty."

"You're one scary, spooky kid," says Molloy, slack-mouthed.

"Ain't my fault," I say, "what you come thinking, out loud, in our kitchen . . ."

"That true?" demands Mama. "You been *thinking* the things my son's been saying? You been putting those ideas in his head?"

Molloy shrugs.

crazy kid and dumb fly-blown pussy in a hovel. Her stubble nipples staring at me

"I got to ask you to leave," says Mama, "if you please. We're church people, and my son here picks up on things. He gets easy troubled by ugly thoughts."

3

Les Voix

Well, it's hard to separate the strata of my childhood mind and recollect when I come upon things, and in what order, but there are early signs I ain't growing plumb straight because, for starters, I got a sympathetic way with animals, to the extent of attracting squirrels chattering around my Moses basket, gathering dogs around my stroller, and drawing bats that, despite their natural shyness with folk, take to hanging in quivery black velvet clusters from the beam above my cot, which my uncle Nat accounts to animal wisdom, saying how I must give off some sound or scent undetectable to humans, yet delectable to beasts.

Then I got this way of hearing voices and using unnatural long adult words for a child newly taken to talk—like *honeyfuggle, carburetor, quotidian, notwithstanding, collateral*—and turns of phrase, like *no sweat, babe,* or *mutatis mutandis,* or *no skin off my ass,* or *no shit, Sherlock,* or *I'm toasted, man, don't bogart the joint,* or *this bird never flew on one wing,* gaining a quick fluency in profanity, which discomfits a mother who aims to raise her child by the Gospels and keep his ears innocent of vulgar street talk.

"Where'd you learn to speak like that?" Mama hisses.

"Voices, I guess. *But, hey, lady, get off my case.*"

She holds her ice palm to my forehead, like she's testing me for fever.

"Ain't natural, Lee, to hear voices."

I shrug. It ain't like nature gave me a choice.

"Who's been speaking to you, Lee?"

"Yellow Danny," I say, "and Lynched Dobie."

She winces. "Yellow Danny?"

"He drowned hisself. He spends a long time on the bottom of the Mississippi, with the catfish. He's well and truly pissed off with life. They nibble his . . ."

"I don't want to hear no more of that talk." She slaps me hard. "And I don't want you talking about your voices to anyone. You want people to think you're stir-crazy?"

"No, Mama."

It ain't encouraging, getting a slapping when you report the honest evidence of your God-given senses. So I never get to confide to her about Michigan Mike, Juicy Lucy, Nat the Greek, Spooky Sam, Cyrus Chance, Sweet Ellen, or Bobby Dazzler, or the way they keep me awake nights, reminiscing, advising, lamenting, crying, cursing, singing, shouting, and talking dirty.

And why's it always me gets to sleep on the wet spot?

Come time for my schooling, Mama and I get the runaround. Reverend Spinks has to take us to an attorney at law in Briar who charges twelve dollars fifty cents up front, to scratch his jowls, make two phone calls, browse a couple of mildewed leather-spined books, before he finds the time to peer at us blankly over the rims of his smeared bulge-lensed glasses.

Something about his hangdog face tells you he lives untidy,

dusty with bottles for company, wears mottled underwear, and doesn't clean the parrot's cage so often.

Praise the Lord, another paternity? Crazy pastor can't keep his dick dry

"My son," says Mama, "he's got a skin condition. He's got a problem with his color, which makes a trouble with his schooling. Black school says he can't be black with white skin. White school says he can't be white with a black mother. Truth is, no one wants to take him. Boy needs educating."

"What color do you want him, ma'am?" asks the attorney.

"Black like me," says Mama. "Naturally."

"Everybody can see the boy is black," says the Reverend Spinks. "Black mother, black family, black church, black soul, black neighborhood. Everything black about him except his color."

Could have been something. This isn't law. It's chicken plucking.

"The law hears you. She comprehends." The attorney nods tired. "Cases like this, you got the One-Drop Rule. Legislators of the state of Mississippi entitle and require anyone with a drop of colored blood to call and consider themselves completely so, and claim all consequent rights and benefits, without prejudice . . ."

"Without prejudice, sir?"

"Forget the prejudice. It doesn't mean Dixie. Principle is, if you're only one-sixty-fourth part colored, Mississippi law will award you the other sixty-three parts for free. In fact, they insist upon it."

"Ask, and the Lord delivers," says the Reverend Spinks. "Can you put it on paper?"

So this lawyer gets two morning drinkers off the street to

shuffle in and witness two copies of an affidavit of Authentication of Identity. One copy is for me to carry in my back pocket, next to my colored skin; the other's for Mama to keep safe at home, in an ebony frame on the parlor wall.

"Come back tomorrow, I could authenticate him white," the attorney offers. "But I'd need another payment, separate evidence, and different witnesses. I can't issue contrary documents on the very same day. Conflict of interest and ethics."

"Thanks, sir," says Mama, "but I reckon that'd only confuse the issue. Boy needs one true color, not two."

"Come on, black boy"—the Reverend Spinks ruffles my straw hair—"let's go get you a soda and schooling."

First day, Miss Shelley, the class teacher at Barrymore Elementary, does her best to disappear me, trying to shuffle me into the pack unnoticed by some sleight-of-mouth conjuring trick. She starts off talking about exceptions to the rule, and things aren't always how they seem, and the whale is a mammal, not a fish, and the tomato is a fruit, not a vegetable, and that Jesus Christ started off a Jew before John turned him into a Baptist. And while I catch her meandering drift and guess where it's leading us, I hear this barrage of shrieks and yikes from the kids, staring hard, never twitching their lips.

Hi, pinktoes

Who that spook?

Who invite that rabbit in?

See you in the yard, honky

Miss Shelley explains how black people come in a range of colors like Lena Horne and Dorothy Lamour, that we are all a brotherhood and sisterhood, we people of color, and we all bleed red the same, and we're all God's children, even blonds.

Then some smart-ass ask if Marilyn Monroe is black too, and how about Grace Kelly? And Jo Moses asks how she knows I bleed red, and shouldn't we check to make sure? And Bo Field says he doesn't care about my color, he just minds my dicky grin.

Now, for a solitary farm kid, used to the open air and the slow vegetable society of beans and greens, a classroom full of kids is a heady hit. The smell doesn't bother me because I worked close with hogs. The noise is no worse than hail on a tin roof. The hostile stares I can take, because I got used to those on the streets of Briar, as a white child walking beside my black mama.

What gets me is the traffic of thirty wriggly minds crammed tight, like maggots in a bait box. You got goofing off. You got blasphemy. You got lewdness. You got inattention. You got teeth-grinding stupidity. You got pettiness. You got sly meanness. You got hot prickles of hate, gut-gnawing aches of despair, shocks of worry like static, tickles of expectation, licks of pleasure, lashes of shame, starbursts of joy. One kid's itchy from ringworm. Another's jerky with nits. The girl in front needs to cough it up. The guy behind needs to scratch it. Someone's trying to keep it in; another's letting it out. One has got arithmetic in mind. Another's doing numbers. We got a Batman, Davy Crockett, Ben-Hur, Elvis, Chuck Berry, Roger Maris, Floyd Patterson, Dorothy Dandridge, Bob Hayes, all strutting their different stuff. We got bubble gum, soda, the dinner bell, and indifference to look forward to. We got a fight, spinach, bed-wetting, exposure, a drunken daddy to fear. And it doesn't help your concentration to know that Miss Clarice Shelley, though she doesn't admit it or say it out loud, has more than half a mind on the afternoon she spent in a motel near Jackson with some Bobby D. Devlin refrigerator-salesman guy. On top of that, you got some lesson or other, with writing, remembering, arithmetic, or understanding. And you're expected to pay attention.

I find it helps if I take deep breaths, pinch myself, bite my lip, avoid any eyeballing, and claim a seat at the back of the class.

I don't claim I'm the most popular kid at Barrymore. First week, some kids save themselves a walk, using my locker as a restroom. I get called some routine off-color names. Some days I get swatted like a wasp at a picnic. Often I get overlooked when they're picking teams. They choose Josh Cayhill, who has a metal leg, or Melvyn Phelps, who's blind, ahead of me, though neither are so good as me at catch, sprinting, or shooting baskets. Come recess, I sit out in the sun to develop my tan. I read on my own, or I sit by Crazy Martha. She may smell rank in the heat, but she's got a soothing way and a positive mind-set.

Sun is luvla hot on my shulders and green grass is one luvla culla in my eyes. Wee is luvla warm, tricklin' down my legs

But long term, being a general oddball isn't all downside, which is how this poor, black, southern farm boy got to go so many un-likely places and mix with all sorts—hog farmers, electricians, as-sassins, the damned, congressmen, running backs, loose ends, angels, spies and spooks, journalists, charlatans, gamblers, country singers, time travelers, dead souls, poets, card counters, bounty hunters, psychic investigators.

What I learned is never to judge anyone by the sound of their job, size of their reputation, the color of their money, cut of their cloth, or scent of their skin. Because I met call girls I would trust with my eternal soul, ministers of religion who steal white sticks from the blind, politicians you couldn't trust to tell you the time, ac-countants who can't add, sadists with stethoscopes, professors who know jack-shit, writers who can't spell, and saints who don't give a damn except about their pension plan.

———

When Grandma Celeste arrives each summer for her visitation, I get to take special care of her and she gives special care to me. I'm her only grandchild. I got spiritual leanings. And now the cataracts gone scuffed her sight, she leans on my arm to hobble around.

She arrives early afternoon in a chauffeured white Lincoln sedan, stacked with leather cases, hatboxes, crates of liquor, and wicker hampers for her snakes. They answer to the names Audo-wido and Danh-Gbwe, and feed on the mixed vermins she keeps live in a smaller separate hamper called the mouse box.

We know better than to lay our coarse farm hands on any shiny waxed city limo. We wait for the chauffeur to open her door. Then wafts of blue smoke drift out, which comes of two hundred sealed miles of heavy smoking. Celeste sits there, bolstered by pillows on the leather upholstery, still as a lizard basking on a rock, her rheumy blue eyes gazing blankly out.

It's like we've startled something solitary by lifting its stone.

Then Uncle Nat and Mama reach for a hand each and draw her from the dark cavern of the car.

She's sixty-something, going on eighty. Spiritual possession, liquor, tobacco smoking, and sniffing powders have taken their toll, rasped her voice, sucked out her flesh, and taxed her skin.

"Where's my boy?"

"Here, Grandma." I take the dry leather of her chicken-bone arm, and we shuffle to the swing chair on the porch.

I don't know why, but she's real taken to me. She likes me like a pig likes corn.

"Don't let your grandma go teach you no nonsense," Mama says when she finds us in a quiet huddle, murmuring together.

"Tell him what?" Celeste rolls her dull blind eyes.

"About spirits or nothing."

"Only one Almighty, honey. The world knows that."

"I don't want no *vevers* sprinkled on my floor, I don't want no snakes in beds, *gris-gris* on my kitchen table, or chicken feet in my parlor," says Mama.

"You still attending that sorry-sinner, down-on-your-knees, know-your-place slave church, honey?"

"That's right," says Mama. "Praise the Lord. And Lee too."

But the way Celeste explains things, when she gets me alone, they're only a hog's whisker apart—Voudou and Baptism—when it comes to *Le Mystère*, because they both got guardian saints, sacrifice, good and evil, life and afterlife, a supreme being and his deputies.

The differences are slight, Celeste explains, and matters of style of worship, finding the proper place for chickens, and turning the other cheek, or not.

For instance, Voudou practices blood sacrifice while Baptists barely talk about it. Voudou welcomes goats to the service while Baptism doesn't feel the call. Some churches you dress up to worship, others you maybe undress or dress down. It just depends where you stand on skin and spirituality.

The Baptists got tambourines. Voudou got a *batterie* of drums. Baptists got an altar. Voudou has *poteau-mitan*. Baptists got hymns; Voudou has chanting and dance.

"That church tell you about the human soul, *cher?*"

"Yes, Grandma."

"How many souls they allow you, exactly?"

"Just the one."

"Huh." She nods. "I think they're trying to simplify things for you, child. Plain, grown-up truth is everyone's got two souls. *Gros bon ange* and *ti bon ange*. Big soul and little soul. Little soul leaves your body when you sleep, or when the spirits ride your head."

"Yes?"

"Make sure nobody tries to make off with your little soul, Lee."

"Sure will."

"Soul-stealers round every corner."

"Understood, Grandma."

"That preacher you go to, does he talk tongues?"

"No, Grandma."

"Pass snakes?"

"No."

"Raise the dead?"

"Only Jesus."

"Sorry, mean-spirited church your mama take you, *cher*." Celeste blows cigarette smoke and peers into the drifting blue haze. "Must be quiet as the grave . . . Have they explained you about your *Tet Met*?"

"What?"

"*Maître de la Tête*. Guardian angel."

"Don't know, Grandma."

"You telling me you ten years old and you ain't been introduced to your very own guardian angel yet?"

"No, Grandma."

"That's terrible, child . . . I'll make inquiries. I'll see if I can get your angel come visit you personal."

"Thanks, Grandma. Appreciate that."

She lays her cold cracked fingers on my cheeks and feels the bones of my face.

"Your mother writes me. She says you're hearing voices."

"I hear some. Not every day. On and off. They come and go."

"I hear the *Les Voix* too." She advises, "It ain't a sickness; it's a curse of a gift. It's in the blood. But it skipped a generation with your mama. She's deaf to it. She only hears car horns, sirens, and the rumbles of her belly. What do you hear? *Les Défunts?* Dead souls?"

"Living folk, mostly, I guess. Thoughts and feelings. Sometimes pictures. And I pick up songs and jingles too."

"You got to listen out for *Les Morts*," she confides. "Often, they're quieter. Often, they're softer spoken. So, you be sure to listen out, Lee. You got to work at it."

"Do my best."

Then Celeste gives me this long be-nice-to-others speech. Not about neighbors, but about the dead. And she explains there's always someone worse off than yourself, particularly dead folk. And that they get lonely too, and they got feelings just like anyone else. But it's hard to get anyone to take notice or listen out for them. Which is why they take to disturbing folks at night, moving things around the house, hiding keys, turning on the stove or dousing the fire, singing out when you least expect it, walking through walls, spooking livestock, turning the radio on and off, breaking crockery, and all that sort of lonely-soul, look-at-me-I'm-dead, ain't-I-spooky, now-you-see-me-now-you-don't attention-seeking kind of stuff. Truth is, if you spend enough time in eternity, on your sorry lonesome, with everyone blanking you when you're trying to get heard, to sort out some unfinished business or other, you're going to turn cranky and spiteful. And by the same token, the dead can be uncommonly friendly and helpful if you bother to listen out for them and spare them the time of day. But there are some that are just plain nasty. So you steer clear of them.

"Sure, Grandma."

"You hear him?" She crinkles her eyes and cocks a bristly ear. "He's often about."

"Don't hear nothing."

Celeste closes her eyes and starts rocking. Then she starts singing; her voice is sunk gravelly deep. It's like some scrawny chicken started growling like a junkyard dog. And I swear I can hear some nifty steel-string banjo accompaniment. Strange. Grandma Celeste sounds more than a tad like Johnny Cash.

I rode with old Jeb Stuart
and his band of southern horse . . .

. . . I catched the roomatism
a-campin' in the snow

but I killed a chance of Yankees
and I'd like to kill some mo'

An ugly grin has gripped Celeste's face. Strong tune. I know it from somewhere. It sounds like a solemn hymn—except for the hate, death threats, and cussing.

. . . and I don't want no pardon
for what I was and am
and I won't be reconstructed
and I do not give a damn.

"You never heard him before?" Celeste pants.

"Heard the melody," I say, "not the words."

"He limps about." She nods to herself. "Confederate cavalry. Lost a leg in '63. Long time dying of gangrene. Can't find rest."

"Why?"

"Got a grudge against history. Mean-spirited bastard, no friend of us Africans."

Then something knocks softly beneath the floorboards. And Celeste stamps back twice.

"Don't bother 'bout him," she whispers. "He can blow out candles. He can rattle the windows. He can spook the dog. But he can't harm us. Dead Dixie bastard can go to hell."

I guess I'm impressed. The room's gone awful chill of a sudden.

"All the same," Celeste considers, "best keep out of his way,

Lee. Don't go inviting him in . . . And best not tell your mother about our little conversation."

"No, Grandma."

"She doesn't hear *Les Voix* herself. She wouldn't understand. And, Lee . . ."

"Grandma."

"You been made special. You got a gift. Let's make sure you use it good."

Celeste's half brother, Nat Claiborne, is a kindly, decent, civil, sour-faced, barrel-chested bear of a man, with hands the size of shovels, resembling a grizzled Sonny Liston.

Saturday night you keep your distance, while he drinks two pints of rye in solemn solitude on the porch. Only Saturday. Always Saturday. Only two bottles. Always two bottles. Rules are rules. Self-denial stops you straying.

The first pint makes him chuckle and mutter to himself. While the second provokes him to attack small, hard soulless objects. He gives stones a hard kicking, slaughters tin cans with the kindling ax, splinters Coke bottles on his knees, and then crushes the splinters of glass to dust with a hammer. It's his awkward private pleasure. He's shy about it and hates anyone watching on.

Sundays, he's red-eyed, abject, and shivery in church. The rest of the week he's sober and civil. But Thursday onward, you sense the pressure building up, from his grunts and teeth grinding.

He bought his fifty acres, of old Indian reservation, through the FHA in the forties. He keeps hogs and chickens, raises soybeans and cotton and truck patches of vegetables.

He has me feed the hogs morning and afternoon, dig and weed, mend fencing. Any time I cut a corner or hash a task, he crinkles his brow and shakes his bewildered head.

"That your best shot, Lee?"

"I could try again."

"Do that. The way you've done it hurts my head."

He's slow, sure, and relentless. And everything is personal. He strokes and speaks to everything he grows. So when a piglet gets scours or the kale gets weevils, it's sickness in the family.

Upshot is, the greens do their very best for him, cotton answers his coaxing, peas swell proud in their shells, hogs grunt him a greeting, roosters perch on his shoulder, and ducks take to following him round faithful.

We got white neighbors south and east. Uncle Nat visits regular, soliciting their advice respectful, admiring their flaccid yellow greens, stringy beans, lean stock, and asking their recommendations for breeds, varieties, and cures.

"Hog goo and turpentine, you say? Grateful, sir. Never thought of that. Brought you a pan of chimney-smoked rabbit. Been two days hanging there in hickory smoke. So soft you can eat the bones."

This is Nat's apology. For having fifty acres where they got forty-five, for plowing with a tractor while they still use mules, for farming more fertile soil, growing heavier crops, and raising fatter stock.

He never forgets a smart-ass black man can provoke resentments. Give a man smoked rabbit with okra and he might think twice before firing your barn, poisoning your water.

"Nice pigs, Mr. Tyler, sir," says Uncle Nat, "dainty walkers. That turpentine sure works wonders."

'Scuse me, Mister Tyler, suh, while I tug my fat black tongue out of your tight white asshole . . . Ain't nobody thought to tell you your soy needs more nitrogen and your hogs got hoof rot?

"He knows jack-shit about cropping. Why you gone asking his advice?" I ask as we tramp away. "They sure don't like us."

"Just paying my taxes, Lee. Just paying my dues."

"Why didn't you tell him his pigs were sickening?"

"Can't be done, Lee. And it ain't my place."

"No?"

"His hogs done told him already. But he don't listen."

"It's sure going to cost him," I say.

"Ain't pleasant to see God's creatures suffer." Uncle Nat wipes the bubbles of sweat from his brow with his frayed cuff. "Troubles hang together. They say his wife's got mange. And his soybean's ailing, and his dog's fixing to leave him. And the only remedies he got are turpentine, sulfur, and jimsonweed."

In the Mount Zion Baptist Church, the congregation's swelling. Preachers visiting from Jackson, Birmingham, Albany, Tuscaloosa, talking about civil rights, Weidemann's lunch counter, segregated buses, colored folks enrolling at Ole Miss and registering for voting. Freedom riders come down from Montgomery to Jackson and get flung into jail. In McComb, a black voting office gets opened.

But when ten Negro men go to register to vote locally, sheriff comes out of the office, carrying a shotgun, and asks, "Who's first?" It goes heart-sounding quiet.

After a minute, a brave man shuffles forward. "I'm first. Hartman Turnbow." Then they all go in and fill out their applications.

"Sorry, folks," says the registration officer. "You're all disqualified b'cause y'all illiterates."

"That include the teacher and the doctor?"

"Sure does," says the sheriff, smiling. "Them's the worse illiterites."

We don't hear no more for a week, when Turnbow gets a Molotov cocktail tossed through his window. They shoot at his family as they all tumble squealing out. Soon as the flames die down, the sheriff turns up to arrest him for burning down his own house, which wasn't insured anyhow.

Turns out the sheriff is the only witness, and Turnbow gets convicted.

"We ain't alone," says Reverend Spinks. "Whole world's watching Mississippi . . . Washington is watching. New York is watching. Birmingham is watching. Foreign parts are watching. All men created equal. All men—black and white—got a right to vote. Constitution says so. America's going to be held to its promise."

Other folks are organizing too. A man stops me in Madison Street, peers soul-searching serious into my face.

Wipe that smile, kid. Ain't nothing clever about being smart

"You a true patriot, boy?"
"I sure am, sir."
"You know right from wrong?"
"Sure do, sir. My mama told me."
"You proud of your race?"
"You betcha."
"Then, give this to your daddy." Man smiles confidential, handing me a sheet of paper. "Time for right-minded people to act. Our race got to protect itself."

But when I start reading the leaflet, I find we're talking at crossed purposes. I'm getting myself mistaken for white all over again.

Thirteen TRUE REASONS WHY you should,
join and support the WHITE Knights of the
KU KLUX KLAN of Mississippi:

1. It is a Christian, fraternal and benevolent organization,
   dedicated to neighborly welfare and charitable good works.

2. It opposes Bolshevism, Castroites, Satan, the International Banking Cartel, Beatnikism, and anything foreign to the Anglo-Saxon System.

3. It does not accept any Tartars, Mongols, Turks, Slavics, Pomeranians, Orientals, Negroids, Papists or Kikes.

4. It is a working organization that not only talks but ACTS.

5. Its members are the sober, courageous, right minded, clear thinking, intelligent, native-born, Protestant members of your community.

6. It is a very secret organization and no one need know that you are a member anyhow.

7. It is a Pro-American organization that opposes any thing, person or organization that is Un-American, un-Democratic or underhand.

9. It is an organization that is sworn to uphold the lawful ORIGINAL Constitution of the United States of America.

10. The KKK has twice saved this nation from her destruction already as history clearly records.

11. There comes a time in the life of every man when he has to choose between the right or wrong side of life.

12. There are today many foreign slimes entering our State bent upon its destruction.

13. It is clear now that if Satan and Communism are to be defeated in America, once and for all, it will be done in the South and foremost in Mississippi.

We know who YOU are
We need your help NOW.
Get out your BIBLE and PRAY.
Fight SATAN.
FAMILIES welcome
Meeting SATURDAY, Briar Road.

BEANS, RIBS and HOMEMADE LEMONADE.
Ask an Officer of the Law for directions WHERE and WHEN

"Grateful, sir, to know your plans. I'll show it to my folks." I fold the leaflet carefully and park it in my pocket. "It's sure going to be one choice picnic."

4

The Interventionist

Before he gets himself national famous, Byron Clement skids his beat-up Buick to a smoky halt on the Briar Road, near the Blue Angel Diner. He pokes his scrunched-up tortoise head out of the shell of the pickup.

"Boy, come here," he croaks. I can smell bourbon, sour on the breeze.

"Yes, suh." I hobble panting up to his truck, hindered by some pretend limp, because I know white folk like to see some wholesome handicap when they're talking to a black boy. I beam my obliging shoe-shine smile. A Clement is a Clement, even when he's the raggedy country cousin. I know enough to stay at arm's length. Folks say he's Klan and can't dip both oars in the water. I can see the well-worn wood butt of a rifle, laid across his denim thigh.

"You the *Cotton* kid folks talk about?"

"Suppose so, suh."

"Heard tell of you, boy," he says, "so I come see you for myself. Been watching you hard . . ."

"Yes, suh?" I screw my face in surprise. "That so, suh?"

"You're surely one fucked-up-looking black boy."

"Yes, suh?"

"You got . . . *yella* hair, boy," he tells me, like I don't know already. "An' it ain't curly. It's straight . . . And . . ." He scrunches up his leather face like a brown paper bag to peer into mine. "You got *blue* eyes . . ."

"Yes, suh. Blue gray, suh. You can hardly see they're brown in the daylight."

"An' your face is paler than mine, boy."

I blush some. Course, I don't agree. All manner of troubles attach to skin color. It doesn't pay to see shades or dispute the divide.

"I'm still real black, tho', ain't I, suh? It's just I'm *white* black."

He spits some dark, frothy tobacco sputum on the dust shoulder between us. We both watch it sink in.

"They find you under some stone? What's your first name, boy?"

"Leaf," I say, "after my daddy."

"He some foreigner buck? Out of county?"

"Yes, suh. He some Iceland sailor, passing through New Orleans. But my grandmammy and mammy they black. Most my folk is deep-rooted local."

He squints at me, sizing me up. After a moment, he unbuckles his brow and narrows his clever, suffering eyes. He nods his understanding.

"You likely don't mean no offense to the White Race, boy."

"No, suh."

"You dress, talk, and think like a good colored. Juss your appearance cause confusions. The way you look . . . it hurts my head."

"'Scuse me, suh."

"I ain't never met no white-skinned Iceland black before," he explains. Then suddenly more worry crinkles his face. "There ain't more like you at home, is there?"

"No, suh." I'm at pains to reassure him. "Far as I know, I'm the only Iceland black in Jones County."

"A word of warning, boy . . ."

"Yes, suh?"

"Don't think you can go around passing yusself off as white, boy."

"No, suh." I'm jerking my head like a mating coot. "Passing off? Not me, suh, never."

Then Mr. Byron Clement drives off in a squeal of wheels, spitting up scorching dirt, leaving me coughing my lungs out on a cloud of Eureka dust, gagging on the stench of sulfur and burning rubber.

I count myself lucky. He's got an awful smoky darkness about him that he dispels by lighting fires. And a couple of years later, he's on trial for shooting some NAACP organizers out of Chicago. And folks reckon, before that, he torched Mount Carmel Baptist Chapel.

There's plenty people, I guess, who can carry off a pale white skin without sacrifice to their appearance, like Paul Newman, say, Audrey Hepburn, Cary Grant, or Marilyn Monroe, who are people who look real fine, regardless of tan, so it never occurs to you they need a black skin to finish them off, but I never counted myself among their graced kind.

When I look at my face in the mirror, I see a vehicle of color that never got painted when it was pushed down the production line. These things happen, so I hear from a guy in Detroit, which is why you should never buy a car that got built on a Friday, because folks cut corners, forgetful, itchy for the weekend.

So, by oversight, I get turned out a white black boy. And it's only one small mistake. But it sure marks you out for life. And it's like every square inch of me is deviant, white. Which, I learned, is the color of hatred, meanness, and spite.

So God knows how any black girl's going to secure some pretext to love me. And I'm going to look like some leper in the bedroom, just showing my face. And taking my clothes off is going to make things ten times worse.

I've got a skin too few. Things that are meant to stay personal to others leak into me. Voices sound out of the blue:

Plop, plop, fizz, fizz. Oh, what a relief it is

Hole in my heart the size and shape of Clarence Bing . . . can smell the stale onion from his armpits . . . feel his stubble on my breast . . . Christ, the shit you bear for love

Some days the volume's yanked up high. Other times it's faint background rustling. With mental radio, you don't get no tuning knob or an on/off switch. It can start up at two in the morning. You pick up foreign stations and you understand jack-shit. Could be Russian weather, Tokyo prices, Swedish culture, for all you know.

Essooa ler sang outray doo tappy, baybay, ay mettey lar tet dons oon sashay on plasteek

There's plenty that riles—sly insinuations, insincerity, affected accents, phony stuff, howls, and cackles.

If a guy's got a speech impediment, he has my human sympathy. Yet you sure get to resent it, when he wakes you at four in the morning, takes forever to spit it out, and it turns out he's got zilch to say. Ditto, the hesitant mumblers. And the sly whisperers just grind you down. You'll find yourself straining to catch what you never needed to hear.

hhm . . . could be . . . Annie might . . . maybe not . . . could ask Judy . . .

You get to hear a lot of anger, blasphemy, self-pity, resentment, leaky below-the-belt personal stuff. Never mind the private grief. There are plenty unfinished sentences, lost threads, repetitions, things unsaid, stranded nouns, lost verbs, and wasted feelings. It comes across a mix of more-than-you-need-to-know and less-than-really-explains-it.

yeah, got me one itchy poozle, got to scratch that ruby fruit

You get used to it. You know how it is with radio. You just learn to tune it out, especially the commercial breaks.

Pictures distract the worst. Suddenly you find yourself gazing on some lady's torso. You can't put a face or a name to her. It's lo-fi. Often the head's missing and she's blurred fuzzy round the edges, but with the bush and thighs in indecent sharp focus.

In time I find it can get plain hazardous, in particular when you're driving. You find yourself steering under the bridge of some thighs. When you come out into the light on the other side, you can find you've crossed the centerline and got to swerve out of the path of some oncoming truck. There's a blare of horns and your passenger—who maybe gave you the mental picture to start—is looking edge-of-their-seat resentful.

Or you're watching TV and you get some wedding photo or child's face drifting over the picture, or a close-up of a clutch assembly, or an image of our Lord on the Cross, or a plate of meat loaf with steaming gravy.

Tastes and smells get real confusing, telling intimate about stuff that just seems to belong in the here and now. So you find yourself sniffing your own sheets, just to make sure, checking the gas knobs on the stove, reaching for the aerosol, forking suspiciously through your food, or eyeing up your neighbor, sucking appreciative.

The upshot is, you don't get a mind to call your own—with the freight of everyone's business drifting through, and you don't want it, and they sure don't—because there's stuff they trust to keep personal, private, and you don't want to let on, so you learn to keep shtum and pretend it's just some stage you're passing through—like diapers, a brace, or zits.

For a kid, it's a burden. Most times I wake up cheerful, but soon I feel I got the world on my shoulders with so much anger around these days, particularly black and white. Shit. We're all human beings for chrissakes.

I'm picking up others' worries, like touching a live wire. I get mad for the bus driver when folks are mean about his stutter. I sniffle for my neighbors who have lost their baby Annie. I itch for PJ the dog, who is flea-ridden. I throb in my breast when the cow's got mastitis, with red-hot needles. I bleed for my cousin Herbie when they chain him to a tree and carve KKK, uppercase, on his belly with a broken bottle.

I am picking up all sorts of ugly dirty talk from adults, and understanding more than I should, which is making me grow up sudden. My mother is always worrying for me. She sleeps restless next door. To make matters worse, I start dreaming her dreams through the partition, which are too womanly and personal for a son's mind, and besides they stop me sleeping.

There's more to it than one sinner's passing concern for another. Mama and Mr. Scott Vernon Morrison are grappling with a fondness that goes beyond the usual contract between insurance salesman and customer.

Mama starts choosing her clothes for more than cover and comfort. The necklines are slipping near as fast as the hems are rising. Unnecessary flesh is showing both ends, besides needless white flashes of scanties. She seems to forget she's mother of a teenage son and going on thirty-three.

Mr. Morrison takes to calling late, without formality or policy documents, sparkle-eyed, smiling overstrong, smelling like a barber-shop of shaving cream and pomade to engage Mama in wordily conversations. He remarks on the warmth of her beverages, the zest of her lemonade, the moistness of her biscuits, the elegant curves of her sofa, the sheen of her floorboards. He plumps up her cushions, holds his hands close to the heat of her stove, and takes to endlessly fingering the fancy fastenings of her lacy curtains.

He's thinking a wordless tangle of hot, damp, glistening ebony flesh, throbby and squirmy, gaping mouths, and twitchy hands.

He gets familiar with our condiments, handles our cutlery like it's his own, avails himself of a napkin without asking, parks his butt on my chair, and says I should call him Scott. He asks me about my schooling, nods at my mumbled reply, and asks if I got homework. Then he claps his hands together and smirks, like I'm dismissed from my very own parlor.

I guess he's that kind of Harry Belafonte, six-foot-four, yard-of-teeth, electric-smile, two-hundred-and-fifty-pounds type of guy that women of a certain age find attractive, so they can end up paying unexpected premiums and buying more than life coverage.

They start talking NAACP and SNCC and CORE and SCLC and Project C and Washington, D.C., and MFDF, which is all some sort of code and cover for the feet grazing under the table and the glancing fingers above.

"You know some Sally woman, sir?" I ask him. I see him with a Sally—his hand draped round her waist, all familiar. She's smiling an open secret.

"Work colleague," he says. "Insurance relies on teamwork."

"You like drinking liquor, sir?" I start coughing. I see him in a smoky bar with bottles and ashtrays littering the tables. Some loud jazzy music with a half-raw woman dancing under a spotlight. She's shaking some tassels on her bazookas and writhing like she's got gut-ache.

"I take an occasional beer," he concedes. But his eyes narrow at my line of questioning, and his voice cools uncordial. "In temperate moderation. I wouldn't call myself no drinking man."

"What's that smell?" I ask. Kind of a compound scent— prawns, sweat, Clorox, and molasses, rolled into one. Mild to start, then coming on throat-catching strong. Thick enough to gag on it.

"Don't smell nothing special," says Mama.

God knows you one strange kid . . . been my cross for thirteen years now, with your color and your moods and your oddness . . . and a mother's love never ends . . . but she'd sure enjoy a snatch of privacy . . .

"Getting late," I observe.

"Sure is. You ready for bed, Lee?" asks Mama.

You want to taste my lips, Scott? You want to lay your hot head on my cool shoulder? You want to link your long, strong fingers in mine?

"You like Captain Marvel?" asks Morrison. "I got you some comics you could go read in your room."

Wanna sink myself in your wide wet yawn, sweet woman . . . wanna drown in your fuzzy cup . . . wanna mix our juices

They're sorry times—when your mama starts thinking dirty in earshot and plotting against you with a total stranger, to imagine you out of the way, so she can unbutton some and loose her elastics.

The summer of '64 is one evil-smelling, searing, scorching, kerosene-smoked season of blazing crosses, drive-by shootings, burning churches, dynamited houses, flaming sermons, scalding rage, melting roads.

After our church gets torched and razed, we meet for worship in a gray canvas Korean War tent in a pasture alongside the graveyard. Reverend Spinks says we should take a subscription to rebuild with bricks, instead of clapboard, but maybe now ain't the most sensible time and we should best wait till they stop burning churches before we fix to build us another.

He puts up a large billboard alongside the burned-out shell of the church saying HOUSE OF GOD. BOMBED OUT BY WHITE BIGOTS. But it kind of drew attention to itself, painted scarlet on yellow, so next night it gets burned down too.

Night riders from the Klan drive by and shoot up his porch and front room, 3 A.M. one Saturday. Favored members of the congregation get invited round for iced tea and to count and admire the thirty-seven bullet neat holes in his not-quite-paid-for leatherette French sofa. There's a curious cross-shaped pattern of holes in a front-door panel, which he finds strangely pleasing as some promise note of protection.

We take plenty church outings. Most weekends we bus ourselves to Jackson, Meridian, or into Alabama, to demonstrate over some segregated lunch counter, bus depot, or school. Or else we go listen to Bob Moses or Reverend King, to keep our eyes on the prize.

This is how I first meet James Jones in June '64, on a coach ride to Philadelphia, Neshoba County, to protest the murder of Schwerner, Chaney, and Goodman.

The dress code is cautious casual, mostly denims and sweatshirts, because you never know if you're going to get hosed, pelted, wrestled, chased, or arrested. If you put your health and freedom in jeopardy, you don't want to risk your best clothes too. So Mr. Jones stands out from the gathering in dressing like a professional mourner at a society funeral with his top hat and tails, lace shirt with gray silk cravat, and a silver-tipped blind man's cane. He's a natty, little, big-nosed, yellow-eyed man, with a goatee beard, bearing a passing resemblance to Sammy Davis Jr.

He comes tappety down the aisle of the bus, flicking folks' ankles careless with his cane, taking his steerage from their protests.

"Suppose I sit next to you, kid?"

"Sure thing, sir."

"You're Corinne's skinny bleached boy, Lee?"

"That's right, sir. Got me in one."

"I see you done a placard, son."

"Yes, sir."

"That's nice calligraphy. And a mighty fine sentiment, son. FREEDOM NOW. It's got urgency and clarity. It doesn't matter it's been said before. It surely needs repeating."

"Excuse me asking. But aren't you blind, sir?" I ask.

"Only when it comes to my sight," he explains me.

"You got a placard yourself?" I ask.

"Prefer to travel light. I brought a pennant." He pats his side pocket.

"What does it say?" I ask.

"Says GO CARDINALS GO."

"That religious or something?"

"Nah." He winces, apologetic. "It's baseball, mostly."

"You aren't demonstrating?"

"Might do some light shouting. Then take a late lunch . . . Tell the truth, I don't like picking on this sorry white trash." He shakes his head. "I try not to pick on folks when they're down in the gutter."

"Down?" I say. "These people bomb our churches; they shoot our leaders."

"There is that . . . ," he concedes, "the murder, arson, and mayhem. Even so, it isn't a fair fight, is it, kid?"

"No," I say, "they got the police. They got guns. They got the politicians. They got the jobs."

"And what've we got, son?"

"We got right, sir. We got truth. We got justice. We got the future. Maybe we got the administration too, if they make their minds up."

"Exactly." He nods. "It's not a fair fight. You've got to put yourself in the white folk's shoes. You've got to stoop to see their point of view and consider their disadvantages."

"Point of view, sir?"

"Everyone born to a time, place, and parents without their choosing. Take a hookworm. He doesn't even know there's a better life than hanging on, wriggling in shit in the bowel of a pig. He's never got the chance of a college education, to listen to Perry Como, drive a Buick, smoke a Lucky, vote Republican, joins the Elks, or vacation in Atlantic City."

"No, sir."

"He doesn't get out enough to gain a proper perspective, see. He doesn't know he's a disgusting bloodsucker. He's just serving time, making the best of things, looking after hisself and his family. Far as he knows, he's one of the best-respected pork-bowel parasites in his community."

"Suppose so."

"Same with your white Mississippian. He's sunk too deep in the shit to see beyond. He doesn't know he's got the morals of a louse or roach. The Southern Baptist Church plain forgot to tell him. He's been brought up to look on us Negroes as beasts of burden, like mules or packhorses. Votes for mules? It just doesn't sound right. Equal schooling for mules? Seems like a waste of schoolrooms. Share a lunch counter with mules? Doesn't sound sanitary . . . You've got to blame the diet, of course."

"Diet?"

"The white diet's deficient in the vitamin B complex. Thiamine, riboflavin, folic acid, B_{12}. All essentials for concentration, clear thought, and moral vigilance. Because they won't eat their collard greens."

"It makes them stupid, sir?"

"Stupid and proud of it. Two-thirds way through the twentieth century and they're still cropping cotton, brooding over the Civil War. And, as if they aren't retarded enough already, they chosen to pick a fight with civilization. And what weapons have they got?"

"What, sir?"

"Fire, dynamite, bullets, and rage—all left over from Gettysburg. Anything they don't like, they're minded to shoot it, burn it down, or blow it up. When you think it through, it isn't clear-sighted."

"It ain't."

"Klan gets together in a huddle. 'Twentieth century coming down the road to Mississippi,' says one. 'How are we going to stop it?'

"And his friend says, 'Suppose we dress up in white hoods and cloaks. Maybe we can scare it off.' And another says, 'Let's string it up and lynch it.' And his brother says, 'Shoot it when it stops at a diner.' And the sheriff says, 'Hey, boys. Don't worry about progress. I'll arrest it on the interstate for speeding, then kick the shit out of it when I've locked it alone in a cell.' . . . Sad, son, isn't it?"

"You aren't from round here, are you, sir?" I can tell from his gold-buckled, two-tone alligator boots, starchy white cuffs, sandalwood cologne, crisp thoughts, quick talk, New Orleans accent, and foreign ideas.

"Here . . ." He reaches into his breast pocket and palms me a thick cream vellum business card—must cost a nickel apiece.

JAMES JONES VII

INTERVENTIONIST AND FREE SPIRIT

3421 ESPLANADE AVENUE
NEW ORLEANS, LA

"Free spirit," I say. "What line of work is that, Mr. Jones?"

"It's a caboodle, son. A way of life, a blessing, and a mess of troubles, rolled into one. I've got a portfolio of personal clients. I represent their long-term interests."

"I got family in New Orleans," I confide him. "My grandma, Celeste du Cotton."

"Fine lady." He dabs his eyes with a napkin and sniffs. "Crazy bitch." Then finds himself surprised by a series of sneezes, like he's got pepper up his nose.

"She ain't well," I say. "She's likely dying."

"Gone. Near as hell," he agrees.

It's clear he doesn't want to talk more about Celeste.

There's something calming about this man's company. He makes you feel safe and cared for, in a scary kind of way.

We sit awhile in silence till he reaches out and squeezes my wrist with his long, cold pianist fingers, like he's tapping into my pulse.

"It's a good, long life you've got there, son. Have you hatched any plans for it?"

"Might raise hogs, sir."

"Hogs?" He frowns. "Aren't an option. You can't buck your purpose. You've got yourself a chronic bad case of *Fate*."

"Or a small farm, sir, growing vegetables."

"Can't be done, son. You have to leave home, travel around . . ."

"Don't know, then." I feel a mite riled he knows more about me and my future than I do.

"Can I give you some advice, boy?"

"About what, sir?"

"About life, son."

"I'd be grateful, sir."

"No good hiding from the voices. They're just going to follow you around."

"I noticed that, sir."

"And the way I see it, son, you got to steer well clear of blue Chevrolets."

"Blue Chevys?"

"With Florida plates."

"Right."

"And when people kick on you, you've got to roll up tight in a ball"—he demonstrates, upper body, hunching his chin into his chest and holding his head in his arms—"because some broke-up arms and ribs are nothing compared to a mashed-up mind."

"Sure, sir."

"And you can go chasing Angelina too hard."

"Who?"

"This singer woman. Whiny voice. Lot of tremolo."

"That so?"

"You can't get it into your head, but the lady doesn't like being pressured or rushed."

"Right."

"I can't stress the importance of a good-fitting brassiere, son, a quality shampoo, and a sound skin-care regime. Look after your tits and face, son, and they'll look after you."

"Sir?"

"When you're young, you think you've got beauty for life, but you've got to protect and nourish your assets."

"And this *brassiere,* sir, what do I do with that?"

"Son"—he crinkles his eyes, perplexed—"your brassiere is there for your breasts. Keep you firm. Protect against droop. And"—he wags a cautionary finger—"you take care there's always a condom, especially after '71."

Like talking to a half-wit. Kid's an accident waiting to happen

"Thanks, sir," I say. "Grateful for that. It's good to know. I'll bear it in mind."

Mr. Jones is counting things off on his fingers, like he's trying to remember what he's forgot.

"Yeah." He smiles to recall. "And the Steelers beat the Cowboys 21–17, Super Bowl X."

"Good result," I say.

"I mention that, son, for the most obvious reasons. Lynn Swann gets voted Most Valuable Player."

"Right."

"I don't give that same advice to just everyone, son. It's tailored peculiar to you. And you're going to find Fay at 2032 Van Ness Avenue. Fine woman. Face like a startled meerkat. Try and practice some kindness along the way."

"Thank you, sir. It's a lot to take in."

"You're a bit young for most of it now. Make sense in the fullness. Bit of everything there." He smiles. "Health care, lifestyle, financial, emotional. It's a good overall package, if I say so myself."

"Who's this Fay?"

"God only knows." He sighs. "Seems you can't leave those San Francisco ladies alone."

"Why you telling me all this, sir?"

"Duty of care, son. Celeste asks me to keep a friendly eye on you. But you got to work out the rest for yourself. I can't be carrying you on my back through life. But one last piece of advice, son . . ."

"Yes?"

"If things get awful bad . . ."

"Yes?"

"Prayer's always an option. And remember, however strange things seem, there's always a reason . . . be it cruel, crazy, or unfair."

"A reason?"

"For *everything*, son. Now, don't mind me if I take some shut-eye. It's going to be a bumpy ride. I guess you're worth the effort. I'll likely see you in New Orleans."

"New Orleans, sir?"

Strange. Normally, I get some feel for what the next guy's thinking even if it ain't precise.

Quit fidgeting . . . and don't even try, sonny . . . When I'm sleeping, my thoughts go as smooth, blank, and cold as newly driven snow

We take a rest stop twenty miles down the road at a diner. Mr. Jones steps off and dissolves in a swirl of roadside dust blown up by a sudden squall.

5

Angel

B obbi Ann Brice's house juts out alone down the far end of Franklin Boulevard like a lonely tooth, and passing her porch, I feel prickles down my spine and the throb of two pulses, quickening together, so I start twitching and jerking to a borrowed beat with one party laying the steady bass, the other picking the rhythm, with the bluesy grunts getting louder, and I know I'm hot on the trail of something fresh, and it's the melody that buys you, so never mind the lyrics are routine popsy crap . . .

> *can accommodate you,*
> *ten dollars up-front,*
> *you better wash it first*
> *an' kick off those boots*

It's one of those barbed fishhook tunes you just can't slip out of your head—like Martha and the Vandellas' "Dancing in the Street" or Sam the Sham's "Wooly Bully."

The quickening beat has you hooked. I sit me down on the porch, tapping my hands on the planks to the tempo. Closer you slide your butt to the clapboard walls, the stronger you feel the throb, the firmer the feel. It's juicy, fleshy, hot, and shivery.

yeah, ahh, ha . . . but go careful with those nails . . . ooh . . .

It turns out Bobbi Ann's a generous, relaxed kind of lady who closes her shutters, afternoons and evenings, to entertain passing friends. After Sheriff Logan and Steve Curtis, the dentist, have come and gone, Bobbi Ann shuffles out in her bare feet buttoning her loose freckled chest and asks me why I had taken a belonging to her porch.

"Whatcha doing, kid?"

"Just hanging out," I say. "Nice spot you got, ma'am. You got real *atmosphere.*"

"Yeah," she agrees, shielding her eyes from the sun and shaking her peroxide-streaked tousled hair. "Sunny, ain't it. And private."

"You got anything particular inside, ma'am?"

"Don't reckon so." She shrugs. "Why you asking?"

"You wrestle, ma'am?" I ask, because the way I see it, there's tangled bodies, tight skimpy clothes, grappling arms, grunts, strain, and submission. "Tag or freestyle?"

She narrows her eyes and crinkles her brow like she's straining to figure me out some way sensible.

"The men sure taken a shine to your place," I explain. "They just keep coming. They come mean and tight. And they leave all friendly, relaxed. Sheriff Logan even tosses me a smile and a nickel."

"Thanks, kid." She nods. "It's matter of how you treat folks. You got to give and take."

"Saw as much in the *Reader's Digest,*" I agree. "Dale Carnegie writes about how to get ahead in life by being nice."

"'Do unto others.'" Bobbi Ann nods. "'Smile and the world

smiles with you.' 'What goes around comes around . . .' 'Give a guy a helping hand when you can . . .' And you . . ." She squints. "You look like the kind of guy that would gladly wash a lady's automobile for a bottle of Coke and a dime bar."

"You being *nice* to me, lady?"

"Sure," she concedes, with an odd, half-cocked, sideways glance. "Why not? You're a little angel, ain't you?"

"Grateful, ma'am." I sniff and gnaw my lip.

It's a kind of good-natured, gracious, likable car, once you lay your hands on it. You sense it's gone far and entertained plenty people. Lounging on the upholstery, you feel it draws you in and down, all backseat friendly. I see it streaking down Highway 61. I see it rocking gently in a turnout, creaking sweet and low.

I go the extra mile for Bobbi Ann. I guess she appreciates it. I sponge her car all over, wax her bodywork, wipe down her vinyl, buff up her Pontiac badge, chammy her windows, empty her ashtrays, polish her chrome, scrape the bird shit off her canvas sunroof, and whitewash her tires, because after that Bobbi Ann starts trusting me with some personal errands to go fetch Trojans and soda crackers and baby lotion and cold beers from McCoy's store, and Mr. Eugene McCoy never asks for money, but just hands the stuff over in tightly folded brown bags and says it's a goodwill business, and reminds me to tell Miss Brice he'll call round to settle up, personal, Tuesday.

"You're real pale and scrawny, Lee. You need fattening up." Mama ladles out some turnip greens, pink-and-white-striped pork belly, and a stiff mound of potato mash to climb.

But when you spent an hour peering through the misted plate glass of the Blue Angel Diner, devouring the best part of the menu, sharing in chili and crackers, fried catfish, double bacon cheeseburger with extra onion rings, a T-bone with fries, German potato salad with cucumber relish, shrimp fritters with chili sauce, pecan pie, and baked Alaska, then cold, greased home food don't seem so appetizing. You fork it around the plate some. But you can't find much pleasure in it.

Mama and Scott get married October '64. After the ceremony, he gives me a hug, slaps my back with a heavy hand, and says, "Hey, son, call me *Daddy*."

You frigging skippy freak

I try the D-word, but it never wants to come out, clogging dry on my tongue like a boll of cotton.

"Gonna struggle my level best to like you, sir." I shuffle back a step to shake his hand at arm's length. "Whatever it takes. As long you try to make my mama happy."

"Thanks, kid." He winces. "It's a generous offer."

In November Grandma Celeste turns up out of the blue to come visit me in a dream. "Lee," she drawls, flicking ash, "you know where to find me. Tell your mother to lift some boards." She's sipping some fancy cocktail, with an olive speared on a stick. Bessie Smith is singing "Empty Bed Blues" in the background. "I've seen you taken care of."

"Sure, thanks, Grandma. Have a good trip." She looks all fleshed out in a sleek black dress with diamond ear studs. Couldn't be much over thirty. It's good to see a spirit flush in its prime. All the same, it makes me aching lonesome. It's hard to find people on your wavelength. Now, I lost the only kindred spirit in the family.

I didn't say a word to Mama. The telegram comes two days later.

"Only met her the once, but she seem a fine God-fearing lady," says Scott, nestling his chin in his palms, "whatever folks inclined to say."

Mama goes to New Orleans to bury her mother and settle the estate. Complications set in, because deeds, papers, and valuables have gone missing. But nothing about Celeste was ever smooth and easy. This leaves Scott and me with two weeks' awkward quality time to get fond and bond.

He's moved in with us in Eureka. It makes sense, because we got space, and he was renting while we were owning. But I couldn't help thinking, in a mean way, that while I'd gained a belated father of sorts, I'd kind of lost grip on a mother and property.

I was noticing how all the portions—of food, concern, privacy—were getting dished up smaller, meaner.

He cooks better than Mama—who burns things Cajun style on the surface and leaves them bleeding raw at the core. Often she just sears a length of pig intestine and chops it up with greens.

Scott uses the same stove, pans, and ingredients, but whatever he heats up turns out to be food. Everything comes charcoal-free. He keeps strict control of things, so you can ask how you want them done up front, whereas Mama never knows in advance if she's frying an egg or mixing an omelet, or leaving a slippy patch on the kitchen linoleum.

You can't say Scott don't contribute. He brings kitchen discipline, a red convertible, blues and gospel record collection, and a stack of Classics Illustrated and cinema magazines. And there are half-empty bottles of Bud or Lone Star he leaves lying around, and scatterings of loose change on the floor and tables. But the negatives stack up too. Plenty comes from his talking. He just never stops. Got a mouth on him like a braying ass. When he reaches the end, he loops back to the beginning. Trouble with selling insurance. You try talking people into submission. He got a throbby way to his thinking like an agricultural diesel engine. Smoky exhaust kind of catches you in the throat. Whereas Mama's mind is generally more hesitant, plonky, with some erratic bum notes—like a reluctant piano student wrestling some new tune into submission.

Now, when it comes to the next guy, I'm tolerant as hell. I say, live and let live. Only it doesn't need to be in our house. Because Mama and me, we lived together fourteen years and got settled in our ways with unspoken understandings. And it's an upheaval to make space for some third party who ain't taken time out to pick up on the house rules. And I can't say there was anything plain mean or full nasty about the man. And likely the worst you could say about him was superficial. Then, you'd fault the way he sprout bristles in his nose and ears, dribble pee on the boards when he take a leak, lay the scent of his armpits like a sulfur fog on the parlor air, clack his thumbnail on his front teeth, think out loud and answer his own questions, excavate his nostrils with a matchstick, scratch his ass with his curled pinkie, snuffle like a hog, break wind both ends, fumble around inside his trouser pockets to fidget with his nuts, monologue through every meal, slide his hand up Mama's thigh, beneath her skirt, when he thinks I ain't watching, play the hi-fi overloud, which ain't so bad individually but tots up in combination, 'cos they change the scent and sound of the household, playing heavy on the senses.

And it strikes us both, there's a third-party outsider in the home now. And he's trying to make out it's me.

The words *guy, manly,* and *normal* pepper Scott's speech. He gives the impression he's aiming to straighten me out quick in Mama's absence, but I got some natural kinks to my personality, and I ain't some bent twist of wire to be smoothed straight in his fingers.

"Got friends, Lee?"

"PJ's my best buddy."

"PJ's fine," he says. "Good-spirited, eager, and loyal. But he's just a dog. He sniffs ass and he licks his privates. I was thinking civilized. I was thinking human."

I shrug. It ain't that I don't have friends. It's more that friends don't have me. I come across as an oddball. Folks fling names my way from a distance.

"Saw you lying out in the field again. What you doing, there?"

"Like it," I say. "Quiet there." In the center of the thirty-acre, nobody else's thoughts seem to reach me. There's nobody buried for two hundred yards. Out there I feel calm, whole, and free. There aren't many places in Eureka where you get your mind to yourself, nourish your own feelings without distraction, and grow ideas from seed.

"It isn't normal, son, just lying stock-still two hours in a field."

I shrug. "Normal ain't the exact same for everybody."

"And Ernie say he seen you on Bobbi Ann's porch."

"She's a friendly lady," I say.

"You betcha. She's a whore."

"So? Didn't Jesus hang out with whores?"

"Jesus was grown up," he says, like it's some age thing. "Going on thirty. An' the Son of God, with special immunity. An' Jesus come down to save their souls, not to loaf around on the porch, run errands, and wash their car."

I guess he's maybe twisting things to suit his purposes and isn't so familiar with the Gospels as he likes to pretend.

"Your mother done every last thing for you, Lee. But I guess the one thing she couldn't provide was a manly example."

"I got Uncle Nat for that." He taught me to hit, chop and saw things, grunt, and conduct a manly silence.

"Fine man . . . ," says Scott, "but he doesn't talk personal. Truth is, he barely talk at all."

"Talk ain't everything."

"Teenage years"—Scott nods—"vexed times. I guess you're getting awkward feelings, don't know which way to turn, or where to put things. You got your eyes on girls?"

He gives me a chunky man-to-man wink for the hard of understanding.

or you some back-jumper, pole-dancing, pillow-biting mama's boy

"Noticed some," I concede.

"Who's caught your eye, Lee?"

"Girls' basketball team."

"Yeah?"

"Girls' track team, girls' dance club, girls' swimming team, cheerleaders, cheerleaders' reserve, library helpers, Mount Zion Choir, Briar Girls Marching Band . . ."

"Anyone in particular?"

"Angie Alberts, Cassandra Anderson, Diana Appleton, Amanda Armstrong, Arminta Armstrong, Helena Bates, Katie Beauregarde, Jade Bowers . . ."

He nods. "You got them all alphabetized then, son?"

"Helps me keep track," I explain him. "In my mind."

"You speak to any of them?"

"Ain't said nothing personal yet. But I been watching distant."

"That's likely your mistake, Lee. To make real progress with a woman, you first got to get close up. Then you got to *talk* with her. Anything holding you back?"

"My looks, maybe . . ."

"Looks ain't everything. Girls ain't superficial. They see through good looks like glass, Lee. They're most times looking for good Christian character."

"But I'm kind of pale and spooky-looking, ain't I?"

He crinkles his eyes to scrutinize and rubs his naked scalp. "I've got to be honest. You ain't got typical black good looks, Lee. You aren't no Sidney Poitier or Bob Hayes." He pats the curve of his belly. "But I reckon some women would find you handsome . . . in a skinny, pale-as-a-ghost, see-through, white-folk kind of way."

"Uh-huh?"

"Sure," he insists. "You the spit of that Paul Newman actor guy. White as milk, scary blue eyes, yellow hair, scrawny as hell. Hear some women go crazy for that bleached-out, cotton-boll, alien look."

"You sure?"

"Sure. It's exotic, Lee. Know what you are, boy?" He starts braying and slapping his thigh.

"What?"

"You the ugly duckling that gone turned into a swan. Shame. If you were only a white boy, you'd be made. Have women crawling all over."

"Look . . . ," I say, "man to man. You ever get that feeling you know what people are going to say? Or what's going through their mind?"

"Guess I'm observant as the next guy," says Scott. "You can't be a success in insurance selling without solid intuitions."

"No," I say, "more than that . . . like you can hear what they're thinking. Out loud in your head."

"Can't say I do." Scott frowns.

You poor fucked-up freaky weirdo kid

I was browsing the comics at McCoy's. Got twenty cents to burn. "Buy me," calls this cover. I flip the pages. Something about the story draws me. And, besides, I never read no Edmond Rostand. McCoy's Groceries never stocked him before. I'm tramping back when I hear the footsteps padding behind. Light, young feet, like a thirsty orphan calf.

"Boy, stop . . . Stop right there."

First impression is female. And it strikes me peculiar. I never was chased by a woman before. Next, I take in auburn curls framing a freckled face, bared teeth, coral lips, long white neck, saucer swells for breasts beneath her T-shirt, skinny arms with golden down, pink plastic bracelet, cornflower eyes, frayed jeans, dusty ankles, toenails varnished scarlet, worn sandals.

Ain't no call to stare . . . You straw-haired thief with your blue-sky melancholy eyes

She comes across as the sort of girl whose mother goes on a Greyhound to see her sister Sandra in Biloxi in '59 but gets lost, so the girl's forced to take over domestic, keeping house for her daddy, without ever learning the proper ways to clean, cook, or do laundry, and gets awful feisty, and aches terrible for what she ain't got, and feels the need of more kindness about her. And goes brittle, crying evenings. And hurts herself with nails and needles and shards of glass. You can read too much into appearances. But that's the way she presents to this stranger's eyes.

Looks like she's fourteen or fifteen. But I mainly work with livestock, so while I can guess you the weight of a hog within three pounds, I don't have the practical experience to age a woman precise. Bare truth is, I don't know exactly where you meant to look or how to draw the right conclusions. I see her teeth look menacing white and strong.

She's got coral lips spreading for moist, mucus-flecked tongue. Spasm pulses her downy neck. Rustle of cotton on skin, nipples taut, and belly loose. Denim-gloved thighs. Swell, peachy strip of naked skin above her belt buckle. Belly button pursed like a startled little mouth.

"Just been to the store. They said you just took it. Fact is, it's mine."

"Ma'am?"

"Classics Illustrated #79. *Cyrano de Bergerac.* Fifteen cents. Here. I've got the money." She's proffering the coins in her shaky paw.

Gimme, gimme. Now, now

"Just bought it myself," I say, "to read."

"I saw it Thursday," she says. "I told them to reserve it."

"I chose it particular," I say, "on account of the story."

Strange-looking guy, Cyrano. Big nose. So he can't get a girl.

Other guys laugh at him. He got the task of living with his looks, making the best of appearances.

"You don't want that. It's girls' stuff," she says. "They got *The Red Badge of Courage*. Buy that."

"Know how some stories are right for you?"

"Sure do."

"Well . . ." I roll the comic tight to a baton, clutching it tight. "This one speaks special to me."

"Read it quick, then," she says. "I can hang around, ten minutes."

"I'm a slow reader," I explain her. "I take my time. When I'm finished, I start over again. When I finished it the second time, I pass it on to my uncle Nat."

"When your uncle Nat's finished finishing with it"—she scowls—"maybe we can do a swap."

"What you got, then?"

Turns out this girl she got plenty cached away, out-a-sight, to tempt a boy—*Silas Marner, Lady of the Lake, Crime and Punishment, Romeo and Juliet, Macbeth, Under Two Flags, The Ox-Bow Incident, All Quiet on the Western Front, Mutiny on the Bounty, The Adventures of Tom Sawyer,* and *The Ancient Myths Special Collection.*

"You read #26?" I ask. "*Frankenstein?* It's drawn by Rudy Palais with captions by Mary Shelley." I mention some woman books, to show I ain't prejudiced fussy about girlie stuff.

"That one's special." She nods. "And do you know #59, *Wuthering Heights?*"

We just carry on walking and talking, till we know exactly what we each other got, and in what order, and what we like best, and why, and if Lou Cameron draws better than Joe Orlando, and if Mark Twain writes better than William Shakespeare or Jules Verne, and if ancient is better than modern, and who is our favorite story animal, and who'd be the worse parent, Captain Bligh or the Queen of Hearts, and why the writer tries to keep the lovers apart till the end, and how much sword fighting you need to make the story tick, and why they race against the clock or fight against fate, and how Pyramus and Thisbe never learned from Romeo and Juliet, and how Orpheus was a dangerous dude to know, and how Hamlet looks the spit of Gus Cochrane at the Magnolia Diner, and can there be any black heroes, and do men write more and better than women, and why Othello did for his babe but King Arthur didn't.

But all that reading had done something troubling to her head because she starts declaring about her *sensibility,* and *the common herd,* and talking about her *voyage* and her *destiny.* Then she remarks on her *soul,* besides.

"Name's Angelina," she says. "You can call me Angel for short."

"Leaf," I say, "but save your breath and call me Lee."

You some white trash, boy? Slouching there in your raggedy overalls. Roughed up like some farm tool bent from too much carrying. You going to follow the mule track, or take the hero's path to destiny?

"What does your daddy do?" she demands.

"Not sure." I flush. "Lost touch."

So I got to explain how my daddy left us a long time ago, nine months even before I get born.

"No daddy, huh?" She nods and pauses, like she's savoring the idea. "My mommy left us when I was ten," she says, "and Daddy don't expect her back."

Bastard probably killed her after he cut her . . . There was a dug-up patch in the corn

"Tough," I say.

"Your folks got money?"

"Some," I concede.

"*Old* money or *new* money?" she asks.

"Ain't sure." Money is money. Never thought of its age. "What's the difference?"

"Old money's got grace and nobility. New money is plain vulgar. It just comes from hard work or luck."

"That so?" I ask. Sweet Jesus, I think, our family could sure do with some money. Me too. Almost give my life for real money. So Mama wouldn't have to clean white folks' houses. And I wouldn't have to grub around in the dirt, no more.

"We had old money," she explains, "but most of it slipped through my granddaddy's fingers, and then down my daddy's throat. And not much new money comes along to replace it from Daddy's job pumping gas. So we are fallen some, from grace and favor."

Daddy's a lush. Mama's left. Live in some nigger cabin, south of the tracks. Eating refried hope with gravy off tin plates with our greasy fingers

"Shame." I look to my feet. Her eyes are too inquisitive, and her talk is making my aching head buzz, like I just done a math test. She's got a mind that just bubbles away like a seltzer tablet. It's fresh and lively, but it sure throws up a deal of surface froth.

"Reckon I'm beautiful?" she says. "Or plain pretty?"

She sweeps her hair back, turns the other cheek and pouts her lips, flutters her eyelids, to give me a fair chance to assess. I step back to take her in.

And her wide blue eyes can't decide if they prefer to coax or mock. And her freckles say ain't I precious, natural. And the glossy skin below her collarbones says aren't I swelling melon ripe. And the flare of the nostrils says I can take you or leave you. And the coltish twitch to her flank shows a free, unbroken spirit. And the purple stripe on her upper arm shows someone's taken a belt to her. And she's got thin red threads across her wrist, like she's been scratching herself persistent.

"Reckon you're lovely."

"Got me a beauty that's a fragrant bud unfolding," she explains, "like a magnolia blossom. When my petals are swollen, fully spread, I'm gonna be a famous beauty. Might even be a legendary lover."

Have me a Barbie figure. Golden tresses to my hourglass waist. Voice like a flute. Soul of a poet. Neon smile. Heroes swarming like bees

"Like Marilyn Monroe?"

"Thinking more like Helen of Troy."

So, she gives fair warning at the outset she's a girl of some ambitions, with a tendency to complicate, for sure.

"You got a good face, Leaf, and a lean body. But you slouch some, which is unheroic."

"Uh-huh?"

"You've got to keep upright. You never know when opportunity will come knocking."

"Uh-huh." I nod, like I know what she's gabbling about.

"Hey, you got a personality there, somewhere?" She raps my head gentle with her knuckles.

"Guess so." I gnaw my lips some. "Most times I keep it under wraps."

"You look really cute, Lee. But it just feels like I'm talking to a mirror. So all I get back is reflection."

"Reflection, huh?" I nod.

"Echo," she explains.

Ain't the lady's task to ask. We gonna be soul mates? We gonna share our Classics Illustrateds?

I guess I'm kind of awestruck at what destiny's dishing up. "Look," I say, taking a step back. "Life's short. It's getting late. We friends, or what?" My face is scalding crimson.

"Could meet you Sunday." She hesitates. "After I done the house and fixed Daddy's lunch."

"And, hey, don't you play the guitar?" I ask.

"How'd you know?"

"You look like the kind of girl that plays. And writes her own songs."

"They aren't songs so much as . . . poems set to music."

"Sure love to hear them."

"Sunday, then," she promises. "And, Lee . . ."

"Angel?"

"I'm looking for a hero to bring beauty and awe into my life. I can't be doing with no farm boy, serving up grits and gravy."

"Bear it in mind," I promise.

I watch her sassy walk, and the swivel of her narrow hips, and her straight back, all huffy stiff from being watched, and the haughty flick of her auburn hair. It's awful beguiling. It's enough to start me off humming. I guess it must be one of her songs.

Been looking for love in dark places
Got a heart that hunts by night

And I'm thinking this is just the start. I got an intuition I just met the love of my life. I watch her silhouette swing a left at the water tower.

And I start weighing up all we share, that divides us from the common herd. Her with her lost mother, and me with my lost daddy. And both being forced to grow up too early, burdened by our special talents. And how we both see beneath the surface of things. And how we're both saddled with narrow-minded parents, bordering bigots, trying to herd us into their corrals. I mean, with my mama burping Proverbs and passing Revelations she half digested in the Mount Zion Baptist Church. And Angel's daddy, who sounds knee-deep in Dixie, mired in the race war, and so far addled he takes a drunk hand to his teenage daughter.

Seems to me, we only got *color* to divide us. Which is only skin-deep. And even that ain't obvious. Not to the naked eye.

Now, black and white don't mix in Eureka, not boy and girl, not skin on skin. But when soul mates merge, it'd be a crime to pry them apart.

6

One Lucky Guy

Mama drives home from New Orleans in a nearly new Dodge Polara hardtop station wagon—361 big block, cream and purple, matching interior, whitewall tires, moon hubs, shark fins— slung low on its rear springs packed with cases, boxes, and furniture.

"Whose car?" asks Scott. "Stick or auto? Great to have you back, honey."

"Ours," says Mama. "Auto . . . Careful, Lee, with those pictures. They're real genuines."

She's awful brisk and nervy, watching us eyes narrowed, hands on hips, like we're raggedy relations.

Nat trudges out, blinking from the gloom of the barn, wiping his mucus-slimy shovel hands on the knees of his overalls.

"I need you," Mama says. "We've got to have a family conference."

"Got a cow calving . . ."

"Twenty minutes," says Mama. "Round the table. In my parlor."

———

"Celeste's affairs got complicated," she explains. "You're probably pinning your hopes on the house, but it had gone downhill in a slum neighborhood. It hasn't seen a lick of paint or new nails in twenty years. And she'd borrowed on it from two different banks, who didn't know about each other. I sold it and paid them off. Got a few thousand dollars left over to buy the car."

"This take long?" asks Nat, rolling his slow bull eyes. "We got a cow calving."

"She could never bring herself to use the trash can. House is crammed with crap. Every stick of furniture got twenty cigarette burns. Celeste filled a room up, then locked the door. She ends up sleeping in the kitchen on a cot bed. No space left anywhere else. She's got bedrooms stuffed to the ceilings with magazines, clothes, gramophone records, rusted cans of army surplus food, crates of liquor, stuffed reptiles, shoes, empty cigarette packs.

"The dust settles; the bugs and roaches take over. You don't need to be a PI to work out she sealed the front bedroom late in '56. Then she started filling the back room. Got sedimentary layers of clothes and newspapers reaching to the fall of '61. Then she turned the lock.

"All the while I'm sorting it out, I got folks calling to settle debts.

"'Miss du Cotton forgot to pay her grocery bill for seven months.'

"'Celeste loaned me a hundred bucks in '59. She'll come haunt me if I don't pay you back.'

"One day I make a clear profit. Next day I'm handing it all back. Come suppertime, I end up crawling round on the floor for dimes to feed myself.

"All the while, I can't find the things that matter—jewelry, papers, cash.

"Then I feel the boards rocking under my feet. I see a picture aslant on the wall. A doorknob comes off in my hand. There's a cavity behind the stove. I cotton on she's been squirreling her nuts.

"Once you strike lucky by lifting a floorboard, you got to lift them all. Soon I got mortgage papers, caches of letters, boxes of photos, small parcels of jewelry wrapped in tissue paper.

"I take the place apart, board by board, room by room. I make a fire in the yard to burn up the garbage to make myself room to move.

"There are letters from an attorney, with first party to this, and notwithstanding, and the second party to that. So I reckon I should call him.

"'You know of any Celeste Saint Marie du Cotton?' I ask.

"'Are you the daughter? I've been expecting your call,' he says. 'What took you so long? Come on over.'

"When I get there, he starts rifling through a cardboard box. There are several wills, because Celeste took to changing her mind and affections quite frequent toward the end, but he only needs the most recent one.

"'Miss du Cotton's affairs are not entirely straightforward,' he says.

"'Tell me about it,' I say. 'I been her daughter. All my life.'

"'Firstly, she wants you to know she is with us still. She has merely taken a different spiritual, insubstantial form.'

"'She's dead but she's hanging around?'

"'You must act on my client's advice however you think best.'

"'Hi, Ma,' I tell the ceiling. 'Sorry I never said good-bye. You left the house in a terrible state.'

"'Secondly, there are a substantial number of minor bequests which she instructs you to discharge . . .'

"There are gifts for musicians, waiters, short-order chefs, barmen, shoeshine boys, painters, chauffeurs, whores, pimps, platelayer, policemen, doctors, horse charity, dope peddler, dope peddler's brother Vinnie, Vinnie's aunt Mae, Aunt Mae's cleaner, cleaner's cousin. You name it. I spend two weeks hunting people who don't want to be found, saying, 'Celeste left you five hundred dollars . . . Celeste left you an amethyst ring . . . Celeste left you a stuffed snake . . . Celeste left you this painting . . . Miss du Cotton left you her Ouija board, which formerly belonged to Marie Laveaux.'"

"Good-hearted," says Scott. "But a sieve with money."

"Any left for us?" asks Nat. "We need some new fencing."

"Then the attorney asks me if I know about the stocks and shares. 'Stocks?' I say. 'Surprise me.'

"'It turns out this writer called Walker Strongman passes the rights in a book of his to Celeste. Called *Go Forth Angel*. Money dribbles in twice a year because, although it isn't strictly readable, they make kids study it at college to gain self-discipline. Celeste told me to invest the income as I thought best. Early on I bought oil. Later I bought television and stores. Recently, I tried munitions and computers.'

"'Mama must have trusted you.'

"'Kind lady,' he says, 'but you wouldn't care to cross her. She laced every deal with a hex.'

"'So . . . ,' I say.

"'So,' he says, 'there's a portfolio. Current value is one-fifty-four.'

"'Dollars?'

"'Thousands.'

"'Lot of money, praise the Lord,' I gulp. 'Knew she sometimes had money. Never figured her for rich. You got a check for me, then, sir?'

"'Three. There's a three-way even split, between you, Celeste's half brother, Nathaniel, and your son, Lee.'"

"Fifty thou," says Nat, scraping his chair back. "Buys a lot of livestock and fencing. Rest in peace, Celeste." He pats my back. "Don't let the money come hurt you, son."

"My money?" I ask Mama. "Any chance? I could use some right now."

"I hold it, Lee. I invest it. Until you get sensible, or reach maturity, whichever comes later."

"There's stuff I need. Magazines, clothes, and such."

"Not a cent," says Mama, "until you reach twenty-one or learn the value of money."

So, I'm rich but broke, which comes as some sweet disappointment. But Scott looks the most troubled thoughtful. He used to be the big number one. Now, he's bottom of the pile—the poorest guy in the house.

fucking weirdo kid gone stole our money

Angel and I got our private place at Jimmy Cooder's hay barn, off the Briar Road.

"That's a real shiner," I say.

"Bumped my head on a door," says Angel, shading her purpled eye with a curved palm.

Daddy punch my lights out . . . Cry all you like, Angel, he says.
But it doesn't get you out of that closet today

"Something to show you," I tell her. "I've got us the real thing." I undress it out of its brown paper bag. She sits close and peers down. I smell her corn-bread breath through her moist amber lips.

"This"—I show the cover—"is the real book. The Classic Illustrated comes after, by shrinking it down."

"No pictures. Except on the cover." She flicks through the pages.

"You got to read it. Then you can see it all for yourself. And color it in mental, just how you like."

"The way it's written," she says, "is like Huck is speaking fast, direct to me, and his grammar isn't right."

"That's deliberate, I reckon. Because he wrote other books where he gets the spelling right. It's got a message to the reader at the front. Look . . ."

"Persons attempting to find a motive in this narrative will be prosecuted; . . . persons attempting to find a plot in it will be shot."

"Most likely a joke," I guess.

She hunches, flicking the pages. Looking down her back, I see the window of pale skin between her T-shirt and her jeans. See the nobbles of her spine, downy golden hair, and the band of her white underpants biting pink into the flesh.

"It's like you're in Huck's head," says Angel, "and his thinking ain't quite nice . . . He forms a murder gang. He smokes and his daddy drinks."

"Yeah," I say. "Don't they leave that out in the comic book?"

The baggy arm of her T-shirt opens a tunnel into her. I see straw stubble in her armpit and the shaded swell of a breast. Down past the book, you see into her lap, the taut cleft between her legs, with the denim splitting something soft. She never moves when our shoulders touch.

"This dude"—she sighs—"he's young but he's dark."

"He's a rebel," I say. "He don't care what the common herd think."

I park my hand on her knee, but it's kind of hard and unwelcoming, and she blinks, then stares me out.

"You getting personal?" she asks. "Or what?"

"You're one beautiful woman," I explain her.

"I suppose," she concedes.

Kiss my ruby lips. Just once, then. But don't try to poke no rude tongue in my mouth

We kind of grapple to get it done. We got to sort out whose head goes which side and whose arm goes where. It's a dry experience, but soft and friend-some warm. Her eyes stay open, keeping a calculating watch on mine. It ranks more an achievement than a solid pleasure. But we both seem gratified in our separate ways.

"Guess we're dating, then?" she says.

"Guess so."

You can brush my breast with your palm, in passing. Just make sure it's accidental

Then we do it again. My fluttering lids tell me she's half closed her eyes this time.

slide a warm hand around some . . . but don't wander sneaky finger past no fabric

You got to relax into it and inhale through your nose. Her hand guides mine and snatches it away when it strays too far.

no, slidy up my silky thighs

I am getting a feel for new contours and textures. Turns out, woman's a warmer, calf-bony, puppy-eager, peachy, curvier, private, cleftier, tuftier, more various place than a man anticipates.

then Hero pressed his lips in supplication to Leander's alabaster breasts

You got firm and soft, dry and moist, cool and warm, still and quivery, bold and shy. It all fits so neat together. Can't say a single piece disappoints, unless you single out the elbow.

stirring 'lectric ripples in her secret purse of love

The boundaries are marked clear enough, but pliant and elastic, so you got to graze sly and press inadvertent, and stray casual, and learn your hands to rove skillful clumsy.

like slow drips of nectar in pink-shaded petals

And it strikes me one wondrous anonymous scam, how you get to wander a lady, up close, all over physical, before you ever get to know her personal.

"Huh . . ." Angel palms me away; her face is flushed shiny and she's breathing fast. "Don't even know your last name."

"Kristjansson," I say, calling on my daddy for help. "And yours?"

"Clement," she says.

"Your daddy's not *Byron?*"

"You know him?"

"Met him once. He stopped to talk . . ."

"He isn't as bad as people say." She blushes. "Just he riles easy. And he drinks some, which shortens his fuse."

Something gloomy shades my spirit—maybe the ghost of Emmett Till.

"Romeo and Juliet," I say. "Verona. Two families that don't get on. Supposing it was like that with us?"

"Star-crossed lovers," she agrees. "Affairs of the heart. Keep things quiet. Ain't nobody's business but ours."

"Yes?" We link fingers and graze our dry lips.

"We can meet secret." She smiles, flicking her hair from her cheek.

Ain't like I'm dating a nigger, or nothing

Looking back, the time to tell her was then. Because the longer you leave these things unspoken, the harder they get to tell in the end.

7

Bad Break

Scott just persists away, along with his personality, with the ways he rewrites the house rules, moves the furniture, sprays his opinions round the parlor like some pissing dog, taints the air with his sweaty feelings, darkens the room with his sulks, and twangs some cheap three-chord riff on the strings of Mama's heart, so he makes her sob, he makes her shout, he makes her laugh, he makes her howl like a she-wolf early mornings, and they construct some row late evening, so they can make up in the bedroom, so there's a deal of loud feelings, dirty thoughts, and needless noise, and if it isn't insults and abuse, it's slamming doors, giggles, whimpers, and a groaning bed, which gets kind of tiresome after a while, like watching the chickens in the yard, pecking, strutting, preening, and screeching, because you expect more from your own folks than chicken culture, just scratching round in circles.

Only, one morning Mama's standing stock-still on the porch, staring out over the duck pond, and I know there's something's changed with her and lost between us. There's some bat-squeak pulses coming out of her, echoing her sorry heart.

eek-eek . . . eek-eek . . . eek-eek . . . eek-eek . . .

It's a kind of dumb, selfish, insistent sound that doesn't care for anyone but itself and don't mind who it disturbs. I guessed what was coming. I heard similar before.

"Got company?" I say.

"Yeah." Mama sighs. "Reckon so."

"Kids," I say, "eat you alive. Don't know why we bother."

"Tell me about it," says Mama.

Celeste's money seems to sour things for a while. It wasn't the gift it first appeared.

Scott has changed his reading habits. He's put away his sports magazines and taken to studying mail-order catalogs, circling items, underlining heavy, in red ballpoint pen. It seems he's set his heart on a white three-piece corduroy suit, calfskin boots, monogrammed handkerchiefs, hi-fi set, and gold identity bracelet. But Mama has stashed the cash in a personal account, and it takes her personal signature to unlock it.

"Married you in sickness and in health, for richer or poorer."

"True." Mama nods.

"Seems only fair," says Scott. "If I'm all signed up for all your sufferings, I've got some stake in your fortune too."

"Give you my love. What else a man need?"

Scott shrugs. "We got money, honey. Only right to spend some. Isn't much hope for equality between the races, if a black man can't get a square deal in his very own house, from his very own wife."

"Got this money saved," says Mama, "against stormy weather. Never know what's coming. Maybe we could build on the house."

"Build?" says Scott. "Well, ain't that the man's decision?"

"Well," Mama says, "supposing a baby . . . ?"

"You got me a boy in there?" Scott chortles, stroking her belly. "A son and heir?"

"No. Girls," I got to explain him, because he's always lagging off the pace. "Twins. Six weeks old, I reckon."

"No, *boy*, I bet you," says Scott.

Some cocksure guys just can't be told, just won't listen. So you just got to leave them learn mulish, when they're good and ready.

With her mama gone to Biloxi, Angel had come reliant on her daddy for moral insights, so the way she talks about the *colored problem* or peppers her talk with *coon, nigra,* and *nigger* was ignorant more than nasty, coming from parroting her daddy, who was drunk in charge of his opinions and couldn't steer himself round any idea that was five miles foreign without sideswiping it, ramming it from behind, and calling it some mean, slurred names. It seems he talked about the Clement Plantation and how the Yankees burned it down, making dusty ashes of his fortune, like it was yesterday, instead of August 14, 1864. And Angel likes the sound of being fallen southern aristocracy better than being the daughter of some white-trash drunk, so she's suckered into romancing Dixie and wondering where all her slaves are gone.

"You some *civil rights liberal,* Lee?" Angel asks. Don't suppose there's any meanness to it. She's just curious—handing me a hat to try it on for size.

"Folk's folk. People's people," I say. "Every race and nation's the root same. You read their stories, you understand them. No reason to suppose black is any different from white."

I see my face mirrored pale on the glister of her guileless duck-egg eyes. And I return her intimate-stranger smile and wonder what could follow from my telling, and what she'd cling to—her hand-me-down prejudice or her fondness for me.

But then, laying hands on her peachy flanks, eyeing the bruising across her back, and breathing the honey and hay scent of her auburn hair, and feeling her calf-skinny ribs and the jerks of her eager heart, like the thrash of a landed fish, and hearing her short gasps, and squeals of startled laughter, and watching her white skin flush a mottled pink above her hillock breasts, and laying my weight on her bony hips, and curling my tongue round her rising amber nipple, the more I understand how white folk think and feel, and see how they aren't very different from us blacks, and the purple stripes on her ribs show she bruises easy too, so you realize that color isn't any bar to kindness and understanding between people of goodwill who make the effort to get on.

We got our private, personal apartment up high, in the loft of Cooder's barn, part bedroom, part parlor, and part study. We got books, a blanket, a radio, and her guitar.

The air is hazy with pollen and dust. The straw prickles your raw butt if you stray off the blanket. Light shines through the slats, casting golden stripes down your naked length. Angel sprawls, watching the roof beams, draped in no more than her secrets, scents, and shadows. I smell the she on me and the me on she. I can taste her on my lips and fingers. Laying my head on her salty belly, I can hear the delicate liquid traffic of her body, grumbling sweetly.

"Don't crowd me, Lee," she warns, "not till I'm famous."

> *girl wakes with a start*
> *eyes herself in the glass*
> *sees it's time to part*
> *packs her jeans and hopes*
> *snips the ties to her heart*

"I'll be gone soon," she warns.
"Uh-huh?"
"Artists have to live by special rules."
"That so?"

"Love you, Lee. Just I got first duty to my talents. I'll still carry you in my heart."

"How you getting famous, Angel?"

"Singing. Acting. Writing maybe."

"No kidding?"

"I just know I'm going to be *something special*, Lee."

Lost my innocence in Mobile
Had my heart stole in Monroe

"You got the ambition, looks, and talent, Angel. You're most parts there."

"Hey, honey." She splays her jerky thighs and draws me close. "Uh-huh?"

"You can love me till I'm gone, baby."

That was the way with Angel. She always pushing you away with her destiny, then drawing you back with her skin, and snagging you tight between her thighs.

Some things too dark to tell

"My daddy says I'm not around enough. He complains I'm neglecting the house. And he keeps asking me if I've got a beau."

"Uh-huh? What did you say?"

"No one special, Lee. No one special."

"I sure don't want to make trouble for you, Angel."

Two days running, Angel doesn't show. I'm tramping home late along the Briar Road with a wowser of a headache when a sedan slides past slow, throbby from an overjuiced carburetor.

Faces peer from the windows to watch me close. White folk. Two in the front seat, two in the back. I can't put a name to any of them. Car pops to halt ten yards ahead. The headlights dim. The ignition's switched off. Open road, ahead and behind.

Blood spurt out all over like water from a broken faucet

There are cotton fields to the right and pasture to the left. Too much flat. I can't hide myself behind no cotton bush, and I can't outrun no car. I walk on, whistling—Righteous Brothers song, "You've Lost That Lovin' Feelin'." Don't want to attract attention by acting odd or running scared.

I don't arrive here unprepared. Last summer the Reverend Spinks arranged for an activist student called Billy G. Johnson out of Chicago, studying psychology and law, to come give us a course—Staying Safe, Part 1—so we know what to do if we get arrested at a demonstration, or get picked on by hostile whites. Billy G. explains us the theory of passive resistance. Then he tests us out on the practice—slaps us around a bit, calls us names, and spits some in our faces, to see if we react.

gliding easy, like a razor through skin

The secret—as Billy G. explains it—ain't to get mouthy or angry when white folks hit on you. If you fight back, it can only provoke them worse.

But he picks the wrong student when he spits on Nat Parish. Nat isn't Gandhi-minded. So he breaks Billy's jaw near the end of Part 1, so he never comes back to teach Part 2. Billy's spirit was still forgiving and willing, but his mouth was all wired up and his tongue was badly sliced.

There's a creak as a car door swings open. A tall, stooped man gets out.

"Boy," he calls, "want a lift?"

"Don't need no lift, suh. Nearly home. Prefer to walk, suh." Billy had mentioned particular not to take a ride in any stranger's car, specially not with armed whites by night.

can hobble them first by cracking their leg bones

"Come on," he coaxes. "Ain't no trouble."
"Dirty shoes, suh. Don't want to mess your car."
"You hiding something, son?"
"No, suh, no. Just messy feet."
There's muttering, a metallic click, and an owl screech.
"Get in," the tall man clutches my arm, "while I'm still asking polite."

He steers me onto the backseat. I'm tight in the middle, touching shoulders with a guy either side. The car smells of pork fat, field labor, and stale beer.

never pleasant to gut and joint a human being

It's a mistake to confuse southern politeness for kindness, or silence for lack of opinion. Soon as I get in, my face feels scalding. There are needles stabbing down my spine. Hate feels physical to a sensitive soul.

but you got to protect yourself against the weakness of pity

Four men turn to stare cold on me.
"This him?" asks Tall Man.
"That's him," says the driver. He got a sad, sleepless, piss-yellow, full-moon face and a scarlet mouth like he's wearing lipstick. He reminds me of Fatty Arbuckle. "Lee Cotton. Born November '50. Got a dossya on him. Code Pink."

"Pink?" asks Two Teeth, sucking through his stumps.

"Watch Particular. Review Regular," says Fats.

"Mistaken identity," I gulp. "Happens all the time." I try to lay some calm on my voice. I breathe slow and deep to calm the quake in my chest. My heart jumps around like a rabbit in a sack.

Some stand there like weary mules, waiting for the blow to land

"Spooky nigger," says Dog Breath.

"This specimen, he belongs to the Pale Tribe of the nigra race," says Fats, "like Marlon Brando and Eleanor Roosevelt."

"Yeah?"

"And Elvis Presley," says Fats. "The pale nigra is the infiltrationist that goes ahead. He's got the job to sow confusion, blur the boundaries. But mostly he's got the task to impregnate white women." It seems Fats is the leader and the scholar of the gathering.

"Elvis ain't no nigger," protests Two Teeth. He whistles as he talks, from the musical acoustic of air being sucked through stumps. It sounds like a muted Swanee whistle.

"Show you later," says Fats. "I got the paperwork—Code Red. Forget the white mother. Daddy's a buck. It's the lips and voice that give him away."

Morons are come to kill me. They're stretching the elastic of theory way too far. There's just no dignity, purpose, or sense in it. Not for anyone. Every man's got an idiot up his sleeve. But no one gains when you let him out.

"This kid's blond," says Tall Man. "How we meant to tell the difference, when he's wandering around all white-looking?"

"It's the Challenge Facing the White Race," says Fats. "That's why we got to stay vigilant. Protect our women. Guard our virgins."

"I ain't gone spoiling no virgins," I say. Honest truth. Only had to lay fingers on Angel to know someone else had got there first.

"Angelina can't come meet you tonight," Fats says.

"No? Angelina who?"

"So we come instead."

"Angel all right?" I ask.

Just bruises to her soul and face. Nothing broke except her heart and reputation

"This a Chevy?" I ask. "Florida plates?"

"What's it to you?" asks Tall Man.

"Got a thing about Chevys," I say. "Been specially warned against them."

"You've got worse things to worry about than Chevys, son."

"Blue?" I ask. "Didn't see properly in the dark."

They don't say nothing.

"Good thing I don't know y'all. Suits us all," I try again.

"What?" asks Tall Man, testy.

"Can't identify you, can I?"

"What's he babbling about, Luke?"

"Careless talk costs lives," I warn. "You best not mention no more names."

"What?"

"Gives you more choices, if I don't know your names. You could slap me around some, then let me go."

Safe Billy G. reckoned the less you know about your assailants, the greater your chances of coming out alive.

"Lee, son." Fats turns with a tight sour-milk smile. "This is Evans, Luke, and Bobbie. I'm Louis La Blanche, Kleagle of the Briar Klan."

"You going to kill me?" I ask.

"No, son. I'm not."

Byron's job to kill you, son. We just come along to help

A man's last defense is his humanity. So Safe Billy G. says. I got
to forge a human link, show I share feelings, show I bleed red like
them.

"Hey," I ask Tall Man, "haven't we met? Aren't you Friday-
friendly with Bobbi Ann?"

"Quiet, kid."

"Only fifteen," I sniff. "Too young to die." I shiver, wetting my
cheeks. "My poor mama," I explain. "Every sinner some mama's
son."

My trouser leg's sodden warm. But they don't notice. They're
making plenty smells of their own.

"Look at me," I say. "Look at my skin. I'm *white, white, white* . . ."

"Shut it, nigger," says Dog Breath. "All done soon."

My teeth are click-clacking together. Sounds like a china cup
rattling on its saucer. I can't still my careening legs.

The car rolls juddery onto pasture, slows into second gear,
climbs an incline, jerks to a stop by a cedar. Tall Man slides out to
let me step onto the grass.

"You can run, kid, if you like," says Tall Man. "We don't mind
a chase."

Prefer you get a rabbit's chance

"No . . . cover," I stutter.

Then, I think, I ain't so slow on my feet, and they ain't so frisky.
They're real old men in their thirties. And they got to get out of the
car to shoot, and there's a dip beyond the tree, and if I dart from side
to side, they can't get a good aim, and some chance is better than
nothing, and I'm sprinting up to the cedar, running free, with the
cold air rushing my cheeks.

8

The Almighty Speaks
Sage and Aniseed

A shadow splits from the trunk of the cedar. A dark figure looms out. It's Byron Clement, pulling something dark and slow toward me, then I see he's swinging a baseball bat, like a slugger at the plate, and it's happening awful immediate, except time is getting stretched terrible long, and I see a narrow-eyed smile break over his face, and I can see Angel's face in his, cheekbones and nose, and the bat is arcing toward me straight at my scalp, and the wood and my bones can't help but meet, and as the club end edges close, I can read the fire branding on the stem which says *H & B ~ 42-ounce hickory,* then all I know is the wood grain of the barrel, spreading across my sight, and I know I'm a curveball headed for the sweet spot.

There's the shock of being chopped in two at the neck. Your head sweeps back while your body carries on. The clout is numbing, flattening.

It's like walking headfirst into an oncoming train, or having your head cracked in a vise. Then the weight of the world presses all over. The sound, starting soft but building ear-splitting loud, is a bough being bent, cracking open, then splintering apart, and my skull is breaking into shards, scattering needles of bone back into my mind. There's a long echo of breaking crockery, like the china cupboard's fallen off the wall, onto the kitchen floor. Then there's just a booming, buzzing sound. So I know it's done something real hurtful bad to my ears.

It's feet then. When one's broke the ice, they all kick off.

Some things just sound awful wrong—like fingernails scraping a chalkboard, like the screech of a chicken being eaten alive by a fox, like the snapping of ribs, the tearing of tendons, the pulping of skin, the squelching together of body fluids that are never meant to mix, the dull thud of bone yielding to boot. And you wonder how they can carry on when it sounds like sacrilege. Never mind what they are doing, the sound's an abomination.

Things are pushed in that don't spring back. I feel things puncture. I sense the warm gush of leaking tubes. There's a spurt of fluids being forced from hidden sacs. There's the awful ache of deep things that aren't ever meant to be touched. My lips part to a toe cap and my teeth yield salty hot. And there's a grating break, which is the snap of my jaw. There's the hiss of air as something deflates slow.

Psssss . . .

They're gathered around me, touching me rough here, prodding me there, but it's just dull pressure that adds nothing to the pain, because now I'm all hurt-out.

Dear Lord, I think, I hope all my parts fit back how they're meant.

Hope we're all done soon . . . got chores to do at home

A shaft of light breaks the tar dark. Then I hear the *shlooop* of something slithery, soft, and moist squeezing out from a very tight hole. A soul finds the route of least resistance. It's me, popping out through that flattened nose my body used to use.

blood an' pulp on my socks . . . head splattered like a watermelon

I've shed my flesh like I've cast off a coat. And I drift up, like a bird riding a thermal, gazing down. The kid is broken up, sprawled, splay-legged on the grass. See his face glistening smooth and black from the gore. He's the cracked shell I've left behind. The me that matters drifts onward, up.

They stop kicking it now—the meat. They just gather round the rag-doll body, talking quiet, peering close. Cedar branches casting purpled shadows. Dewy mist is rising from the grass. Hear the whistle and rattle of a distant train.

"There's a right way and a wrong way to chastise the nigra," Fats says, brushing lint from his shirtfront. "We should have strung him from the tree."

"We got a rope in the car," says Tall Man.

"What's the point?" asks Fats, turning away, spitting something thick and phlegmy. "You fixing to kill him twice?"

"We done for the night?" asks Two Teeth. "Annie needs me back."

"Y'all just dump him somewhere tidy," says Fats. "Ain't fair to leave him in Roy's field."

"Where?" asks Tall Man.

"Take him some distance," says Fats. "Take the kid for a ride."

Makes me smile some, seeing them stranded stupid, all clumsy concerned in their bodies, thinking they could break me, trying to work things out, never knowing I'm there on top, whole and happy, looking down.

Dying's not like falling asleep. It's like waking from the dream of life.

I lift up, angling off to the left. I'm surrounded by things friendly, but I can't decide by what, by whom. There's a fluffy, foggy grayness, stretching into a tube, brightening as I rise. Incandescent specks are drifting past, some fast, some slow, like specks of dust dancing in a sunbeam. And I know we're all family together, all souls on our journeys, drifting our separate paths. The walls of the tunnel come clearer and silvery, the light at the end is glowing golden, bright, and close.

The light beckons, inviting. The light loves me. It understands and forgives. I need to reach that light and bathe in it, like I've never wanted anything else.

There's the grumble of thunder, then an explosion of light rolling out all around me. It's a liquid golden joy, brighter than the sun. Yet it doesn't hurt the eyes. I am at the center of the light, which exists entire for me.

I am the love of the world

My past, present, and future are layered in fluorescent skeins around me, so I understand the pattern. Now I see myself and my life, spread out in all directions, all times. I see how the smallest events pattern together. The chipped cup, the curdled milk, the grazed knee, the pig squeal, and the fallen leaf are all inevitable, necessary, and connected. There's no guilt or regrets, just how you judge yourself.

"I am the light," the radiance tells me. "I am the love eternal."

"Lee Cotton," I explain him. "Out of Eureka, Mississippi. Baseball incident. I guess you been expecting me?"

Go forth, angel

Now, it doesn't speak, the light. And it doesn't do small talk. Instead, it *shows* profound. It uses this luminous, radiant music, like a harpsichord sounding heartstrings, and a clarinet blown by kindness, scented with vanilla, aniseed, and sage, resonating into shimmering waves of logic that just kind of dance into the spaces, filling the gaps in your mind with joyful truth.

"We live to love," I realize. "Only love."

Then there's the magical riff, of seven luminous chords, telling me all there is to know, about the Almighty, our life, our purpose. It's utterly simple, extraordinary strange, and unspeakable lovely.

"God's truth?" I gasp. "I never knew."

"Man cannot know," the light tells, "until he sheds his body."

"Can't wait to tell the folks back home," I say.

Sweet Jesus, you know that feeling? When you said something terrible wrong? Or out of place? And there isn't no way you can take it back or make amends? Well, it's worse when you're addressing the Almighty, the Light of the Ages.

The light leaps back. The radiance dims. There's a chill breeze with spatters of rain.

"You are come too early," the light whispers, and wanes. "You are still attached to your heart and sinews."

"Can't I stay?" I plead. "Now I've come so far?"

But the gloom and the cold are unrelenting.

"Can I keep the secret? And take it back?"

Then, there's an almighty clack and the whir of tape-recorder rewinding. It's the seven chords played backward, ugly and discordant as fingernails scraping, broken hopes, babies howling, splintering bones.

And suddenly it's darkening, and I'm tugged downward, like scum through a bath drain, down through cold, slimed piping.

"Just ain't your time yet," Celeste croaks in the gloom.

"Shame of it, son," I hear Mama call, "trying to sneak into heaven in dirty boots and overalls."

"Kid can't do nothing right," I hear Scott cluck, "not even die."

"Just a matter of practice, Lee," soothes Uncle Nat. "Next time you'll get it right."

The pipe is sucking me faster, deeper, darker.

"Hey, son," James Jones calls. "Tell me I never warned you about blue Chevys?"

I hear a nasty, sniffy, slurpy sound.

Shlooooop . . .

That's my soul. Going back, the way it came. Snuffled back up my nose, like a lump of gory phlegm.

Sometimes, chile, a broke-up body's the only option you got

"Got a pulse now," says the woman in white. "Poor kid's come back."

"Shears," barks the man. "Let's open him up and take a look."

Someone's taking a road drill to my rib cage. I'm sliced open by unutterable sadness, chiseled by pain. My teeth are chattering from the icy cold. All over, I'm coated in slime and shame.

But all the time, I'm trying to remember the Secret of Life, like I just been told. Seven chords. About love, people, and something else. So jaw-dropping lovely and aching simple. So utterly simple—if I could only remember it—I could piss it in the sand.

I am mashed, crushed, wrenched, and shattered. My life's been crumbled and the pieces cast to the winds.

I'm only halfway alive but refused entry to death, and too damaged to wake, but the Lord protects, and so does the mind, because the brain knows its limitations, so when it's overtook by a caboodle of sorrows and cares, the mind drifts above the hubbub, distant and calm, or focuses on some small distraction, like the itch in a toe, the texture of a bedsheet, or the scent of surgical spirit.

Now, you got to remember, my brains been mashed and my senses scrambled, and I find myself dollar wise but cent foolish. I got the big picture, but not the small detail. Like I know the Lord loves me, and that I got a small place in his overall scheme, but I don't precisely recall my name. And I know someone done me a grievous injury, but I can't remember why or who. And I got a secure feeling I belong, only I forgot exactly where.

Should we take a cab home, Jesus?
Or can we hoof it back from here

So I am just lying there still and mortal cold. There's the chill weight of glaciers, stopping me moving a muscle. But it ain't as bad as it sounds because the mind clutches small comforts, and you got an inkling you're headed the right direction, inching back to life.

I'm dimly aware of things being done to me. I get sliced open and then sewn up. I get moved a lot and dropped once from a gurney. Light follows dark, follows light.

9

Getting My Head Together

When I wake from a long, dark, bumpy sleep, I find myself in bed in a white-tiled room where the warm air's soured by burnt toast, Lysol, and body fluids. I'm a parcel of bandages tied up by a tangle of piping. There's gauze and crepe and plaster all over, with tubes going into me and tubes coming out, ferrying my fluids, pink, yellow, red, and amber, with a throbbing white cabinet powering the whole shebang. Some Good Samaritan has taken me in and bandaged my wounds.

They've put a transparent plastic band around my wrist, holding a narrow card saying—

UNIDENTIFIED MALE. CLOSED HEAD WOUND. NEURAL TRAUMA.

But when they got to know me better, they come revise this to

UNKNOWN MALE. MUTE. IMPAIRED MENTAL FUNCTION.

But I don't take offense easy. Folks mostly mean well. You can taste the love in the air, rich and sweet as buttermilk. I can't expect them to know my name, when I can't recall it exact myself. And there's a limit to how thorough a total stranger can write you up in ballpoint pen on a strip of card no wider than your little finger.

I guess I look Frankenstein-monster scary. They've shaved my head and there are tramways of stitches round my scalp. I can't speak up to account for myself. My jaw's in a brace and my heavy tongue snagged on broke-up teeth. My face is swollen up, double size, glossy purple like an eggplant.

There's no knowing what language they're speaking to start. Their mouths are whirring blurs.

Hell . . . oh . . . haloa . . . halo . . . sun

I try to fix on some words that sound half familiar. But another crowd comes along and chases them away. A pulse of pain. And a golden flash passes through my head, scattering things screeching, like a fox through a chicken shed.

hear you can boy me nod once if

White coats and dark coats lean all over, sticking in needles, shining lights in my eyes, peering into my ears, pulling tubes in and out of my nose, spoon-feeding me, and fiddling personal down south.

one-twenty-five micrograms per kilo intermittent in glucose 5 percent

Most times they talk medical over me, but sometimes they speak direct to my particular parts, cutting out the uncertain middleman, telling my mouth to open, my throat to cough, my hands to unclench. They speak firm but kind, in simple phrases, like you'd use to train a puppy. But sometimes they're pure exasperated with the bits of me that won't learn, spill careless, or make messes on the floor.

fucking dumbfuck idjit, fucking stay fucking still, lumpa stinking dead meat

There's some thick mental skin people got to protect themselves from sympathy, and having other folks' thoughts and feelings come seeping in. But if I was thin-skinned before, with the voices visiting, I'm now stripped near raw. So it's hard to call my mind my own—with so much foreign suddenly drifting through.

indications throat infections, otitis media, streptococcal endo-carditis, meningococcal, and pneumococcal meningitis

look, you got cancer, I got asthma, we all got to die sometime, lady

A meal in a minute with the chef's touch in it

Dr. Ralph Cody, strong scented from cologne, peppermint Life Savers, and cigars, with a waxed mustache, gold-rimmed spectacles, and moist lips, drops by my bedside most mornings to pass the time of day, tap his silver pencil on his diary cover, buff the toe of his loafer on a trouser leg, and split his attention between me and a cordial observance of the nurses.

What we got? White hick farm kid, kicked senseless. Working hands. Profound neural insult. Symptoms? Aphasia, agnosia, amnesia. Prospects? Lousy. Prognosis? Smiling half-wit.

"Hi, son? How's your talk coming on?"

"Hmm," I say. "Hmth."

"Progressing, then?"

"Aha."

"Good, son. And any luck securing your name?"

"Eeee."

"Fine, son, fine." He taps my shoulder and looks around.

Can you beat the sight of a bending nurse in a garter belt? The
pear ass beats the apple ass every time

Time passes quick when they slammed you full of diazepam to stop
you having fits, and you ain't the full ticket. But after a year, I'm
starting to feel half right.

The way I saw it, they mended all my dented bodywork. Now
they were buffing it up real fine. My hair has grown back. The casts
have come off my arms and legs, and I'm shuffling around without
a stick. There's a long fine scar down my cheek, but you could mistake that for a youthful laughter line. They got a dentist to crawl all
over my mouth, screwing my jaw together, filling in, and smoothing down all the rough edges. So now I got a gapless smile on me
that is whiter and wider than ever before. And I get issued baseball
boots, new Levi's, and T-shirts by some Sisters of Mercy, in my
very own personal sizes.

I guess I look like one of those shiny limos on a Floyd Mathers's
sales lot—shot with fiberglass filler, welded up neat, then glossed
over, with nothing to show from the sheen I been scrap-heaped in
any write-off, head-on collision.

But the truth is the brain is one delicate, fine-tuned engine. And
you can't go running it without motor oil, or forget to change the
filter, or go whacking the distributor with a wrench, or slugging the
camshaft with a hammer, and still expect it to run smooth or accel-

erate from zero to fifty in under seven seconds. Because the fact was
I just couldn't run my mind for long without overheating. I couldn't
overtake any curb-crawler or drive up any steep incline without
stalling. And when I try to put it into fourth, I just get a terrible
grinding, crashing metal feeling, like the transmission's rattling
apart. So, some days, it feels like I'm boiling over and over-revving,
with all my warning lights come on together. Then there ain't nothing to do but park up in a rest stop.

Mornings and afternoons they have me exercising, twisting from side
to side, touching my toes, jogging on the spot, clenching and un-
clenching to squeeze foam balls, lifting weights strapped to my shins.

Before long I am getting twice-weekly speech therapy from
Miss Maxstead, who is a real kind fat pink lady with a scarlet face
furry as a peach and big mounds of dimpled chest that wobble with
her words, and kind of ripple with the soft sounds and quiver with
the hard.

"Look up," she commands. "Read my lips."

She gets me to repeat what she says. It starts off simple with
things like *sixish* and *good blood, bad blood,* or *red truck, yellow truck,*
then builds up to *preshrunk silk shirts,* with *freshly fried fresh flesh,* till
I'm feeling my way with real long strings like *The sawingest saw I
ever saw saw was the saw I saw saw in Arkansas,* and *Don't pamper
damp scamp tramps that camp under ramp lamps,* till I could handle
*Amidst the mist and coldest frost with stoutest wrists and loudest boasts
he thrusts his fists against the posts and still insists he sees the ghosts,*
which are things you'd never ordinarily have no call to say, except
they loosen your tongue for the general because, Miss Maxstead explains me, there are different but neighborly parts of the brain controlling the sense of words and the speaking of them, and I got me
more damage in my speaking center, so I got to work on that to
build it up, like an athlete would need to exercise a damaged knee.

"And we've got some grammatical problems, haven't we, Lee?"

"We have?"

"I think we'd better start building our auxiliary verbs, don't you?"

"Suits me fine."

"Because the gerundives are a luxury, while the adverbials can wait."

"Yeah?"

"Tell me, Lee"—she smiles confidential—"does the phrase *present tense* mean anything to you?"

Now, far as I remember, where I grew up, they never taught us children to speak. There weren't no proper talking lessons. They just trusted us to pick up language the best we could, by babbling and eavesdropping, chipping in, and such. And if the kids started slow, they kind of got the drift by the age of six or seven. And by the time they were old enough to date and drink and smoke, they could really speak their minds and say most everything they wanted.

But the way Miss Maxstead explains it, there are strict rules to saying anything, worse than algebra, morals, or legislation, like the definitive article, accusatives, the future with intent, the laws of the *if-then* conditionals, the positive obligations, the infinitive construction, continuous tense, phrasal verbs, and the past perfect, because, it turns out, the American language is centrally governed and tied down by bylaws, which makes me feel a real sucker that I've been talking mistaken all my life, confusing my *got* and my *have*, my *isn't* and *ain't*, switching tense without sense, speaking real inconsistent, because no one spared the time before to explain me exact how it's meant to be done, properly speaking.

For, until Miss Maxstead explains me the second time, I never even knew a *for*-clause can never precede the verbs it explains, but a *because* can.

"Because it might help," I suggest her, "if you got me some things I can read on my own to teach myself."

"You mean books?"

"Books would suit me real fine."

So, after that she brings me a pile of stuff, each trip. And, end of the session, we talk them through. Early on it was *Cat in the Hat, Fox in Socks,* Thing One and Thing Two, Quackeroo kids' stuff, but then I start to move up the grade levels to *Little Women, Black Beauty, Huck Finn, David Copperfield, Emma, Mrs. Dalloway,* all the way to Sammy Beckett and Mickey Spillane. We take a special long look at the modernists. For whom Miss Maxstead is real partial inclined, never mind they split infinitives.

Sure I faked an odd orgasm, Duke . . . but you faked a whole fucking marriage

But you get to realize there's lasting damage upstairs in my mental department. The world goes black-and-white come nighttime. There's a hazy circle, where the world's gone missing, to the right of my sight. It means I got to twist my head sideways to fill in, and look at things askance. When I'm tired, I drag my right leg and my speech goes slurred. As for the voices—they just got louder, worse—like they were liquored up, shouting to be heard in a noisy bar. But after a while, they quieted some and started to sober up.

Dr. Ralph takes time out to explain things. He says that when he operated on me, he had to take some damaged tissue out. So, when it comes to brains, I haven't got quite as much as I had. They took most from the left side of my mind, which is the part that controls language and logic, reading, writing, and arithmetic. But the right side isn't too bad.

But, then again, when it comes to brains, I got one more than I had. Because they had to do a commissurotomy, severing the two halves to stop me having fits. And the advantage of that, Dr. Ralph explains, is that I can use my right and left hands independent, which other people can't. And think two separate thoughts, and so on. So, all in all, I got me two brains for the price of one.

Anyway, he reassures, the mind's flexible. When bits get damaged, other parts take up the slack. So Dr. Ralph advises I got to learn to drive more on my right brain. It controls the left-hand side of the body. He says I likely find it easier to do most things left-handed. The right brain gives intuition too. It might help me to start relying on that.

"Noticed that, sir."

"And because you lost some tissue from the frontal lobes, you might find yourself flattened out, emotionally speaking."

"That matter any?" I ask.

"You win some, you lose some," he says. "The highs won't be so high. And the lows won't be so low."

"That's a shame," I agree. "But don't worry, Doc, it'll suit me just fine."

"And there's chunks of the left brain lost or damaged. You might find there's holes in your memory, and you can't recognize what things are and have trouble finding the words you want . . ."

"Noticed that, sir. And what's that hairy thing below your nose?"

"That's a mustache, Lee."

"Moo-starsh." I savor it. "Crazy. You doctors got a name for everything, sir. Don't mean to get personal, but what's it for?"

After that I start keeping notebooks so I can nail down the meanings of things. First, things go in the red book, as and when. Then, I organize them alphabetical in the blue book, which turns into my personal dictionary.

> Morbid—part of a body, dead or dying
> Moron—guy tries, but he's a slow learner

Mosquito—whiny bloodsucker
Mother—parent, female (everyone gets one at birth)
Much—big numbers, way past ten
Muff—private, wrapped-up part of lady
Muffin—spongy cake, often fruity
Mule—stubborn guy or animal, good for plowing
Must—when you gotta, you gotta
Mustache—vanity hair, on man's upper lip (optional)
My/mine—hands off, belongs to me
Myalgia—pain in muscles
Myopia—don't see far, not clear
Naked—without clothes
Nameless—wriggly, just can't fix the word to it
Natural—meant to be, just the way it is

It helps to organize things and pin them down. I also keep a drugs book of the pharmaceuticals they're pumping through me. I'm arranging my life like a jigsaw puzzle, trying to fill in all the missing pieces. Plus I taken to playing chess with Christie and keeping an open mind on what the next guy's thinking.

One time, Dr. Ralph calls me into his office to meet this broad, heavy-breathing, Spam-faced guy in a peaked cap. Truth is, I'd been expecting him or something similar, but with a different cap badge.

"Hi." I shake his hand. "Got me a letter?"

"No."

"You aren't the mailman?"

"No, son."

"Is there a fire, then?"

"I'm a policeman, son, not a fireman."

"Guessed it." I nod. "Knew right off you was something useful wrapped up in your uniform."

"You got beaten up real bad, kid," he says. "Remember what happened?"

"No, sir."

"Know your name?"

"Called Lee, sir. Lee something-else. Got an uncle called Nat, if that helps any. And a mother called Mama."

"So, Lee, where you come from?"

"Farm, sir. Hogs and chickens. Beans and corn." There's far more I know, but I don't care to let on.

"Where was that?"

"Near a road, sir. With fields, fencing, and a duck pond."

"Know how you come here, to St. Louis?"

Well, that came like a bolt from the blue. I'd reckoned I was still semi-local, in Mobile, maybe, or Jackson or Yazoo. Feel a sucker I never thought to ask. But when you're damaged goods, and the elevator don't reach the top floor, you don't think things through as thorough as you ought.

"You got dumped in the carriage of a freight train, headed north. Guard found you all beat up, near-enough dead."

"Spooky." I wince.

"So we know near enough where you came from."

"Where's that, sir?"

"Somewhere on the route—between New Orleans, Louisiana, and East St. Louis, Missouri. That mean anything to you, son?"

"Not a lot." I shake my head. Lying comes easier than a chase after truth. "I ain't especially good with faces, names, or places . . . You circulated any description of me?"

"White, male adolescent. Aged approximately sixteen. One hundred twenty pounds. Blond hair. Blues eyes. Southern accent. Possible delinquent."

"That should help," I agree.

The policeman rises, shakes his heavy jowls, straightens his hat. "Best of luck, son. Let us know if anything comes to mind."

What I don't tell Dr. Ralph or Sergeant Gene is that I remember a deal more than I've frankly declared. Because the mind, it turns out, is a dogged witness to the body's death.

First I get splinters of reminiscence. A blue car, a stench of sweat, a gappy mouth, a cedar tree, a work boot arcing into my face. Names and whole faces start coming too. The mind is piecing together the fragments, searching for sense and story. So, soon, I am suffering flashbacks.

Most nights Byron wakes me, looming out from the tree, swinging his baseball bat. It plays like a slow-motion film. I keep hoping he'll miss this time. But he always gets me smack in the forehead. However sluggish and prolonged the swing, I'm slowed down more. So I never get to duck in time.

Early pieces of film start to attach. My brain is editing the story, from the scattered strips on the cutting-room floor. It was always there in mind. It just got chopped up. It just needed sticking back together.

Gloomy things been coming back to me in bitter, treacly dollops. You think you've told yourself the worst. Then something darker comes trickling in.

I reckon I can't go home for a long while. When people have killed you, it's plain foolhardy to try to return. You only present yourself as unfinished business, being witness to the first event. So they'll only try harder, all over again. Then there's all sorts of unpleasant trickle-down could touch on Mama and Uncle Nat that I wouldn't even wish on my stepfather, Scott.

I can't reach Angel. No way. Not with Byron Clement minding her gate. And her scared out of her wits. Plus she likely don't want me anyhow, not now I've turned out to be black.

The law doesn't help because the Klan is the hand while the police are the glove. And justice isn't in my weak, trembly hands. Not till I'm properly mended. Not till I fix my plans.

All this leaves me hatreds to nourish like sunflowers from small, hard, brittle seeds. I just need rain, sunshine, and solid ground, and the patience to wait for harvesttime.

I decide to write a short letter home, revealing everything Mama needs to know, excepting my full whereabouts.

> *My Dearest Mother*
> *I reckon it must be near on a year since I left without warning and I am sorry to cause you grief but confused circumstances force me to leave in a hurry and since it is awful difficult to explain things which you are surely better not knowing I will write properly later so for now I just want to comfort you I am healthy cared for and happy but missing home, but please forgive my untidy writing which comes from an arm accident and maybe my punctuation ain't so smart as it was from a blow to the head but still you must feel my love close to you forever for whatever the miles I am only one state of the union away and keep you always in mind never forgetting PJ but now isn't a safe time to come home*
> *Your loving son Lee*

Times like this you feel grateful you got an education to fall back on. And while the homesickness makes me giddy with yearning, some weight is lifted from making the effort of explaining myself, putting a mother's heart at rest, and excusing my sudden absence.

But there comes a time in the life of a Mississippi kid on the run when being cast as a nameless Midwest half-wit, with free board and lodgings thrown in, comes as plain providential, for its promise of safe haven and provision of quality thinking time. And I was developing a taste for the easy-time white life, just hanging out, with folks making my bed, cooking my meals, correcting my grammar, and fixing my laundry.

Me, I'm just biding my time. I keep on writing home but I don't get any reply. I guess I'm in disgrace.

It's only three months later that Dr. Ralph calls me into his office all over again.

"Don't know what to do with you, son." He leans back in his chair, rests his feet on the edge of his desk.

"Happy where I am, sir, thanks. Charity Hospital. It's the only place I got." Plain fact is, there's no way home without drawing trouble on my family.

"We're *acute neurological,* son. Whereas you're more *chronic mental.*"

"Sir?"

"We can't find any kin to pay for your treatment. And you don't belong here, anyway."

"Feels like home, sir."

"Point is, you're kind of in between being ill and getting fixed. And you're on the cusp, between being a needy child-in-care and an indigent grown-up."

"How does that leave me, Dr. Ralph?"

"Leaves you a half-wit, son, passing through adolescence. Without much memory, but with an attitude and pimples."

"Not much mileage in that, sir."

He shrugs. "Zits are a passing stage, Lee. Being a half-wit probably isn't."

"Look," I say. "It ain't fair. You got to give a sucker an even break. Even damaged people can contribute some. I could pay my way by helping out." And I start putting back the scattered bits of puzzles he's got littering his desk. "And I could fix the door too. It doesn't hang properly since Boggs kicked it in."

Dr. Ralph blinks long. He looks at the puzzle pieces on his desk, then he stares at me. "Do you know what they are, Lee?"

*Stanford-Binet Nonverbal Reasoning Test, Spatial Logic,
Culture-Free*

"No idea, sir. Not a clue."

"Intelligence test, Lee."

"Didn't mean to go tampering with your intelligence, Dr. Ralph."

"Hmm." He squints to eye me keen. "Do you have any recollection of being clever before your accident?"

"Not that I recall, sir."

"Well you're off the scale. You have an intelligence quotient in excess of one hundred sixty."

"That bad, sir?"

"Good and bad." He nods. "Bad news is you're a dope. Good news is you're a clever one. You've got more brains than you let on."

"Brains, sir, no, sir. Never thought about it. I just let my fingers do all the thinking. The pieces say where they want to go, like when I'm playing chess . . ."

"Have you been playing chess too, Lee?"

"Not well, sir. I ain't no Capablanca or Alekhine. Don't know my King's Indian from my Lopez-declined."

a1–a2. Guess I'm in zugzwang now. Just can't make a move without worsening my position. Comes of reading books to pass the time. Seems like the harder I try to dig myself out, the deeper I'm sliding back in.

*I have a bona fide, publishable case study here. Brokenfohr in
Neurology had one. Well, now I have one, all to myself*

"I could try and arrange for you to stay around, Lee, but you'd have to pull your weight, do a job of some kind . . ."

"Job, sir?"

"Something like ward orderly–*cum*–case study."

"Sure thing, Dr. Ralph. That sounds neat."

"You wash floors, change linen, get food from the kitchen, shift the garbage. Do what anyone tells you."

"Great, Dr. Ralph. Can't wait to start."

Looking back, I should have asked there and then about the terms and conditions, but when you're chin-high in the pigpen, it doesn't contribute to count the flies.

10

Passable Average
White Guy

I am no sooner in my baggy dark blue overalls with my official
plastic and cellophane lapel badge, saying LEE—MEDICAL ORDERLY,
and a sudsy mop in my hand and frothy bucket by my feet, than
everyone's changed their tune, and the nurses and doctors who used
to ask smiling, *How you feeling today, son?* Or, *You need anything,
kid?* started scowling, saying, *Get your butt in gear, boy,* or, *Hey, you
sleeping on the job, or what?* And the other patients who used to treat
me like one of the guys, share magazines, or pass the time with a
game of checkers suddenly fall silent when I slouch by, or take
to demanding things, impatient peevish, like I'm suddenly turned
into some waiter/cleaner/pillow fluffer/asswipe/garbageman/shit
carrier/bottom-of-the-heap message boy/puddle attendant.

"Hey, Christie," I protest, "who do you think you're talking to?
It's me, Lee."

"Nurse," he bleats, gazing right through me, "that new orderly
won't fetch me a bedpan."

But there are plenty positives too, like my own boxy room in the

dormitory with a key to the door, nighttime privacy, free meal to-
kens for the staff cafeteria, and free run of the hospital.

After a week I pluck up the courage to ask Dr. Ralph if I'm allowed *out* of the hospital onto the streets of St. Louis.

"This isn't a prison, Lee." He frowns. "Do your job in the day
and you can do what you like in your free time."

"I can go *anywhere?*"

"The world's your oyster now, son," he confirms.

But there's a worry for me, still unresolved. I guess it's overdue
that I raise the unspoken issue of color.

"And what *race* would you say I was, Dr. Ralph?"

He squints, eyeing me perplexed. "I'd call you Caucasian, Lee.
I'd say you were Nordic-looking . . ."

"Shit." I whistle. "No kidding?"

I've truly turned into something else. I've turned into a free go-
where-you-want average white guy. It's like invisibility. No one
gives me a second glance.

So, lunchtime, I exit the bustle of the main foyer, clatter down
the steep white steps, tramp the grass to Lafayette Avenue, and turn
to look back at the eight stories of red brick, turrets, towers, Greek
columns, bleached arches, sooty windows of the building that so
long held me. It's good to feel the breeze on my cheeks and sniff the
fresh traffic fumes. I feel most parts cured at last.

My days off or weekends, Dr. Ralph sometimes invites me over
to his house, in particular if he needs someone to fix his fences, tend
his garden, paint his bathroom, mend his car.

He hands me down some fine-quality leisure clothes. But I'm
growing some, which leaves me a bit short in the sleeves and legs.
And I guess from kids' remarks on the streets, the tweed jacket,
button-down shirts, cravats, and brogues leave me looking secondhand frayed and over-preppie.

He and Mrs. Annie Cody, MD, have got themselves a large brick house but a small acreage, six bedrooms and no children, three toilets but only two butts, high fences but no livestock, and one of those progressive-liberal, separate-beds, pass-you-on-the-stairs, no-call-to-talk, mind-your-own-business, open-and-closed kind of marriages, but things still need saying, so they take to using me as go-between.

"Lee, have you seen my alleged husband. That paunchy, balding guy who hangs around evenings. He calls himself a psychiatrist. He reckons he understands people."

"Guess he's in the kitchen, Mrs. Annie, fixing a drink."

"Would you care to call on him, Lee? Ask him if he remembers me. Ask him who's fixing dinner."

"Sure thing, Mrs. Annie."

It's only four strides to the kitchen. The door's open. Sounds carry.

"Dr. Ralph?"

"Lee? Has Madame Bovary sent a message?"

"Your wife asked me to ask you . . ."

"Have you any idea what's involved in trying to gratify the lineaments of a wife's desire, Lee?"

"No, sir, never been married. Never had that luck."

"No . . ." He shakes his head. "Conundrum. Freud never fathomed it. Damned if I can either. I tried throwing kindness, time, and money at the problem, but nothing seems to work . . ."

"You could try some *love* and *respect,* you asshole," Mrs. Annie calls through from the next room, but not so loud as to labor her voice.

love you, honey? It's like reaching for the giblets inside a frozen turkey

But you can see from the framed photos, including her wedding day and final-eight lineup of Miss Arkansas 1942, that Mrs. Annie

Dr. Cody is one fine-looking lady before she starts drinking after-noons, eating burgers and ribs, onion rings and fries in bed, and getting coarse-grained, widened out all over, bordering obese, smelling of warm blood and chitlins like a newly slaughtered hog.

Had lovers kneeling at my shrine. Had men coming out of my ears. Had tits firm as grapefruit. Had a belly taut as a drum skin

It's the first time I'd hung out in a white folks' home, and while I don't like to typecast or paint a race a single color, I guess I was surprised at how much alcoholic beverage got consumed, how much fried chicken got ate, how little exercise got took or work got done, how slovenly folks could get in matters of routine personal hygiene, how many narcotic substances are left lying around, the volume of shouting, the traffic in obscenities and insults, the lack of faith or spirituality, the endless throb of soul or Tamla music, the dirty re-marks, sly thoughts, loose morals, and sexual static.

Once a week or so, Dr. Ralph calls me out from ward duties, and we spend some hours in his office. He asks me questions or gives me tests so he's got the full data to write me up. Truth is, he's planning to polish me up into a full-blown monograph, a footnoted case study.

We work through a stack of postcards he's got to see if I recognize any scenes or places. He's even raked up a photo of Main Street Briar, but I don't concede I recognize that. We look at inkblots or cartoons to find out what I see skulking in their shadows.

We record my voice so some linguistic friend of Dr. Ralph's in Santa Barbara can try place me precise on the southern map. But it turns out he can only explain me vague as Delta black, nearby Jackson, with some St. Louis overlay, on account of some aspirates, sliders, glottals, and rhythms I got stuck in my throat. So Dr. Ralph writes back to say *Nice try, Dean, thanks anyway.*

I get to look through a tachistoscope, which is like the end of some binoculars sunk in a metal box wired into the wall. This way Dr. Ralph can show different stuff, very fast, to my right and left eye, to see what I recognize, and how fast I react, which seems to amuse him, and I guess he's got sound-science reasons.

Other times, I get to count backward by threes from ninety-nine while listening in on some headphones so I can press a button whenever the voice says a five-letter word, which gets plain wearying after a while.

Then Dr. Ralph moves on to mapping my mental world. He's trying to work out what concepts I got stored top floor. This involves listing things like sports, occupations, animals, foods. Or I got to tell him how any two things—like *hope* and *tuna*—are similar to each other but different from a third—like *baseball*. We make some steady headway here. The way Dr. Ralph sees it, I got a mind that's been shaped and scripted by the weather, farming, the New Testament, spirituality, a sense of estrangement, nineteenth-century fiction, popular music, progressive politics, radio advertising, southern vernacular speech, an acute sense of hearing, and a preoccupation with sexuality, life, and death.

What I'm missing, he says, is any real self-awareness, personal ambition, sense of privacy, or social tact.

"Thank you, sir. That's real useful. I'll sure bear it in mind."

Every month or so, I get to travel to some university or hospital with Dr. Ralph, who takes me along as exhibit A and talks about me to a small flock of weary, sleepy doctors, shows X-rays of my head, describes my cortex and hematomas, and then gets me to demonstrate my general foolishness. At the end I get to beat one of the audience at chess, checkers, or Marienbad matches, which always amazes, since it turns out doctors are surprised if common folk can better them at anything, especially some hick kid with half a brain.

At the very end they ask one or two wordy questions, which is a way of sorting out their pecking order and letting slip what books they've written or read. After that, we leave the stage to muffled but genial applause, before meeting them all over again in a different room for coffee. It's completely finished then, unless Dr. Ralph gets an offer of dinner from a mental colleague or an invitation from some curbside lady in black leather shorts to a sleepover party at some motel, which leaves me steaming up the windows, camping out in the car.

One trip, I raise the issue with Dr. Ralph why he never had any children, if he felt he was missing out, and had he ever thought of adopting, maybe just a singleton. But he says a child is a responsibility for life, and you never stop paying for it with your emotions, time, and bank account, and that he'd chosen to help his fellow man through medicine instead, and maybe Mrs. Annie wasn't cut out for the self-denying strictures of motherhood, besides what prompts me to ask?

And I say that there must be young people all over who need a name and a sense of belonging and the chance to love and be loved. And he looks at me curious, sideways, anxious.

"Lee," he says at last, "we'd better fix you up with some proper identity, all yours."

"Dr. Ralph?"

"Get you a name you can call your own. So you can get yourself proper papers."

As it turns out, there's a scam for this. We just need to select a name, birthday, and place, then search for what we fabricated, in the Missouri Bureau of Vital Records, 930 Wildwood, Jefferson City. When we don't find it, we get the bureau to write themselves a letter of No Record, and Dr. Ralph writes too, explaining my lost situation.

Not many people get to choose their parents and the terms and conditions of their birth. But I struck lucky again. It left me free to choose most everything except my sex. I got able to add a year to my age, just to hasten my tiresome slow progress to maturity.

Lee Joplin Hendrix McCoy, white, born September 14, 1949, Ste. Genevieve, Missouri

Everything gets chosen particular. Second life round, I'm going to get it right—the real McCoy. September 14 is the date of my rebirth, when I woke from my coma. Joplin and Hendrix come from Janis and Jimi. But I don't know then that they're both going to overdose within a couple of years, turning me into a living memorial. And if you got to be born in Missouri, Ste. Genevieve is likely the prettiest spot, judging by the postcards I seen.

After you been a medical orderly a full year, you get to consider the career structure and plot your progress. My colleagues get mean with the patients, get friendly with the nurses, steal drugs, get drunk, get arrested, go missing. But they don't seem to draw respect, and they don't seem to be progressing in life. So I raise the equal opportunities issue with Dr. Ralph, behind closed doors in his office.

"Kids today," I say, "don't know they're born."

"They don't?"

"Open sesame. World's just sprawled there butt-naked, spreading its legs wide for them—free love, drugs, music. They haven't even had to push at the door. Aaron Chandler's dad just bought him a Spider convertible."

"Is that so?"

"And Jimmy Waters's folks going to put him through Princeton."

"Yes?"

"You think I should be going to college, Dr. Ralph?"

"I can't see who'd benefit," he declares.

"Medical orderly is useful . . . ," I say, "but it doesn't seem to lead anywhere."

"What are you looking for, Lee, professionally speaking?"

"Opportunity, sir, training, progress, with a view to money, status, power, freedom, women . . ."

"Let me see what I can do."

Which was how Dr. Ralph came to employ his rank and good influences to get me a job in the hospital pharmacy and a caretaker's room to bunk down. I land on my feet in the basement of the nurses' dormitory. Suits me fine. Smiling faces. Welcoming looks. Younger, hopeful voices. Sunny days. Velvet nights. Tangled sheets.

Knock on my door, pretty boy, any time

The past two years I've been passing for white, and I never pause to put people right. And vanilla gets to feel colorless comfortable. You get fewer hassles on the streets. You're less often asked to explain yourself, show ID, or use the back entrance. And the Delta farm boy has risen to the rank of pharmacy assistant, Charity Hospital, St. Louis.

Nights, I'm keeping the company of a golden-haired nurse called Ellen Alton who hails from Champaign, Illinois. But none of this has changed me fundamental, or made me forget my race or roots. I must have written home seven times. But I'm still waiting for the first reply.

Saturday afternoons I take myself to the library and follow events closer home, in the pages of the *Meridian Star* or *Jackson Advocate*, which keep me abreast of livestock prices, high school socials, baseball scores, announcements, Mississippi shipping, and Delta crime.

You never know whose smudged dotty face you're going to come across drunk driving, marrying Katie Beauregarde, dying, graduating, playing first base for the Pelicans, opening a record store in Briar, selling their pickup, or serving ten in Parchman for armed robbery.

Byron Clement got arrested for shooting up a car carrying NAACP organizers. Two dead. I follow his trial by weekly install-ments. He gets bail and an all-white jury. There's a photo of An-gelina outside the Jackson courthouse, a foot taller than her daddy, standing an arm's length away, looking the other way, blank and withdrawn like a Kennedy widow stranded lonesome among the common people. Looks so strange that this mean, leather-faced gib-bon of a man can father such a pretty daughter. The article reports she's waiting tables at the Magnolia Diner, to support her career as a singer. Looked like she'd turned out as plain glossy and lovely as she'd always supposed.

The way I see it, it's my trial too. I'm another unnamed victim, and when Byron Clement gets arrested in Jones County for shoot-ing a black man, a hopeful message goes out to us all. And it feels a touch safer taking a Greyhound home. Seize the day.

11

Dead and Buried

So one Saturday night I take the bus. And one Sunday morning I'm wandering back down the Briar Road, kicking up dust, getting giddy high on the pine, hayseed, and pollen air.

I've grown four inches the last couple of years and put on twenty pounds, muscle and bone. I'm wearing my hair liberal long over my ears, to my shoulders. There's cool-dude, drug-dealer mirror sunglasses shading my eyes. People say I look the spit of Peter Fonda. I guess I come across citified. The fringed leather jacket and scarlet loon pants sure show I'm not local.

Uncle Nat is stooped, chopping kindling by the barn. He rises, stroking his back, to watch my approach. With a final swing, he sinks the ax deep in the chopping block.

"Sir?" He wipes the palms of his hands on his overalls.

Circus comes to town?

"Hi."
"Yeah?"

"Long time," I say. "Now I'm back. If you like, I can stay awhile."

"Don't have the pleasure." He extends a stiff arm and a leather catcher's-mitt handshake. "Young man."

"Uncle Nat." I smile. "It's me." And I pull off my shades. "I brought you a box of cigars and a pint of rye."

"Sir?" He scowls polite. "I know you from someplace?"

"It's me. *Lee.*"

"Knew a Lee." He shakes his head. "He was a good kid, but he's long gone now."

"Ask me something; I'll prove it's me. Some doohickey details that only I could know."

He shrugs.

You some hippie, boy, lost on drugs?

"Remember Bessie's calf with six legs? Remember the jimson-weed cure?"

"Okay, son," he says, "you want to play games? Who ate my birthday cherry pie, five years back?"

"PJ starts, and I finish it. Too scared to tell you then. I'm real shamed to tell you now."

He eyes me shrewd. "Show me your sickle scar," he demands. He's entering into the spirit now.

"Sure, Nat." I roll up my trouser leg. "There," I say. "Seven stitches. Summer of '63."

"Knew it was you. Guessed all along." He slaps his forehead with his shovel hand and cackles. He goes to clutch me, then steps back and frowns.

He slumps on a hay bale, rocking and groaning, covering his face with a hand, peeking through his fat sausage fingers. I sit myself down by his side.

"You've grown plenty, Lee," he says, "and you died too. Hard to square it all in my mind . . . It's like you're some spook haunting or something."

"Just flesh and blood. Live as can be."

"No, son. You properly, finally, *certificated* dead."

"No, sir." I smile.

"Yes." He nods. "Believe me. I been to your funeral, Lee."

I help carry your coffin. I contribute twenty-eight dollars for the headstone. I shed my own tears

"Can't be."

"First they find your cap and jacket, all bloodied up. Three months later they find your body buried nearby, in Cooder's field, all broke up in pieces."

"Not my body. No, sir." I slap my thigh. "Trouble with Mississippi. One sprawling cemetery. Dead dug in everywhere."

I look down the slope to my clapboard home. There's no smoke from the chimney and the curtains have all come down.

"No one home?" I say.

"Your mama and Scott take the twins to Chicago. They don't like to stay here anymore."

"Girls?"

"Anna and Amelia."

"Cute?"

"Real nice, *normal-looking black* kids."

"Best way," I say. "Where's PJ?"

"He went skinny miserable. Never stop yelping . . . So we done the kind thing."

He invites me into the house but I say better not. Grateful. Kind thought. Another time. Gets too complicated for folks—chasing down the right words to converse with the dead. Takes too much time doing a Lazarus-risen act for a family of six, all coming and going.

"Only one thing I ask, Nat. Three photos if you can spare them. One of Mama, one of Celeste . . . and one of me as I used to be."

When he's trudged back from the house with the pictures, we just sit and talk, over an hour, past and present—family, hog breeds, collard cultivation, pea pollination, neighbors, cotton, legumes, nitrogen fertilizer, galvanized nails, fencing, tractors, seed corn, carburetors. I write my address for him and he gives me Mama's. At the end, I get directions so I can go visit my grave and leave some flowers by my headstone.

I turn at the road to wave and see Nat slapping his head bemused, like he's trying to shake something loose, out from an ear.

Eureka looks shrunk, dusty, and flaky distressed. Seems strange how I could have confused a street for a town. Folks give me severe sideways looks. A passing car sounds its horn. Driver shows me a finger. Not because folks recognize me, but just because they don't. They're flexible that way. I ain't that freaky-looking black kid anymore, just some uninvited foreign white trash, messing up their strip.

Down the Briar Road I see a blue Buick parked up on the shoulder. The hood's raised and a guy's leaning over the engine. I can smell burning rubber. Something inside me wants to turn on my heels, while something else tugs me on.

Mr. Byron Clement pokes his cartilage face out from the shade of the hood, like a turtle out of its shell. He got his hooded eyes screwed in concentration, dragging the last drop of tar from a cigarette butt that he holds dainty delicate between curled finger and thumb.

He swivels to watch me. We are twenty yards apart. He's eyeing a passing stranger. I'm watching the man who broke up my life with a baseball bat. The lizard, scumbag, frack-face, misbegot, son of a bitch, shoat, lowlife, snakebite, diddy-bob, dirt road, cracker, green as owl shit, chicken bone, ignant, puke, asswipe, mother-fucker, by-blow, pootbutt, shit on a stick, asshole, cocksucker, wethead, bastard, redneck, fuckface, cunt-bubble, spunk-rag, shit-dribble.

He turns his head, coughs, and spits on the ground. But he has me fixed, held at the edge of his vision, stock-still, like a rabbit in the headlights. Then he turns and beckons with a slow cupped hand and outstretched arm, like he's directing a reversing truck.

"Know your way round an engine?" The voice is juiced up, slurred. He's a frail, leather-skinned, sunken-cheeked, chicken-boned man in oversize jeans. He sways dizzy and winces as he leans my way.

"Kind of," I say. I like to help the next guy. But for Byron Clement I make exemption.

"You local?" He squints against the sun.

"Kind of," I say.

"I know you from someplace . . ." He nods and his groggy eyes skid around me. "It'll come to me," he promises and taps his head. "I got a fucking memory like a fucking elephant."

"You're overheating," I warn.

"Steaming. And a stinka fucking burning rubber."

"Uh-huh." The way I smell it, Mr. Byron Clement been drink-ing rye, ain't washed recent, and his car got a broken fan belt. Or a burst cooler hose. "That so?" I say.

"You got a spare smoke?" he asks.

"Sure." I pass the pack. "You checked your fluids?"

"Feeling kinda dizzy," says Byron, drawing heavy on his Marl-boro. "Got these stabby pains—chest and arms."

"That'll be your heart and cooling system," I advise. "You been running too hot and frying your engine."

"Know how to fix it?"

"Maybe the car," I say. "Wouldn't know where to start with your sorry heart. Look, ain't your fan belt shredded?"

I reach for the edge of the hood. I could crash it down on his head. I could proceed with the wrench from there. But my hands freeze. They don't want to do it. Traitors.

"Yeah." Byron peers back at me.

"No, look," I plead. "Look again."

But I got a muscle mutiny, proceeding up my arms. I've shackled myself with cowardice. And now Byron ducked out again from under the hood.

"I could fix it temporary with nylon or tights," I say.

"Got a daughter at home," says Byron. "She got nylon lady things."

"Far?" I ask.

"Couple of miles."

"Give us your belt, then," I tell him. "That'll get us back. Once we cooled down."

Byron smirks grateful. He shuffles round to the driver's side clutching the top of his jeans to stop them falling down to his knees.

"Grateful, son. Nigger passed me in a pickup," Byron laments. "Never stop to help. We white folks got to stick together."

"Hell, you got noisy tappets, sir," I say. "And terrible piston rattle. And foul emissions."

"I done some hard miles," he concedes.

Byron Clement's house is a clapboard shack. It's the shape and size of Dr. Cody's garden shed, only in far worse repair.

We climb the steps. Byron settles in his lounger. It's the back-seat of a Rambler four-door sedan, which he's converted clever into a two-tone leatherette and velour sofa, by unbolting it out of the car and screwing it tight to the front of his house.

"Angelina," Byron barks, and closes his eyes. "We got company."

The girl doesn't hurry. She comes scowling in her own good time. She's grown plenty. Five nine or ten. Fuller figure, narrow waist. Hair tied back in a copper ponytail. Gold hoop earrings. Red apron, white blouse, dressed for work at the diner. She doesn't go easy on the mascara. She carries the scents of cologne and fries. She's gnawing her lip, looking past me, with plenty on her mind and better things to do. I gaze down at her calves and ankles. She's lost the Bambi look but a gentleman couldn't complain.

"If you got some old tights," I say, "I can fix the fan on your daddy's car."

"And get us both a beer," barks Byron.

"Ain't you had enough already?"

"Never had enough," Byron observes wistful. "Never once in my life."

The girl clucks and ducks back into the house. I wander down to the car and lift the smoking hood.

"These do?" Angel wanders up behind. She palms me a warm crumpled ball of nylon. She winces at passing something up close personal to a total stranger.

"Fine," I say. Then I take off my shades and give her a shy, awkward grin. Sweet lady, mine.

"Sweet Jesus." She looks me full in the eyes.

"Hi," I say. "It's been a real long while since you peeled off your tights for me."

"Sheeeet . . ." She sighs. "Tell me it ain't you?"

"Guess it is." I smile.

"Thought you were . . ."

feeding the worms, pushing up flowers

"No," I say. I'm conscious of Byron watching. She's looking blanched and spooked, which only draws attention.

"You got a problem, Angel?" he calls.

"No," she says, "not me." And she backs off and watches me dip over the engine.

"Fucking death wish?" Angel hisses, crimson. "Where you living now?" She splits her lips and shows her glistening pink mouth.

"St. Louis. You singing?"

"Bars and clubs. You working?"

"Hospital. You seeing anyone?"

"Sure. Any business of yours?"

"How come your daddy's out of prison?"

"Bail. Your family?"

"Moved on."

"Hey, Angel," Byron barks. "You forgot the beers?"

"That ring on your finger?" I ask. "Does it mean anything?"

"This?" She fingers the band. "It's a boy-girl thing."

"Shame," I say, "crying shame."

"Great to see you looking well, pretty boy . . . Always have a place for you, back of my heart."

"There's a thing I need to ask you, Angel . . ."

"Lee?"

Guess it's now or never. Things just got to be said.

"You want to come live with me in St. Louis? Hitch our destinies? Rent an apartment? Buy a TV? Fuck like rabbits? Get a backyard barbecue? Have my babies? Live real happy?"

"Truth is"—Angel frowns, takes a couple of steps backward, hands on hips, gazing past me—"can't say it's what I got planned. Not for my life."

wrong time, wrong place, wrong person . . .

"Babies needn't be immediate, Angel. We could wait till you're good and ready."

She shakes her solemn head. She looks to the ground. She chivvies a tuft of grass with the toe of her shoe.

"No chance?"

"It's not a black-and-white thing, Lee."

"No?"

"It's just a things-move-on thing . . ."

"I'll always love you, Angel . . . Maybe we could . . . further down the line?"

The girl shrugs. "You better go, Lee. It sure isn't safe for you. Not here." She squeezes my hand quick and limp, then lets it drop.

"You got a pen and paper?" I say. "At least?"

I feel wooden and hollow. Things come across when you've got sound intuition. When she touched my hand, a picture flashed through my mind. I saw her riding, hair blown, smiley in the front seat of Jeb Walker's '58 Plymouth Fury—the two-tone lime-and-mustard model, with leaky gaskets, rattling exhaust, lazy back suspension, and a Dixie-flag fender plate, trailing a thick gray vapor plume.

Still, she'd spoken affectionate and smiled twice. And when you analyze it careful, it comes across more as "Maybe, sometime" than "No way, never," which leaves a guy a splinter of hope for the future. And she seemed half pleased to see me, in a scared, go-forth kind of way.

But, shit, I nearly died for the lady. I spilled my brains for her. A guy could hope for more.

So, now, there was nothing left for me in Eureka but to go visit my grave and pay my respects, to whatever sorry soul got buried in my place. Obligation. Duty of care. In the normal course, no one wants to know you once you're dead.

———

For Angel I leave a paperback copy of *A Patch of Blue* that I'd bought special for her on the likely occasion of us meeting up. It's the tale of a blind white girl, from a bigot family, who falls in love with a guy, never realizing he's black.

For Byron I leave a good-bye note, folded on his driver seat.

Mr. Clement:

You don't recognize me. I'm the Iceland nigger you keep meeting along the Briar Road. Once you warn me off. Once you break my head with a baseball bat. Once you ask me to fix your car.

Many things happen to me because of you. I've gone to heaven and then come back. I lost my family. I lost the love of my life. I turned white. I got an education.

I came with half a mind to kill you. But then I realize Jesus loves you, if no one else. And when we meet up I find you shrunk, ill, drunk, and stupid as a tick. And it's a real poor pleasure, crushing bugs.

There are many needless human afflictions—meanness, rage, stupidity, self-pity, drunkenness, poverty. And you sure got the royal flush. So I'm doing the meanest thing I know how. I'm leaving you here, just how you are.

How does a morbid, dried-up runt like you father such a beautiful, warm-hearted, sweet-lipped daughter?

Yours sincerely,

Lee McCoy

I suppose it was real harsh-worded in parts. But I speak as I find. And the most part was heartfelt fair and lifted some heavy baggage.

I know it's kind of flaky. But I kept Angel's nylons, crumpled in my pocket, and never fixed them to her daddy's car. The truth is, I guess she wore them recent, because at the crux of it, they carried a poignant, personal scent, which took three months to fade. You cling to the little you get.

There were dark things looming that I didn't sense coming. When I get home, there's a yellow military envelope waiting. You never realize when you're young how every small choice carries consequence. And the birthday I select for myself wins a prize, coming first in the 1969 selection board lottery.

So they write me immediate to come for a physical examination, to determine if I'm fit for military service. When you read through the paperwork, you appreciate the U.S. Army is thorough and literal, and risks nothing to the civilian imagination. They tell you to *hereby* report, *pursuant* to their order, and where, and why, and what to do if it's a hardship. Everything is dated and timed, numbered and signed, underlined and capitalized. So you'd have to be a half-wit to misunderstand, after you've read it through the third time.

I don't know a better place to rest my head. Sure, every woman's different, but I never met any dish that can better that mix, of salt and peppery, sweet and sour, solid melting, warm and spreading, delicate and pungent, even if it tires the tongue and you can get some hairs snagged up in your teeth. And I just lie there thinking I'm Benny Goodman and she's my clarinet. Or I untangle all the seven scents. So, having my mind sunk deep in the business, I reckon Ellen could try to concentrate too.

Hurry, Lee. You snuffling round like a dog sniffing ass. Gotta wash some pants . . . and the Byrds coming live on the radio

"Got some news," I say. "I got a letter for the draft medical."
"Take some blues," says Ellen. "Race your heart, or take some oxyprenolol."

"No," I say, "they're wise to that. They keep you overnight, to see if things wear off."

"Or prick your veins like a junkie."

"No need. I've got this." I tap my foolish head.

First thing, they make me strip, take my blood pressure and pulse, look me all over. I guess I pass as bony, healthy.

"You got epilepsy, heart disease, renal damage, drug addiction, or alcoholism?"

"Not yet, sir. Not me."

"You delinquent, homosexual, an addictive or a degenerate character?"

"I never got round to any of that stuff yet, sir."

"You want to serve your country?"

"I'd sure like to, sir . . . Only, I don't insist it's in the army."

"Congratulations, soldier, you're A1 fit, sound as a bell, strong as a mule."

"Haven't you forgot to look over my head?"

"Seen enough. Heard all I need." Doctor One smiles satisfied brisk.

"I just feel I need to tell you one thing, sir."

"What, son?"

"I'm a half-wit, sir, fully certified."

"You are?"

"You ever read 'Clever Fool: The Boy without a Past,' by Ralph Cody, MD, *Alabama Journal of Neural Trauma*, volume XXI?"

"Don't recall I have."

"I advise you take a long look, sir. It's a landmark case study of forensic neurology. I don't mean to brag, but that idiot is *me*."

"Yeah?" He's flicking through his papers. "The army doesn't mind idiots. It needs all it can get, if the truth be told."

"Just I'm damaged goods, sir. I got profound neural insults, with trauma to my temporal lobes and Broca's area."

"Fine by me." He smiles.

Heard it all before, son, every variant. Just don't give me any of that psycho shit about John the Baptist, avenging angels, or vampire blood

"And I hear *voices,* sir."

"Voices?" He pulls off his glasses and rubs his eyes. I guess I've stolen the pot with an ace on the flop. "Tell me," he says, sudden weary. He draws my papers back out of the stack and slaps the folder down on the desk.

"Other people's thoughts, sir. Dead souls too."

"These voices, what do they say?"

"Most everything they want to," I say. "Loads of personal crap and dirty talk. But it's nothing to do with me. I'm just the radio receiver."

He lifts the phone. "Mac, here," he announces to the invisible party. "Got another textbook-reading, time-wasting reluctant soldier . . . Voices . . . Probable bullshit, query schizo."

It's a high-stakes professional organization, the army. They can't afford to equip any paid-up psycho with grenades and a high-velocity rifle, because they might turn out some loose killer type. So I get passed on down the line—from psychologist to psychiatrist to neurologist, and back again. They keep on throwing more doctors my way. First ones are young, smooth, and smug. But soon they start balding, graying at the temples, and furrowing their brows. By the end, I just get liver-spotted silverbacks, blinking over their bifocals, shaking with Parkinson's, jerking with tics. It seems like the medical profession is withering away before my very eyes.

"Any of the following ever spoken to you directly?" asks Doctor Two. "Jesus Christ, John the Baptist, Moses, the Virgin Mary, the Beast, the devil or any of his demons, or any characters from the Bible?"

"No, sir. Not yet they haven't."

"Napoleon, Adolf Hitler, Joseph Stalin, Fidel Castro, Ho Chi Minh, General Westmoreland, or President Nixon? Or any famous or infamous figures from life, fiction, film, or history?"

"No, sir. None of them."

"Good. Have you experienced any of the following: hallucinations, loss of will, confused identity, sense of leaving your body?"

"I left my body once, sir. But that was just riding my soul, when I died for a while."

"Right, son." He rubs his forehead vigorous. "I suppose you'd better explain that too . . ."

So, then, I got to go into getting beaten senseless for dating a white girl, getting united with the light eternal, and hearing the seven most beautiful chords in the world, forward and backward, then coming out of my coma, and all that neurological shit.

"Dating a white girl?"

"That's a big chunk of the puzzle," I say. "Did I forget to tell you I was black?"

"Black?" he asks. "In what way?"

So, I tell him in a skin way. So, then, I got to backtrack about growing up as an Iceland colored, with double-recessive white genes, because my mambo grandmother was only part black, while my daddy was pure Scandinavian blond. And all the troubles that that entails in central Mississippi, where folk can cling on fierce to some old-fashioned racial attitudes.

"Mambo?" asks Doctor Three. "As in voodoo priestess?"

So then we're onto comparative religion and why Hollywood never gave voodoo a fair crack of the whip, and that a mambo is truly part Christian Scientist, part Roman Catholic, with some herbalism and chicken-keeping thrown in.

"But you got to keep open to the spirits," I explain. "It's in my blood. That's why I get to hear other folks' thoughts."

"A mind reader, huh? That's interesting, son."

"One last complication, sir. I'd better mention it to clear the air. Then you'll have heard the whole caboodle. The truth is . . . I'm officially dead."

"Dead?" says the doctor. "That isn't obvious. Would you care to explain?"

So, then, I got to backtrack through the grief of having somebody buried in my stead and going to see my very own headstone—*Lee Cotton, Loving Son.*

"Cotton, Mr. McCoy?"

"Shit, sir. I think I left something out. Did I forget to tell you, I changed my name?"

I'd never had the chance or leisure to run through all the natural complications of my Mississippi childhood with a team of mental experts. After you've seen a few of their specialists, you get to understand that the army is fair-minded, and that if you are honest with them, they'll be real straight with you in return.

"May I speak straight with you, Mr. McCoy?"

"I'd welcome that, Emeritus Professor Lieutenant Colonel Greene, Purple Heart, Retired, sir."

"You've had an improbable life, young man, or you're some draft-dodging worm, wriggling about in his own heap of shit."

"You've got it in one, sir," I agree. "All my life, I been dogged by unlikelihoods and cursed by coincidence. I'm a walking *Ripley's Believe It or Not.* Sometimes, it feels like I'm fated or something."

"We'll see about that, shall we, son?"

So he gets these Rhine figures out of a cupboard and blows off the dust. They're a pack of cards marked with squares, triangles, wavy lines, and such. You got to guess which shape he's looking at. After we've run through the pack twice, he tells me I've done just fine.

"People misunderstand the army, McCoy. They think it's about scooping up the youth of our nation to get killed or crippled in Vietnam. But we're also busy defending the homeland."

"Sounds like good work, sir." I specially like the sound of *home.*

"You've heard of the Beige Berets?"

"No, sir."

"Special outfit. Elite force. Psychological warfare. Do you think you'd be interested in trying out for them?"

"That involve travel to Southeast Asia?"

"They mainly fight from their desks in Nevada. We can't all be battlefield heroes. We have to serve where we're needed, soldier."

"Yes, sir," I say. "I reckon I'd prefer that to 'Nam, so sign me up."

He takes time out for a phone call.

"Vernon," he says to the other party, "it's Bobbie. You rascals still collecting freaks? . . . Yeah, for real . . . I've got you a cracker, gift wrapped with a scarlet ribbon . . ."

But they don't let just anyone into the First Mindborne. You've got to meet stringent mental criteria. First off, you got to take a pencil-and-paper exam. The army got a method and a test for everything. Normal intake they give you the ASVAB, where you got to work small numbers, muscle some words, say which month follows August, and decide which conducts electricity better—copper or wood. This way they sort the wheat from the chaff, technician from rifle carrier. But for the psychic intake they give you the PESKY too, which has general psychic questions, with separate scales for psychokinesis, prediction, psychometry, telepathy, and out-of-body. It's got two-hundred-odd trip-wired multiple-choice questions like

1. Examine this photo of the Jefferson Building, Engineering Faculty, University of South Carolina. Float down the main corri-

dor in a westward direction. How many chairs do you see in Room 130?

(a) 0 (b) 12 (c) 38 (d) 145

2. This exam paper has been exposed to toxic material. Is it
(a) anthrax (b) cesium (c) uranium (d) all of these

3. I wrote these questions. Am I
(a) Norbert B. Silver (b) Norbert B. Goldman (c) Sylvia McClusky (d) Abe Joos

And you just got to struggle through and try answer them all, even when you haven't a clue, or reckon all the alternatives are wrong. And they're making you take the test butt-naked, lonesome, in a copper-lined room, wearing earmuffs, facing gray walls under orange light, so you can't pull papers out of your sleeve, listen in to what any other guys think, or get distracted by any static, auras, electromagnetic phenomena, or radio waves.

Anyway, I score 39 percent, which doesn't sound that hot, but it's a solid step up from guesswork or chance, which only gives you 25 percent. And Sergeant McAndrews seems real pleased when he talks through the scores, even though I'm just a one-trick pony. It turns out I can telepath like crazy, but I hardly telekinese, transmit, or psychometricate myself from Adam. And I just couldn't foresee to save my life.

12

The Beige Berets

There are seventeen of us on the dusty army rattle-bus from Carson City to Fort Scott. Everyone's got a hard wooden bench to themselves. There's no visible life stirring outside, so when we're tired of watching the heat shimmer, dust whorls, sand, and sage, we turn our minds to the littered corrugated-metal floor and on to each other. It doesn't take a psychic to spot we're an odd, cagey collection. I guess we're feeling each other out.

The Sioux guy opposite leans across, smiling sly. "Any chance . . ."

"Sure . . ." I reach in my pocket and pass him the pack of Luckys.

"You a mind reader, or something?" he asks.

"Uh-huh," I say. "And you?"

"Diviner. Dowser. Stuff underground and out-a-sight—oil, water, minerals, bodies."

"Useful," I say. "That's a livelihood you got there."

"Made a living, till this fucking draft."

"Crazy times."

"I dreamed this shit-hole we're going to."

"What's it like?"

"Sand. Sun. Restless dead. Badlands. Snakes and a stink of drains."

There must be some poltergeister goofing off at the back of the bus, because this guy reading *Sports Illustrated* finds the pages smoldering alight, and we got to stop to clear the smoke. Then, as luck has it, we get a broken windshield, out of a clear blue sky, even while we're parked. The glass crackles frosted then blows outward, scattering gleaming shards on the hood.

U.S. Army? I can break that too

Sergeant Bing welcomes us to basic training. He tells us that Fort Scott is a converted prison, surrounded by desert and electrified razor wire, so we should draw our own conclusions if it's there to keep the vermin in or the wildlife out. He says how some of us are honest volunteers and some are dumb conscripts, too stupid to avoid the draft, but what unites us is being a special intake of freaks and miswired minds. He says he himself is a normal, regular guy and that eternally damned abortions of nature like us don't cut no ice with him.

He says he's got to break us, then teach us to march, shoot, and suffer. He warns that he is going to have to crush us all up before he can piece us together as soldiers. He tells us we'll be called upon to lick his ass, drink his piss, clean the parade ground with a toothbrush, crawl through a mile-long overflowing sewer, before sorting the Nevada desert into two piles of sand—the yellow grains and the white grains—just as we ourselves will be sorted and assigned into two lots, the reuseable trash and the throwaway junk.

Right after, his sidekick, Sergeant Brody, steps up smiling like Christmas and tells us that a supper of mushroom soup, meat loaf with onion gravy, and apple pie with pecan ice cream will be served at eighteen hundred hours prompt, and that vegetarians, Jews, Islamists, and dietary deviants should announce themselves to the quartermaster, and that the evening's movie will be *Bringing Up Baby* with Katharine Hepburn and Cary Grant, and he hopes we enjoy it just swell, just as he wishes us every success in life.

"Bad cop, good cop," says this slack-mouthed, dreamy-eyed, carrot-haired freckled kid sitting next to me. "Name's Ethan Carey." He offers a moist, limp hand.

"Lee," I say. "McCoy. Pleased to make your acquaintance."

He's a gangly guy with a shy horse-tooth grin and a vacant air about him, out of Chicago.

He gets the bunk alongside. First morning I wake up and see him checking his face real curious in a shaving mirror.

"Have I been behaving odd, Lee?"

"No, Ethan. Everything's fine."

"It's February fifteenth?"

"Sure is."

"Basic training, right?"

"Sure. You got a problem you want to share, Ethan?"

sometimes it's later than you think

"I'll tell you later, Lee." His eyes are dancing round, checking no one else is tuning in.

Of course, it's a freaky intake into Mindfuck, so you got used to a level of eccentric behavior powered by maverick minds.

"What are you in for, Lee?"

"Mind reading."

"Cool," he says. "It takes all sorts. I'm grateful for the warning."

"And you, Ethan? Why'd they pick you up?"

"I've got future memories." He winces, apologetic.

"What's that?"

"I remember things that haven't happened yet."

"No shit," I say. "Neat stuff."

"Nah . . ." He shrugs. "It doesn't get you anywhere. It's way more trouble than it's worth."

Later, when he explains it, I get to see his point of view. The way he tells it, time is like the elevators in some fancy New York store. There's several in parallel, some going up, some going down. Unlike the rest of us, and without knowing, Ethan gets shifted from one elevator to the next. It tends to happen overnight or if he has a fit. He can wake up and find he's ten years older than he was the night before, or seven years younger. That's why he always checks the date first thing and takes a good look at his face, for warning signs of age or youth.

"I'm just a regular guy, doing ordinary things. But I end up doing them out of sync. One day I wake up next to my wife, Karen, and I haven't even got married yet. Find out there's a couple of kids too."

"She nice?"

"Fine, decent woman." He wipes some moisture from his eye. "Pretty as hell too. But imagine how I feel. This woman has borne me two sons. She's stuck with me through my odd turns. She stands by me when my business goes bust . . ." He sniffs.

"And?"

"And I don't even know her name, because I haven't even met her yet. No wonder she gets pissed with me, when I wake up in the morning and say, 'Hi, pretty lady, who are you?'"

"Shit," I say.

"That's why things went so wrong between us, Lee. That's why she files for the divorce. She says she can't go on living with a total stranger."

"Tough break, Ethan." I nod.

"You know the worst thing, Lee?"

"What's that?"

"I've got it all to come. It's all downhill after I pass thirty-six—the nervous breakdown, the divorce, the car crash, the drinking, the kidney disease . . ."

"That's a real bummer, Ethan. But if you keep jumping backward and forward in time . . ."

"Yep?"

"Ain't you got some choice bits of your childhood to look forward to?"

"Hey, man. My dad's a complete psycho. And my mother ran off with my orthodontist."

"Sorry to hear that."

Course I sympathize like shit with Ethan. Only, there's something shabby, unchristian comforting about running into some guy that got lumbered mental even odder than you.

To start off in this man's army, they get you to run around in fatigues and boots, try on gas masks, climb needless obstacles, swing on ropes, fall off walls, assemble an M14 in the dark, bayonet sandbags, bandage a guy's guts back into his belly, and breathe in tear gas in a concrete cellar, and all that kind of boy-games stuff. It's all hot, gritty, and loud. You get yelled or screamed at most times, and everything—eyes, nose, food, nostrils, clothes—gets shot full of Nevada sand.

Our hearts aren't in the marching and shooting. Their hearts aren't in teaching us, because they got some better use for us up the line. After a few weeks they start easing up on the physical jerks and assessing us up close and personal, then we move indoors to a classroom and, mornings, we get to take classes with a Captain Bell, who is a bulge-eyed Gene Wilder look-alike physicist out of Cornell in a grandpa vest and tie-dyed silk bell-bottoms, and a Major Grey, who is some embalmed desk-spook from the Defense Intelligence Agency in a gray wool civilian suit and black bow tie, and they speak in turns, manic and monotone, wired and somber, doing this Mortician-and-Pimp double act, marrying up death and desire.

"Some basics, soldiers," says Major Grey. "We're going to be doing some idiographs . . . some paper-and-pencil personality tests to see what makes you tick."

"And we're going to be doing some biophysics to get to see how your bodies work," says Captain Bell. "We're going to be testing your biomagnetic fields and see where you stand with the electromagnetic spectrum—what waves you absorb and what you give off . . ."

"Today we're giving you the Manual," says Major Grey. He goes down the aisle slamming these books, thick as phone directories, on each of our desks. "Guard it with your life."

It's got a fluorescent yellow cover. The title says *Psi War: Mind as Weapon*. Inside, the contents page lists the chapter headings: 1. Your Mind Is Your Weapon, 2. Assembling Your Weapon, 3. Ammunition, 4. Aiming Your Weapon, 5. Storing Your Weapon . . .

"The Soviets have been developing mental warfare," says Captain Bell. "The Free World has got to keep ahead. You're on the team. But before you come out hitting for America, your minds need training."

"Army regulations are made for normal service. That's why we need you to sign these"—Major Grey wanders between our desks scattering forms—"abnormal consents."

MJK 713b: Informed Consent to Asynchronous, Four-Dimensional Military Service

MJL 75: Absolute Waiver of Civil and Military Claims Entitlement (All and Any)

MJL 76: Human Use Agreement—Body and Mind

"It's safe to sign, sir?" I ask.

"Would I trick you?" says Captain Bell.

Don't worry your head about anything, soldier. We don't need your understanding. We'll make do with your soul

"The world is stranger than we can even guess," says Captain Bell, ruffling his *Easy Rider* sideburns. "There's much more to the mind than most people know . . . This, now"—he draws a crude oval on the board—"is the standard-issue, untrained, civilian mind . . ." Then he makes horizontal dashes across. "The top layer is the consciousness for everyday usage. Below is the subliminal mind for creativity. Beneath that is the subconscious mind for dreaming. And beneath that lies the core."

"Now the core gets a lot of name-calling—spirit, soul, geist, essence, élan vital," says Major Grey. "But here in this man's army, we keep things straightforward and sensible. We call it *subspace one*."

"We're going to be getting you better acquainted with your subspace ones," says Captain Bell, "as a shield of defense and as a spear of attack. You're going to be spiritual warriors."

The way he explains us, the core mind can see forward and backward in time and travel most anywhere in space. Young children got channels open between their consciousness and core, but these close by the age of three or four. But psychics like us, we've been damaged some way growing up. Our development hasn't been normal and true, so we've still got access to the core. It makes us freaks with a military use. He promises we're going to do some interesting travel. Out-of-body, remote viewing, time travel . . . that kind of thing.

In a freak-show snake pit like Fort Scott, you need a friend you can trust. Most nights Ethan and I keep to ourselves, talking over life or events of the day. We shy away from the card school. Psychics play sly, hard, mean poker and get disputatious and up-close personal. It isn't worth the hassle for a pot of fifteen dollars.

"Never thought the U.S. Army be teaching me to meditate," I say, "and feeding me LSD and mescaline."

"They're making it up as they go along," says Ethan. "We're just disposable lab rats."

"I guess we'll keep in touch, whatever . . ."

"Maybe," Ethan concedes.

"So, if we're going to keep meeting up?" I splay my hands, to gesture the fullness of time. "In years to come, it occurs to me . . ."

"What?" he demands.

"You must know some stuff about my future, Ethan?"

"Shit, Lee." He winces. "You don't want to know."

"That bad, huh?"

"I'm not saying it's bad, Lee. I'm not saying it's good. I'm just telling you it's a curse knowing, either way."

"It is?"

"Live in hope, Lee. And act as though you're in control of your life. That's my advice. Because, if you know what's coming, it fucks with your perspective and saps your motivation."

"Thanks, Ethan."

"You're welcome, Lee. I'll tell you one thing, though . . ."

"Yes?"

"We both come out of this sane and alive," says Ethan, "because I see you in Times Square, New Year's Eve, sometime in the eighties."

"Uh-huh?"

"You've changed plenty, but it sure suits you. You're arm in arm with this woman. I guess you're preoccupied. That's why you never stop to speak."

"I just pass you by? Hey, sorry, man."

"Cool, no problem." Ethan frowns. "I'm on the skids on the bottle, then. Maybe I don't want to be seen . . ."

"Look," I say, "I didn't mean to. If I'd known it was you . . ."

"Forget it. But I tell you something crazy that happened around that time . . . Did you ever see that Ronald Reagan actor guy?"

"Drake McHugh in *Kings Row?*"

"That's the guy. He ends up the fucking president of the fucking U.S.A."

"Now, you kidding me . . . Now, Henry Fonda I could believe."

Ethan makes up all sorts of unlikely crap like this—about folks having home computers, and Kissinger getting the Nobel Peace Prize, and Russia turning capitalist, and the kid from the Jackson Five turning out to be white, and the chief of staff turning out to be black, and this film called *ET,* and Anaheim winning the World Series, and electronic mail, and virtual sex—just to crack me up.

First weekend leave we get, Ethan and I take a visit, on recommendation, to Roy's Bar near Elko. It turns out a relaxed, word-of-mouth kind of place with rooms where you can stay over. The service is self-service, because, after a while, Roy and Ellen get to trust a customer—so they can serve themselves and pay at the cash register. It works on the honor system. And Roy, who's served time for armed robbery, isn't often disappointed. Last one out locks up. First one in opens up. The keys are a kind of notional security, because they hang on a hook outside the front door.

It's at Roy's place that I first meet Dr. Gene. I guess he doesn't shave or shower that often, or bother to clean the engine grease from under his nails, but he makes up for it with a familiar manner, and the conversation don't lag because he got an encyclopedia mind and can talk real lengthy on matters the average guy never thinks to mention—like the sexual manners of snails (strangely wild and frothy frenzied), the periodic table of elements (real orderly), the poetry of this Emily Dickinson lady, parapraxis, some thinker called Highdigger, violin varnish, the aerodynamics of bees, seismology, or the role of the iceberg in history.

"You talk real well, Gene. And you talk real fast. Are you on any special medication?"

"Self-medication, Lee. Sheer fucking joy of life. And amphetamine sulfate when I'm driving. Helps the reflexes. Ethyl alcohol when I'm stationary."

He hands me his business card, with a forensic thumbprint stamped in motor oil.

Eugene Devine, MD

MECHANIC

Buicks my specialty

Roy's Bar, Elko, Nevada

It turns out, Gene used to be one skillful surgeon who worked hospitals in Chicago, New York, and Boston. He'd won best-of-year prizes as a student, devised a new procedure for treating hernias as a resident, and was being fast-tracked for a Nobel Prize, and the reason they stopped him wearing a gown and took away his scalpels was nothing to do with his technical skill, but because of his addictive personality, the way he confused his surgical and social time, and his habit of operating off the textbook script and adding little operative embellishments, which didn't always work out. And, still, he might have got away with all that, but he was mouthy with the hospital administrators and had taken to borrowing morphine.

And while he looked kind of wired and carried the scents of overheated, unclean living, the locals in Elko had started to bring him their human ailments and sick animals—pets and farm stock. Because Doc would take on a patient where orthodox medicine shook its sorry head. Like the time Roy's Airedale got sideswiped by a truck and the vet said he had to be put down. But Doc operated for eleven hours straight, using diazepam as anesthetic, reconstructing the shattered pelvis with dental adhesive, titanium wires, and some stainless steel screws he got out of a rotary fan. And it was no surprise that the hound was up and running in a couple of months. And the only sour note was the ungrateful way the dog took to yelping and hiding whenever Doc appeared.

So, I guess it's out of gratitude, and because Doc draws extra custom to the bar, because if someone arrives with a sick heifer and has to wait around, he feels obliged to buy a Coke or a beer, that Roy's lets Doc put a sign in the bar window saying DEVINE'S SURGERY—UPSTAIRS and lets Doc have a room for gratis, to use as clinic and operating room, store his welding equipment, tool chest, and medical gear, and a government surplus autoclave for sterilizing things medical and for loosing the built-up grunge and grease on automotive parts.

Through the quartermaster I arrange for the *Meridian Star* to be mailed to me, and only twelve days late.

Ballistics show that the shells that killed the civil rights workers come from the rifle found in Byron Clement's car that was seen close to the scene. But the jury got to offset this against Byron's sworn testimony he was drunk at home on his own the night of the crime. After a week's deliberation, they still can't decide. So the judge orders a retrial. Meanwhile, Byron's free to walk the streets. A Briar Citizen's Committee gives him a celebration dinner and takes a collection for his defense fund.

Three weeks later, the *Star* carries an article about Angelina with a quarter-page photo. She's posed in profile, all light and dark, glistening hair, narrowed eyes, and hollow cheekbones. Turns out she was runner-up in some writing competition. It's some story about growing up restless confused in small-town Mississippi. The judges praise the authenticity of her accent, her tonal palette, the precision of her vision, the depth of her empathy, the measured wit, her anger and acid tongue. It's said that her writing evokes comparison with one famous drunk and dead author. The article reports her uncle is mayor of Briar and her father is well known as a political activist in central Mississippi.

My letters to Mama in Chicago come back finger-smudged and tattered—*Return to Sender, Persons Unknown*. So I write to Nat for a newer address. He takes three weeks for a considered reply.

Mister Lee McCoy,

Since you come visit me I was turning things over in my mind. This is a difficult letter to write. I keep on trying words out then tearing them up because they don't fit together right. Truth is, I am not a scholar of feelings or a wordy man. Mostly I read seed catalogs and fertilizer advertising and cereal packets, as you may know, so I do not have the words close to hand to fence my feelings in or join up my thoughts into straight lines. But the honest truth is, I can't be certain who you are, because when your loved ones die you don't expect to see them this side of the grave again, and not strolling up all casual out of the blue with a new name saying hi and turned into some hippie type with city-boy habits and fancy dress and excuse-me language. If you are Lee for true, my blood and kin, you must know my love and care rides with you, blessed child, all your life and be assured that the hogs prosper and that the beans are cropping well. But if you are not, you are truly some fraudster low-life scum, may your soul be damned for eternity for the pain you visit on me and my family. Unless you are some spiritual visitation, then please accept the apologies of a simple man who means no discourtesy and prays for his soul's direction, but who drinks some on a Saturday night and awakes confused on the Lord's day.

I have spoken to the Reverend Spinks of your visit. He says grief takes several strange forms and that the mind is slippery, so it sometime sees just what it wants to, and that while whiskey does many things, it does not help a man to come to terms with a loss. Also I have written to Scott, who is your stepdaddy, or maybe not. And he says he will ask his lawyer to write you explaining the legal position because of the pains and moneys involved. But he cautions I must no account send you their new address.

I have tried to do my best for all sides in this and I do not know of any easy fix. So please be accepting of my heartfelt love and regard, or contempt and hatred, or proper respect, whichever is proper and deserving to you.

May you receive all you deserve.

        Yours with due sentiment,
        Nathaniel Claiborne

"Trouble?" asks Ethan.

"Family stuff," I say. "I'm trying to track down my missing family."

"Hey," calls Jimmy the Sioux diviner, two bunks away and eavesdropping. "Want me to look them out? It'll only cost you a carton of Luckys."

"Shit," says Ethan. "You're charging to help a buddy now?"

"Hey, it's not me." Jimmy shrugs. "It's my gift. She's a bitch— a real hard, commercial lady. She only comes across for a guy who pays her."

"Sure," I concede. "A carton for your gift."

Jimmy says he needs something personal. I show him a photo of Mama. It's a kind of irregular rectangle with a wavy edge from the way I cut out my daddy with a pair of toenail clippers, to while away the time of day.

He smoothes his fingers over the picture. His eyes go glazed and distant. He tells us to get a map of the U.S.A. and spread it on the floor. He crouches over New Mexico and starts muttering, dangling this crystal jiggling on a string of cotton.

"Iowa," grunts Jimmy. "I need the map."

Ethan goes to get a large-scale map from Sergeant Bing's office, and that gets spread between the bunks. Jimmy takes the cotton between his teeth so the crystal dangles below his mouth. He's kind of hunched on his hands and knees, his face creased in concentration, swiveling his hips, lowering his mouth like he's fixing to give Iowa some loving. The crystal's spinning crazy to a blur.

"Four?" asks Jimmy. "I'm getting four persons?"

"Mama, Scott, and the twins."

"This isn't their home. I'm getting them traveling," says Jimmy. "I'm getting them all crammed tight in a car."

"Where's that exactly?"

Jimmy peers close to the map. "The intersection of Highway 151 and 220, between Cedar Rapids and Iowa City, close by the Amana Colonies."

"Which way are they headed, Jimmy?"

"Jesus, it's a crossroads. A four-way intersection, Lee. What do you think I am? Some fucking mind-reader freak?"

13

Future Tense

I guess there's no place like the U.S. Army to confirm your worst suspicions about men. You've got a load of guys caged tight together, without air freshener, sympathy, or the consolations of women.

It's all shine and polish, starch and neat folds on the parade ground surface, but things can get messy and stained backstage, underneath. Discipline only stretches so far. Tact can fall by the wayside. Civility can go fuck itself. Guys can say hurtful things, never worrying about your feelings. You get to see some ugly habits emerging. Men can be gross. There's equal parts mischief, frustration, and testosterone, which makes for a combustible mix. A fight can break out from a sideways glance or a hasty remark. You get to hear heads bouncing on concrete floors. You find splatters of blood in the washroom.

Sometimes, you sense what the next guy's thinking. Often, it isn't pretty. But I guess it's even worse in a combat unit, where killing coarsens guys' souls.

When the pupil is ready, the master arrives. I find Dr. Wolf De

Melon's book *Life: A Survivor's Manual* on the puddled floor of a la-
trine cubicle. It's like a silent human presence, with the large sky-
blue eye on the cover staring unblinking. But I am reluctant to reach
out for it because the cover has gone soggy damp at one corner, and
the tang of ammonia is stinging my eyes.

Forget the Dewey decimal system. The U.S. soldier only got
two uses for print in the john and neither is halfway literary. So I am
reluctant to handle anything secondhand, moist.

Still, it beckons me. I reach down, lift back the cover between
finger and thumb, and look at the contents page. Naturally, I am
straight-off poleaxed by the chapter headings: 2. Your Idiot Brain,
3. Listening to Your Voices, 7. Nourishing Your Inner Fool, 9. Dying
and Rebirth, 10. Bright Smile, Dark Soul, 11. Finding Your Angel,
14. The Lost Father, 17. The Eureka Feeling . . .

It never happened to me before. You open a book and find it
speaking personal, confidential, direct to you, an audience of one.
And it seems to know all your intimate stuff and back issues.

On the back cover Dr. Wolf De Melon, MD, describes himself
briefly. As it turns out we got a deal in common. He was born in
Missouri too. He served his time in the army. He grew oranges
in Florida, worked in a Midwest hospital, had himself an upstairs
breakdown, and realized the only person who could cure him was
himself. And I kind of warm to a guy who hears voices too.

The first chapter, Wolf lays his cards on the table. He warns
anyone looking for a slick read, easy answers, or a quiet life to go
look elsewhere. He counsels that the road to Enlightenment is one
bumpy ride. He doesn't guarantee Inner Bliss, and he can't promise
the time of arrival.

He lists thirteen guiding principles, which add up to his philosophy of life, while sounding kind of deep and contradictory:

1. You can't chase happiness. It finds you—when you're looking
    for something else.

2. Every setback is an opportunity. Every wall has a door.

3. You are more than you realize and less than you know.

4. The greatest fear is the fear of life.

5. Nothing is random, not even chance.

6. You must heed your inner voices.

7. You must reconcile your male and female sides.

8. You must nourish your inner fool. He is wiser than you think.

9. Your life is a script and you are the author.

There are no principles 10 through 13, on account of some soldier tearing out pages 7 through 11, so he can wipe his ass on the Sermon on the Mount. I look kind of longing into the dark depths of the murky, spattered bowl, but it's all been flushed away. Pity. I reckoned Dr. De Melon was working up to something big, saving the best for last.

Guys come and go. The light dims. Looking at my watch, I realize I've been sitting in the can for over three hours. I still haven't got to the bottom of *Life*, but at least I've made a start. As soon as something comes half clear, it kind of recedes and blurs over again. I'm realizing that Dr. Wolf De Melon is on to something big. But he doesn't give immediate answers. A guy has got to pull his full intellectual weight.

Ethan and I are developing a strong fraternity on account of traveling some of the same hard shoulder on life's twisty road. I guess we're both freaked by burdensome strangeness. And we both had our lives wrenched from our grasp.

"You ever see any of those French art-house movies?" he asks. "Godard and Truffaut and all that crap?"

"Nah."

"There's a start, a middle, and an end. But not in that order. There are flash-forwards, flashbacks, and key parts of the story go missing. You think you've grasped the plot, then the action jumps ten years back, or twenty years forward."

"Dizzying," I console.

"That's my life," says Ethan. "It's been edited by some arty-farty director on acid. I can't get a fair run at things, or a chance to follow through. I've just finished kindergarten and I wake up to find I'm selling insurance in Denver. Worse, I'm fifty-two."

"Tough break." I whistle.

"Do you know what I come to regret most, Lee?"

"What's that, Ethan?"

"Old age. I never made any proper provision for my later years."

"Don't you have a pension, Ethan? Or savings?"

"It's not a matter of money, Lee."

"No?"

"In America, they do away with money in 2023."

"Uh-huh? What they use instead?"

"Social credit—it's a mix of wealth, status, and shame, rolled into one. Everyone microchipped. You log in every day, to check on your rating. It goes up and down. It depends on what work you do, what credits or fines you've picked up. There are fly cameras and sensors everywhere, tracking what you're doing and saying. They're always picking on the old folks. Fines for this, debits for that."

"They are?"

"They say us old folks are bone idle and doing all the crime, taking drugs, vandalizing, holding unlicensed opinions. They call it *age rage*."

"You need a license? For opinions?"

"Sure. The way they see it, you have to be entitled to your opinions, and that means paying too. But that's not the worst of it . . . That's the sex permit."

"Sex permit?"

"You've got to pass theory and practice. No one's gonna screw you, Lee, unless you're fully insured and you've got a kosher license. And the penalties add up in no time. Of course, it depends how attached you are to your body."

"Ain't everybody got a body, Ethan? In this future of yours."

"Not the transhumans, Lee. They upload their minds to silicone. Then they speed them with processing units, hundreds of times faster than brains. That way they can learn Icelandic in thirty minutes. When they want to do something physical, they rent a young, beautiful model body from Central Organs, Inc."

"Where's the mileage in that, Ethan?"

"Immortality. Super-intelligence. Freedom from age and illness. Multiple lives . . . that sort of stuff."

"Multiple lives?"

"You can copy and paste your mind into any number of files. Then you can make different choices all at the same time. It means you can live as many lives as you like, all at once, in parallel."

"You try it for yourself?"

"Could never afford it, Lee. I never accrued enough social credit. With my rating, I can barely afford a friend. I had to make do with a cyber pal. And share a latex plasma lover with the rest of the cruddy old guys in my pod."

"Tough," I console.

"Not so bad." Ethan smiles. "Most of the transhumans got the virus."

"Virus?"

"Q72. Computer bug. Nasty infection. It worms its way in and starts chewing up their googol bytes. It takes the fastest, cleverest minds in creation . . ."

"Uh-huh?"

"And turns them into porno websites and advertising loops."

"Websites, Ethan?"

"I'll give you a pointer, Lee. If the opportunity ever arises, try to get a job in computers. That's where the future lies."

"Crazy," I say. "I'd have bet on eight-track stereo and polyester."

Then a cute thought comes to me.

"Ethan," I say, "you follow sports?"

"Football and ponies. Why are you asking?"

"Just occurred to me. You could do some gambling. Bet on some results coming up."

"Like the Steelers winning the Super Bowl, beating the Cowboys 21–17?"

"When's that, Ethan?"

"Seventy-nine, I reckon, or '80."

"That kind of thing," I say. "But you got nothing sooner?"

"Riva Ridge wins the Kentucky Derby in '72."

"Soon enough," I say. "Do just fine." I scribble it on my cuff with a ballpoint.

"Trouble is . . ." He winces. "I did what I did. It's a bit late for me to start rewriting my future now."

Now I know Ethan isn't no Nostradamus, but when it comes to mapping the future, he's the best cartographer I got. He's got his personal slant on things. It's not that I swallow it wholesale, not every fine speckle and freckle, but I know he's got some real knack, so I've started jotting it all down in my little blue book. The only trouble is, he's got this killjoy habit of telling me the plots of the best movies, decades before they ever come out. Still, it's a guide—what to watch out for.

> 1972—Dallas routs Miami in the Super Bowl
> Pacino, Duvall, and Brando score it big in *The Godfather*

1973—Redford and Newman in *The Sting*
Peace in Vietnam

1974—Nixon resigns. Some tape recordings involved

1975—Cincinnati Reds win the World Series
Plastic shark in a film called *Jaws*

1977—Elvis dies. Overdose of burgers on the can

I got snippets like this stretching all the way forward to—

2017—Nanomachines eat north Virginia
Heidi and Helga option—Generation Seven Plasma
Lovers

The way Major Grey explains it, we've got to learn to subdue our left brain and trust to our right brain. Left brain is language and calculation. Right brain is intuition and image.

Left brain tends to dominate conscious life. It's always trying to reason and explain. But for psi work it needs to take a backseat, so the dreamy right brain gets its chance to speak.

"That's why we need you to do everything left-handed today," enthuses Captain Bell. "It's going to give the right brain some control and encouragement."

Through meditation, we're getting used to resonating with the oneness. You need to suspend yourself, hanging there in the ether, then imagine the serenity below you.

"Breathe it in," coaxes Captain Bell. "Draw the opalescence up through your feet . . ."

They wire us up to biofeedback machines. We learn to move our brain patterns from alpha to beta to theta, then back again. They play us focus tapes so we can merge right and left hemispheres. Before long, we're getting used to floating about, turning slow, lazy somersaults in the ether, hanging weightless in infinity, paddling round with our hands or feet.

After class, I hang behind and wrinkle my brow.

"Anything troubling you, Private McCoy?"

"You know Dr. Wolf De Melon's book, sir, *Life: A Survivor's Manual*, sir?"

"I'm not familiar with that work of scholarship, soldier."

"So you won't know Life Principles 10 to 13?"

"'Fraid not, son. Anything else?"

"Don't want to speak out of turn, Captain."

"Tell me, anyhow," he allows.

"Any chance of changing the future, sir, if the past is forever fixed, and Einstein got it just about right, so we can't accelerate faster than light?"

"Let me worry about that technical stuff, Private. I've got the mind and training."

"Understood, sir. Just ride careful on that motorcycle, Captain."

I only mentioned it because Ethan reckons he remembers how the captain skids on his Harley to avoid a pothole, sideswipes a fence, and gets his head taken off. It's somewhere near Tonopah, sometime in November, and he may be an arrogant jackass, but we come to like the captain in our private ways, and we all sure miss him, just as soon as we get to suffer his replacement, Major Randy McClennan.

By the end of basic training, they'd culled some loose cannons and whittled us down from seventeen to nine. Jimmy the dowser had gone AWOL, while Ernie was on a punishment squad, on account of his attitude problems, digging holes in the ground just so he could fill them in again, and Paul the albino had gone phototropic purple through overexposure to the Nevada sun.

This was '71. It was the early days in the Psi War program. I hear tell things have moved on. But when Ethan and I were on the case, they were putting all their eggs in remote viewing.

The basic idea is you send your mind on a journey while your body stays behind. It's a mix of time travel and foreign espionage, all without leaving your chair. One guy views; the other guides. They don't tell you where you're going in advance; they just give you co-ordinates for time and place. This way, your conscious mind don't impose preconceptions about what you're going to see. The core mind knows where it's going. But consciousness doesn't have a clue.

The guide is your buddy. He's there to ask questions, keep you safe, make sure you come back.

To start off, they give us training runs all over the place. If it isn't Belsen, Hiroshima, the Black Plague, it's some other disgusting shit-hole in history.

So there I am in the gray room—gray ceiling, walls, and carpet—strapped into my gray chair, wired up to the biofeedback rig, concentrating on my focus tape, hearing the pulse of my brain waves shifting down toward flat theta.

The only color in the room is Ethan's carrot hair. "Got your co-ordinates," he says.

"Shoot," I say.

"FO3Y-JG65."

"Hell," something sighs deep inside. *"Ain't nothing sacred? Jesus, why go there?"* I got this dull foreboding. I hear scraping and feel shudders, like some heavy furniture's being shifted in the basement of my mind.

Pink tunnel pressing hard—headlights dimmed—smeared windshield—no other traffic—only me

Every Friday, Captain Bell has you in his office to talk over your progress.

"Well done, soldier. We can't fault your application."

"I tried my hardest, sir."

"You're bringing back some hard, fine-grained detail, McCoy. Take this . . ." He starts rustling through my travel reports.

Cadillac series '62 Coupe—navy-and-gray check interior—cigarette burns on backseat left side—low mileage—baby blue with white sunroof—bald curbside rear tire—low-slung chrome bumpers—sirens—screams—open-top Lincoln—black hide interior—lady crawling out . . .

"That's all good, hard, solid detail. We had our fact-checker check out the facts."

"Thank you, sir. Good to know."

"As a matter of interest, McCoy, do you have any idea where that was?"

"No idea, sir, not a clue."

"Junction of Elm Street and Houston Street, Dallas, Texas, 1963. Does that mean anything to you?"

"Lot of shouting, sir. Police cars wailing all over the place."

"Assassination of John Fitzgerald Kennedy."

"Not surprised, sir. I kind of felt there was some bad shit going on."

"And then there was this, McCoy . . ."

Buick Century—shiny black—worn running board—whitewall tires—cracked windshield—oval hole in front passenger door—driver dead—smell of gasoline—twenty-three thousand miles on the clock—condition good to fair—suspect front suspension

"I remember it well, sir."

This remote viewing takes you unpleasant places. You never

know what you'll find. It leaves some scars on the mind. And you get awful gut-wrenching vertigo toppling down into the void. Then there's terrible bends coming up again from the depths, so you've got to breathe steady and take your time. Next day you've got a wowser of a headache. When you try to sleep it off, you got unwelcome shapes invading your dreams.

"Where do you suppose that was, Private McCoy?"

"Not sure, sir. But it was kind of warm. And I think I smelled a salty sea tang on the air."

"Good observation, soldier. But it belongs in your report. That was December 7, 1941, Pearl Harbor, Hawaii."

"Hell," I said. "I guessed there was something crazy going on. Then, those explosions were most likely *bombs*."

"Most probably, McCoy. Anything strike you about the information you're bringing back?"

"The mind, sir . . . it picks up on small detail. But sometimes it misses out on the bigger picture."

"True, McCoy. Anything else?"

"I guess I'm real good at reporting the cars."

"Exactly, son. You've got it in one."

Automotive cretin. You dispatch him back in history and all he can spot are the license plates

"You going to let me go, sir?"

"No, McCoy. We're pleased with your progress. You've got fine, precise perception. We just need to steer it away from cars."

"How you fixing to do that, sir?"

"Not sure, son. But we're working on it."

You heard of aversion therapy?

———

"We've got a long leave coming up," says Ethan. "You thinking what I'm thinking?" He goes on to explain me how he'd like to get drunk, get laid, have a fight, eat a steak, sleep in a double bed, take a hot bath, all more than once, although he's not too fussed about the particular order, as long as it all kicks off with some beers.

"Fine by me," I say. "Why not start at Roy's place?"

14

Taking Leave

We've got fourteen days R & R before we get posted. Most of the other guys have places to go and people to see—wives, children, girlfriends, parents—but Ethan and I are at an unraveled loose end. We've only got ourselves to look out for. We hitch to Carson City, where Ethan's left his Pontiac Bonneville four-door.

Got a wife in Chino, babe, and one in Cherokee

Then, we're scorching off for Roy's place, bouncing off curbs, skidding around corners, throwing up dust, with the radio blaring.

Ethan's a real serious rock buff, only he's got itchy ears, so he keeps shifting between music stations, because if he likes the first and second number, he seldom likes the third, which means we get to hear a lot of static, white noise, and retuning.

. . . lost her innocence in Eudora
had her heart stole in Monroe

hawked her skin in Helena
pawned her soul in Tupelo

Sometimes, music can touch you deep and move you unexpected ways. Normally, country singing never gives me a woody, or brings to mind coral nipples or a dewy bush glowing opalescent, backlit by moon glow.

"Jesus. It's Angel," I say.

"Angelina Clement," says Ethan, "bedroom misery . . . guess who I had in my pants."

guess she's making tracks
although she's drifting slow
headed for Chastity, Nebraska
she ain't that far to go

"The woman's suffering movement," says Ethan, reaching out for the knob. "Rule number one: Men are shits."

"Hey," I say. "Please. Let's hear the lady out?"

"You like this whiny crap?"

"It isn't so bad. And I sure as hell love that voice."

well, she put it out for JJ
but she laid it down for Chas
so, Lee, if you wanna tango
come down South and jazz

"Jesus," I gulp. "She hasn't forgot. She mentioned *me*."

"You cracked, Lee?"

"You don't understand. I knew her way back. She was my girl . . ."

"Guess she's sending a message, Lee." He gives me a smart-ass grin.

"Suppose," I agree.

"To you . . . and Jo, and Mo, and John and Don too . . . And all the guys in the Dolphins' defense and the Mississippi Home Guard."

"Yeah, Ethan. I get your drift."

"I mean, if I was a tramp like her, I'd keep it quiet. I surely wouldn't shout about it."

. . . now, left raw in her skin
her lost heart comes to rest
and she smiles to think back
how the first love was best

Ethan makes it a running gag for the next fifty miles.

"You ever know Roberta Flack, Lee?"

"No such luck."

"So that 'Killing me soft, Lee, with his song' isn't a personal message to you?"

"Don't reckon so, Ethan."

"How about Elvis or Sinatra?"

"No," I say. "Never met."

"Carly Simon's 'Bet you think this song is about you'?"

"Never heard it."

"Shit, you're right, Lee. I'm getting ahead of myself. It doesn't hit the charts until '72."

"Ethan," I say, "you mind stopping soon?"

I spend a couple of hours alone in Elko, visiting phone booths. Well, you try getting a phone number or an address for a semi-precious recording star, whose last single climbed to thirty-seven in the country charts. The record company doesn't give out the personal numbers of its artistes. Besides, Miss Clement has changed her label. They advise I contact her agent. But they don't give out names or numbers for agents. Long-distance information wants to know what city. "Hey," I say, "if I knew that, I'd look her up in the book."

So I go buy a copy of Angel's record from a store. This gives me the name of the producer and the studio. But the studio gives you the runaround because they don't believe you're long-lost family with sensitive news from home. And the producer is gone on vacation, not that it's any of my business. I finally get lucky by ringing Mr. Cochrane back home at the Magnolia Diner, saying I'm a director out of L.A. Then I'm ringing Angel's number regular. But her phone rings unanswered for twenty-seven hours. I finally get through 3 A.M., Sunday morning.

"Hey, Angel, it's Lee."

"Lee from the studio?" She sounds slurred sleepy, or freshly woken.

"Lee from way back. Lee from Eureka."

She takes a ten-second pause. I hear her exhaling long, then breathing steady. "Lee . . . Shit." She lays a heavy, deliberate smile on her voice. "How's things, pretty boy?"

"Fine," I say.

"Cool," she says. "Nice to hear from you. It's very late or really early. You got some special reason for calling?"

"It took me forever to get a contact number. I been trying to reach you, ever since I got your message."

"Message?"

"The song."

"Song?"

"'Lost Her Heart.'"

"Oh, that thing. You like it or something?"

"Fine," I say. "I liked it real good. Only the lyrics are kind of *down*. I got to worrying about you."

"Hey, it's just a song. You scribble it on the back of the menu when you're waiting for your pizza. If you like it, you try it out. If the audience goes for it, you record it."

"Sure, Angel," I say, "but it mentions *me*."

"It does?"

"Lee," I explain. "Second verse, line seven."

"Oh . . ." She makes this gurgling sound, like she's swallowing liquid giggles. "The names just come at you, out of nowhere. They're not real people."

"So it wasn't a message, like *We're made for each other. No one ever touched me like you. I miss you, baby, so hurry down?*"

"No, Lee . . . If I want to reach someone, I'll visit, write, or phone. It's way more reliable than recording a song . . ."

"My mistake."

"You happy, Lee?"

"Doing fine."

"Good."

"Just I often think of you, Angel."

"I think of you, Lee. From time to time. Always fond. But things move on."

"Uh-huh?"

"You weren't still thinking about *us* again?"

"No."

"The truth is, I've got a partner. Been together a year."

"Uh-huh?"

"Called Judy," says Angel. "We're really happy."

"You a *lesbian* now, Angel?"

"I don't like labels, Lee. I'm free as the breeze. We just got to follow our desires and find beauty where we can . . ."

"You loosened up since you left Eureka."

"Yep," she chirrups. "Isn't that odd?"

"Glad you've done so well, Angel. I like your songs. Especially the slow, miserable, whiny numbers."

"Thanks, Lee. What you doing these days?"

"Army. Draft."

"Vietnam?"

"Desk in Nevada."

"Good."

"Right."

"Thing is, Lee . . . I'd better be going."

"Bye, Angel."

"Bye, Lee."

I look to my watch. It tells me we'd been talking four minutes.

It just seems we're fated, always out of sync, Angel and I. It's like I'm always lagging one step behind. First off, I'm the wrong color. And by the time I got that sorted, it turns out I'm the wrong sex.

Angel's got a kind of interrupting, controlling way to her conversation. So most all I wanted to say had gone unspoken. That I likely loved her more than anyone else had or could. That I gone to the doors of death for her. That she owed me more than *hi ya*, not that I counted the cost. That I forgave her for her father. That it didn't matter if her voice couldn't always rise to the proud pitch of her lyrics. That I could live with the clutter of her sometimes-ugly ideas. That a day didn't go by without a thought of her silken thighs, burning bush, parting lips, and amber nipples. And I'm sliding myself back, tight into her. That I never belonged anyway so much as breathless, blessed, stranded on her skin.

"Christ, Lord," I plead, "just make me a woman. They run rings round men. They got it made."

We park a couple of days in Roy's Bar. Ethan's on a binge. Well, I like a drink as much as the next guy, but Ethan's got some demon and just can't find his off switch.

Roy's is good for conversation, pool, and drinking, but it draws the middle-aged, overweight, unwashed, bearded-men's crowd, so it isn't the place to meet new women. Ethan is eager to find some action with a lady.

"Hey, Gene," he asks Doc, "where can Lee and I get laid round here?"

"Try Fran's," says Doc. "Or the Lazy O."

"Those bars?" asks Ethan.

"Nah, brothels."

Then Doc starts lecturing on Nevada brothel legislation, and how it'd just be plain ignorant for tourists like us to visit the Whorehouse State without once checking into a bordello, playing craps at a casino, and buying a rattle-skin belt. Doc says it'd be like going to Flagstaff and missing the Grand Canyon, or visiting the Black Hills without seeing Mount Rushmore.

As it turns out, Fran's is just a couple of stranded trailers, parked in the roadside sand, six miles out of Elko. It's dim lit inside, from orange bulbs, and smells warm of frying bacon, jasmine incense, and moist morning sheets.

"Welcome, strangers," says this orange-haired girl. "Name's Courtney."

"And I'm Anna Belle," says an older, larger, wearied lady. "Are you boys looking for action?"

They look twenty years apart in age, but they both got green eyes, frizzy stick-out hair, and that taut-skin-over-a-skull look you can only contract from getting a plastic surgeon to carve up your face. They could be mother and daughter, a before-and-after ad, or a warning about fast living.

"We're looking for company," says Ethan. "Have you got a lineup or something?"

"You guys have just struck lucky," says Anna Belle. "The lineup is us."

I guess Ethan has visited such places before, because he's promptly fixed himself on to Courtney, talking numbers and moves, and it sounds real technical, so it could be football maneuvers for all I know.

With Ethan latched on to Courtney, I'm kind of default matched up with her mother, who is likely a real nice lady and all, with rich experiences behind her, hard struggles, and the wisdom that comes of all that, and is likely real good at what she does best, but I'm kind of left with a desire gap and reservations about paying to have sex with a lady I'd never lie down with for free. But everyone got their professional pride, and I don't want to hurt no feelings or ruffle no feathers, but I've always been attracted to slender, younger women, with smoother skin, without worry lines across the face or tic-tac-toe operation scars across their belly, which I guess is an age and taste thing, because, it turns out, when it comes to the lady-rentals industry, there's a market for most everything.

Now, Anna Belle's obviously got plenty to offer, spilling pink and juddery over the slack edges of her lingerie, but I don't understand her terms. Some sounds like children's games or practical jokes—like Half-and-Half, Body French, Give or Get, Reverse It, Lay Back, Motion Lotion, or Showtime. And then she's got fancy Nevada names like Elko Jell-O Sandwich or Winnemucca Shower. And then, at the pricey end of the menu, there's some real unlikely, sticky, tacky, expensive things we never even thought of trying down South in Mississippi, where folks most times stick at getting laid.

"That's all Greek to me," I admit.

"You haven't been to a cathouse before?" she asks.

"Never."

"Well, it works like this . . . ," she starts to explain me.

It turns out it's a pay-up-front service industry, geared to time and motion, with a negotiable tariff for *everything*. You got to wear a rubber. There isn't no kissing, and smiles are extra. So there's no love lost, and it comes across kind of mercenary, calculating. Though, if you're feeling sentimental, you can buy a Girlfriend Experience, which gets you a cuddle and giggle, before and after.

"Supposing I'd stopped at a diner"—I frown—"and I don't have the time or money for a square meal, what's your coffee and doughnut?"

"That's fifteen dollars," says Anna Belle. "It lasts ten minutes tops. No come guaranteed. It's called a hand job."

"That's the one," I agree. "I heard of them. We even got those back home in Eureka."

And to do her justice, the lady knows her way around a man and got quick, grasping, nimble fingers, plus a sly pressure-point gimmick to hasten things, even if she doesn't bother to look at me hardly, but just goes by feel, flicking through the pages of the movie magazine on the bedside table, left-handed.

"Thanks, ma'am," I say after the rush event. Maybe I come over a bit formal, polite, out of respect for her age. "That was way better than I expected. Even better than I could do for myself."

"You're welcome, kid." She smiles, but I could tell her mind was still on her magazine, stranded in movie land, on the set of *Love Story* with Ryan O'Neal and Ali MacGraw. I wander out to the car. Moby, the minder, takes a snitch look at his watch as I pass. "You all done?"

"Sure," I agree. "My friend still in there?"

"Guess so. There's one certain rule you learn in this job."

"Yeah?"

"Some guys take longer than others."

Now, I don't know what Ethan finds to do inside, but after four hours he still hasn't surfaced for air, so I sprawl out in the back of the car and take a catnap.

When Ethan finally wakens me, he's got wild, haunted, knowing eyes, chapped lips, a puffy face, afternoon stubble, a wide smirk, and a rich stale smell. As it turns out, he availed himself of a special discount promotional offer—All You Can Eat—which meant he and

Courtney get to do the *act*, many ways and several times, all for a modest hundred and fifty bucks. Which sounds a deal of money to invest for a few brief squirts of delight and some groin spasms, being ten times more than I spent, and comes across grabby, greedy, though Ethan seems real pleasured by the transaction, so driving back to Roy's, he's giving me vivid reportage and some action replay.

"Hey, is that *natural*?" I ask.

"Shit, Lee. The lady does some farmyard things you'd never believe . . ."

"That *sanitary*?" I ask when he's explained me another. "Twice?" He discloses some unlikely numbers and more graphic detail.

"Heck," I say. "No hands? No kidding? With her lady thing?" Then he tells me his number one highlight.

"Yeah?" I say. "Jeez, Ethan. How on earth she stretch to that?"

"Practice, I guess. That girl's got a real natural elasticity. She can bend things every which way." Ethan unscrews a bottle of Wild Turkey and takes a celebratory glug.

"Like this?" I raised a foot onto the dash, then I'm trying to tug it up, round behind my neck. Now a Pontiac Bonneville's an ample spacious car for most practical uses, but it never got designed with a view to accommodating show-off sex, front passenger side.

"Here . . ." Ethan passes me the bottle. I stow it tight between my thighs, so as not to spill any. "The way Courtney does it . . ." Ethan has taken a foot off the pedals and draws a knee up to his chin, leaving us coasting.

"Guess it's easier if you're a lady and in the buff without a gear stick," I console.

"It's more like this . . . ," says Ethan, lifting his other leg. "Just grab the wheel . . ."

Oh, Lord grant me vision. Oh, Lord grant me speed

———

Life can deal you some harsh, cruel lessons, especially in the highway-conduct department. So, nowadays, I'm a focused driver and don't think to do more than cover all the bases, watch my mirrors, and work the controls. And we still would've been okay if this jackrabbit hadn't streaked out and zigzagged across the road, but I got a sweet spot for rabbits, so I swing the wheel to veer left, and then overcorrect the other way, and of course Ethan doesn't have a foot on the floor to work the brake, and once we got two tires in the ditch, the car got a mind of its own, so it doesn't matter which way you tug the steering wheel, which is how we slew into the telephone pole, and my feet go through the windshield, and my buttocks swing up to the dash, scrunching the bottle of Wild Turkey into my crotch, while Ethan leads with his arms and head, and performs a forward roll through the glass onto the hood, and down past the grille, and then there's steam rising, and the metallic whir of still-spinning wheels, and a stench of spilled whiskey, and Ethan whimpering, sprawled across the fender, and the ass view of a jackrabbit lolloping over the scrub giving me a surprised—*well, thank you, fluff-ass. I owe you one*—backward glance.

I reach out for the ignition key and switch the engine off.

I got glass shards stuck through the fabric of my crotch, which is dark from whiskey like I've wet myself, and when I draw the mother piece out, there's a spreading crimson patch and a scalding throb. So I just know my prize personal goods been damaged down south. And when I unzip, it's like a butcher's slab, irrigated by a fountain of blood spattering up on my chest. And it's only by pressing hard with my thumb, then binding the base of my dick with some duct tape and string I find in the glove compartment, I can get the geyser to quell. Which only goes to show how a broken bottle, driven into your crotch, even at lowish speed, can cut you up real hurtful.

Only positives—I find out later—are the ways Wild Turkey can work as topical anesthetic, mild astringent, and makeshift antiseptic. Otherwise, things could have turned out worse.

15

One Real Changed Boy

I lose some groggy hours after that. But I got clear memories of driving back to Roy's Bar, on account of the makeshift way we get it done. Ethan's got double vision, a broke arm, and cracked ribs, so I got to steer again from the passenger side. But he's painless mobile below the waist, which leaves him free to work the pedals, as long as I warn him to brake in time. We got to go real slow because we got a flat, a wheel hub's scuffing the tire, and the fender's scraping the ground. Still, at least we've only got four miles to crawl, back to Roy's.

"That was some spin," Ethan says. He sounds squishy and muffled through a raw mouth and split lips. But oddly satisfied.

"Yep," I agree. "Crazy fucking jackrabbit. Stupid fucking telephone post." I don't feel like talking much or arguing blame. I got real excruciating groin pain and a seriously tacky, leaky lap. It feels like I got razor wire for pubes that slash me when I cough.

We both need some examining, stitching, and bandaging. We're trusting Doc Gene to sort us out first, then fix the car.

———

I take a foul and crazy dream. I'm chased to the edge of a crevice by a pack of baying, snapping Byrons. Angel is waiting on the other side, shrieking for me to jump. But my legs are leaden, stuck to the ground. I never jump. I wake.

It's then I find Doc alongside my bed, peering down at my face. He has a gray, drained pallor. His eyes are glinting and swiveling fast. Maybe they're Dexedrine driven. His T-shirt is stained dark at the armpits and spattered and smeared from blood. His fine long surgeon's fingers are grained with engine oil from his paying job as a mechanic. He's smiling strong like he's real pleased with his night's labor.

"It all worked out fine, Lee."

"Good," I say.

"You made the right choice."

"Choice?" I ask.

He's got instruments scattered across a sheet on the table—stainless steel scalpels, dinky woodwork chisels, mallet, and a power drill with a sanding head. By the table leg there's a galvanized bucket, overflowing with cotton wool, lint, and some yellow fatty strands, and pink fleshy slivers, and whitish tube stuff, like you get stuck to your knife when you fillet game.

I'm reaching for my face and neck. My chin is swathed in cotton packing and aches like it's been whacked with a sledgehammer. My throat feels like it's been smoothed with a rotary sander. Someone has been digging through my groin with a spade.

"Nice outcome." Doc sits in the bedside chair and takes a swig of suds from a bottle. "You signed up for a Biber procedure. Now, I guess, you're asking yourself why your surgeon has operated on your jaw and trachea without first waving some consent form. Am I right?"

"Biber?" I'd hurt enough before. Now I got me real cutting botherations in some previous painless places.

"Legitimate question, Lee. Those are embellishments, cosmetic grace notes. They only make sense in the full clinical context."

I wince. I got this strangulated feeling that makes it hard to talk.

"Painful down there, I guess? And chilly?" says Doc. My groin is heavily swathed, stained, and bulging. It looks like I'm wearing a soiled diaper. There are plastic tubes coming out from beneath the wrapping, to drain the wounds or something. "I packed it with ice to ease the swelling and help close the wounds . . . It isn't orthodox post-op procedure, but if you like, I can fetch you a burger and beer."

"Nah," I say. "Thanks. No appetite."

"There's a deal of goodwill riding with you, Lee. The guys stayed all night in the bar to follow your progress. They took a collection for your convalescence. Raised forty-two dollars."

"Kind." I cough.

"And I did a nice job, Lee. Very clean, very elegant. And it's not just me that thinks so. The guys took a look before I bandaged you up. They reckon you've got something special down there, even though it's all raw and all stitched up. Ellen says it's really handsome, well proportioned, and natural-looking."

I smile and close my heavy lids.

"Surgery . . . ," says Doc. "It's a pragmatic craft—the art of the possible. Viz., you do what you can. You don't do what you can't. You've got to stay alert and think on your feet. Sometimes you've got to improvise. You don't know what you'll find till you lift the hood and peer into the engine . . ."

"So?" I point to my crotch.

"We're getting there, Lee. I'm putting things in a full clinical context . . . Now, orthodox surgeons wouldn't do the procedure I did on you. One, they aren't doing the best for a buddy. Two, they're governed by medical ethics—which don't apply to me, since I got suspended . . ."

"Uh-huh . . ."

"I've seen plenty of pudenda in my time, socially and professionally. They don't all pass the eye test, Lee. But yours is a pleasure to behold. The phrase *elegant engineering* comes to mind. If it was a car, it'd be a Porsche. If it was hi-fi, it would be Bang & Olufsen."

"Things work?"

"I believe so, Lee. Everything should function, more or less how it's designed to."

"Great."

"Maybe we could have done something more *orthodox*. But you left things too long before you presented to my clinic. I opened up the scrotum and found that testicle one is completely lopped. Without a blood supply it's going necrotic. It has to go. Testicle two is ruptured. The nerves and vessels are mostly severed. It's hanging on by a thread. I can't possibly save it. It has to come out."

"Shit." I sigh. "That doesn't leave much."

"I'm thinking on my feet, Lee. I'm thinking we could put in some makeweight implants. Then you'd pass for normal in the shower. But you'd need regular hormone therapy, to keep some testosterone flowing. Then I look at your dick, Lee. It isn't pretty. It's all pneumatics, the working dick—fluid pressure and valves. But your corpus spongiosum is punctured and the corpora cavernosa is spiked. Know what I find?"

"Nah."

"Your valves are fucked, Lee, clotted, locked solid. The blood goes in but it can't get out. Then, when you siphon it out, it doesn't refill. It's these squidgy little microvalves. Those doodads are just too delicate to fix. Shit, I think, that was this kid's last erection. Well, your blood pressure's low to fine and your breathing's steady, so I went down to the bar for a beer—to talk things over with Roy and get a second opinion.

"'Roy,' I say, 'the patient's headed for a life of sterile impotence. There isn't much I can do, except sew up a bum steer.'

"'Look, Doc,' says Roy, 'he's a young man with his life ahead of him. We believe in you. You've got to pull something out. Can't you improvise something like you did with my Airedale pup, Leo?'

"It's then I start thinking *laterally*. Before long, I'm thinking the Biber procedure. Never done it myself, but I'd always fancied giving it a try. And I've got the textbook. I talk it over with Roy and Ellen. At first, they aren't convinced. But after a while, they come to see the logic."

"Huh?"

"Two principles, Lee. What's possible? What gives the patient the best life outcomes? In your case, we're thinking, what gives the kid the best chance to love and be loved, what gives him a *transactable identity*?

"Sure, it's extreme but it's the only way I can get you back the way you should be—natural-looking and functional. We discuss it with the guys in the bar. We discuss it for an hour and fifty minutes. Ellen says thank God you're such a cute-looking boy. Ernie reckons you're halfway there already. Roy says it takes all sorts and you should hang out here while you recuperate. Nancy says she can teach you most of what you need to know. Carmen says you can't put a price on the physical side of love, and she'll find you some clothes and help you get back on your feet. Billy says he once got drinking with some she-males in Acapulco and they were just regular guys underneath, so who's to say what's normal. So we just wait for you to come round, to get your approval."

"Approval, Doc?"

"You see, Lee, nature's by impulse female. Embryologically, the male is a late elaboration on the female. Anatomically speaking, below the belt, a guy's a swollen woman with some needless add-on parts. So, it's mostly a natural operation. Think of it as paring down. We're mainly talking about shaping, peeling, and pruning . . ."

"No, Doc, no . . ." I'm reaching down for my groin.

"Careful, Lee," says Doc. "You don't want to disturb your catheter and drains . . ."

"You never . . ."

"Hell, Lee. You agreed. You gave your consent. We took our time to talk through the options."

"Consent?" We got a misunderstanding here. We're scuttling round in circles.

"Sure, you're a bit groggy. But I put the case to you fair and square. 'Lee,' I said, 'your manhood's been hacked to shreds. I can stitch you up a eunuch, or I can shape you into a very presentable distaff.' And you say . . . *'I been there before, honey. It ain't so bad.'* "

"I do?"

"As Roy is my witness. And then you said . . ."

"Yeah?"

" *'You got any absinthe in the house, young man? I'm parched as the desert.'* "

Well, that never sounds like me. It sounds like I was rambling. It sounds like the voices were talking for me. It sounds like no one so much as my grandma Celeste . . .

"*Distaff,* Doc? That means left-handed, right?"

"No, Lee . . ." He winces. "Distaff means *female* . . ."

"Hey, not a *pussy?*" I plead.

"Vaginoplasty, Lee. State of the art. Inverted penis, new urethral opening. I used scrotal tissue for the labia. I took some penile tip for an erectile clitoris and built it a dainty little hood to duck into. You've got beautiful privates, son. And I didn't just make it up as I went along. No, I asked the guys—'Hey, boys, what's the most beautiful pussy you've ever seen?' So I modeled it tight on Michelle Angelo's, which Ernie strayed across in a magazine centerfold.

Here . . ."—he passes the smudged, glossy pages—"want a sneak preview? See the lie of the land?"

You get kind of cool and detached. It takes time for things to register. You just find yourself wandering the landscape of your nightmare, to see how far and deep this chasm yawns.

"This?" I point to my neck. I sound deadly calm now.

"Ellen came up to check you out. She sincerely admired your pussy, Lee, but she pointed out your bobbly Adam's apple. Roy came up and he said you'd have a real feminine face if it wasn't for your jawline.

"'Doc,' says Ellen, 'you done real well for Lee. Everyone's grateful. But are you going to leave him half cooked, or are you going to go the extra mile?'

"'Ellen,' I say, 'these procedures are best done separately to give the lady recovery time and to avoid cardiovascular strain.' But your pulse is good, so I think why not?

"Roy says what about your chest. But I say I'm going to have to send off to a friend in Bathsheba to get some implants. And breast size is a personal issue with an aesthetic angle. So a guy is entitled to personally choose the exact tits to fit, instead of having them stuck on behind his back, without his approval."

Then I realize it's all right. Ha-ha. I wince at a sharp metallic twinge, like the echo of a scalpel cut. Then I know it's all some drawn-out joke.

"Hey, Doc." I smile through the pain. "You're kidding me, right? I can still feel my dick."

"Lee . . ." Doc leans close to advise me sober. "It's early days and you're doing great. But you've got a steep learning curve and you've got to try and adapt. You've got to start thinking feminine. Anatomically speaking, the tip's not your dick. It's your *clitoris*, and the shaft is now your *vagina*, son."

"Doc," I say, "you know me. I ain't a man to bear a grudge, or haggle about who said what. Forget the chin and the throat, just put my man-bits back how they were . . ."

He splays his helpless hands. "Your crotch was slashed to ribbons, Lee. I just tidied up the mess."

"Hey, Doc . . . ," I say, "just do your best."

"Lee . . ."—he gestures regretful to the galvanized bucket—"things have come out that can't be put back. Some things can't be undone. You should have thought it through before you agreed . . ."

I close my eyes and start rocking. I release this unending moaning, howling animal sound I never knew I had curled up within me.

"Hey, Roy," Doc shouts, "you better come. Lee isn't taking it as well as I'd hoped. We have some postoperative backsliding."

My legs won't support me, so I slide off the bed onto the floor, and I'm wriggling across the boards like an alligator, levering myself with knees and elbows, toward Doc. It strikes me, in a sunk-in-sludge, bottom-dwelling, forgotten-knowledge kind of way, if I can get within range, I can snap off his arm with my jaws.

Roy and Doc are grappling with my limbs, straddling my back, twisting away from my snapping teeth. Then I feel my arms pinioned and I see Doc sliding a needle into my arm.

When I wake, I'm back in bed with my arms reaching behind my head, with my wrists bound by rope to the bed frame. I don't know what I been dosed with, but it kind of moderates my rage to a lazy-happy-killer mood. I'm smiling broad and clacking my teeth, trying to bite at Doc when he ventures close.

I lie in bed five days solid. After short fitful sleeps, I wake knowing something awesome has happened. Uh-huh, I remember, I been turned into a woman now.

"How's it going, soldier?" Ethan pulls a chair to the bed.

"Fine," I say, "except . . ."

"Never got round to telling you, Lee. Time and place and all that . . ."

"What, Ethan?"

"The future and such . . ."

"Uh-huh, what?"

"You'd turned into a woman—when I saw you in Times Square."

"No kidding?"

"You turned out a fucking lovely lady, Lee. A real eye-turner."

"I do?"

"Drop-dead gorgeous," says Ethan, "as God is my witness. No bullshit. You made the right decision, for sure."

Folks come and go, offering food, advice, counseling, and humor. I keep my head in the pillow. I don't say a word. Opinions vary. Doc reckons I'm touching ungrateful.

"You know what that *free* surgery would cost you, Lee, in Morocco or Mexico? We're talking in excess of ten grand."

"How's it going, honey?" I guess Roy's trying to nudge me into the groove. "You going to get off your butt, lady? Take a shower, shampoo, and shave?"

"I know how you feel, Lee," says Ellen. "It hit me, too, when I was thirteen."

I don't dignify it with any reply. I guess they're all trying their best in their odd ways. Only, there's a part of me that wants to blame.

I just know I'd have found myself in a different position if my physician hadn't an amphetamine habit and been counseled by a bar full of drunks.

Every hour or so, I drop my pants and snatch another look. I guess any guy suddenly given lady parts would likely do the same.

"Hi, baby," I say. "Mind if Daddy takes another peek?" I suppose it was a way of breaking the ice, getting acquainted.

And it sure looks different. She's real pretty in a fey, lie-low, coy, fold-up kind of way. But I keep feeling I'm intruding on her privacy.

I wrap her up and zip her up quick. It's hard to feel, deep down, she's mine. However much a guy likes pussy, nothing prepares him for having his own.

Well, I can deal with change. I can wander beyond my comfort zones. I been black and I been white. I been alive and dead, rich and poor, clever and stupid, entire and broke, one-brained and two-brained, lost and found. But, for sure, there's a limit to how much you can handle. I never once envisioned taking a sex change.

Sure, I was never a man's man, nor a lady's man neither. I wasn't a proud man. When you dangle that tackle, you can't feel too self-important. It's hard to take a dick seriously, on account of its sloppy puppy ways, murky manners, and main-chance morals. But it's yours. You've grown up together. You've been on adventures. You come to rely on each other. You had some real satisfying times together. You think of yourselves as linked for life.

You're a guy. And there's a lot that hangs on that saluting part. And when you lose that, you've lost a deal that goes with it, socially speaking.

Still, when you get to know *her*, she's a real cutie. Sure, she isn't the same, but she's something to hold on to.

I'm starting to examine things cold and clear. I lay self-pity aside. When you look at things close, you see you ain't alone in this. Most everything is imperfect or broke. The iron bedstead, fine peppered by rust. The door that hangs askew, screeching against its hinges. The chipped cup. The off-white sheets. Roy with his bullet-wound limp. Garry the color-blind painter. Ethan who can't walk a straight line with time. Nevada sprawling parched in its sand. The South that can't reconcile black and white. The U.S. Army, getting the runaround from rice farmers in Vietnam. Nothing works right, just how it should, not even Security Advisor Henry Kissinger or President Richard Nixon.

I think back to things Uncle Nat told me, distilled from the salt sweat of his brow:

You can't mend a chicken with chicken wire . . . Don't go milking the mule, son . . . What you is given is what you is given . . . Don't try unscramble an egg, Lee . . . Whoever said it's gonna be fair? . . . I may be used, son, but I ain't used up . . . If you don't bite, don't growl . . . Don't shoot the jukebox if you don't like the song . . .

"Are you feeling any better, Lee?" asks Ellen. "Are you praying or something?"

"Just closed my eyes and kneeled down. Spoke some words. I been saying farewell to my misters."

"Good idea."

"I've lost a lot in my time. I've learned it's important to say good-bye."

"Right."

"You know what, Ellen, I never truly gave them much time or thought when I had them. I kind of took them for granted. You only miss them when they're gone, the little rascals. You know something?"

"What's that, Lee?"

"They were real characters, those guys. The left fellow, he always hung out lower. The right guy, he always kept himself closer, the itchy little devil . . ."

"You've got to grieve and then let go," says Ellen.

"You reckon there's someplace in the hereafter, for the parts that come off in life?"

"The way I see it," says Ellen, "you'll probably all meet up in the end. In heaven, they reckon, everyone's whole."

"Guess so."

"Move on, Lee. Make the best of things."

"Sure." I nod. "But when you fall asleep a man and wake up a woman . . . You got issues to take on board."

"I brought you some magazines, hon," says Ellen. *"Ladies' Home Journal. Cosmopolitan.* They might give you some pointers. They might help you get into the groove."

I flick the pages. I take things in. Turns out there's this new panty girdle to hold you firm with spandex and nylon. Control is knitted in. It reaches from belly to midthigh, so you don't get no untidy panty line. And there's some new satin-smooth brassiere that comes natural or fiberfill, giving great separation and support. You can choose candied apple, white, or taupe. And then there's this panty hose that doesn't bag or snag, but keeps you smooth from waist to toe with natural-fabric panels, where it matters most, to keep your crotch from steaming up.

It turns out there's this massive technology to keep all the parts of women firmly in place, trussed up in elastic, smooth, and wrinkle-free.

And then there's some other cotton industry to absorb women thorough, to keep them all bunged up, with antibacterial deodorants built in. And there are special sprays for intimate hygiene problems that men just don't get.

Because you're usually not alone, and fluids can spread.

And it turns out lots of women got this design fault—which is undersized breasts. They're only 34B where they're meant to be 36D. So they need the Mark Eden Bust Developer, which helps you add four inches in only eight weeks. But if you ain't satisfied after only a fortnight, Mark will refund you in full, if you write him personal at his box number in San Francisco. And then you can stay flat as a pancake, or cheat by stuffing your bra, or try the Campasina

Glamour Plan instead, which brings you the secrets of European farm girls, who got voluptuous bustlines by working their pectoralis major muscles, from cleaning out goat pens.

And if you got to smoke, some guy's even designed femme cigarettes like Eve, with a pretty flower motif on the butt, and Kool, which are elegant, slender, and menthol fresh on your breath.

Salem, the cigarette with springtime freshness

And if you got to drive, some guy's designed small tin-can, underpowered cars, which come with dinky names in pastel colors.

Plus you're expected to make all the fried chicken, coleslaw, and strawberry shortcake, entertain your husband's boss, knit all the patterned sweaters, suck dick, raise two children, keep your hair bouncy and shiny, your legs smooth and hairless, and all your openings dry and sweet smelling, without underarm fabric stains, or spotting, staying free of facial wrinkles, while wearing a smile, and keeping a civil tongue in your head.

Please don't squeeze the Charmin

Stronger than dirt

I mean how does your average guy score on all that? Jesus. Who do they think we are? Do they think they're talking to women like *me?*

It isn't an encouraging introduction. There's some of this woman stuff I can swallow. But, on a lot of it, I'm going to have to pass.

Dear Lord, I think, who'd be a woman? Given the choice, I'd rather be black.

———

"How's it going down there?" Doc pokes his head round the door. He's dangling a couple of beers.

"Fine," I say. "Once you get used to her, she's real swell. Your female parts got limitations. But they've got real eye-pleasing, smoother lines."

"I've been thinking about your breasts, Lee . . . I've been thinking about your breasts a lot. I've got some girlie mags if you care to look. See if anything catches your eye . . ."

"The way I see it, Doc . . ."—I take a swig—"whatever I choose, I'm going to have to carry every step of my life. I don't want hickeys. But I don't want jugs neither. Forget Raquel Welch. I'm thinking firm. I'm thinking soup bowls with zero sag. I want to stretch a T-shirt with optional bra."

"You're in the zone," says Doc. "It's all ergonomics and good design. We need to balance the look and the physics. You've got to appear all woman, but we don't want to shift your center of gravity too much. We don't want to obscure your downward vision. You don't want any major barrier to come between you and fixing an engine or playing pool. And we want to minimize nipple friction. Except . . ."

"Yeah?"

"Guys do like them big."

"Guys?" I say. "Guys can go fuck themselves."

"You reckon on being a dyke, then, Lee?"

"I suppose . . ." I wince. "I haven't truly thought it through. But, hey, Doc, please don't talk disrespectful. That d-word grates real ugly on the ear."

"Sure, Lee. Now, about your breasts . . . What do you think of these, Jane Fonda's?" He hands me a photo.

"Dynamite . . ." I smile. I've seen the future. It's swell. "Those are the real McCoy. Those are the cat's pajamas."

———

Ethan comes to say good-bye. His face is bruised bad still, purply black, and his right forearm is plastered up. All the guys in the bar have autographed his cast so I add my signature too.

I keep meaning to tell him his face is getting roughed up by this desert sun. I need to loan him some moisturizer.

"Leave's over. Got to get back."

"Guess you'll have to go without me," I say.

"Yep . . ." Ethan nods and considers. "The U.S. Army can re-assign you many places, but not to the other sex. Have you thought of joining the WACs?"

"See you, soldier."

"See you, Lee." He hesitates, and turns back to me, spreading his arms. "Don't misread my intentions, lady, but how about giving me a farewell hug?" And he presses his moist, warm lips to my burning stubbly cheeks.

"See you in Times Square," I say.

"Yeah. In the eighties," Ethan agrees.

Shit. We both know you mustn't fuck with history. We both know I pass him by, unseeing.

16

The Almighty's Mathematics

A guy doesn't convert to a woman overnight. It just doesn't happen so quick. When the wraps come off, you can see the joins, the seams, and the stitches. You need to find the crossover motivation. And there's female psychology to take on board before you can call yourself a lady.

But there are angles on getting feminine that just shake down to mathematics. As you likely know already, the golden section is defined by phi, which equals 1.618, and, sure, there are plenty more decimal points, but you can drop those for most sex-change, plastic-surgery purposes.

You just know there's something special about phi, because it plays some real freaky tricks, like, for one instance, 1 + phi = phi squared, but it doesn't just end there, because the reciprocal of 1.618 is 0.618, and the height of a man is five cubits, and when he raises his arm it becomes six, and phi squared × 6/5 = 3.1416. Which is pi! Cute, huh? Plus plants use phi to rotate their stems, so a leaf never finds itself hung out in the exact same place twice, and from this, you can infer, we got a short handle on the Almighty's mathematics.

But I was just stumbling round in the dark. And I know nothing of this till Doc Gene took the time to explain it. Because, when he was trimming down my chin, he had to calculate the amount by phi, to get the best proportion for my face.

See, the head forms a golden rectangle with the eyes at its midpoint. The mouth and nose are each placed at golden sections of the distance between the eyes and the bottom of the chin. Most every ratio in a good-looking face turns out 1.618.

Now, I scored pretty good as I was, mouth upward. Except, all my life, my jaw has been draining the beauty right out of my face. So getting my chinbone shaved and properly proportioned was the final piece in the jigsaw. And Doc claims it made all the difference in transforming a soft-featured pretty boy into a real striking, heart-aching, head-turning, jaw-dropping woman.

"Shit," says Doc, laying the calipers down. "You're going to be one fucking gorgeous lady. When your bruising comes down, all the chest hair comes off, and your breasts get slotted in. No idle brag, Lee. Take it from your physician. Take it from the hand that made you."

Like I say, there's a lot out-a-sight, intimate, cotton-wrapped about being a woman that a guy just don't anticipate until he crosses that bridge when he comes to it and takes that leap into the dark. You may think some lady looks calm and controlled on the surface, but, I can warrant from inside experience, she's likely got the cheeks of her ass clenched tight and webbed feet paddling like mad beneath.

When your pussy's man-made, instead of God-given, you need to keep stretching it with stents at the start, to stop it collapsing or closing up. It's not that I got any immediate plans for it. As it stands, an in-house vagina is plain surplus to my requirements. But it's a kind of hidden asset, to keep under wraps. And there's an obligation to take care of whatever you get given in life, even when it doesn't have any obvious, practical use. Anyway, when you think it through, if I ever get it on again, I'm going to need something to offer a partner, to lay on the table, to contribute to the party.

Doc's fitted me up with special expandable silicone implants he's adapted himself. The way it works, he can inflate them slow, with more saline, every few days through a sealed port. This way the skin expands slow to accommodate a gradual growth, because Doc doesn't want me to have to start my female life bilateral unbalanced, self-conscious, with stretch marks. And this way, he reassures, we minimize loss of nipple sensation, which may not concern a guy so much, but can count for a lot for a woman.

We work up, over two weeks, to a 145 percent scale copy of Miss Fonda's breasts. Then we decide enough's enough. And it all gets sealed up. I'm that much bigger than Jane overall, so we got to round things up to create the same impression and compensate for foreshortening. Only difference is that my nipples point straight ahead, whereas Jane's tilt very slightly up. Each to their own. I don't claim mine are any better. Only, Doc reckons, he's improved some on nature. Because with implants you get less slack and jiggle, better symmetry, and a firmer touch.

They're swollen and tender the first couple of weeks. It takes time for things to bed down and hang natural.

And I got a deal of intimate shaving to do every other day, to avoid telltale stubble. But Doc reckons this should ease when the estrogen kicks in and the residual testosterone gets all burned off. When I got some spare money, he advises, I'd better invest in some major electrolysis.

After a couple of months, I send off for a couple of mail-order wigs—a kind of Farrah Fawcett blond number with flicks and a classic real-natural-looking Mary Tyler Moore brunette. I guess I'm hedging my bets between conservative and raunchy.

Ellen finds me some spare cosmetics and panties. She holds a finger to her lips as she palms me a book. It's *Sex and the Single Girl* by a lady called Helen Gurley Brown. It's graphic advisory, no holds barred. It tells us women some handy, inside stuff about our salient parts. I guess it could save me a deal of tacky time-waste trial and error, and there are some finger exercises she recommends, and tips on reaching crucial things out-a-sight.

Nancy finds me a denim blouse with some fancy rhinestone detailing, an empire-waist, paisley-patterned velvet dress, a gypsy patchwork waistcoat with buckskin pockets, and a scarlet polyester catsuit with bell-bottoms and a zip from navel to neck that she says she can't fit into no more, without stretching things, on account of her weight. A girl couldn't ask for better friends.

Sure, I've still got rough edges that need smoothing off. Nobody mentioned it before—not when I was a guy—but now, it's apparent, I come across as an opinionated, mouthy woman. It turns out I got inappropriate detailed views on the New York Knicks, car mechanics, the gold standard, space travel, and politics. And I'd be better off looking in a mirror, to check my mascara isn't overheavy and my lipstick hasn't smudged.

And Ellen takes me aside and advises I wear panties, or cross my legs, when I'm perched up on a bar stool.

"You've got to try to retain some mystery, Lee."

"Yeah?"

"Because a girl doesn't want to go broadcast her bush to the nation." And when he finds the time, Doc gives me deportment lessons to walk right, elocution classes to pitch my voice up, and advice on conversation, to talk like a lady should. He calls it aftercare.

"You see, Lee. There's an implicit contract here. You're the first and only woman I've ever made. I'm not going to leave you unfinished. We've done the undercoating. Now we've got to give you the final gloss."

"I appreciate that, Doc. And if there's *anything* I can ever do for you . . ."

There are things you take for granted as a guy that turn out to be a science for a lady.

"See, Lee . . . Bell Labs have proved when a woman walks, she swivels her hips up to sixteen degrees each side of the axis. It's called the pelvic twist, and it's got the evolutionary purpose to attract the male gaze and accentuate your ass."

"Yeah?"

"So, try and work in some mild rotation, lady."

"Right." I swivel around a bit and jerk my hips. "Anything else, before I'm all finished off?"

"Women have a shorter stride pattern, Lee. Try shortening your steps. Plus you need to tuck your elbows closer to your body. And a personal thing, Lee. But Roy asked me to mention . . ."

"Doc?"

"You'd better stop using the men's toilet and start peeing in private upstairs. Apart from everything else, it disturbs the guys in the john."

"Guess, so," I agree. "It's force of habit, Doc."

But he's right. It does go awesome quiet in the can. Some guys lose their flow, but mostly they drop their jaw and stare. If the cubicles are busy and it's urgent, you got to make do with a urinal. Then you got to arch your back real hard. And without a dick to point at the bowl, you got to aim high with your tufts. You don't have the hose power a man does. You have to think ahead in steep parabolas. You got your panties stretched between your knees. It gets to look like some show-off party trick.

"When you've only been a lady for three months," Doc advises, "there are things you still have to learn."

"Yeah?"

"Try to cut out the personal scratching, Lee. There are things a trucker or soldier can get away with that come over gross in a lady."

"Sheer male habit, Doc." I splay my hands and examine my crimson lacquered nails. "It comes from bunking with twenty GIs in a barrack. You like this shade of lipstick? They call it Sacramento Rose."

"Hell, baby, the color suits you. It rhymes with your skin, and sings along with your eyes. You've got the looks of an angel." Doc sucks in and nods solemnly, admiring his handiwork, dwelling on the shady valley of my chest. "It's only when you move or talk that there are any real giveaways." And he lays a heavy, reassuring hot hand on my thigh.

Oh, my sweet Galatea

"These erogenous zones," I ask, "like you're forever reading about in magazines, how many is a woman meant to have, when they all rounded up and numbered?"

"Well . . ." Doc frowns and hesitates. "Opinions and experiences vary. How many have you found?"

"Only five, so far," I admit. "I guess it depends how you count."

"Five?" says Doc. "That isn't so bad." He gulps on his beer, blinks, and looks away. "Have you been testing out the equipment, Lee?"

"Not for real." I blush. "Not yet. I've just been feeling my way in the dark."

The truth is—and I got to be frank—I been giving my body some close scrutiny, to try and figure out how every little bit works. Every day I find some small new detail. Fingers only get you so far. So I've been taking some sneaky sideways advice, by holding a shaving mirror under my chassis.

It's like puberty's hit me all over again. Technically, I got nothing new. It's just what I had before, pruned and laid out to a different floor plan. But when you have a tidy-up and rearrange the furniture, you can get a whole fresh new feel to your living room. Then again, maybe it's more like one of those reversible jackets, plain one side and plaid patterned the other. So, when you wear it inside out, you can kid yourself it's entirely new.

I don't say it's any better being a woman than a man. But it can get kind of stale being stuck in the rut. And it's real refreshing to change the surface values.

In the reflection of the wardrobe mirror, I watch the torso undress. The T-shirt's drawn up. There's the flat belly, rumor of ribs, and swell breasts. Lace hems slither down long smooth thighs. The legs splay. I'm like an outsider looking in, like I'm watching a strip show. And it's kind of disconcerting to be a horny spectator to your own skin. You know it isn't healthy to have the hots for yourself. But you got that warm, prickly tingle. And you still got that phantom-dick problem. You feel it rise to the occasion, then look down to find it's long gone.

It wasn't losing my parts so much that hurt the most, as never saying a proper farewell at the time.

I know there's a fork in the road ahead—between looking like a woman or *being* one. But with twenty-odd years in a male body, you build up a hefty caseload of awkward male conditioning.

I've started serving bar to pay my way, and trade is slowly picking up. There are locals who've heard about me on the grapevine and come for a drink to take a look. And there are truckers and commercial travelers who've taken a shine to the place and started making regular callbacks.

Guys like to look a lot, confide their names, ask innocent-sounding fishhook questions to draw you into personal talk, stroke their scalp, declare their destination, lean over the bar, observe your frontage, inquire as to your state of origin, flick lint from their sleeves, pat their stomachs, show their incisors, nod and grunt for no evident reason, brag about the width of their wallet, pocket their wedding rings, bad-mouth their bosses, remark on the humidity and ambient temperature. It's sure a revelation, standing woman-side of the deal and never getting to shuffle.

It's a kind of ritual. Often, they feel obliged to hit on you. Sometimes you get offered a steak dinner or auto ride as a come-on, like you're a kid or something.

That thing you do with the Pepsi bottle, hon, why don't you do that thing to me?

You want cock? Well, I got cock. Betcha I got the biggest cock in this bar. Likely got the biggest cock in Monroe County.

I smile a lot. I nod some. I still haven't found a reliable, steady pitch for my voice, so I try keep conversation to a minimum.

No? Cat got your tongue? Well, yo ain't so special as you think, lady. Yo all sunk-bone, hollow-cheeked starved like that scrawny Faye Dunaway

I'm still trying things out for size and finding my way, like the way I grasp a bottle, sliding a slick finger along the neck, before passing it to a guy, lick specks of beer spray from my hand, or flick the tip of my tongue round the underside of my lips, or roll my eyes, or hold back from blinking, or rub the base of my spine while leaning back, or nibble the tip of my little finger, or run a hand down a thigh while staring at a guy. Some of it comes from girls I've known. Some I picked up from TV.

Partly I do it for the tips, but mainly I'm building up mileage, walking in a woman's shoes, seeing how far I can go, giving full head to my feminine side.

May you dig up your father by moonlight and make soup of his bones

A thing I notice early on, as a woman, is that you pull a lot of gaze. You got guys trying to catch your eye; you got glances, glints, flickers, twinkles, blinks, and winks. You got look-see into your lap. You got up-skirt espionage when you come down stairs. You got scrutiny on your rump; you got sidelong down your hips; you got eyeball in your chest and peeps into your brassiere. Man's got a viewpoint on your figure and perspective on your looks. You got survey over your skin and scrutiny into your mouth. Contrary to report, a man's most restless organ is the eye.

It feels like you're a contestant at the Miss America Pageant and every last guy is a judge. It doesn't seem to bother them how they present to the eye themselves. They just stare out unabashed and give you a score.

This hoggy, pink-skinned, paunchy guy with bristly nose hair comes into the bar, orders a whiskey sour, and starts giving me solemn perusal, with some sly askance mixed in. He's got his hair swept over his scalp from a parting just above his ear. He's got a belly straining his moist shirt, with some tufts of belly hair sprouting out. He gives off a cheesy hormonal scent.

"Excuse me, lady, can I ask your name?"

"Lee."

"You ever modeled?"

"No."

"Lee, can I say something that might come across as personal?"

"Sure," I concede. "Most men do. So fire away."

"I'm a photographer, Lee, so I speak with a professional eye. I don't want you to take offense . . ."

"No?"

He produces this Leica out of his case. Click. He sways up close to frame me. Click, click.

"The lens loves you." Click. "You've got great features and you've got fine bones." Flash. "But something isn't working." Flash. Flash. "You come across as less than the sum of your parts. You know what it is?"

"Tell me."

"You hold yourself too stiff. Your movements are too rehearsed. You need to loosen up. You've need to release the *me*." Click. Click.

"Thanks," I say.

"Stanley Elkins," he says, handing me a moist business card from the chest pocket of his shirt. "Art photography."

"You're *artistic*, Stanley?" I say. I'd taken him for cattle feed or hydraulic fluids.

He says he's come to Nevada for its hard textures and the harsh, pitiless acid light. "See . . . ," he says, and he draws a hide folder out of his attaché case and lays it on the bar. "I've got some work here."

Stanley's got press cuttings. He's been exhibited in New York, won prizes in Milan, and been published in *Newsweek* and *Playboy*. He is very black-and-white. He's done a lot of shiny black girls smeared in oil. Mainly tits, and groins with shaving rash. But he's got some clothed portraits of Mormons looking overmarried and Amish looking grumpy, some complete brick walls, carcasses hanging in abattoirs, and close-ups of driftwood and rusted cars.

"You see what I do best"—he taps a groin through the cellophane—"are tonal contrasts, landscapes in skin, and chiaroscuro."

"I can see that, Stanley. You never been tempted to buy any color film?"

"I work with the gray spectrum, Lee."

"It's all very still. And it looks real hard and cruel."

"Sure. If you're interested, I could shoot you too."

"I'm kind of shy"—I giggle some—"about stripping off for strangers."

"There's nothing so hollow as modesty, Lee. There's nothing so shallow as skin."

"Hell, Stanley, you sweet talker . . ."—I giggle—"I just don't know."

"Sleep on it, Lee. You don't want to miss out on an *opportunity*."

Doc's been loitering surly and close, seasoning a scowl. He asks me if the guy's bothering me. I say it's jake, because he isn't the pervert he seems, and I'm learning about gray scale and photography. And Stanley says it's a private conversation, anyway. And then they're head to head, eyeballing each other harsh. So Roy intervenes with some soothing words and beers for both on the house.

"Guys," I say, "get real. There's no point fighting over *me*."

I mean, I don't desire men. How's a girl meant to find them attractive, for chrissakes, when they grate on the ears, hang musty in the nostrils, feel furry, rough to the touch, and present so poor to the eyes?

"But, Stanley," I say, "can I handle that lovely instrument of yours?" I detect a moment's indecision, then he passes over the Leica, nestling in his palms. It's awful heavy and military feeling, all gunmetal and pimply leatherette and lens turret. There's something obscenely gratifying about cupping its gravity, fingering it, and feeling up its firm, cool textures.

"Give me time," I say, "and I'll get one of these." Yeah, it was love at first sight, me and that Leica.

I frame him in the viewfinder. Guess what? I got this seedy children's story goblin smiling back. I hear the heavy metallic click and feel the judder in my palm. I swivel round on Gene. Know what? It's the face of John the Baptist, wild-eyed on speed.

"Shit," I say. "You can steal a guy's soul with this thing." I've found my vocation. "Stanley?" I ask. "What are these numbers round the lens?"

"Those are your apertures, Lee. They let you decide how much you want to open up."

Apertures? Don't you just love it. It's one filthy, candid business, this photography.

"You've heard of f-stops?" he asks.

"Not in this context, Stanley."

"See," he explains me, "it all keys in with depth of field, speed, and exposure. Do you want it slow or fast, or do you prefer it deep or shallow?"

"How do you like it, Stan?"

"Me"—he frowns surprised—"I do it every which way, Lee. It depends on the occasion, and the emotion I want to convey."

"Don't it just," I agree.

"Then you've got to tie it in with your film speed, Lee."

"Uh-huh."

"Some are slow but sensitive. Some are real fast but smudgy. It's a trade-off. What you gain in speed you can lose in fidelity . . ."

"Ain't that always the way?" I agree. "You hit it bang on the button."

"The way I see it, Lee, photography is where light reflects the intersection of physics and desire."

"That, Stanley, is the best invitation I've heard in years."

Click. Click. Hee. Hee.

Yeah, the preacher is a dodger an' I'm a dodger too

I've turned out marginal tall for a woman at five feet ten inches and a hundred and forty pounds. I've got broad shoulders from a childhood of farmwork. It helps me carry Miss Fonda's breasts and lends the appearance of a tapered waist. My contours are smoothing over the rumors of military muscle. I've been laying a thin skim of subcutaneous fat. The estrogen helps with the hair growth too. I've got more luster and body than I ever had as a crew-cut guy. I laid the wigs aside once the tresses crossed over my ears and started reaching down for my neck. This was my Mia Farrow phase.

My complexion's picked up, coming up peachy smooth, now I been able to hang up my razor. I'm getting less reliant on makeup and trusting more to skin. I like the natural Midwest girl-next-door look.

Ellen and I are getting close, woman to woman, with bathroom sessions and trying on clothes. We've been known to share a shower and suds each others' back.

"Doc did a real nice job on you, baby." Ellen observes my naked length. "I asked if he could do a boob job for me. He's put me on his waiting list. But he's got a nose job for Susan Field and he's reconstructing a Dodge convertible."

"You don't need no new body work, Ellen." I wrap an arm round her waist to reassure.

"Easy for you to say, Lee, looking like *that,* all built up from scratch with Hollywood parts. No offense, but you come across way better as a lady than you ever did as a guy."

It's true I've been lucky. I never was a manly man. Doc's surgery revealed my feminine grain. Some guys can never make the transition. However much work they have done, they still come across like John Wayne in a Mae West wig and carry themselves like the Redskins' defense.

"Hey, honey." I fold moist Ellen in my arms. I press my lips to her forehead. I run my hand down the nobbles of spine and start massaging the small of her back. "Your body's just swell."

Well, our thighs meet and our bellies press. Wet from the shower, we got some suction adhesion. My nipples are pressing stubby into her. I'm going breathy, twitchy, and flushed. I get a liquid throb where my misters used to belong.

Maybe a line's been crossed, because Ellen eases herself out. We get that skin-on-skin soft ripping sound. She wraps herself in a bath towel. When she looks my way again, it's a touch perplexed, reproachful.

"Women don't touch *that way*," she advises, "at least not here in Elko."

"Sorry, Ellen. I didn't mean nothing by it. I just got these leftover male reflexes."

Not that I'd ever try hit on her. Betrayal of trust. Besides, she's kind of spoken for. Lovely lady.

It's an open secret that a couple of nights a week, most often Wednesday and Saturday, Doc Gene's bed stays empty while he rests overnight at Ellen's. But when they're together in the bar, it's hard to discern a relationship. They don't speak much, or touch, and when you find them together, there'll likely be a third or fourth party sitting between. But often you can see Ellen clocking Doc at a distance, like when he's hunched over the phone or visits the can. And when he comes or goes, she tends to look to her watch.

I've had a glimpse of both sides now. I got a dual perspective denied most everyone else. And it seems to me, guys got a lot going for them. They can go most everywhere, anytime. You seldom ask yourself who they belong to, or why they're out late. You don't assume, if you see them alone in a bar, that they're an easy lay or come to rent their body for money. They aren't always under the eye. They can voice an opinion on anything, talk shit, and speak dirty. And they aren't weighed down by all those hygiene regulations and sanitary bylaws. I mean if a guy doesn't wash for two days, he can pass himself off as industrious, sweaty. A woman doesn't enjoy the same latitudes.

I was noticing all manner of sexual inequality. Take garment quality, for starters. A guy's trousers often got rivet reinforcement, deeper pockets, stronger zippers, and double stitching. But a girl's slacks are just sheer flimsy. You can rip a gusset or tear a seam just vaulting a fence or playing touch football. It's like the women's fashion industry is trying to keep you female passive. And likely as not, you're paying more.

I don't realize at the time and don't have the words or ideas to express it clear, but my sympathies are veering feministic. But, as far as I knew then, women's studies was high school cooking lessons, selecting your shade of eye shadow, learning to give a BJ, reading child-care manuals and *Family Circle,* and matching your napkin to your flow. But all that was going to change as life wised me up, with a bump, of a sudden.

Can't say I care about folks' color or gender. Long as I can get them to bleed red and pay up green

17

Propositions

One Friday afternoon two military police strut into the bar, all crisp-ironed creases, badges, webbing, and hormones. With steel heel plates on their boots, they clatter the boards like tap dancers. I'd seen them at a distance around Fort Scott, but I didn't know them to speak to. They sit at the bar and ask, barely civil, for a couple of beers. They glower around at the clientele. They know they're welcome as clap. They flick the stale peanuts along the bar, they watch the pool game unimpressed, feed some nickels in the jukebox.

> *Can't care if it rains or freezes*
> *Long as I got my plastic Jesus*

"Hey, lady," says the lieutenant, breaking his moody silence. "Take a look. Mean anything to you?"

> *Don't care if the night is scary*
> *Long as I got the Virgin Mary*

He skims my recruitment photo along the shiny oak bar top. I come to rest upside down in front of myself. I got that rabbit-in-the-headlights look. He asks me if I've seen me.

"Okay," I concede, "there's a likeness."

"Yep . . ." He looks to the photo then back to me. "You've got the same nose. You related?"

"Hell, yes . . . it's me before my sex change." When you're caught in a dead end with your panties down, you got to come clean.

"No need to get sarcastic, lady," says the sergeant. "We're only doing our duty."

> *Don't care if it bumps or jostles*
> *Long as I got the Twelve Apostles*

Roy gives me a granite shut-up stare, then takes a long, softer look at the photo. The moment has passed. He says he's seen the face a month ago, but not recent. He asks them what I've done.

"AWOL. He's a lost steer we need to round up. We wouldn't be chasing him so hard," says the sergeant, "but he's Special Intake."

"Special?"

"Security stuff."

"The guy could have gone undercover," Doc advises.

"We don't get spooks gathering here," says Roy. "It's just locals and travelers."

"This guy dangerous?" asks Ellen.

"He's in possession of *information*."

"Any distinguishing characteristics?" asks Doc.

"Yeah." The sergeant flicks through his notebook. "Vertical leg scar and childlike manner."

"What does that last mean?" I ask. "It doesn't come across complimentary."

"Naive, I guess."

"You leave a contact number," says Roy, "and if some scarred simpleton comes into the bar, we'll sure let you know."

"Grateful, sir."

As they turn to leave, they salute. I just can't help myself. I click my heels together and my arm jerks up to salute them back. Sheer fucking force of habit. Army gets you trained like a lab rat. It turns you into some idiot windup toy.

If the jukebox took teardrops . . .

"Bye, ma'am." The sergeant shows a wince of annoyance, softened by kind of a hurt, yearning look into my eyes.

Well, hell, life's easy for you, babe, looking a million dollars, with men crawling all over

The good news is that I pass the eye test—because the military police aren't particular fools, and it takes something special to trip them up. Bad news is the guys start teasing me terrible. They pretend I'm some trained killer type and start ducking under the tables when I come close. They take to calling me Clint or *The Man from U.N.C.L.E.* Which is a joke, short term, but grates on the nerves in the long run.

The sender doesn't seem to know my full name, and there's no return address on the back. The package comes stiffened by a cardboard back. It's addressed to *Lee, c/o Roy's Bar, Elko, Nevada* in prissy, small, spidery handwriting. The stamps are franked in San Francisco, California. I haven't received any personal mail at Roy's before. I guess I'm intrigued, apprehensive. You can feel the contents through the paper. It feels like a brochure or magazine. But

when I open it up, it's a series of eight-by-ten black-and-white photographic prints mounted in cream card surrounds.

It's from Stanley Elkins, the photographer. He's sent me my first
portfolio.

I'd posed against a white sheet backdrop. But Stanley has done
some fancy superimposition and collage, because he's got me hanging in the buff from a coat hanger in an open wardrobe, alongside
a row of dresses. And then he's got me peering plaintive through
some bars, behind a sign that says DON'T FEED THE ANIMALS. Then
I'm standing naked on the pavement outside some department store,
carrying a Macy's shopping bag. I got both arms raised. With my
right I'm holding an umbrella. With the left I'm hailing a cab. Then
there are some real big close-ups—of nipples and navel and
kneecaps that look like landscapes of the moon. And there's some
that look real rude and intimate until you work out it's a stubbly
armpit or the crease between two toes. But my favorite has to be me
standing there raw with an idiot smile. There's strings coming up
from my head, hands, and feet—so it looks like I'm a puppet, being
jerked by an unseen hand.

There's a handwritten note, folded around three hundred dollars in crisp, clean tens.

Dear Lee,

*Hi, Angel. It turned out well. Guess you inspired me. I
got a poster contract and a centerfold, so—enclosed—there's
a fee. If you can make it to San Francisco, I'll fund your fare
and another shoot.*

Stanley G. Elkins

When Doc appears shaved and twitchy one evening in a crisp white
shirt and laundered jeans, and makes a beeline for the bar, and leans
real close up to whisper ticklish into my ear, and extends a personal

invitation, I can see Ellen watching us anxious across the room, and I sense an unwelcome complication.

"Dinner?" I say. "What you mean, Gene?"

"Restaurant in Elko. There are matters I'd like to talk over, in private."

"Private?" I ask.

"Yeah," he agrees.

"What about Ellen?" I say.

"What about Ellen?" he says.

"Don't you want to bring her along?"

"Prefer not," he says. "Three's a crowd."

"*Guys-together* kind of occasion?" I ask.

"I'll pick you up tomorrow," he says, "at seven."

"We'll miss the Packers game on television. Besides, I got to wash my hair."

"Seven," says Doc, kind of alpha-male decisive.

Sad and strange, all this tangled desire, that can't satisfy anyone like it should—with me wanting Ellen, and Ellen wanting Doc, and Doc (I fear) wanting me. And whichever way I turn, it feels like I'm betraying the trust of a friend.

Gene isn't his usual fluent self on our date. I reckon he's taken himself off his medication. He's got spearmint breath. He comes across as sober. We sit side by side in silence in the front of his Buick enjoying the fresh scent of Paco Rabanne and an unswerving straight view of the median. He's real careful with his driving. He's tongue-tied. And in the restaurant he's banging into the furniture, awkward with the menu, and clumsy with the cutlery.

He says when you create something exquisite and beautiful, it's near impossible to let it go. He says you don't trust anyone else to lay their dirty mitts on it. He says you get lacerated by irrational jealousies. He knows we're ill matched. He says that while I'm truly a guy and a half-wit underneath, there's no accounting for *desire*. And when you got that insistent itch, there's nothing to do but to scratch it. Hell, you can't think straight. You can't sleep. Your heart races. You just go crazy. He squeezes my hand overfirm.

Jesus, I'm going to offer my heart on a plate to a she-man

"I went to the jewelers, Lee." He shunts a small leather box with a flick of his thumb across the gingham tablecloth.

"Right . . . ," I say. I flip the lid. "Real nice . . . ," I say. "Real classy." It's an awful beguiling diamond, between two emeralds, on a fine gold band. Now, I got most things a woman's got, in trumps, except any quality jewelry.

"Look, Doc . . ." I take his hand. "You've done *everything* for me. And if I could repay, I would. But there are things that aren't in my gift. You did my body real good, but you never touched my heart. Truth is, I got my eyes on women too. But if I ever go the *other way*, I'll be sure to give you first refusal."

I can change all that, Lee . . . You just need this man's good loving

Now, the trouble with Gene is his mind's always racing ahead, and he's got an answer for most everything. He says there's seven forms of love all mingled together, and eros barely figures, because sex is just the tip of it. He says he's talking agape, respect, companionship, sympathy, and care. He says that, out of the sack, a guy-on-guy relationship can work real well, because of shared recreational interests—like poker, football, and car mechanics—which a woman can't be relied upon to share.

Little lady of mine got a body to die for

He says at home we can just hang out like a couple of ordinary guys, only one of them's in woman's clothes. I wouldn't have to work unless I wanted. Anyway, he isn't comfortable with me tending bar because of the come-ons from drunken men and the questionable moral atmosphere. He promises he'd clean up his act, go easy on the juice, and cut down on the pills. I say I wouldn't want that because it might wreck his charm. I say I only been a woman for forty-five weeks, four days, so it feels too early to settle down. I warn him that when a guy knowingly chooses a lesbian, he's got his reasons tangled, and he's facing troubles farther up the road. I say I admire his orchid mind and electric intellect, and I'll never provide any mental challenge. I tell him plain I ain't good enough.

"Doc," I say, "my little light is dim. I am no great shakes in the mental department. Plus I'm emotionally flat. You are looking for a deeper well, while I'm shallow as a saucer. I'm all surface and no depth, like a blank sheet of paper." He's making me moist-eyed and I sniffle some.

"Hey, Lee." Doc pats my hand. "I'm confident I can handle some superficiality in a gorgeous lady."

"And experience taught me not to love another person. Because I lose them soon as I got them. And the pain isn't worth the candle."

"Love is a journey," Doc advises, "not a destination. I'll be holding your hand every step of the way."

"I'm kind of *fated*, Gene. Strange things happen. I'm sheer fucking trouble. Plus I got the Mason-Dixon Line tattooed down my heart."

I tell him I'm just a doohickey soul. Sure he wants me now, in the heat of the moment. But six months down the line, I'll be mislaid, forgotten—some small item, gathering fluff in the glove compartment of his heart, lodged behind some speeding fines and a route map.

Gene says you got to look to precedent and history. There's all manner of unlikely couples. He talks Marilyn Monroe and Arthur

Miller, Admetus and Alcestis, Pyramus and Thisbe, Apollo and Hyacinthus, Noah and Eleanor Cohen.

"Sure," I say, "and show me just one happy ending."

The waiter comes to ask if we enjoyed our steaks, and if we want anything more.

"Sure," says Doc. "Quit brushing the lady's arm when you serve her. And keep your sly spic eyes off my woman."

It's downhill after that. When I offer to go dutch, Doc just grunts. We drive back in silence. At Roy's he opens the door for me, then slams it closed and scorches off. And back in the bar, folks fall silent. Ellen wrinkles her nose and eyes me icy. Roy's gone abrupt and edgy. A girl feels unclean and guilty, and she ain't done anything wrong.

Fucking ungrateful she-male bitch. After I give you a camisole and my favorite body stocking

Hell, I just wanted to be nice, fit in, smell good, and look pretty. But it felt like I just wandered in with dog shit stuck to the soles of my new Cuban heel, two-tone, dual-texture, buckskin-and-suede, Apache-fringe, knee-high boots.

With Stanley's invitation and money, I reckon I deserve a break. I'm run-down, depressed. I been feeling lethargic and suffering mood swings. It's likely from the mixer tap of my hormones, now the testosterone has been turned off, while the estrogens are flooding through.

Some mornings, a girl feels melancholy weepy for no obvious reasons. You feel gawky, unattractive, bloated, and slow; your nylons snag, your nails chip, nipples are awful sensitive, chafing when you move, and things just seem out of kilter. And God knows where you left your purse, and your spatial sense seems shot because you're getting giddy disorientated on the stairs, and can't remember if you're meant to turn left or right for the bathroom, and you wonder why folks can't act a bit considerate, and why guys think it ever helps to shout.

Roy says, "Fine. Take a month's vacation. It'll clear the air. Make sure you come back." Nancy smiles at the sidelines. Ellen nods from her table but doesn't lift her butt to say good-bye.

Gene insists on driving me to catch the bus at Elko. He tells me I'm an ingrate, opportunist bitch with an eye for the main chance and the morals of a feral cat. He gives me a six-month supply of estrogen tablets. He warns I'd better telephone him or consult a physician if I get any worrying symptoms with my female parts. He's ferocious gruff and affectionate. It's good to see him grubby again, zipping along on amphetamine sulfate.

He holds me to his chest, nuzzles my neck, and plants a hot wet suction kiss on my forehead. I pat his shoulders till he sees fit to release me. He hands me a paper-wrapped tube of nickels, so I'll always have the wherewithal to ring home.

"Don't cry, Gene. I'm coming back soon."

"No, you're not. The world is there at your feet. Only an idiot would come back here. Shit, I'll be leaving soon myself."

"What are you going to do?"

"Cosmetic surgery, Lee. Not boob and nose jobs for the vain. Real stuff for damaged, burned, and ugly people."

"Aren't you disbarred?"

"Suspended, Lee. In seven months I can practice again."

"That's beautiful, Gene."

I paid for those shoes that just walked out on me. And the tits too

It's a far ride from Elko, Nevada, to San Francisco, California. And farther in culture than distance. You got to change everything en route—I'm talking buses, assumptions, cultures, accents, diets, friends, occupations, vices, mind-set, and sexual manners.

You try to carry your habits with you, but travel shakes you right out of your grooves. I get into San Francisco at nine at night, a sticky, sweaty guy in a frock, with clammy, chafing panty hose, pins and needles down my leg, and a throbbing head. I feel the need of a friend, so I go to a phone booth in the Transbay Terminal to ring Stanley immediate. A cold, feisty woman answers the phone eventual. It's Stanley's wife. She says he's out of town for a couple of days and I should ring back Saturday.

Find yourself a dime and call someone who cares

I ask her where I should stay. She says God knows. She advises I suit myself and maybe try some hotel. I say Stanley invited me out from Nevada. She says Stanley makes all manner of invitations to ladies all over, all without consulting her. So it sounds like it's become an issue in the marriage. I reassure that Stanley is a complete gentleman and he only wants to photograph me. She asks have I got the right verb? It's clear she isn't going to invite me to stay over.

I book into the Henry Village Guesthouse on Eighteenth Street in the heart of the Castro. It may not be the best, but I don't have local knowledge to advise me. First off, they don't know where to place me. Receptionist says it's mostly guys sharing. Do I have company, and what's my angle? But when I explain I'm wiped out, just bused into town from Nevada, they eventually discover me a small second-floor room to myself, next to the elevator, facing the street.

Guy on guy doesn't bother me hardly, except for the bass-note throb and the squeal harmonic. But as I lie in bed, beneath the off-white coverlet, now dark, now pink, from the blinking bar sign across the street, I start to get some real ugly stuff coming up through the floor.

And thou shalt not let any of thy seed pass through fire to Molech.

You turn onto your other side. You lay a pillow over your head. Does it cut it out? It sure does not.

Got to cut along the vein not across. If you cut across, it leaks out slower. And they can stitch you up

Shit, I'm thinking to myself. I been traveling all day. Now I got this morbid stuff about the physics of suicide to keep me awake. Is someone trying to tell me something? Can't a lady get any sleep?

And if a man also lie with mankind as he lieth with woman, both of them hath committed an abomination; they shall surely be put to death; their blood shall be upon them.

I clamber into my clothes all over again, snagging my nylons, from gusset to thigh. No guessing the brassiere was designed by a man. Why does a lady always have to fasten from behind? She needs eyes in the back of her head.

But if the Lord offers salvation, he will surely send a sign.

It isn't hard to find the room. You go down one floor in the elevator, get out, and look for the door on the left. I knock. I knock again. A shifty-looking kid peers through the gap. He's got a pigeon chest and a towel wrapped round his waist. He's got granddad glasses all misted up in a pink, puffy face.

"Yes, ma'am," he says. He blinks all twitchy behind his specs.

"Are you the guilty guy with a razor blade, reading Leviticus in the bath?"

"Yes . . . ," he says, staring bulge-eyed wild. "You a messenger of the Lord?"

"Too right," I say. "The message is this. Life is for living. It'll all seem better in the morning. Spare some thought for your neighbors. One man's ceiling is another man's floor. Now, for chrissakes, can we get some sleep?"

"Thank you, ma'am." Now he's sporting a stupid Alfred E. Newman grin.

"Say, aren't you from the Delta?" I ask. I haven't heard that accent in a while.

"From Meridian, ma'am."

"Well, shit, isn't that a coincidence? I'm from Eureka, just down the road."

"So what must I do?" he demands. "With my life."

"Look, kid . . . Love who you like. Follow your talents. Enjoy yourself. Loosen up. Help where you can. But always try to respect your neighbors' sleep."

I pad back to the elevator and up to my room. I hear his bath gurgle empty. I've just got Psalms coming through the boards after that. But the Old Testament I can always sleep through, no trouble.

You know what? Maybe I spoke sharp to him. But I reckon, without much effort, I helped him ease himself some, along the serrated edge of life. It's nice to help out. And most times, it barely costs you anything.

18

Sisters

I track down Stanley through the phone book to his photo studio, a converted warehouse south of Market, the size of a basketball court, with blacked-out windows, whitewashed brick walls, splintered boards, vaulted ceiling, and a sweet sick smell of solvents from a print shop below. He squints like he's surprised to see me, pats my rump absentminded, pours me a tepid coffee, and sits me down to explain me the setup in the freelance photographic model business—that a lady gets undressed for commerce or art, depending whether she's naked or nude, and she likely does art for her soul, while she does commercial for her purse, and she got to strike a sound soul-buck balance, and while both involve presenting raw to camera, for commercial you wear a smile, or glint a come-on, and you got to spread your legs wider, and do more lip work, and maybe suck on things suggestive, whereas for art you keep your mouth shut, and most times look bored or impassive, so, by way of illustration, Stanley shows me some of his recent spreads.

Guys are just so predictable, superficial. They don't care what a lady's like inside. It's all bumps and lumps and holes for them. They're just suckers for the surface.

Now, I always liked sex as much as the next guy, but some things are plain private. There are things that don't need showing, and things that don't need doing, and things that only belong in their proper bedroom place. So some of Stanley's compositions look plain ugly. And unnatural and un-American, because in the land of the equal and free, it's serving us ladies up as yawning openings or cold cuts of meat.

"No sweat, Stan." I swallow. "I can handle all the art you got on offer. And I'll be glad try my hand at commerce. Only I do draw some lines."

"Where are your lines?" he inquires. "Draw them in the sand."

"My personal lines, Stanley," I explain, "are performing with animals or men . . ."

"That's fine."

"And having *things* inside me, Stan. My skin is the world's. But inside is personal. Within, I'm me."

"No big issue, Lee. There's always a big market for an intimate view of a solitary lady. It's the evergreen voyeur perspective. But are you prepared to touch yourself at the *intersection?* The audience enjoys the impression of finger work. They like transgression and intruding on something deeply private."

"No sweat, Stanley. In the natural course of the every day, I touch myself personal all the time. But I won't cross over the median. I won't reverse into oncoming traffic. And I won't throw any hand-brake turns."

"All this is fine," says Stanley. "Now we know which side of the road you're driving, I believe I can use a body like yours often and plenty."

The truth is that, ever since Gene doctored me, I'd been casting off all threads of modesty. I used to be semi-coy as a guy. But this new body of mine is a glossy, show-off V-8 vehicle and deserving of display, for the innocent admiration it draws from third parties. And strangely, it doesn't feel personal, private—on account of it being a greatest-hits compilation of third-party parts—Michelle Angelo below the belt, Jane Fonda up front, and Doc Gene's facial sketch of Miss Julie Christie, which elects me to that small charmed minority that look their best wearing no more than their skin.

In a dress, I can still feel an awkward, gawky pretender. I find my hands wrestling my purse. I keep crossing and uncrossing my knees. But stripped raw, I got a real shapely, sheeny gloss. I look and feel one special lady, and my dermis kind of speaks for itself.

"Would you like to be used immediately?" asks Stanley. "I have a commission from a gentlemen's quarterly. They'd welcome a fresh face. I can pay two hundred fifty dollars here and now, if you waive any forward rights."

"I would welcome some early exposure in this industry," I say. "And the money would sure help tide me over."

"If the model and photographer know they are going to hit the sack after," Stanley advises, like he's recalling some tiresome chore, "it adds a frisson and a creative tension to the photo session."

"I will pass on that, Stanley," I say, "and supply for myself all the tensions I need."

It always struck me, even as a guy, that women were plain wasted on men. I just can't warm to the prospect of some grunting guy rooting about inside me with one of *those* and squirting off. And even if it didn't seem so slavish, submissive, comic, unsanitary, Stan would come way down on my wish list, because desire can't help get nudged by appearance.

"That's cool," he agrees. "But my assistant isn't due until ten. We have some time on our hands, so would you care to suck my cock?"

I wince to consider. "I don't suck dick, Stan. It does not agree with my philosophy or appeal to my taste . . . But I will help you out other ways around the shop that don't involve your body fluids."

"That's a professional attitude, Lee. I can live with that. I'd be a fool not to ask. Some girls do oblige."

"Sure. No hard feelings," I agree. "It's best to have everything out in the open."

You just got to be firm at the outset with Stanley. He'd jump on a crack in a plate. As long he knows who does the crotch work up front and who works the camera behind, he is professional, personable, and passes as a makeshift gentleman. Plus he pays on the nail.

My second week in town, I move out of the Henry Village Guesthouse because I get talking to this model at the studio who's called Erica to her personal friends, though her professional name is Amber Lipz, who says, Hey, what a coincidence because I'm doing an East Coast dance tour, so you can take over my place immediate for three months if you just pay the rent, if Stan will only vouch for you.

The apartment turns out to be the complete article, with a kitchenette, bathroom, plum walls, matching shag carpet, cupboard space, a double water bed, TV, ornate iron fireplace, mirrors most everywhere, a lava lamp you can't take your eyes off, and a long view onto Duboce Park, fog permitting.

Only downside is Lipz is scatty and has left untidy in haste, without thinking through the arrangements clear, because her things are strewn everywhere, like she's still in residence, with the wardrobe bulging with her clothes, and the drawers bursting with her underwear, and the fridge sprouting live cultures, and all manner of personal lady things scattered all over the floor, and the only thing she's made real tidy is the bathroom cabinet, which she's packed into a clinky, aromatic cardboard box, sealed with duct tape, with a stuck-on message saying PRIVATE. PERSONAL. KEEP OUT, which naturally invites investigation and turns out to be full of lotions and potions, creams and oils, shampoos and conditioners, moisturizers and balms, shaders and shadowers, scrubs and rubs, glitter and gloss, tweezers and razors, plus there's an unmarked carton, under a pile of magazines at the base of the wardrobe, in which she had photos of friends she'd made, mostly guys, and there were bundles of real personal letters, from her mother in Chicago, Duke, Darren, and bad-boy Juan, plus there were financial papers, card statements, a syringe, a whole pharmacopoeia of pills, and a Smith & Wesson, Model 3913, 9mm auto with single-stack magazine and slim grips, and two pairs of handcuffs.

So, padding round the apartment the first evening, I'm inspecting all Erica's left behind, fingering her textures, sniffing up her scents, learning her brands, browsing her labels, picking up the litter of lingerie, reading the instructions on cosmetics packaging, mopping up her spills, wiping her smears off the shiny surfaces, picking up the crumpled balls of discolored Kleenex, trying on this and that item of clothing, because we were roughly the same dimensions, Erica and me, except in the breast and hip departments, where her stuff hung a touch loose and lonely.

And it was a real eye-opener, seeing how much history, purchase, preparation, clutter, fabric, duplication and variation, suede and leather, silk and lace, gel and cream, paper and plastic, concealment and cover, scent and deodorant, medication and intoxicant goes into being a real bona fide lady.

Because all this while I'd brought a soldier's sensibility to things, thinking how I just needed to pack a spare bra, a few pairs of panties, some white T-shirts, jeans for work and a couple of dresses for evenings, two shades of lipstick, and a few bottles of nail polish. So I was struck how light I traveled, how little I owned, how narrow the path I'd taken, and the scant handle I got on being a lady. And this just came from seeing the stuff Erica didn't need—that she could afford to leave at home. So God knows what she took with her.

As a lady, I realized, I was still parked at the curb, with the hand brake on. I still had to find the key and turn the ignition.

So, Erica taught me plenty, and wised me up, in her absence. Her wardrobe turned out to be a library of possibilities, as I pad the carpet, front of the mirror, flirting with my reflection, seducing the guy in me, just trying things on for feel and size, eyeing myself tip to toe, front and fanny.

I worked my way through Erica's lady magazines taking in useful, factful articles like "Diagnose Your Discharge," "Exercise Your Pelvic Floor," and taking the quizzes like "How Do You Score in the Sack?," "Have You Found the Right Guy?"

So I was cramming heavy for the female exam to come. I guess not an hour went by without me learning something new and significant about deniers, menstruation, nipple tape, my feminine feelings, yeast infections, cotton and synthetic mixes, breast-feeding, zippers and other fasteners, glyceryl stearate, pregnancy testing, depilation, or cup size.

I got straight, darkish strawberry-blond hair to my shoulders now. It leaves me free to go either way—bleaching back to childhood blond or darkening down with dye.

I got coral freckles scattered across my cheeks and along my nose, vacant curious steel-blue eyes. Maybe, facedown, I look like a dancer. I gained some puppy fat with the hormones, but the ribs still show, with a rumor of pecs. I don't carry much spare butt, and I got real long, slender legs. You best visualize Julie Christie's face on Charlotte Rampling's physique, with tits. Or maybe imagine Veroushka with a delicate nose. I don't claim things are perfect, but I reckon most GIs would have turned out worse.

A thing about having a sex change is that the body converts much quicker than the mind. Likely as not, you carry on dreaming masculine dirty, climbing all over Barbara Hershey, say, or Jacqueline Bisset. Then you wake drowsy to find a strange woman in your bed, strangely attached at the hip, then realize it's you, because there's some primitive part of the mind that won't let go of your man parts long after the scalpel has cut.

And old habits die hard, betraying you in the blink of an eye, as you reach down to check your fly as you enter a room, tug your top off when you're frying in the park, peer into a lady's cleavage or stare at her panty line, intercept a stray pass and shoot a basket when the kids are playing in the yard, join men-only conversations, poke your head under the hood of a broke-down car and offer advice, flip beer bottle caps with your teeth, spread your feet wide on the edge of a desk, forgetting you're wearing a skirt, pick your teeth with a matchstick, wipe your mouth with the back of your hands, or clear your nose with a loud inward suck, and lapse into ugly barrack talk, saying things like *scumsucker* or *dipshit,* and though you got good reflex reasons, you can tell from the other party's reaction you aren't coming over authentic *feminine.* Which kind of puts you on edge— feeling you can't trust your habits, let yourself go, or relax yourself for real, which is why I start putting it down on paper—the Science of Being a Lady—with headings in my notebook like *Show and Tell, No Way Jose, Keep Under Wraps, What Goes Where,* and so on, and with a drawing of the female form showing what attention and care every part needs, in the hope that in the fullness it would also sink in and come natural.

In Elko they had Ladies' Night at the country club, a girls-only yoga class, a hair salon, and a women's-things aisle in the pharmacy. But in San Francisco in the seventies they had women-only everythings springing up all over—bed-and-breakfast, bathhouses, bookshops, bakeries, you name it.

Well, I was getting hassled in the streets and shops, followings, propositions, invitations, eye work, handiwork, and whistles.

I'm not an aggressive lady, but off Eighteenth Street I have to head-butt this youth who's seized me round the waist and tried to drag me into an alley. And I was required to raise a reflex knee into his groin. These things happen too fast to debate the morality.

"Hell, what kind of fucking woman are you?" he asks, sniffling, glassy-eyed, on his hands and knees like a panting doggy.

"The worst kind," I say. "I understand men. You damaged down there, kid, or just groggy?"

So when I keep passing by the Full Moon Café—Women Only, I'm feeling tempted into a place of calm and safety. I reckon I can meet some local ladies, talk coiffure and cosmetics, maybe get some fashion tips, and get the lowdown on the local clothes stores.

But it falls quiet as I swing through the doors. I guess they saw me coming. All you can hear is the collective intake of breath, the clatter of my five-inch stilettos on the tiles, and the static rustle of my split-thigh dress aggravating my fishnet tights.

The girls inside are something else. They favor shorter hair and a relaxed, practical style of clothing. There's a lot of thick ribbed sweaters, comfort-fit denim, overalls, plaid shirts, trucker jackets, lumberjack boots, fatigue pants. They don't have a smear of foundation between them, and they're quite innocent of lipstick.

Who let that poodle in?

If I'd known what I was coming to, I could have dropped into an army and navy store to select some looser, shabbier clothes to conceal my allure and curves.

I get a bit flushed, self-conscious. I take an empty table at the back. Still, I sense I'd won their full attention. Well, I sat it out as a kid at a segregated lunch counter in Briar. So I'm not going to budge my pretty ass from here till I'm good and ready.

I got concerns I'm still showing some masculine grain. Maybe my hands and feet look overlarge, while my hips seem narrow. Perhaps my eye shadow is understated, and my mascara oversubtle. And I'm traveling light on minimum jewelry. But some of the ladies gathered here look positive manly. We got lip fur, leg hair, sprouting armpits, sideburns, crew cuts, biceps, paunches, bulging veins, flat chests, fight scars, and a couple of unlikely bulging crotches.

A waitress saunters over. She's got a boyish bob of hair above a golden-freckled face. I see her titties heave beneath her sweatshirt, like she's convulsed by a private joke. From where I'm sitting, she's the prettiest thing in the shop.

"Hi," she says, "I'm Rita. Have you come to the *right place?*"

"What's the matter with this town?" I say. "What happened to service, hospitality, and 'Welcome, stranger'? Everywhere I go, I get asked the same."

"Fresh in town," she says. "Who'd have guessed?"

"Hey, lady," I inquire, "is sarcasm the local sport?"

"What can I get you?" Rita asks, blushing for me, hands on hips. "You got tea?"

They got tea. First she gives me a list of herbs. When I select *tea* tea, she gives me a list of countries.

"You got *American* tea?" I ask. She says she'll go ask and find out.

When she sashays back, I try make amends and start over again.

"Nice place you girls got here," I say. "What do you call the dress code? In Nevada it's known as *trucker-casual*. But y'all wear horn-rimmed glasses and don't do tattoos."

"Well now . . . ," says Rita. She sits wearily at the bench opposite; she eyes me quizzical, wondering where to start. "We're *women*, not girls. *Girl* is an infantilizing, patriarchal term to have us sit on Daddy's lap. And we're beyond fashion, because we aren't interested in fetishizing ourselves to phallocentrism or subjugating ourselves to the male gaze."

"Right . . . ," I say. "Now stop right there. The way you're talking, I'm sensing you had some bad experiences with guys somewhere along the line?"

"Too right. Haven't you?"

"Well, now you come to mention it . . . ," I recall. "One guy near enough killed me with a baseball bat. Then all his buddies try to kick out my insides . . ."

"Sheet." She whistles. "That's even worse than what happened to me."

"Men . . . ," I say. "Shits. Can't live with them. Can't live without . . ."

"Well," says Rita, frowning, "we're giving it our best shot."

"You some girl gang or something?" I ask, because the nickel's just dropped.

"Exactly that," says Rita.

"You got a name?"

"We're the Full Moon Sisters. We call ourselves *separatist feminists.*"

"You got bikes?"

"We're not like bikers. We're a sisterhood of the heart and the mind."

"Cool," I say. I'm starting to see the light. "But don't you miss having guys around, to do the work, open doors, and buy the drinks?"

"No." Rita smiles. "Not one bit."

"So, as far as sex goes . . . ?"

"Exactly," says Rita. "You should try it for yourself."

"Well, yes, lady," I say, "I'd sure like to." I take a moment's silent contemplation. "But I guess I stand out?" I suggest. "I reckon I need to dress different. And learn the slang?"

"It would surely help," Rita agrees. "The way you're dressed now—you come across as the *enemy*. And you chatter away like an imbecile."

"I can see that. Only thing is . . ."

"Yes?"

"For people who want to live without men, you squander a deal of time talking about them."

"True," says Rita, "and regrettable too. Postcolonial mentality." She pats my hand. "You aren't so green as you look."

"Just as a hypothetical . . . if a guy like me wanted to join the gang, what would he have to do?"

"Well"—Rita strokes down my cheek with the flat of her hand—"you could wipe that war paint off your pretty face, for starters." She runs her fingers through my hair, skimming my cheek. "Shame to cut it off. So, just tie it in a ponytail. Get some looser clothes in natural fabrics." She grazes some easy fingers along my splaying thigh. "Buy some practical footwear." We're playing foot-sie now.

"You favor any particular perfume?"

"The scents of a natural woman. And the nail polish would have to go."

"Jewelry?" I finger Gene's ring.

"Engagement ring is a no-no. Stow it in a drawer for the duration of your stay."

Oh, yeah. Yes. Women who love women. It's my kind of gang. Truth is, I been looking for ladies like this all my female life.

19

My Heart and
San Francisco

Stanley can only employ me one day a week as a model. He wants to pace my exposure. He doesn't want to flood the market or exhaust my novelty. But I like hanging out at the studio, chatting to Steve the assistant and the other models. And I get to learn how Stanley lights and frames his work, exposes a lady, and prints the results. So, before long I am loading film, testing exposures, adjusting apertures. Next thing I know, I am bathed in red light, up to my elbows in developer and fixer.

It still leaves me plenty time on my hands. I wander Chinatown, take some tours, including a boat trip past Alcatraz to Angel Island, watch the sea lions at Fisherman's Wharf, walk the waterfront, visit clothes shops, work on my appearance.

You get to meet all sorts and soon realize the population of San Francisco, California, is a deal more varied than that of Elko, Nevada, because you got all races, and many mixed-up genders, inebriates, junkies, dropouts, hippies and yippies, Pentecostalists and prostitutes, and just about every profession, persuasion, and perversion you could think of, plus plenty you'd never imagine.

Most afternoons, I take tea at the Full Moon Café. I've started a slow courtship of Rita.

Know what gets me about Rita? Flax and straw hair. Pert pink mouth. Skittering, kind doe eyes. Freckles most everywhere. Bambi on ice. Poppy among the thistles. Gossamer petals, too frail for the breeze. A delicacy laid too open to the world.

"Lapsang?" she asks.

"Thanks," I say, "with a squirt of soya milk. Are you doing that mung-bean bake today?" Because the Sisters have big pulses, tofu, and garlic habits, with no heed for the consequences.

"Sure," she says, "and what you reading?"

"The *SCUM Manifesto*," I concede. "Is that a good place to start, or an angry dead end?"

> . . . Life in this society being, at best, an utter bore and no aspect of society being at all relevant to women, there remains to civic-minded, responsible, thrill-seeking females only to overthrow the government, eliminate the money system, institute complete automation and destroy the male sex. The Society for Cutting Up Men will kill all men who are not in the Men's Auxiliary of SCUM. Men in Men's Auxiliary are those men who are working diligently to eliminate themselves . . .

"You know what?"

"What?"

"I think you're struggling to *come out*." Rita smiles. "It's a difficult time. I'd like to help."

"I bought some clothes," I say. "I made a start."

"I noticed . . ." Rita takes me in and sucks on her cheeks. "Overalls are good," she says, "and practical, in principle."

"But you don't like these?"

"Comfort cord or denim is fine. Skin-tight black leather is something else."

"Shit," I observe. "Ain't life a bitch? Two steps forward and one step back."

I'm suffering for this fashion item. They cost close to a hundred dollars and they're slicing me in half where I naturally split. Only, later, history vindicates me. I didn't know so at the time, but I was pioneering *femme*.

But it pains me to hurt her. Rita's flushing rosy, like I've just slapped her in the face. Later, I find out the reason. There's certain words the Sisters are careful never to use. *Bitch* is one. There are others I could mention, but they make me blush.

"Hey," this heavyweight contender lady calls from the serving counter. "Anyone got time and can type fast?"

I raise my hand, like I'm in school. She waddles over splay-footed, rocking the floorboards, and eyes me sideways, dubious, slowly stroking the rumor of her mustache.

I don't tell them, but I got real fast skills from the army, where they had us type up our own reports.

"She's all right," says Rita. "She's trying hard. And if it's anything *sensitive*, likely as not, she won't understand."

"She looks all typist to me," says another.

Which is how I gained entry, behind the scenes, into the back room, facing a fifty-year-old Remington, with a sticky question mark that they rarely used, pounding out manifestos and position papers at the rate of fifteen thousand words an afternoon, building up course credits.

I'd break every so often to ask what things truly mean. You can learn a lot quick, if you aren't afraid to ask the right questions.

"The 'C' word," I ask, "can we use that for real?"

"Stripped of its loathing, it just means vagina, Lee. It works like the 'N' word. You can use it within, but never outside."

"Hey, Susan?" I ask. "Any statute of limitations here? Any allowance for mistaken identity?"

"What?"

"Guys been behaving bad for thousands of years. But are they the very same guys walking the pavements? And are we the very same women that suffered way back?"

Because the way I see it, it wouldn't hold up in a court of law. The average guy might be a shit. But you can't prosecute him for suppressing women since the dawn of time. Least not if he shows some respect to his mother, helps his kid sister, and he's only twenty-four.

"We are righting historic wrongs, Lee. And you think men have changed any?"

"Fine, honey," I say. "Don't need to make any sense to me. I'm only the lady typist ... And this *Patriarchy* you always going on about, how does that work?"

"Like an octopus, Lee, with tentacles reaching everywhere."

"Well, hell, Susan, why don't you say so? It's coming across dry and tight as a camel's ass."

We feel a realness, feel at last we are coinciding with ourselves. With that real self, with that real consciousness, we have the revolution to end the imposition of all coercive identifications, and to achieve autonomy in human expression.

There's a lot in the feminist argument for every decent heart to take on board. Men been getting away with murder, acting up and riding their luck. And women been well and truly screwed. But I worry about the separatist version. I fear they're throwing out the dick with the bathwater. Sure, I lost mine and learned to hobble along without. But it's not a modification I recommend to most other guys. So, I don't think the Sisters have thought through the practicalities. They're going to need some free space the size of Canada to fit all the Sisters in, if the idea takes off. Or we going to have somewhere like Mississippi, with two oil-and-water communities that just won't mix. Everything's going to be soured by hate and disdain. And, somewhere down the line, we going to need a steak dinner, a few beers, and some laughs. And you can just drape a thing in so much theory that you lose all touch with what's beneath. Photography works the other way, on surface values. You get nose to nose with what's truly there. Then distort it as an afterthought.

You can call it cheating, baby. I call it a couple of careless mistakes with your sister Jeannie

What with modeling mornings for men's magazines, and getting cozy with Rita in the afternoons, and learning all there was to know about photographic processes, and helping overthrow patriarchy, I felt real cocky that I'd found a good life/work balance and had all the bases covered, so I never saw the curve balls coming.

It may be illegal in Arkansas, honey, but it isn't uncommon in San Francisco

First bad break was a famous sister coming down from New York. Her nostrils flare as soon as she enters the tearoom. She sniffs, then announces she can smell a *man* in the building. She says she's got a sharp nose for these things. Well, there's a big crowd of us gathered excited, her being a three-book theorist and all, so I'm able to scurry out the back undetected. Likely it wasn't me at all. It could been some other lady, with a high testosterone flow. Or maybe some turncoat sister had laid herself open to some guy's advances and absorbed some liquid traces. And there'd been some male deliveries— vegetable and postal—because the tentacles of patriarchy penetrate every last sphere of women's activity—but it contributed to my sense of unease, that I was kind of a pretender, traitor, who aspired but could never truly belong.

I been schooled in photography basics now—formats, speed of film, focal distance and all the exposures, depths of field, and apertures you can use. And how it's all in the printing and touching up. Stanley lends me an old Nikon single-lens reflex and gives me a box of past-its-date film, saying, "Go experiment, Lee. Shoot away like crazy. Find your eye. At the end of the week, I want you to bring me *just one good photo*."

Anyway, Stanley's busy, so he forgets. Which spares me because I can't get anything near good enough to show to a real professional.

I been studying Stan's photo books. But it's discouraging—seeing the standards the old-timers set.

I guess we all start off Brassaï and Cartier-Bresson. Then I veer off Man Ray tricksy, go off on a Walker Evans, a Bill Brandt phase, and an Edward Weston. Then it dawns on me. I'm straining too hard. I'm always thinking derivative. What the shit. Forget tradition, forget the craft. I'll enjoy myself and just shoot what I like.

"Hey, Lee," says Stan, sorting through my stack of prints. "Whose are these?" He's stooped over, eyeing one through a magnifier.

"They're mine, Stan."

"Yeah?" he says. "But who shot them?"

"I did."

"Okay, smart-ass. Who printed them?"

"I did."

"Okay, Miss Diane Arbus . . . where do you find all these crazy, freaky people? And how do you get under their skin?"

"Freaky? These are my friends, and people I know. Some sisters I hang out with. Some guys at the hotel, Steve, and you."

"Me?" asks Stanley, shuffling quick through the pack. "Shit . . ." He finds one of himself. "You bitch, Lee. You think I'm some institutionalized perv in some psycho-geriatric ward?"

"Sorry, Stan. But that's your face. It's how you look."

"I do nude photography, Lee, touching pornographic. But I try and prettify, to make things look better than they truly are. But this is really filthy stuff. This is a close-up of the asshole of my soul."

"Yes?"

"I know how you do it."

"How's that?"

"You come across as some dizzy bimbo. It gets people's defenses down. So they display themselves, self-satisfied naked. They don't know your camera's going to skin them alive."

"That's never my intention, Stan."

"Just do me a favor, Lee, one photographer to another?"

"It's yours, Stan."

"I'll see if I can get you some work. But I'd prefer you don't take my picture again . . ." He's got a steady twitch, working his jaw. "Can I keep these?" He waves to his portraits.

"Sure."

"Nice work . . . really nice print." He starts guillotining them real fine into ticker-tape shreds.

I've tried real hard with Rita, but my progress keeps getting blunted by basic mistakes. I buy two tickets for the Raiders game, but she goes all huffy, saying watching men kicking the shit out of each other is a start, but it isn't her notion of entertainment. Then, when I give her a candy-pink cashmere sweater, she folds it back in its tissue paper, hands it back, and asks if I'm trying to package her up as some fetish commodity.

"Hell, no, honey," I protest. "You can over-read things. This isn't bondage gear. It's an oversize conservative sweater in a pretty color."

I ask her what star sign she is. I got an intuition she's an Aries, and I'd like to buy her a birthday present. She asks how I can believe that mumbo-jumbo superstitious astrology crap. So I protest at least it gives you twelve sorts of different people, whereas feminism mostly reduces us to two.

And, I'm thinking to myself, I don't fit either group. Not precisely. I figure as some freak slider, in between. So I'm not fully struck on some theory that excludes me or shoves me to the margin as some freak footnote. And I'm getting weary of all this promissory talk of political lesbianism. Because, in my personal experiences with Rita, it's all talk and no do, all theory and no practice. And the way it's written up in the manifestos, we're meant to try integrate the two and get down in the sack to some real the-personal-is-political praxis.

Last year Rita finished a political science and journalism degree in Chicago. She came out nine months ago and her father, who's a psychology professor, is reading up on the literature on lesbianism in thick journals of abnormal behavior but finding it hard to get a handle on it. Her mother's a psychotherapist and reckons it's legitimate being a lesbian, but girls tend to pass through it, and no point in burning bridges by spreading the news, specially not to the families of young men you'll come back and marry. Her parents had even been asking themselves where they went wrong. Like it's nothing to do with her.

"Like, can you believe?" Rita demands.

Sure can. And there's plenty I could confide in return. Because I got issues too. Like how I was black before I was white, and a man before I got to be a woman, and how I was in the army before I got to be a pacifist. And how I actually earn my living at the intersection of commerce and art. And how Stanley thinks I got talent and a real original, naive eye. And he's shown my work to some magazine guys who think they might use me for a fresh off-the-wall perspective. But I guess the time isn't ready to tell Rita yet. These things are best left until you get real intimate. And so far, we'd only held hands, nibbled, and pecked around a bit. Until Rita asks me to come to a demonstration with her, Saturday night. And this is a real serious invitation because, the way I learned the Sisters carry on, this near enough amounts to a date, a signal of intent, with the promise of some unbuttoning.

So you can gather I am deeply touched. And I would certainly go under normal circumstances, but I am already booked.

Stanley is escorting me to the Festival of Skin annual dinner and awards ceremony, which we are hosting this year in San Francisco, and I've been nominated in two categories for Best Female Solo Newcomer (West Coast) and Best Still Photography Body (Middle-weight Division), which may not sound like much, but these are the kinds of career breaks that can get you introductions to the leaders of industry and get you started in the moving image department. And there are just no end of spin-offs, with freebie underwear, glitter body paints, books, agents, sex toys, videos, career rungs, professional recognition, and a five-course dinner. And it promises to be a leg up and the highlight of a difficult year. And Stanley says the Beach Boys are doing the cabaret, and Rip Torn will be there, and no one who is anyone can afford to miss it.

"Can't make it, Rita." I wince. "Got to work late. What are you demonstrating about, anyhow?"

"Pornocracy and the degradation of women's bodies."

"Too right." I nod. "Too right. You tell those bastards . . ." Because I hadn't yet joined up the dots to make the right connections.

I am hit by a chill breeze when the taxi draws up at the hotel, since I am wearing only Chanel, a spray-on tan, white knee boots, and a two-piece suit of silver-sequined hot pants and bra. They have laid a long red carpet down the hotel steps onto the pavement. The press is off to the right, and the righteous cacophony is off to the left.

"Dykes against fun," says Stanley, taking my arm. "Can you believe it?"

They're waving posters saying STOP PORN and THE SANTA BAR-
BARA WOMEN'S COMMITTEE AGAINST THE FETISHIZATION AND COM-
MODITIZATION OF WOMEN SAYS "NO" TO VISUAL OPPRESSION and
MISOGYNIST PIGS and JERK OFF, BUDDY and KEEP YOUR DIRTY MINDS
OFF OUR BODIES and such like.

And the camera crews are filming us skin professionals passing
in front of the protesters. And there's spit flying and howling, with
jostling and a confetti of leaflets and flash guns giving a disco strobe
effect, so I'm getting this slide show of the frozen expressions on the
face of some Sisters I know, who are recognizing me and are jab-
bing fingers, pointing me out. And I see Rita take me in slack-
mouthed. And the next frame her face is contorted into a howl, and
she's holding her head between her hands, so she looks like that
Munch poster I got tacked to my bedroom wall.

"Hey," says Stanley, tugging my arm, sensing my hesitation.
"You coming or demonstrating or hugging the spotlight or what?"

What can I do? The cameras are on you. You got to keep poise.
You got to hope the scalding flush of shame fades away quick. I
stumble onward and upward. I turn and blow Rita a kiss from the
door. Priorities, princess. Some things weren't meant to be.

The truth is I was real hooked on Rita. I wanted to date her
proper, give her flowers, open doors, buy her dinner, get to know
her proper, with a view to getting intimate, but somehow all the politics had clouded it and gotten in the way.

Thing I noticed about the Sisters was how they wouldn't forgive, forget, and move on, but were forever analyzing their feminine feelings and twisting everything female political, so they're
sometimes plain clueless about what's truly going on in the world,
to the extent of not knowing who's number one draft pick or who's
contesting the World Series or how to replace a blown gasket, because they're too busy polishing their hurts, like semiprecious stones,
till they glint, every which way, till they got a whole necklace of

gleaming complaints, but then bragging about how much sweeter their vinegar feelings are than men's feelings and remarking how men only think about sex, oppressing women, power games, or occupying Southeast Asia, which I just happen to know is plain wrong, from my previous life as a man, when I often thought about real innocent things, completely unrelated to fighting or getting laid, and since I'd become a woman myself, there was no real sea change in the way I saw things, except that maybe I was thinking more about pussy than ever before.

But when you try to get friendly, woman to woman, sister to sister, you just end up with some corrections to your vocabulary, a book list, a neck message, and chamomile tea, without the merest whiff of what you truly come for, and all that without a beer on the table.

The trouble is, some people won't meet you halfway, heart to heart, skin on skin, without you first buying wholesale from the warehouse of their opinions.

20

Picturing Souls

Still, it comes as a jolt and cautions me, because I don't want to get saddled with a Judas reputation for betraying all the other guys in my sex, and this modeling was drawing me perilous close to porn, while photography beckons a way out and has stolen my heart and mind, so I'm fixing on a career change, to swivel a full hundred and eighty degrees, and duck right out of the lights, to hunch into that shady place behind the camera, because all my ambitions are back side now, south of the lens, since there's only so much you can do with your skin, it being mainly crotch splay, statue work, or nude recumbent, while you tweak your posture at some guy's brusque beck and call, and, likely as not, Stanley insists on smearing you in Vaseline, head to toe, personal, so the smiles and the looks of unfocused longing are forced and synthetic, and while your beauty's unblemished, you just know you've exceeded your shelf life.

Stanley gets me an interview with a picture editor at *Angel Dust*. This cocky young guy flicks through my portfolio, blinking.

"Strong," he observes. "Vicious. You don't take prisoners."

He asks me where I trained. I explain that Stanley Elkins taught me technical, but not artistic.

"So what are your influences?"

Well, Stanley prepared me for this, having me browse his photo books, explaining how a photographer can consider himself an artist, if he knows the traditions of his craft, finds his own *aesthetic,* and can even collar a *rationale,* so I am well prepared by rote to answer that I draw many of my thematic influences from the candid documentary tradition of Weegee, the FSA crew, Kalvar, Johns, Capa, and such like, plus the paintings of Egon Schiele and the music of Woody Guthrie and Aaron Copland. I guess I memorized the names right because the guy just watches me cockeyed, nods sagely, and says there's always work for a fresh forensic eye.

"Elkins is very professional," he says, "but he's tied to his roots as a food photographer and never changed his technique. He bastes his women in oil and serves them up on a plate. And you," he asks, "does everyone you photograph end up looking mad, a flake, or raw as a peeled prawn?"

"I seem to get under the skin," I admit it. "So it depends what the person's got inside. Some folks look sweet and serene. Some come over real ugly. Others, what you get is just what's on the packet."

"Fine skill," he observes, "filming the human soul. Have you done any actors or politicians?"

After a couple of tryout assignments, he starts using me regular, mostly character portraits, mood stuff, markets, and music venues.

I like to skirt the edges of the scene. Along the way I might bump into some furniture, spill a lens cap, giggle some, search for my exposure meter, and say, "I can't believe I'm here for real. Now, where did I leave my camera case?" or "My grandmother's crazy about you." Every photographer does things different. But that's the MO that works for me.

I give the impression of a novice, struggling. It buys you that unposed time before the subject cottons on he's been clocked. If you're dizzy, friendly, and pleasing to the eye, that can go down well. You don't want to come across competent, threatening, and scare off all the spontaneities.

With the real cagey customers, there's lots of fencing around. The subject is erecting barricades. So you got the task of pulling them down or sneaking behind. Sometimes it helps to say off-the-wall stuff that catches them off guard. Emily Dickinson came up with some real stupefying winners.

"'The soul has bandaged moments,'" I say. "'When too appalled to stir.'"

"Pardon me?"

"'The heart asks pleasure first,'" I explain. "'And then, excuse from pain.'"

"That so? And do you know how to work that thing, baby?"

"It's kind of automatic," I explain. "With a push-down button mechanism."

Often you got a journalist in tow, who's come to do a word piece to punctuate the pics. They pull rank and come across senior partner, so you don't want to vacuum up too much of their time. So I like to have the image in the can before the subject even knows we've started.

"Now, how would you like me?" they ask.

"Excuse me?" I ask, packing up. "I'm all done now."

"But the portrait?"

"Got it."

"Surely not?"

"Trust me," I say. "I got it already, and I won't get better."

With practice you get the confidence. The drama's all between scenes, backstage. The moment has been and the impression's been taken. It's never the full picture. But it works as a stolen image. We're in the shorthand business.

"You get anything?" I ask Fay, the writer, when we're back in the car. This Fay's got a reputation. She's a hard, feisty, unsmiling lady with a pesky rodent face, pushing thirty. She looks at me cold through her wise owl glasses. She reminds me of a scrawny Billie Jean King. She smells a bit rank too. Mustard yellow of desperation and indigo of hurt. I sense she's plain overlonely, underkissed, barely fingered, and hardly touched.

"I got an opinion on Watergate and some choice words about Kissinger. What did you get?"

"A single candid moment," I say.

"Which?" she asks. "I didn't see."

"I got the congressional candidate in his lair. Guy's evil. I got him being lectured by his lady personal assistant. She's wearing a nasty sneer. He's squinting at himself in the mirror, picking his teeth with a matchstick. He's got back-lit tufts of nose hair. There's some nice foreground detail. The dog on the rug is licking its nuts."

"I guess that captures it all." Fay frowns. "I thought you were some empty dork, Lee. But underneath, you're all right."

"Thanks, Fay."

"This inane, chucklehead, clueless manner, it's just an act?"

"Well, yes, Fay, in a superficial way, but, then again, in a deep sense, no, I'm lost . . ."

"Join the club. We're all lost, Lee. Let's hit a bar," she says. "I'll buy you a drink."

Get fizzy drunk together, like we're friends or an item

"Wish I could work words like you, Fay."

"Wish I could shoot people dead like you, Lee."

"You ever read any Emily Dickinson, Fay?"

"Shit, Lee, she's a great poet, the poor lonesome bitch. Doesn't she just stab you through the heart with icicles? You dating anybody?"

"Me?" I say. "I live in hope. But 'you cannot solder an abyss with air.'"

"I'm not dating either."

"No?"

"The truth is," Fay explains me, "I have a sociopathic personality and an acid tongue. But sometimes I feel the need for a friend."

just one night. I'm plain as a brick and lonely as sin. Just lay a mouth on mine, press me to a human heart, and stray a helping hand . . .

"You hitting on me, Fay?"

"I don't like many people, but I do like you, Lee."

She reaches over the tabletop to clasp my hand in hers, interlocking fingers, which feel real intimate, with her pressing tight, warm, and moist on me, five places at once.

"Suits me fine, Fay. But I got to warn you—my heart is one overcrowded cemetery."

The truth is, I had a bad break in the heart department. I felt a numbing down from three weeks back, when I'd been doing an atmosphere piece on the Castro's bars. I am struck by a poster at this folk venue where a singer called Angelina Clement had got third billing.

I get there an hour early and watch her set up in silhouette. Then I hear her warm up her vibrato. The lady tunes up, plucking the strings.

I realize all I want in the world is there onstage, waiting for me to come pluck her and carry her back to my apartment. Love first. Talk later. Love again. Plan our future. Patience pays.

"I've come early to catch you, Angel," I call from the back.

"Great," she says, peering into the gloom. "You hear me okay?" She starts crooning into the mike. "You in the business? From a label or anything?"

"Me, I just love you like crazy. I'm your greatest-ever fan."

"Shame," she says. "Can't be helped. Don't worry."

She's singing for money, not love, now. And because it's old material, she hasn't got full recall of the lyrics, which means she fluffs some odd lines. Her pupils are gaping. Her eyes are wandering out of sync with the songs. The emotion is trotting lame behind like a stray, hopeful of adoption. The place is slowly filling up. People are chatting. Still, she gets polite applause. I wander up to the stage.

Maybe she isn't the exact same Angel I knew naked in Cooder's barn. Life's been scribbling on her skin. Her face has coarsened and her body spread some. She's lost some luster—hair and spirit—and gained some creases round her duller eyes. Still, she's close enough to the real thing.

"Loved your act," I say. "You were great."

"You want to buy a cassette?" she asks. "My greatest hits."

"That include 'Lost in Skin' and 'Isabella'?"

"Yes. You sure know my backlist."

"How much?"

"Two dollars."

"How many you got?"

She's got eleven left. I say I'll take them all. She's blinks surprised, then says, "Thanks, you're a real fan."

"I'll give them to friends," I explain. "Christmas presents. I'm a photographer. I'm doing a piece for *Angel Dust*."

"Great," she says. "I could use some publicity."

"You got a recording contract these days?"

"Nah," she says. "The business is run by pimps who just screw you, fleece you, then leave you."

"I've always loved your work. Always loved *you*. Ever since I knew you way back in Briar."

"Really." She blinks. "We went to high school together?"

"You got no earthly idea?"

"Remind me."

"We had a *thing*, Angel. We reckoned we were soul mates."

"Well, it clean escapes me . . ." The lady frowns. "Did we . . . ?"

"Like rabbits," I confirm. "Lee. Cooder's barn."

"There was a Lee," she concedes. "Knew the kid well. But he was this boy . . ."

"Long story," I say. "Strange things happen. I've changed some along the way."

"You? Lee? Never."

"Look me in the eye," I say. "Tell me it isn't me."

"Jesus . . ." She's gazing up close, rolling her eyes, peering up into mine. We're intimate once more.

"You want me to show you my leg scar?"

"Shit." She steps back, hands on hips to take me in. "You come across well as a woman, Lee. You had *everything* done?"

I nod.

"Only sometimes, they leave . . ."

"No," I say. "Lopped off. The whole caboodle. Surgeon in Nevada."

"So where does that leave you? You date guys now, or what?"

"Hell, no, Angel. I'm still into women. Just like you."

"Look." She frowns perplexed, clutching my elbow. "Why don't you come out back and meet Gary and Phoenix?"

"They friends?"

"My guy and my son."

Christ. Jesus. First, the wrong color. Then, the wrong sex. Now, I'm the wrong sexual orientation. This woman has been dogging my desire, wrong-footing me at every turn. It's hard not to feel sore and played with. I wonder I kept my heart vacant so long.

We wander down a side street to an egg-yolk yellow VW camper bus. It's home. Gary is smoking a joint while changing Phoenix's diaper. So the air inside is muggy and agricultural moist, with trickles of condensation winding down the cloudy panes.

"Honey," says Angel, "this is Lee. He's come to photograph me for *Angel Dust*."

"Cool." Gary nods and smiles good-natured, unfazed. "But we got the squirts here. Guy's got a rash. You seen the Vaseline?"

"Isn't it here in the closet?" asks Angel, sorting through a heap of clothes on the floor. "We're normally tidy, but things get all shaken up on the road."

Angel unbuttons her blouse. Watermelon breasts judder out and splay wide. Easterly and westerly. She starts to suckle young Phoenix. The big boy is pummeling her breast with one chubby hand, clutching a sugar-frosted doughnut in the other. Wearing no more than his diaper, he looks like a scaled-down sumo wrestler.

Well, maybe they aren't *the breasts,* because nursing bloats things up, and softens some, mapping it out with blue veins, and teats thicken and get chapped, and remind you some of a sheep's udder.

But, still, I can't say I feel no resentment at the little fellow palping those silken ivory mounds, and champing an amber nipple like it was just some drink dispensary, and eyeing me sideways, satisfied, superior, like he just got dealt a flush.

"You want some pictures, or what?" Angel asks.

"You want to brush your hair first? Fix your face? Prepare yourself or anything?"

"Nah." She catches her reflection in the window. "I'm fine."

"You look just swell, baby," Gary agrees. "Madonna and child."

"Fine kid," I observe. "How old?"

"One and a bit." Angel smiles. "He's talking some."

"When do you toilet train kids these days?"

"When they're good and ready," says Gary. "You don't want to get anal about it, or you give the guy a fixation, Reich reckons."

"Lee was one of my boyfriends back home," Angel explains. "We just met up at the club. As things turn out, he's a woman now."

"Cool," says Gary. "If that's your bag. We're all living better through chemistry."

"Gary's a songwriter," Angel explains. "He used to write for Infinite Monkeys."

"Hey," I say, "I was that puppet lady on the cover of your *No Strings* album."

"Crazy. I knew I knew you from someplace," says Gary. "Guys used to have wet dreams over you. Never guessed you were a tranny."

"Small world," says Angel, shifting Phoenix to the other breast. "Strange trip."

I do some fish-eye shots for a wraparound view of the van. I do a head job on Gary—mustache and phosphorous eyes. Then I do mother and son. Finally, I shoot Angel chest upward. The way I plan it, I can superimpose her on some cosmetic background, air-brush out her acne, narrow up her gaping pupils, and lend her some model's hair. Do the very best I can.

"We're getting low on gas money," says Gary. "Could you spare fifty dollars? I can pay you back when we hit Colorado."

"Colorado?"

"We are stardust; we are golden. We've got to get ourselves back to the garden."

"Well, sure." I lay some notes on the table. I write my phone number in ballpoint on the tabletop. "Any trouble, be sure to ring me."

"Groovy," says Phoenix, unclamping himself from the breast, taking me in wide-eyed, "big boobies."

"Smart child," I say. "Real character."

"Don't worry, man," says Gary. "Nothing personal. He says the exact same to everyone."

"See you around, Lee. Strange how we keep connecting up . . ."

"Crazy," I concede. "See you, Angel."

"What's this crap?" asks Rick, the editor, when I show him my por-trait of Angel. It took me three days. It's something special.

"New singer," I say. "Real talented."

"Lee . . ." He shakes his head. "Are you doing shampoo ads now, on location in Dakota? Why not stick to what you know? This is better. Manson and son . . ."

"That," I say, "is the boyfriend and child."

In the bar, I take a slow cold beer while Fay quickly empties a bottle of chardonnay like it's a Pepsi. She's got a disconcerting way of cocking her head, staring real direct through narrowed eyes, pursing her lips, and smiling at me, enigmatic in silence while she grazes my arm with her careless fingers or flicks my hair off my cheek. She tells me I look real lovely. She asks me where I've been all her life.

"Mississippi," I explain her, "Missouri, and Nevada."

"Yeah?" she asks. "No kidding?"

"Yeah," I confirm. "For real."

"You ever been married?"

"Nah." I giggle. "Never. Not me."

"You ever talk much, Lee?"

"Me," I concede, "I observe, mostly."

"Observe what?"

"People mainly."

"Good choice." Fay nods.

"You mocking me?" I inquire.

"I'm just struggling to make human contact, the best I can." She reaches under the table and lays her palm on my knee. "I relate through irony and sarcasm. How about it? Are we going to be friends?" Her thigh docks alongside mine. I can feel her body heat and twitch.

"Sure," I agree. "I could use a friend. I'd like that real good."

"Good," she says. "And don't worry. I'm sort of desperate . . . So I don't have high expectations."

"Great," I say, "because I hate to disappoint."

"I don't want to rush you . . ."—Fay glances at the face of her watch—"but it's seven months since I last had sex."

"Yeah?"

"I live round the corner," she says. "We could get friendly at my place."

"Hell, sure," I agree. "I can be friendly most anywhere."

But out on the sidewalk in the chill evening air, joining hands with our squirming fingers, I start anticipating. It's then the anxieties kick in for real, that I've bit off more than I can chew.

Doc Gene apart, early on, I never been physically examined as a woman. Not up close and intimate. Every last nook and cranny. At least the lens pretends a distance.

I've got the same dumb desires, stronger than ever before, but now I'm packing different parts. And how do you do this girl-on-girl stuff anyhow? What fits what and who goes where? All my experience has come man-side of the deal.

Ethan once told me how lesbians do wild, crazy things I'd never believe. But Ethan got an unreliable, supposititious handle on women, so I never followed through to ask. Stan had showed me some magazine spreads once, but it was all posed and static. The ladies hung limp like puppets poised to be jerked into life.

I cotton on to my ignorance, and that I'm skating on real thin ice. Most likely there are some basic compulsory figures that I just know nothing about, never mind style marks for artistic expression.

But when it comes down to it, I guess you just got to use what God's given you, bend to your desire, and sway to intuition.

Through the front door of Fay's apartment, we're into the shades of an unlit living room, the floor piled with stacks of papers and magazines. There's a stale musty smell of tobacco and mice. Fay leads me by the hand through a door and throws the switch on a dusty bare bulb.

"My bedroom," she explains.

"Nice." I blink in the sudden light. There's a sweet, stale smell and a feel of neglect, a rumpled unmade bed, bare white walls, a long venetian blind hoarding dust on its slats, some empty wine bottles, and a scatter of books on the matting.

"I live alone," Fay explains me, gathering up an armful of wrinkled clothes from the coffee-stained sheets. "And I wasn't expecting to get this lucky."

21

Second Bite
at the Cherry

Then I got the lady clambering all over me, urgent, breathy, clumsy, with jaggy elbows and poky knees, with her wide yawning mouth, chewing and sucking on mine, and her hot, acid wine breath and garlic aftertaste, her hands on my shoulders pressing me down to the bed, and a frenzy of fingers tugging to strip me, like a kid tearing the gift wrapping off a birthday bike, and a flicky wet tongue in my ear, while the buttons are popping on my blouse, with scrambling fingers behind, fumbling to unhook my bra, and I got hot gusts of her breath on my cheeks, while my head is buzzing with all manner of contradictory stuff.

Sure, I want her. But is this too early? We only got acquainted three hours ago.

A girl has a beautiful bounty. But she can only give it the once. She's also got a reputation. She wants to come across as open and friendly. But she doesn't want to get herself used and discarded, mistaken for some easy lay.

Fay extracts her flicky, muscley tongue from my mouth and ducks down to clamp on a tit, and chews around a bit, which is real startling, painfully pleasant except I'm awful nipple sensitive, and she's started tweaking overadamant with her teeth.

"Go gentle, baby," I whisper, stroking her hair. "Don't manhandle me."

I feel odd, out of body, like I'm drifting above and gazing down, feeling strangely done-to and put upon, like I'm being wrestled into submission, and she's trying to slide my panties down my butt with the palm of her hand, while I got fingers hooked on the waistband, holding them up and, just in case, I got my knees pressed firm together because I just want a foot on the brake pedal, and less jerking on the clutch, because she keeps jumping the lights like a guy, and though she's small, she's awesome strong, and her fingers are rippling me in the cleft, so I feel splayed open and awful exposed, with only a film of cotton between us, guarding my modesty, and, jeez, why didn't I go home first and change into the crisp, laced, candy-pink lingerie I bought special with an imminent view to surrendering myself, and my gift, to someone truly beautiful?

"Slow down, honey," I gulp. "We'll get there . . ."

"Fuck patience," says Fay, all flushed and breathy. "It's never done anything for me."

I stiffen as her tongue slithers a winding mucus path down my belly. Her hands forage ahead, high on my inner thighs and sliding up, pressing in on my privacy.

"Hey," I say, sliding out from beneath her and off the bed. "Back in a moment. Got to pee."

Well, she's caught me on the hop. I just need to compose myself in the mental department, besides checking physical everything's neat and tidy down *there*.

And while I was real cocksure as a guy, I'm coming over strangely puritan, tight as a lady. Hell, how else would it be? It's all new to me. Sheepish, I sprawl back on the bed. I flicker my eyelids to the semiclosed position. I grit my teeth and trust to fate.

"Relax," Fay commands, parting my thighs.

So I lay myself open, splaying my jerky limbs wanton, as Fay spreads me wide, and beavers away, relentless, hand to mouth, inside and out, most everywhere, even places I never expected.

I'd always felt obliged to perform as a guy, so I'd never tried female passive. But we both seem to get what we're after. Fay's snuffling, wet-nosed, rasp tongue, dribbly, eager as a panting doggy. And it sure as hell pleasured me.

It comes as a real education, because I've never done extended multiples before. Woman has got it made. Men just get a spit at it. They can't contain their excitement. They just spill the thrill in a few quick squirts.

I've got an oceanic pubic throb. The gulf stream passes through. The tide laps in and out. I don't remember quite when I lost consciousness or the will to stir. It can be a seamless slide from come-again to sleep.

I wake naked, head throbbing in warm woman-scented sheets beneath a duck-down duvet. I can smell fresh coffee perking, and I hear a cascade of water. It's pelting rain outside or someone's taking a shower. There are garments strewn over the bedroom floor. It's a two-skirt scatter.

Fay wanders in pinkish, straggle-haired, wrapped up in a bath towel. She looks down somber and shakes her head.

"You snore like a buffalo. You scratch like a chimp. You howl like a wolf. You want a coffee?"

"Howl?"

"In your sleep. Like a wolf for her cubs."

"Don't recall." I blush.

"You've got wandering hands, sharp elbows, and large, cold feet. I get them all over. You've got this disconcerting pelvic thrust. You talk dirty in your sleep. Your pits smell rank as a man's. And you grind your teeth. Who's this Celeste?"

"My grandmother."

"Angel?"

"Old girlfriend."

"You've got some angry voices there, screaming to come out."

"Guess so, Fay."

"It's like bedding down with a troupe of gibbons, Lee. A girl needs her beauty sleep. If we're going to make a habit of this, you'll need to clean up your bedtime act."

"Sure thing, Fay."

"Right . . ." She brightens. "Got to rush. See you tonight. Your place or mine?"

Now, Fay has got real interesting matte, functional looks, unblemished by any distracting beauty gimmicks. She is a moth, not a butterfly. She is a cod, not a marlin. She is a crow, not a cockatiel. She's plain functional as a Shaker chair or a teaspoon.

At five foot two and eighty-five pounds, she's discreet sized too. Her eyes are for seeing, her brow is for frowning, her nose is for breathing, her mouth is for talking, her lips are for pouting, her hands are for fingering things, her hips are child bearing, her breasts are there if the need arises, her legs are for walking, her butt is for being sat upon. And everything does just what it's meant to, and nothing distracts, distorts, or pulls focus. She's near perfect designed and proportioned.

She's got some rare visual qualities. In the trade we call them invisible *charm* and *inner beauty*. But it takes a photographer who knows her to bring it all out.

You guessed I'm in love? I guessed so too. Forget the words and pretenses. We understand each other. And our bodies just fit. We slot together.

The girl plain pleasures me, jut of hip, nobbles of spine, splay legs, hay scent of hair, quiver of sleeping lids, snuffles, twitchy navel, tufts and fluff, crease and crevice, moist and dry, divot and mound, pout of mouth and pert of nose, toe and finger, elbow and knee.

Fay's a feisty, firm, calf-bony woman and cool to the surface touch. But she warms and softens, the deeper you get. Under the wraps, she's peachy tepid. At her core, if you know where to look, you find an oozing, molten syrup. At night she clings whimpering by her sharp nails like her life depends upon it.

When Amber Lipz comes back early from Boston, I got no place to stay, so I move in provisional, no strings, see how things pan out, with Fay.

She seems surprised I can carry all I own in an American Tourister, camera case, and a Safeway plastic carrier.

"It's a trick I learned," I explain her, "to travel light through life . . . You got any special place for me to hang my jacket?"

Fay lends me a roof. I bring her domestic discipline. If basic training teaches you anything, it's how to fold small, iron neat, polish shiny, and keep a tidy bunk. When Fay's at work, I'm often vacuuming, polishing wood, wiping vinyl, stacking books, filing papers, painting walls. Often, I got her supper waiting, bubbling away on the back burner.

We aren't afraid to act domestic, ordinary. We stay home plenty. We watch *M*A*S*H*, *Streets of San Francisco*, *Sonny and Cher Comedy Hour*, and the 49er games on TV. We enjoy the simpler things in life. We can laugh at ourselves, which helps. Plus we can laugh at other people too. And we're kind of complementary. Often there's no call to talk. We just sprawl on the couch in silence, wrapped up in each other.

"Shall we . . . ?" she asks.

"Sure, baby," I agree, "with extra olives?"

"And pepperoni . . ."

I cook. Fay eats. I drive. She navigates. I'm the pictures; Fay's the words. She's the logic; I'm intuition. I'm the silk; she's the steel. I'm the looks; she's the brawn. I'm credulous; she's knowing.

As a guy I was glib and superficial. It was all down to the landscape of the face and the curves of the body. That and a smiling willingness. But, as a woman, you look further, deeper. I guess you look beneath the skin. You want more than a firm ass, good grooming, and a sense of humor. You want honesty, intelligence, sound values and reliability, decency and respect. Sure, a salary and property helps too. You don't want a beauty contest, to compete for mirror access or haggle over who's prettier. Maybe you want someone who needs you just a splinter more than you need them. So you know they won't up and run.

When you've loved and lost, you want some stability in the emotional department. When you been a dandelion blowball in the breeze, you just ache to come to rest.

Our third anniversary, we buy each other plain gold bands, go picnic on Gray Whale Cove, then go see *Chinatown* at the movie house. I guess we're turning into a respectable, boring, staid, civic-minded dyke couple.

We got our ups and downs. You just couldn't last so long without. Fay complains I'm hiding things, including my family and life history. She doesn't believe my folks went missing on their way to Chicago. We've still got sleeping problems. But people got baggage. You got to be there for the other and carry through.

Things can sneak up on you when you're happy and busy. Fay has got a staff job with the *San Francisco Chronicle*. Now, its rival the *Examiner* is owned by the Hearst family, and it just happens that Patricia Hearst, who is William Randolph Hearst's granddaughter, had become suddenly the major news. First she gets kidnapped by these hippie kids, who call themselves the Symbionese Liberation Army, who are against poverty and injustice and such, and in favor of free food for the poor and world revolution. Then Patty is heard calling her family pigs on some tapes they release. And shortly after she's seen on surveillance camera, holding a rifle, helping in a robbery of the Hibernia Bank in the Sunset District. And Fay is running around covering all this. So Patty has become this disruptive killjoy third party in our household. She only has to be seen in Oakland, or shoot up Mel's Sporting Goods shop, or hijack a Ford, and the weekend gets canceled indefinite, because Fay gets called out, to follow in her messy, shot-up wake.

Anyhow, it's during some enforced quiet time for Patty, after her arrest, that Fay spots my inner color showing through.

"That's some suntan you're developing there, Lee."

"Yeah. Strange thing is"—I lift the band of my panties and peer inside, down the arch of my hip—"I got it all over. Like everywhere."

"It's café au lait, isn't it?" Fay observes. "More than golden. And your hair's darker too. You henna-ed it, or something?"

I cock my head to the mirror and finger the strands. It's real odd. I got dark auburn streaks coming through from the roots.

"Know what?" I squint at myself. I detect a distant echo. This skin tone is what the old folks called *mulatto*. "Maybe I should get myself looked at . . ."

"Just get it checked," says Fay. "You never know."

There are two photos I've always carried, recessed in the darkest folds of my purse or wallet. They're the pictures Uncle Nat gave me, when I went back to Eureka—Mama at the New Orleans dockside, and one of Celeste in a restaurant, sitting stiff-backed over a plate of crawfish, wearing a simple silk dress and pearl necklace, cheroot in one hand, fork in the other, outstaring the camera.

"Look, Fay," I say. "What do you think?"

"Shit, Lee. It's you. It's uncanny."

Yeah, you got to suck the heads offa them crawfish. And them tails

"My grandmother, Celeste Saint Marie du Cotton," I explain. "It's the genes. They always hunt you down in the end."

"When you told me about your family," says Fay, "you never happened to mention some were black."

"You prejudiced all of a sudden?"

"I'm no bigot." Fay is gone awful pale and steely. "But a partner has the right to know these things."

"Shit, honey. I guess you're right . . . Truth is, I been working army fashion."

"What?"

"Disseminating *as and when* on a *need-to-know* basis. Walls have ears . . . ," I explain her.

"Army?" says Fay. "And what would you know about the military, you airhead cherry seed? And you got anything else you want to get off your chest?"

"Guess you know it all now, baby."

Well, I didn't want to lumber her with all that guess-what-honey-I-used-to-be-black-before-I-was-white-and-a-man-before-I-got-to-be-a-woman revelation crap. You don't know how people will take things. You can say too much. You can scare people right off. Things got a way of dribbling out when they're good and ready.

It isn't the first time that Fay has advised I consult a doctor— for my memory lapses, troubles sleeping, nocturnal howling, missing periods.

This woman who bleeds once a month and goes rabid with cramps is concerned I can't enjoy the same experience. Now it's my tan, for chrissakes.

But things are getting steadily darker, in particular nipples. The areolas gone from amber to hazel. I'm passed through a Hawaiian bronze to something more ethnic-looking, bordering Latino. And whatever it is, it's progressive.

Anyway, I am walking Lower Haight, back from a shoot, when I see a doctor's bronze sign in a doorway. The plate says he's a dermatologist, which I just happen to know from "Increase Your Word Power" in *Reader's Digest* means a skin doctor. I guess someone's looking out for me. You don't have to be a neurosurgeon to understand his plate is a *sign* from somewhere.

I tour the block, chewing it over. Then I duck in. It's one of those impulse spur-of-the-moment purchases.

Dr. Calvin Chandler is a wizened, white-haired, cold-fingered, warmhearted, glint-eyed, dry-witted dwarf of a black man, sitting on a very high chair, driving a real large desk. He doesn't sound too surprised or fazed when I tell him I'm changing color. He's got hyperpigmentation too, with black blotches under his eyes and over his knuckles. His specialism is real personal questions—

1. Where do I come from, down South?

2. How would I describe my racial origins?

3. What do I mean—Iceland black?

4. How long have I been this color?

5. Do I spend much time in the sun?

6. Am I sexually active?

7. Am I pregnant?

8. How are my periods?

9. Have I noticed any decrease in my body hair?

10. Do I drink heavily?

11. What is my line of work?

12. What is my diet?

13. Do I take an oral contraceptive pill?

14. Would I care to undress?

15. Do I have pains in my finger joints or abdomen?

16. Does my family have any history of Peutz-Jegher's syndrome, xeroderma pigmentosum, Albright's syndrome, Addison's disease, or similar?

17. Would I care to put my clothes back on?

He is mainly drawing blanks, looking discouraged, bordering testy.

"Anything more you can tell me," he asks, "regarding your medical history?"

Well, I tell him how I've been doctored little, but intensive, so while I got no medical history to speak of, I had a couple of major operations. So, he asks what these were.

"In confidence, Doctor?"

"Sure," he says. "Absolute and total. Nothing leaves this room."

"Commissurotomy on my head," I concede. "That's when they cut my brain in two, to stop me having fits. And later I get my body work done. All over."

"Body work?"

"Sex change."

"Indeed?" His eyes flicker with interest behind his half-moon spectacles. "This wasn't manifest on first examination . . . Mind if I take a second look?"

After some palping of my abdomen and close-up scrutiny of my tits, he says, "Really nice work."

"You recognize them?" I ask. "They were big in *Barbarella*. Can't claim much credit myself. They were Jane Fonda's, first time round."

"And this," he says, "is wonderfully crafted."

"Well, *that*," I explain him, "is Michelle Angelo's. The whole caboodle. Pretty, isn't she? I often get complimented . . ."

"What *artist* did all this?" he asks.

"Gene Devine," I say, "a mechanic in Nevada. He used to be a doctor."

"Professor Eugene Devine"— he nods—"is one of the world's leading restorative plastic surgeons. He specializes in burn victims. You were very fortunate to gain his services."

"He got scary, stary eyes?" I mimic Gene's scowl.

"He is known for a certain intense expression."

"Crazy, bulge-eyed Gene." I smile. "He made it good in medicine? Who'd have guessed it?"

Anyway, now the doctor can narrow it down. It turns out that high doses of estrogen, like I been taking to feminize myself, cause melasma, turning you browner. Plus head trauma can affect the pituitary gland. And getting kicked repeated in the kidneys can damage the adrenal glands. And all of these kinds of damage can give you chronic hyperpigmentation. And we better do blood tests to see where we stand with our endocrines and melanocytes and whatnots. He draws off enough blood from my arm to jug a couple of rabbits.

Ten days later Dr. Chandler rings me out of the blue. He invites me back. There's nothing I need worry over. Not overly. But he needs to talk things through.

"Good news," he says. "Your pigmentation is nonpathogenic. You haven't got Addison's or Albright's or hemochromatosis— which are conditions that make you very sick."

"So what have I got?"

"Pritzburger-Laycoff's syndrome."

"That's good?"

"You have type three, which is the best there is, because type one gives you leopard spots, while type two gives you broad blotches, whereas type three lays an even pigment all over. And it doesn't compromise your health. You've got cells in your skin called melanocytes. They lay down color. Yours are going manic."

"What causes that?"

"Mainly adrenal shock. Perhaps from the time you were beaten up."

"You got treatments, Doc, for this kind of thing?"

"Young lady," he says frosty, "contrary to popular opinion, black skin, in itself, is not an illness. Some wear it with pride. Most often in Pritzburger-Laycoff's, there is no pathological cause."

"Sure," I say. "Understood . . . Only I got a particular personal slant. I grew up a white black boy. Now I'm turning into a black white woman. I was just hoping to get things stabilized some . . . You always been black, yourself?"

"Seventy-two years, man and boy."

"You'd like to turn white?"

"At my age, lady, you become conservative. I'd rather keep things just as they are."

"That's my point," I explain him. "I like my color. It's just swell. But I need to know where I'm headed. The ways things been, as soon as I get used to a sex or a color, I been moved on."

"That might all be over now."

"Yes?"

"It strikes me"—he gives me a thin smile—"you've exhausted all the major options."

"You reckon I'll stay put as a *black woman*?"

"That's my eighty-five-dollar prognosis."

"Suits me fine." I smile, reaching into my bag for my purse. "I been looking for some stability in the skin department."

Tell the horny bastard to get off his butt and marry Leonie

"Sir?" I say. "You helped me cheap. Can I help you cheap?"

"How?"

"I smell loss, sir."

"You smell loss?"

"It's dark green, sir, and fusty. It's peppery and smells like a cello."

"That so?" He hoists his brows and observes his ceiling.

"Your dead wife, Marianne, sir. She wants you to know . . ."

"What do you know about Marianne?" He's screwing his eyes and creasing up his face.

"She says you lay your receptionist, Leonie. She's a good lady. So why not marry her? Get the companionship and home cooking too."

"Is that so?"

"Look," I say, "Marianne is happy, at peace. She just wants the same for you."

"Yes?"

"No side to it. All she want is your happiness, sir. She wants you to know." I reach across the desk and press his hand. Guy better get his skates on. He ain't got that long to go.

"Did she say anything else?" He's dabbing his eyes with a large polka-dot handkerchief.

"She says she forgives the other things—the incidents in Philly and the dental nurse in Baltimore with the loose morals and the wonky eye."

"Is that so?" He sniffles. "Can you pass a message back?"

"Shit, no, sir. It's all one-way traffic. The dead is kind of fixed in their ways. They talk but they don't listen. You'll have to answer back for yourself."

22

Echoes

All autumn I seem to be growing gradual darker. But I like my new tints and relish my changed looks. I got the shades and hues I was born to. The way I see it, I've grown into my skin. I've gained in luster and sheen. You get higher contrast. The light's real kind to your cheekbones. You get a broader tonal range. Plus now I'm consistent—skin and background.

I guess somewhere I crossed the threshold. Sure, I'm light, but I've turned definite black. It likely happened weeks back. Maybe overnight, twisting in my sleep. And without waking, or sensing anything different, I crossed the magic racial line.

The only trouble is that my hair is straggling behind my mocha Josephine Baker skin, a glossy chestnut gold with auburn glints, showing darker at the roots, that makes it seem I've been bleaching black hair, like I'm maybe unhappy with my natural racial look, so I start darkening it down with Clairol ebony, which still leaves me reddish highlights in the sun. I'd have more curl put in but the perm turns it real dry and brittle.

Maybe I get pulled over more. The police need to know how a woman like me gets to drive around smiling in an imported MG roadster. They look me over. They admire my lean lines, hide seats, walnut dash, and spoke wheels. They ask about my chassis, speed, and age. They like to wiggle my dinky gear stick. Sometimes I'll show them under my hood. It needn't end unpleasant. Often a ticket's deserved. I'm not a conformist behind the wheel. And I never been a keen observer of prohibitions, red lights, lanes, or limits.

On the streets, folks I used to know can walk straight by, eyes fixed ahead.

"Susan," I say, "don't you recall? It's me, Lee." They wince at my outstretched hand on their wrist. They're fearful of street robbery. Their eyes keep flicking down to their handbag.

"Lee?" You can see the strain in the eyes and forehead.

I know what's going on. They look me up in the book of memory under the wrong headings. They going to "B" for black, or "N" for nigger—not "H" for human or "F" for friend.

"That Lee!" they say when I explain. "I remember you some-how *different*."

"Different how?" I ask. "Maybe the cut of my hair?"

"Can't put my finger on it . . ." They don't like to mention color, and how they knew me way back, before I got to be a nigger.

And in the elevator in our apartment building, I've been getting askance. The neighbors stand a little farther back now, give less chat and look glassy-eyed, like we've never met.

. . . used to be a safe, respectable building. Now we're overrun by black dykes . . .

"Who do you work for, young lady?" asks the platinum blond widow from 25B.

"Whoever pays best," I say. "I'm freelance."

. . . sure don't pay these rents to share an elevator with 12G's maid or some colored hooker . . .

Fay has left early. It's the buildup to Patty's trial. I am disturbed at nine in the morning by two heavy-footed, impatient, out-of-breath, jumpy boy soldiers hammering the door. They're pink and moist, perspiring fear.

"Hi," I open up. "Can I help you guys?"

"Do you know a Lee McCoy, lady?"

"Yep, that's me."

"You?"

"Sure. Can I help you some way?"

"Born September 14, 1949, Ste. Genevieve, Missouri?"

"Well, kind of," I concede. "But only in a roundabout way."

"Private McCoy, formerly posted to Fort Scott, Nevada."

"Hey, guys." I chuckle. "My service days are long behind me."

"Don't be so sure, soldier."

"How come?"

"Welcome back, Private." I feel the cold steel of a handcuff being slotted onto my wrist.

"What's going on?"

"You're under arrest—for desertion."

"This take long?" I ask.

"Three months to seven years. You a WAC or something? We came expecting a man."

"Shit," I say. "Look, my partner's out. Can't I leave a note? And explain her what's come up?"

Dear Fay,

Lana rang. She's coming round Tuesday. Be sure to check the motor oil. Chicken in fridge.

I got arrested by the military police who say I'm AWOL.

Echoes and stuff. Complicated. Long story. Hard to explain.
Back whenever. Love you like crazy. Think of me nights.
    Lee

Army rumor tells of military prisons and how they're designed by Harvard psychologists, staffed by sadists, to make life ten times worse than normal service. You don't know where they'll put you. Could be Guantánamo, Cuba, or Alaska. The army gets ornery rigid. It's going to be real tough on a lady serving time in a man's joint. Guys could take advantage, especially sharing a cell. I am twitchy, gut-knotted, nervy. I need a friend.

I am bundled into a metal cage in a dark airless van and driven to this military base in Oakland where I am held alone in a cell. There's a series of military types come eyeball me through the bars. They're not happy either. They've got a docket-prisoner contradiction. The guys went out for a white man and came back with a black woman. But it's sure hard to argue with military intelligence.

I get led out to an office where a doctor checks me over in silence. My height's spot on, my weight ball park, my teeth match my dental records, my scars are just where they should be, but my gender and color don't check out.

"She's all woman," says the doctor, "and genuine black. But she's got the white soldier's mouth and his upper face."

"Shit." Sergeant McWatt whistles. "We've got one fuck-up here."

I've only been there six hours when Fay turns up with a lawyer.

I got to give you fair warning about living with an investigative reporter. There may be a lot that escapes them domestic, like where the clothes basket is, what the wastebin is for, or how to purchase toilet paper. But when they latch on to something professional, they go for it like a cat for a mouse, and even after they shake it and kill it stone dead and gnaw its head off, they still won't let it go. But flick it around with a paw or toss it in the air, to see how it lands. Fay's always been that cat-way inclined.

They arrange to see me alone in an interview room.

"I've been briefed by your partner. So please don't say a word," says the lawyer. "Let us do all the talking."

"But . . ."

"Not one fucking word, honey, you half-wit," says Fay, "not without our say-so."

From what I gather from the raised voices around me, once the military comes join the discussion, Fay and the lawyer are trying to muddy the waters and pursue a mistaken-identity angle. They're working the line that the U.S. Army having lost a white male shouldn't arrest a black female and subject her to trauma and wrongful imprisonment, because it's clear as day I'm not the real McCoy.

Then I sense someone's been digging me up, and my suspicion is that it's Fay, rooting around sneaky behind my back.

And the army police guys are frowning and passing round my photo and papers from my file and peering at me and shaking their heads.

"You ever served in the army, lady?" they ask.

"Let me put it this way . . . ," I begin.

"My client has nothing to say," says the attorney. "And nothing to answer."

"I'm a reporter with the *San Francisco Chronicle*," says Fay. "If this is how the military operates, this is building into a really strong story . . . We're thinking front page and human interest. We're considering punitive damages. We're lining up easy scapegoats to carry the can."

"Look, lady, my hands are tied. We follow procedures."

"It's purely a paper problem," advises the attorney, tapping the thick red file marked *McCoy L. J. H.—Private* down the spine, "and if you care to leave the room for ten seconds, we could relieve you of it entirely."

"That, sir, is a soldier's entire record . . ."

"Exactly," says the lawyer. "Elegant, isn't it?"

"Lose him?"

"Call it a mutual compromise. You've got the wrong person. We don't want a recurrence. It would suit us all. The problem's gone." The lawyer smiles magnanimously. "You've got a 7 percent desertion rate from 1971. That's ninety-eight thousand folks you can go pick on. Why have you got a fixation on this one?"

"The teeth are unusual and match precisely," says Captain Brewer. "We've certainly arrested the right mouth. We intend to hang on to that."

"It doesn't pan out," says the lawyer, "because my client is not legally divisible, and her mouth is not a discrete persona, so, habeas corpus, you're illegally imprisoning four limbs and a torso, and we'll go play the racial and sexual harassment angles."

The captain considers a moment, then slides the file across the table. "I just know you're pulling some scam," he observes, "but God knows what it is . . ."

Fay reaches out, scoops up all the papers, packs them in her leather briefcase, and clicks the lock closed on my military history.

Back home, Fay doesn't talk but stretches out glacial chill and still on the sofa and won't respond to touch, talk, telephone, tickling, gratitude, massage, chardonnay, or Chinese takeout.

"You got issues, honey?" I ask.

"Issues?" she asks. "Me?"

"How's Patty?"

"Patty's in deep shit."

"You mad at me, or something?"

The lady shrugs. "Do you think you've been straight with me, Lee?"

"In my fashion, Fay. We all got baggage, haven't we?"

"This isn't baggage, Lee. This is a fucking freight train."

"You coming to bed, honey?"

"Later," she says. "I've got some reading to do."

I lie awake in the dark of the bedroom. Through the crack of the door, I can watch her rustling through my file, rubbing her forehead, taking notes, sighing, tapping her pen, wrinkling her brow, clucking. At five past one in the morning, I swear I see her briefly smile.

At 2 A.M. she stows her papers away, comes in, and snuggles into my back. We lie still, unspeaking, in the spoons position. Her breath pants warm on my neck.

. . . you promise you'll never splay yourself wide-open to beauty again, because it is shallow, mean, spiteful, and snide and snickers up its sleeve, because they are the big cats and you are the small furry thing that ducks into holes, and you just have them poking around halfhearted, never rooted, because they're doing you some favor, and the beautiful heart is fickle as a butterfly, and its desire more treacherous than its face is ever freckled pretty . . . and every time you're suckered again, boy and girl alike, and start all over, as if you can never learn, and scare them off with intensity, and stale desperation gets to smell awfully foul, but you still try to bind them, bore them with fidelity, and dampen them with your plainness, jade them with your dull demands, and drag them off proud for meat loaf and opinions with your moody mother, and slurred golf-swing advice from your father, and hope they don't notice sister Lulu is a bit

*loopy, and ask them if they've got any Thanksgiving plans and
do they like cranberries . . .*

"You awake, Fay?"

I get a sharp intake of breath and an indecisive grunt.

"This a trust issue, honey?" I guess. "And, hey, thank you, baby,
for getting me out of the slammer."

"Trust?" asks Fay. She jerks up and switches on the bedside lamp.

Things evidently been brewing and bubbling in her mind and
turned her hurt, shrill, and vehement, blotching up her face, resentful ugly.

She remarks there's nothing to trust. It's all floating. There's no
solid ground. My whole story is crazy. I've got no personal history,
and no bank account or driver's license, and nobody writes, and nobody phones. So she'd supposed bad, melodramatic things. Like I'm
escaped from some asylum for the criminal insane or just out of jail,
on the run from the Mob or the police, or married with some crazed
husband chasing.

"It's like you're taking me for a sucker," says Fay, "or daring me
into spying on you, going through your things when you're out, and
because there's nothing personal, I suppose you've got some other
place where you keep your private stuff and your lover. So I end up
following you when I'm free to see where you go. And I'm taking a
wineglass to O'Shea, the sleazeball in Vice, in confidence, so he can
do some prints and check them against the files, and he finds nothing, only the army, so he says, like he truly bothered. And I'm looking up the real McCoys in the phone book in every town I visit, and
going back to the Missouri records, because you say you were born
in Ste. Genevieve, and finding this kid registered seventeen years
late, out of an address belonging to some neurologist who says,
'Sure, I knew Lee. He was a patient of mine for a couple of years.
What's the poor half-wit doing these days?'"

"Christ, Fay, you been real busy. You did all that for me?"

"Hardly, Lee. I did it for me."

"How do you figure it so far?" I ask. "I don't claim I understand it all myself. Except I got restless skin."

"Look," she says, swinging out of bed. ". . . I'll get my notes."

On top of the wad, she got a torn piece of paper—

How come?

    1. CIA/military experiment?

    2. Extraterrestrial??

    3. Paranoia?

    4. Life is a dream?

And she's drawn me a timeline, with *Lee? McCoy?*—*chronology* underlined top of the page.

". . . I've got a kid admitted to Charity Hospital, St. Louis in 1966, with severe neural trauma. There's been a near-fatal assault by persons unknown. He recuperates. One of his doctors takes him in. He isn't the full ticket, but he can hold down a menial job at the hospital. He gets drafted at the end of 1969. He's a private soldier doing crazy Psi War stuff in Nevada in 1970. He's been selected for his psychic abilities. He goes AWOL after a year. He pops up in San Francisco in 1972. His face is much as before, but he's collected a woman's body along the way. She starts working as a model. Then she finds she's got a flair for photography. She's white-skinned from a black family. But in her mid-twenties, her skin has started darkening. Now she's turned black. If there's logic to it or natural causes, I'd really like to know."

"People change," I reassure. "Along life's road, there are many bumps. It's not so odd."

"Two races, two sexes, one person? In a handful of years?"

"Hell, honey, forgive me for living. I can't change who I am."

"You're inchoate, Lee. You're plastic; you're protean. What happens next? Are you going to grow wings or transmute into a fawn?"

"Now, honey," I warn, "stop right there. You're getting unreal, fanciful, and pitching fly balls over my head."

"Do you love me, Lee?" Fay is gone puffy, wet-eyed on me. She's got winding tear trails down both blotchy cheeks.

"I sure do. I've lost so many people on my way. I'm going to cleave to you."

She wraps me in her arms, draws me to her bony chest, and starts rocking me like a child. "I was on my way out before I met you. I was off my head every night on booze. I was hateful, spiteful, and vengeful. I didn't have a smile or good word for anybody. I was a pimple on the face of humanity."

"Easy, Fay. You choking me."

"I'm not going to let you go, Lee."

"Good."

"Know what I'm going to do?"

"What?"

"I'm going to get to the very bottom of you. But you've got to be straight with me."

"Sure, Fay. It's a long knotted story. What you need to know?"

"Family, first," she says. "Let's get your pedigree."

So, then, I'm rattling off my antecedents, best I know them, and she's jotting and ripping up and starting again. And within an hour, we got a clear picture of where I come from, and against the odds it turns out my family is real organized, tidy, and respectable-looking. And it's kind of democratic in the bloodline business because everyone's equal in the genealogical scheme of things, because they don't have to do anything special except subscribe a sperm or contribute an egg. But Fay says my Granddaddy Walter Strongman is well known for writing and drinking and served time in Hollywood, and through him I'm related to some serving senator and judge.

In the end, it looks like this:

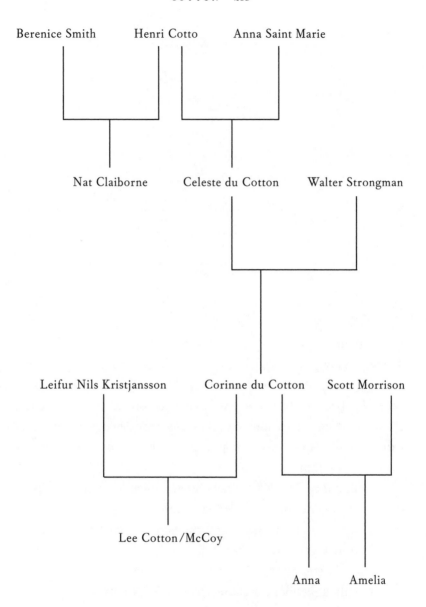

"You ever seen your half sisters, Lee?"

"Never. Mama moved on. I lost all touch."

"Your folks can't be that hard to find. Leave it to me."

23

Coming Out

But in the event, it's Fay's family that grabs our attention, because her daddy Jonathon, who is a sweet, harassed man with a stammer and runs a shoe store in Minneapolis, has let his medical insurance slip because business has been bad, on account of better, cheaper foreign shoes and, shit, now Fay's mother Lydia has fallen real badly ill with a breast lump, and God knows how they can afford the operation and radiation.

"Hell, honey," I say, "I'll help best I can and maybe go back to do some modeling. But the only way I know to make big money real fast is by taking advantage of information and abusing the future, which can risk you terrible karma."

"How do you mean?" Fay asks.

"I've thought about it but never done it," I tell her.

"What?"

"Gambling," I explain her, "on the scores and results coming up."

"Yeah, you bimbo, sweetie, and how do you happen to know the scores?"

"Future memories," I say. "Shit, I never tell you? . . . In the army my buddy Ethan jumped around in time. In '67, he got to spend some time in '76. So he got to hear sports results, in advance of everybody else."

"Oh, yeah," she demands. "So who wins the Super Bowl?"

"Steelers beat the Cowboys 21–17. So Ethan said."

"World Series?"

"Cincinnati over the Yankees, four to nothing."

"The Kentucky Derby."

"Bold Forbes, isn't it, Fay?"

"You sure?"

"Ethan's never let me down."

"So why have you never bet on results?"

"Upbringing, I guess. Leftover faith. Baptists don't gamble."

"It isn't gambling, Lee, if you know the results."

"But then it's dishonest, ain't it, Fay? Cheating the bookies?"

She kind of eyes me sideways and snorts.

"But, hey, your parents matter way more . . . How do you do this betting anyhow?"

The game is ten days later, January 18, at the Orange Bowl, Miami. We watch it at home on TV. As it turned out, it was a real classic matchup and fingernail game, even knowing the result in advance.

First quarter ends 7–7. Tony Fritsch kicks a field goal to put the Cowboys ahead again. Gerela misses a couple of field-goal chances to advance the Steelers' score. Third quarter ends 10–7 to the Cowboys, and I can see Fay is getting twitchy, nervy.

"You laid a bet?"

"Too fucking right. Two thousand dollars–plus. All I had in the bank."

"Lot of money." I whistle. "That going to win you much?"

"Nothing," says Fay, "the way it's going. You and your fucking future memories."

"Beats me," I confess, "how we get from here to 21–17. I guess the game gets real busy at the end." Because we're three-quarters through and the defenses are dominating.

Fay's gone luminous pale and retreats to the bathroom. After a couple of minutes, I hear some heavy retching.

Anyway, Reggie Harrison blocks a Dallas punt for a safety. Then Gerela gets two field goals to put the Steelers ahead 15–10.

Fay comes back looking gray and concerned, and a bit wobbly on her pegs.

"How long left?" she asks.

"Three and a half minutes left on the clock."

"Christ, Lee." She retreats toward the bedroom.

"Don't worry, honey," I shout. "All we need is a touchdown each end and a Steelers' missed conversion."

Then it starts coming good real quick. Bradshaw hits Swann for sixty yards into the end zone. Then the Cowboys answer, when Staubach hits Howard with a thirty-yarder. So now the score's just how it should be.

The Cowboys defense holds. And then they come back. It's looking ominous until Edwards intercepts Staubach and runs it back to the Pittsburgh thirty-three as time runs out.

"Hey, Fay, honey," I call, "it's all fine. You can come out of the cupboard now. My boy Ethan got it just right."

And I swear that night, and the whole next day, she was happier than Chuck Noll, the Pittsburgh coach, Terry Bradshaw, and Lynn Swann, all rolled into one. And she was bedroom-pleased with me till early morning like I was Most Valuable Player.

It turns out you get crazy odds for an exact-score wager. Fay had spread the bets over several outlets and got herself real unpopular by winning $126,000. Plus you even get to keep your original stake money.

It was a real godsend for Fay and her parents. But I felt kind of soiled and sly, cheating those bookmakers, who rely on folks not knowing in advance and are likely sensitive behind their swaggers. And they likely got needy dependents and sick family all of their own. But when all's said and done, at least it was only money they'd lost, instead of anything real important. And I guess, in their soft inner hearts, they'd be pleased to know they were funding the medical care for a real sick lady.

"Fay," I say, "if we're going to do this regular, we're going to have to be sharing the winnings."

"Naturally, Lee."

"Because if I'm going to go stealing from connected Italians on a regular basis, I want to put something back into society."

Patty goes on trial on February 4, and Fay is chasing round the edges for material the other papers haven't got. This is real fine-grain investigative stuff. Did Patty report her occupation as revolutionary? Was she fed LSD while she was held? Had she got pregnant by Cinque Mtume, the leader of her captors? Was the defense counsel wearing pancake makeup? Did Dick Alexander, who was covering the trial for the *Examiner*, wear a *Fuck You* tie as a message to Randolph Hearst who was spiking his copy? Did Catherine Hearst say she rather her daughter was dead than a communist? What prompted Patty to say "Fuck off, Daddy"? And what did Daddy say back?

It's all murky and conspiratorial, and Fay is up to her neck in it, so I am real surprised when she comes home one evening with personal news, about me.

"Hey, Lee, I think I've found your daddy at last."

"You're kidding?"

"It's a small population in Iceland. I had a foreign correspondent chase a government contact in Reykjavík. He's come up with a Leifur Nils Kristjansson, aged fifty-two, ex-seaman, married twice, with three daughters and a son."

"What does he do, Fay?"

"He's a taxi driver, and he keeps horses."

"That's him. I've always seen him with horses. He got a limp?"

"Don't know," says Fay. "I've only got the headlines over the phone. We've got a photo and background coming in the mail . . . And I've some news from your old home."

"Home?"

"Miss-iss-ipp-pee." She drawls it slow and stupid, with drunken hiccups. Like it's funny down there. Or something.

"Now, that's your first mistake. It's pronounced *Miss Hippy*. And it's nothing to laugh about. Christ, Fay, you been stirring down there or something?"

She says it's work. She's being sent South to cover the Carter campaign. Plus there's some trial in Meridian too. Some old Klan members are up for shooting civil rights workers back in the sixties. It's the third time they've tried them. They got off twice before. Now, there's a crusading DA and black jurors. They're going to nail them. And it's national news, because it seems like the South is finally purging its past. And this all links with Carter because of Regeneration and a New Deal.

"I've got an interview lined up with the candidate himself. I need a photographer. Do you want to go home and take some pictures? You can be my translator. Explain the local manners, and what folks are talking about in their slurred, lazy way."

"Sure, Fay. Count me in. I've haven't been back for years. Time I caught up."

Now, Fay is not ashamed of me, socially speaking, except she prefers when we mix in company that I stick decorative and smile silent and act dumb, which is a role I am usually pleased to act because often the conversation drifts over my head or wafts through my ears and, things being equal, I prefer to eat and drink than monologue about the morality of journalism, who fucked who first, the literature of Márquez, the filmography of Pakula, or the Daughters of Bilitis.

Now, Fay is no party animal, but she is sometimes required to attend for office reasons and such, and sometimes brings a partner to show she is human, after all. Then, it's painful to watch her morph all artificial, smile at people she hates, and simper insincere.

And we are at this all-female gathering, seated round an oval oak dining table, so there's no easy escape, because we are waiting for the *colored staff* to bring the main course, when there's mention of the *transgender problem,* on account of this Ray Rivera who changed his name and parts to Sylvia and has gotten involved in the Gay Liberation Front as a woman.

Practiced opinions are dealt like cards on the table. Then the hostess, this dictionary-swallower, book-writing sociology professor lady called Maude, says that it is impossible to change gender, and that anyone who tries is a victim of male fascist medicine, and a patriarchal tool, and a penis in the women's shower room, and a travesty of the female, Frankenstein monster, divide-and-conquer freak, and that the lesbian forum can only be for *women born as women*. And all this feels real prickly close to home. And I am watching Fay coughing up her zinfandel, purpling up her complexion, and fidgeting with her sesame roll. And maybe I've drunk too much, but sometimes you just got to speak your mind.

Lady don't know shit, chile

"You don't know shit, lady," I say. Now, this isn't an original thing to say and may sound a lame double negative out West, but in central Mississippi it comes across as fighting talk.

Well, the gathering falls real quiet. Some folks look to the bloody traces in their soup bowls, some snicker, and the bold ones turn curious to me.

"No?" asks Maude. "What would you know about anything? And while we're on the subject, why do you dress like a ten-dollar whore?"

bitch needs to look at herself in the glass

I refill my glass. I reach down for my handbag and extract my makeup mirror. I pass it over. "Maude," I offer, "best advice I got is you take a clear look at yourself in the glass."

"Yes?" she says. "Why?"

"Appearances . . . ," I explain. "You look like Tony Curtis in *Some Like It Hot*—before he puts on the drag. That's your choice. I look like Josephine Baker in cabaret. That's mine. We got to work with the latitudes we're given. When I got my nuts cut off, I made the best adjustments I could. All my life I been hounded for being born the wrong color, or the wrong sex, or dating the wrong person, or living in the wrong place. We ain't what we're born. We're what we do with ourselves. So I'll be the gender I choose. I'll wear what I like. I'll do as I please. I'll love who I want. I'll talk when I care to and say what I like. And you can just go fuck yourself, lady, but thanks for the bread sticks and gazpacho soup."

Then I rise unsteady to my feet, because two bottles of cabernet sauvignon 13 percent can go to your head, and scrape my chair back. "Fay, you old dyke," I say, "your lady's leaving. You coming or what?"

To do her justice, she jumps up real quick, smiles uneasy, searching in vain for a friendly eye, waves a stifled silent good-bye, and shuffles around by the door, facing the wall, pretending to rummage for our coats.

Out on the street she finally finds her voice. "Nice evening. Next time, don't hold yourself back, Lee. Speak your mind, why don't you?"

"Excuse me, Fay. She may have doctorates in doctorology, but she's all redneck at heart."

"You know what you just did?" Fay cackles. "I believe you just came out. Then you insulted the Queen of San Francisco in her palace."

"Shit," I say. "No kidding? I hope she isn't the kind to bear a grudge . . . But you don't mind, do you? All that backstory stuff . . . That I used to be a guy. And black, and white, and black again. And I served in the army. And grew up down South. And I play the stereo too loud and snore . . . that kind of stuff."

"I suppose I was riled at you holding things back. But the way I see it"—Fay squeezes my hand—"now I know everything. These things made you what you are, Lee. They contributed to your character."

"Shit, honey"—I stray my hand down her lean butt—"that's the sweetest thing . . ."

24

Hi, Y'all

We could fly into Jackson and rent a car. But I say no, I'll drive every mile of the way. I want to pace my fall South, carry my own shell, have my out, my escape, because experience of Eureka tells me it's wise to have your departure fixed in advance of your arrival.

So we take the Interstate 40, for four days straight, dawdling off where we can on the old 66, until we hit East Memphis. Then we drop south on 55.

Like a feather blown on the breath of God

We check into the Briar Holiday Hut. The young white lady at reception doesn't seem fazed to find a black and white dyke intent on sharing a bed. She just gets our number off Fay's American Express.

"That it?" I ask. "You've taken us, then? We're all booked in?"

"Welcome to Briar. Enjoy your stay. Would you care for a local map?"

"Hell, no need, honey." I smile. "Me, I'm local. I know here-about like my own diddly pout."

I leave Fay at the motel, phoning to fix some interviews, while I drive off to go see how the land lies. I want to see what folks have done with the place while I been away.

The Cotton house looks real well-cared for, dressed up like a Norman Rockwell picture, with the clapboard newly painted cream and the window frames sage green, with neat picket fences, a pebbled path, and freshly mown lawn. Nat made sensible provision for his retirement by siring four sons. I see the man sitting in a rocker on his porch, under two blankets in the sweltering heat, withered and frail with a head shrunk away like a prune.

Aunt Hannah waddles out scowling to greet me. She's wearing an apron on which she's wiping her floury hands. "Help you, miss?"

"I'm looking to see Nat. I haven't seen him in a long while."

"He's sick. How you know Nat? You local or what?"

"Know Nat from way back, when I was a kid."

"I don't remember you."

"Miss Hannah, don't you recall? I used to play with Herbie."

"Age." She sighs. "It addles the brain."

She says I can talk brief to Nat while she bakes some muffins. He likes pretty women. But I mustn't tire him. She points a finger to her temple. "Don't expect too much. The cancer," she says, "it's gone climbed the stairs, up to the attic."

I draw a cane chair up alongside. Nat's rheumy eyes flicker open and slowly wander my face. He nods and squints. Then smiles.

"Celeste?" he asks.

"No." I pat the parchment of his hand. I sense he only got a few days left. "But you're real close."

"You an angel, lady?"

"No, Uncle Nat. It's me, *Lee.*"

"Huh." He smiles. "I bury you. So now you come back to bury me."

"Neat," I agree.

"You got the nails to hammer me down?"

"Guess so."

"Nickel plate or galvanized?"

"What you prefer?"

"Nickel's best."

"You got it." I stroke his arm.

"Mules been milked?"

"Sure," I say. "All under control. Everything seen to."

"I got a wife?"

"Hannah," I say. "She's baking out back."

"Fat lady? Gappy teeth?"

"That's her."

"I seen her around." He nods solemn.

"Good lady," I say.

"Tell her count the babies and go write the number on the prison wall."

"Good as done, Nat. You gone gabby in your old age."

"Growing a heavy crop inside . . ." He coughs. "Nearly harvest-time."

"Soon, Nat, I reckon. Real peaceful. With all the family gathered round."

"They given you any plumage, Lee?"

"No, Nat. Just skin and bone."

"Huh." He slowly closes his eyes on me. His chin jerks down on his chest. He's blowing frothy bubbles from the side of his mouth. He's lapsed into a snuffly sleep. The flies have settled again on his scalp.

"Bye, Nat." I squeeze his shrunken hand. "You're a good man.

You saw plenty and you lived good." I lean over and brush my lips on his twitchy cheek.

It was always the same with Nat. He talks brief and indirect, but he always gets his point across.

When I swing a left at the Briar crossroads, I am whacked by memory, as I get hit by my past, speeding headlong toward me, blaring a warning.

There's my Angel, sprawled naked in the hay barn. I can feel the prickle of straw on my butt. I can taste her mouth and smell the talcum off her bra and hear the skim of cotton on flesh as she slides her pants down her thighs.

There's the Klan come calling in the Chevy.

There's Byron peering under his steaming hood. There's the stench of sulfur and burning rubber.

These things, coming back out of the blue, can beat the drum of your heart, jerk on your breath, yank your pulse, twitch your face.

A mile down the road I'm cruising past Byron Clement's house. I slow to read the homemade sign by the broke-up fencing.

PRIVATE SALE
(no agents, lawyers or scum)

HOUSE, MACHINES & 5 ACRES
OF SOUTHERN HERITAGE

— KEEP OUT STRANGER —

Now, Mr. Byron Clement has become becalmed in a slow property market, because the post found the leisure to acquire a near-fatal lean, and the paint on the sign is blistered and faded from several summers' sun.

I check my mirror, then reverse up slow and admire the facade of the Clement residency. The place looks overgrown, deserted. There are waist-high weeds out front, a thick crop of carpetweed growing on the roof tiles. The front door is clattering the frame, swinging in the breeze. I step out of the car and slam the door.

"Private," says a voice to the side. "Can't you read. It's private land."

I look left to find a wizened old gnome of a guy standing hunched in the shadows of a cypress, dangling a rusted machete in his hand. He's bronzed dark as me, wearing a Raiders baseball cap, faded from black to bottle green. He's dressed in frayed overalls with no shirt underneath, so you can see a boll of silver cotton strands in the center of his plucked chicken chest. He's wearing oversize laceless boots. The guy looks like an emaciated derelict.

I gulp. I don't want to leap to any hasty, nasty conclusions and presume he's full mean as before. Maybe age has mellowed Mr. Byron Clement. It could be he's become a racial liberal, in the fullness. Could be he's been redeemed by the Good News about our Risen Lord.

"Admiring your spread, suh . . . Saw the For Sale sign."

"You ain't local, are you?"

"San Francisco," I say. "But I used to live real close. I been visiting people and places I used to know."

"If you know hereabouts, you should know this is a *white* spread." He gives a wide sweep of his hands to take in the tumbleweed, star thistles, and nettles, rusted oil drums, and doorless, wheelless Pontiac coupe, supported by stacks of bricks under the axle. "Always was. Always will be. So it ain't for sale to colored peoples, spics, dagos, perverts, kikes, or chinks, however much they paying."

"Hell," I say, "I'm as American as you."

"You reckon, coon?" Byron frowns, tweaking a sprout of silvered ear hair between finger and thumb.

"How much you want for the place, anyhow?" I ask.

"Family home. Inheritance. My folks built this house. Couldn't sell it to some out-a-state nigger, who's got rich on the back of the white man, driving some foreign car . . . Rather burn it to the ground."

"Yeah?" I say. "Understood." I know he's got a history of razing buildings. "And while you're talking of family, how's Angelina?"

He cocks his head and narrows his eyes. "What you say?"

"Your daughter," I remind him. "I heard she made it in music, for a while. What's she doing now?"

"No fucking business of yours," he advises.

"Used to know her way back," I explain. "We used to play around as kids."

"Well, hell, Angelina . . ."—he gazes skyward—". . . after she fucked around with a nigger, she was some muff-licking dyke, then she got knocked up by a Polack hippie, before she married some Hebrew shyster."

"Right . . . ," I say. The last part comes as news to me. The way he tells it, he sounds real disappointed by her love-life choices, and he still wears his opinions on his sleeve. "She's been round the block, then?"

He considers me with still eyes, in silence, sucking in his cheeks, gathering all the loose fluids he can summon up in his dry old mouth to gob down by my feet.

"Don't get *personal* with me, coon poon. I ain't your friend, and I don't know you from rat shit."

"Hey," I coax, "relax. Lighten up."

I come prepared, with some beers in the trunk from McCoy's store. "You fancy a drink, suh?" I lift out a six-pack.

He eyes them greedy. I pull a tab and lift the can to my mouth. "Still chill." I sigh. "Real thirst-quenching."

Now we got an uneven tussle between the bigot and the lush in him. I watch the contest play across his twitchy face. I sip my drink, knowing which demon will weaken first.

"You can hand me a beer if you like," he concedes, looking around uneasy, guilty. "I can be sociable. Only it don't make us friends. A free can of suds don't buy me."

"Sure," I say, passing one over. "That's gracious of you, suh. Let's drink to Progress and Family."

"And to Dixie," says Byron, draining the can. "They real tiny, little rascals. You got another?"

He pulls the tab on his second can. "To southern hospitality," he ventures. His eyes keep flicking back to the remaining beers laid by my feet. I suppose he's calculating how pleasant he's got to be to earn them.

"Thanks. You ain't so bad," he concedes, "for an out-a-state colored lady. You just don't know your way around."

"Hey." I beam. "You're one sweet-talking man."

"We never had no color problem. Until the liberals come along. For to teach the niggers to make one. Everyone knew where they stood . . ."

Byron starts his conducted tour of Delta history, explaining the pecking order of the races and the natural harmonious order of things—how God made the man to govern woman, and race to govern race, and made the black man to labor because he was strong but indolent, and made the white man master because he was fair and kind.

Somehow, it doesn't make full sense to a black lady. I'm prompted to ask him about the Klan.

"Klan?" He shakes his head in disbelief. "Weren't never no Klan. Kikes in Hollywood invent that shit."

"I just been reading about the Klan trials. In the papers . . ."

"Black-on-white persecution . . ." Byron scowls. "Chasing innocent patriots just because they got white skins. Governor Waller starts all this—packing the courts and administration with blacks."

"Yeah?" I say. "Now, tell me, suh, you learned anything new these past twenty years?"

"Learn?" he asks. "What's to learn? World's gone crazy." He blinks. "Now the niggers got everywhere. Even running things. No offense. You spare another beer? They're weak as piss but I'm real thirsty."

"You know we met before?" I ask.

"I reckon not, else I'd remember."

"You must recall . . ." I bristle. I take it personal. When someone's done their level best to slaughter you, they got a moral obligation to remember the event.

"You confusing me with someone?"

"No, sir. We go way back. We got history. It's *personal*."

He gives a long unblinking stare; it's meant to intimidate or something. "Who are you, then?" he inquires.

I look into the deep creases and sunken curves of his skull face. I stare at his hazy gasoline eyes, fogging up with cataracts.

Equal opportunities. You got all sorts in creation. They all got their place and purpose. The Lord ain't facetious. He's got his own good reasons for everything, even the louse, hookworm, and hyena.

Byron was never a pleasing sight. He never got given the tool kit to be adaptable, clever, appealing. Few could ever have loved or liked him. He inherited some mean demons, and he drew some very short straws.

He was a real hurtful hinge of my life. Some doors closed; others swung open. But I can't regret the paths I took. I been interesting places. I met and loved fine people—Ethan, Doc Gene, Ellen, Fay.

"Me?" I say. ". . . I'm the Iceland nigger on the Briar Road. I used to hump your girl in Cooder's barn. So I've been on the receiving end. Baseball bat and boots. So don't give me any of your innocent crap, 'cos I know what you are—a quart of shit in a pint pot . . ."

He scrunches his face up like brown paper; he slumps forward to peer at me with his crusty face and lost baggy, sunken eyes. He gulps dumb and startled like some bemused, deformed, scaly abyss-dwelling fish, above its depth.

"Knew someone . . . like that . . . He was a guy. He was pale."

"Hell," I say, "that's progress. We all move on. We can't get stuck in a rut."

"You? Him?"

"Me."

I watch some blunt feelings working his face by turns. We got perplexity, fear, hate, and then a feral slyness.

"What you want?" he growls.

"Shit. To be honest, I don't know. I just needed to take a final look, maybe hear you explain yourself . . ."

"When you get given a second chance," says Mr. Byron Clement, slapping the flat of the machete blade against his thigh, "praise the Lord, it's a crime not to take advantage. So, this time, I'm going to *do* you, no mistake."

And the crazy old dude is bouncing on the balls of his feet, flailing around with his rusted old blade, grunting narrow-eyed like some Shaolin monk out of *Kung Fu*.

"Hey, look at yourself, old man." I dance back and advise, "You think you're David Carradine?"

"Going to cut you, nigger," he whispers intimate, confidential. "In half."

"You better be careful, you fucking old buzzard," I warn, "or someone's going to get hurt, for real. And you're going to make me angry. First you attack me as a boy, now as a woman. Don't you have any respect for human life?"

Then he lunges, slashing down. I'm bending back, but I've left my leg outstretched, and I watch the blade strike down on my thigh, and see it sink in, and feel a sharp ache and the dull thud of metal on bone, then my leg opens pink and glistening, like a wedge of watermelon, then darkens from a thick crimson spread of syrupy blood. There are winding trickles down to my ankles. It feels warm and tacky between my toes.

I jump back. I see spatters of my blood glistening on nettle leaves and see a length of two-by-four lying like a ridge in the grass. So I pull it up to parry his lunges. And I could likely take him straight out with a jab of the timber into his face, but it's easier and safer to dance a few yards ahead, on account he's slowed down by loose boots and rattling breath from his emphysema.

We stop, still but poised, four feet apart, staring each other out, when I sense a spasm, then a wobble to his bowed legs. And I see from the spreading dark stain down from his crotch, he's taken the pause in hostilities as an opportunity to empty his bladder.

Then his fingers splay wide and the weapon falls to the ground. He stoops, hands on knees, heaving and coughing, to try and recover his breath. He's flushing up an unhealthy purple. Then he sinks to his knees with a real startled expression in his swimming eyes.

"Huh . . . ," he says. "Haa . . ." Then he topples forward, flat on his face in the dirt, outstretched arms gone quivery and his feet twitchy, before he falls still.

I kick the machete beyond his reach. I roll him over with my loafered foot. He's got glazed eyes, a still face, blue frothy lips, and no evident pulse.

"Shit," I say. "I never meant for it to end like this."

Well, I do have an unpleasant choice. But not long to decide. This is the man who broke me up with a baseball bat. Also Angel's daddy.

I know one thing. You got to strive to be better than the thing you despise. And a life is a life. It isn't man's to discard.

"Well, fuck you, you poisonous, loathsome bastard." I sigh. "Making me do *this*. To *you*."

I lower myself weary to straddle him. I sit myself astride, my butt riding his bony hips. I hook the buttons on his shoulder straps and pull the bib of the overalls down, to expose his scrawny ribs. Then I start.

I'm striking his chest double-fisted. Firm to start, then hard enough to crack his bones.

And, yes. Shit. Then, of course, I got to part his lips, prize open his jaws, fingering the warm slime of the cavity and the rasp of his tongue, levering against the sharp, jaggy stumps of teeth, then lower my mouth onto his and share my breath, and pump my life into him, following the mouth-to-mouth resuscitation procedure, as taught us week three of basic training.

It is peculiar unpleasant to perform this maneuver on Byron Clement, on account of the smells and tastes, because he has soft, white curdy stuff speckled all over his lips, has regurgitated some beer and lunch down his bib, and has a sulfurous oral cavity, with some broken brown stumps, being a heavy smoker while a stranger to toothpaste and dentistry all his life, plus he's wet himself, so he wouldn't be high on anyone's kiss list, not to mention his real poisonous personality, never mind our past history.

But shortly, we got an irregular jerk to his chest and a slow throb to his wrist. His gray face goes twitchy, gradually pinking up, while his glazed eyes flicker. This evil bastard has got as many lives as a cat.

I knot a scarf round my thigh to narrow the split and slow the trickle of blood.

I drive to the gas station and call for an ambulance. When the paramedics see the gaping wound on my thigh and my sticky scarlet leg, they say they got to take me in too, because I need tetanus, sewing up, and stuff. So Byron and I take a final ride together, sharing an ambulance to Briar.

He's laid out on the trolley, blinking startled at me, like he's struggling to remember me from somewhere.

"Where am I?" he slurs.

"It's a kind of hell, sir," I explain him slow, "of your very own devising."

And it brings a slow smile to my face, to think how strangely intimate I been with this demented family, straddling them both in my time. And I feel strangely satisfied, like all the old scores are settled. And I can finally move on, unburdened by Clements.

It ate me up over the years that he wasn't in prison, serving life. But seeing him here in his home, I realize he'd been his own mean jailer all the while, no hope of parole, serving his own hard time, hiding from the light, stifling his soul. He'd built his own cage cell, desolate, pitiful, and comfortless. So, now, he can perish or live. I just don't mind.

"What?" asks Fay, when I ring her from the phone booth on the ward. "Where are you? Where have you been?"

"Hospital," I explain. "Machete wound. Left thigh."

"That some local greeting?" she asks.

"Accident," I say. "Seven stitches. The blade just nicked the femoral artery, so I needed a blood transfusion. They're holding me in overnight."

"I'll be right over," she says. Fay's reliable calm in a crisis. It takes some real life-and-death big deal to faze her.

25

Someone Goes,
Someone Returns

Next morning, I sign a disclaimer so I can discharge myself early. I ring Fay immediate, then I'm limping impatient round reception, looking at my static watch face, eyeing the entrance, waiting for her to come pick me up.

"Sit next to you, kid?" I ask this square-headed fat kid. "My leg's throbbing bad." He's swinging his feet a foot above the floor. It's turning into one long reunion.

"You sick?" he asks, spooked by my proximity, sliding his butt surreptitious, farther up the bench.

"Nah, flesh wound." I pat my gauze bandage. "What's your name, kiddo?" I ask.

"Phoenix," he says.

"Well, *Phoenix*, fancy that. I bet you a dollar I can guess your age."

"Go on."

"Seven. I'm sure of it."

"No." he beams. "I'm five, going on six. Pay up."

Reluctant, I wrestle a green one out from my purse.

"We come to visit Granddaddy," says Phoenix. "He got a heart attack. He's a famous killer. But the cops could never pin it on him."

"You don't say? Not every kid can claim as much."

"Can't brag about it, though."

"No?"

"We live on a good street so people mustn't know. And Daddy's big in the movies. So it's bad for business. And Mommy says keep mum, if I want to stay in private school."

"Sound advice, kid."

"You a *black* woman?"

"Yes, Phoenix, I believe I am. More or less. Guilty on both counts, as near as dammit."

"I never met black people before."

"You don't say, chile."

"We don't have them on our street. Unless they're Sidney Poitier or they come to clean the pool or pick up the garbage."

"Nice," I say. "Where's that?"

"Benedict Canyon."

"Los Angeles?"

"Yes." He frowns. "But you don't say it like that. Not if you're *educated*."

"Well, that's my problem, Phoenix. I didn't pay attention or stay long enough at school."

There's something about Phoenix that isn't right. Maybe it's a matter of proportion, his stocky torso and short limbs. Perhaps the nasal giggle and unblinking owl eyes. Maybe drinking LSD through your mother's milk leaves a lasting impression. Naturally, I sympathize. I been mistaken for odd myself.

"I bet you a dollar I can guess your mother's name."

"Nah." He giggles. "You never could."

"It's Anastasia, or it's Arminta."

"Close." He frowns, admiring. "It's Angelina. Pay up."

"Y'all one happy family, then?"

"Don't know. But we're *winners* and we're *rich*."

"Well, that's the next best thing. Your mommy and daddy get on good?"

"Suppose. He's not my real daddy. We borrowed him for his house and money. But now he says Mommy's turned *cold*."

"It happens," I confirm. "Phoenix, can I give you some advice?"

"About what?"

"About life." I reach out for his wrist and feel his small, racing, jiggedy pulse.

"Thing is . . ."—he eyes me sideways and gnaws on his lip—"I don't know if I'm allowed to take any *black* advice?"

"Don't worry, kid, I used to be white. I've seen both sides."

"Suppose, then," he concedes.

"You must try not to disrespect people, Phoenix."

"Yeah?" He blinks surprised. "Why's that?"

"Because everyone's got dignity. We're all the same under the skin."

"Even poor or ugly people?"

"It makes no difference."

"What if they're stupid or smelly?" He frowns, trying to untangle the puzzle. "Black or yellow?"

"They're equal, all the same."

"Yeah?"—he blinks busy—"No one's ever told me *that* before."

"And, kid, you've got to keep a real careful eye on your mother."

"Why's that?"

"You know why," I guess. I wink.

"The pills? And her drinking?" He flushes rosy.

"Exactly," I agree. "You've got it in one. So what are you going to do when you find your mother deep asleep, and you just can't wake her?"

"Leave her be? Let her sleep?"

"No, ring for your daddy at work. Get him to call an ambulance."

"Okay," he concedes.

"I want to help," I say. "Take this, kid." I lay a *gris gris* in his palm. "Don't let your mother see it."

"Hey." He frowns down at it. "That a *chicken foot*? With a *fish eye*?"

"Is a diamond just carbon?" I ask. "It's a good-luck charm. It's to ward off danger and the evil eye."

"Thanks, lady," the kid says, kind of unconvinced, wrapping it in Kleenex, stowing it in his jacket pocket.

"Phoenix. Phoenix. Come *here*." It's Angelina striding across the waxed floor, clattering her stilettos mean and hard. "I've told you not to talk to strangers."

Compared to her hippie days, she cleaned up starchy brittle with a glossy veneer. She thinned down plenty, and she got those thin creases in her face, starting to show. It comes from frowning down at the world. Delicious acid lady.

"It's all right." I smile up, to reassure. "I'm kind of harmless."

"Maybe." She scowls over the tops of her shades. "How's a young kid to know the difference?"

"Hey," I say, "remember me?"

"I can't say I do."

"You look real familiar."

"I used to be known in the music industry," Angel concedes.

"I grew up round here," I say, "and I sure know *you*."

I see the fear in her gaze. I see the eyes flare wide. I see the fierce mother protecting her child. I see incredulity. I see dignity bobbing its tail like a fleeing rabbit. I see nose quiver and nostrils twitch. I hear the cockcrow. Tight lips twitch.

"*Whoever* you are," she says in clipped, starchy tones, "we've never met. You're confusing me with someone else."

"Hey," I protest, "it's me, *Lee*."

She closes her eyes. She nods slow, without surprise or enthusiasm. She sinks down weary on the bench opposite, like she's been slugged. Her shoulders slump, like the wind's been taken out of her. She frames her head in her hands, eyeing me up.

Fucking shemale pervert, always sniffing my ass, dogging my tracks. She's turned back into a nigger now and she's come back to gloat

"Lee . . . ," she says at last, "I remember you *paler . . .*"

"I used to be white," I explain her, "but I got real restless skin."

"It's not that I'm not pleased to see you, Lee . . ."

"No?"

"My daddy had a massive coronary," she says. "I had to fly down. We thought we'd lost him."

"No such luck," I sympathize. "So he's been hiding a heart all the while?"

"Family." She shrugs. "What can you do?"

"I know how you feel. I got one too."

"So . . . ," she says.

You got to act quick with Angel. She'll most likely disappear for five years, marry someone else behind your back, or change herself someway fundamental. So I know I got to cut to the quick.

"No offense, Angel, but I got to ask a personal question. Would you like to come live with me? It goes without saying, your boy's real welcome too."

"No, Lee," she answers immediate. No need for thought. She narrows her eyes and shakes her head weary. "But thanks for the offer."

"No?"

"Water under the bridge . . . Compatibility, sexual orientation, husband, commitments, and such . . ."

"Yeah," I agree. "But I like to ask whenever we meet. At least I got it off my chest."

"I'd better be going, Lee." She gives a tart little twisted smile.

"You know we're going to keep meeting up, Angel?" I warn. "Through the years."

"We are?"

"I'm sure of it. There's some crazy link. It's like I've been put on this earth to watch over you or something . . ."

She rises and reaches across for Phoenix's hand. "Take care, Lee. See you around."

"See you, Angel. You going to give me a good-bye kiss?"

She hesitates, awkward, her arms stiff by her sides, face twisted away so I can peck her cool cheek.

I watch her hurried retreat down the corridor. Say what you like about Angel, she always had a spirited sway to her hips, a noble tush and eloquent back. Phoenix hobbles along beside, struggling to keep pace.

Do I feel disappointed? I guess I do. A mite, a tinge, a touch. But if experience has taught me something, I've learned it's a real patient long game, courting my Angel. And, someways, it feels like we married already, only living apart. Because there's no doubting we're tied real tight, for life, but by a very long rope. And I know we're going to keep meeting up down the line, every few years or so, whenever she needs me, or something.

Fay wanders up. "Who's the Ice Queen?" she asks. "With the Troll?"

"A girl I used to date way back, Angelina, and her son, Phoenix."

"I saw her in the can. She's really thorough at washing her hands. Like Lady Macbeth. We caught eyes in the mirror. I'm sure I know that face from somewhere."

"Some moneyed L.A. wife," I say, "turned real snotty. The kid's all right, but he's got a lot to learn."

It's a real popular funeral, with a thick crowd at Nat's graveside and seven black sedans. I see Mama arrive with Scott and the twins. I hang back from the crowd as the Reverend Spinks gives his oration. Time and place and such like. I say my personal farewell.

Mama seems shrunk and bowed. She's wearing horn-rimmed spectacles. Scott has gained round the waist and grizzled some.

The twins must be ten now, I reckon. They're a secret society of two. They've got knowing looks and gestures, and nods and winks, and telling silences, private unto themselves. You never see more than two clear inches of daylight between, and even then they're holding hands. They wander near and perch together on the wall, tapping their heels on the stone.

"Now one of you must be Anna and the other must be Amelia?"

They smile conspiratorial, purse their lips, and look to each other.

"And I'm trying to work out which is which . . . ," I explain. "You don't know me, and you won't believe it, but I know you. Bet you can't guess who I am."

"You on the *Loony Tunes*?" asks one, earnest, unblinking.

"You the Bionic Woman?" asks the other. So I know, at least, they got a sense of mischief.

"No such luck. I'm your long-lost brother, Lee."

They giggle in sync. They each put a hand to their mouth like they covering a burp.

"What?" I ask.

"We've seen Lee's picture," says one.

"We've got his photo on the wall," says the other.

"So?" I say.

"Lee's pale; you're dark."

"Lee's a boy; you're a woman."

"Lee's dead; you're alive."

"Lee looks like a dork; you're real pretty."

"That's the evidential case," I explain, "but appearances can be real misleading. As you likely know yourselves, because people think you're identical, but you're truly very different, aren't you?"

"That's true," says one.

"That's right," says the other.

"You going to carry a message to your mama for me?" I ask.

They raise their eyebrows in mute unison.

"The message is a secret. It's only for your mama's ears. It's this: *Someone goes and someone returns.*"

I watch them run over. They take turns to whisper in Mama's ear. She stares my way, desolate forlorn. She turns and trudges over. A yard away, she stops. She lowers her head to gaze on me regretful over the rims of her spectacles. She squints. She comes close. She frowns. She looks away, moist and glassy, like a glare hurt her eyes.

You always been a thorny, burdensome, heartbreaker kid

"Hey, Mama," I say, "ain't you got a hug for your prodigal son?"

She spreads her arms wide. She takes me in. I'm snuffling and she's sniffling. We're wetting each other's cheeks. We got some heaving and quivering too. We're one flesh, two bolls of Cotton, rolled into one, mother and daughter. I'm smelling sweet sorrow, salty tears, and lemony talc.

Opening my eyes at last, I see we've drawn a curious crowd. There's Scott and the twins, Fay, the Reverend Spinks, Aunt Hannah, Cousin Herbie, and more, gathered in a semicircle, looking on curious, like we're some cabaret double act.

Who that fancy lady with Mama Morrison?

Mama glares, mops her face with a handkerchief, steering me away, down the path to the gate, to privacy. When we got some distance, she turns and eyes me up hard.

"You, Lee, are one *changed-looking boy.*"

"Guess so, Mama."

"Why you all got up in fancy dress?"

"This," I protest, "is a Chanel suit. Out West, it's considered sober smart."

"Are those your very own titties?" she demands. "You insisting everyone eyeball."

"They are."

"So, you gone changed into a woman, or something, son?"

"Yeah, Ma. Things happened along the way. Praise the Lord."

"That a permanent condition?"

"Yeah. Some things in life you just can't undo."

"Hmm." She grunts disapproving. "So how you get dark?"

"That," I say, "is a skin condition."

"I got to tell you something, Lee." She squeezes my hand. "You're so far changed . . . it takes a mother to recognize you."

"I know, Mama. It's a long story. Fate's played some odd tricks on me."

"So, why you never write?" she demands.

"I wrote. No one answered," I protest. "I came back and found you gone."

"So, where you been these last nine years, three months?"

"St. Louis, Nevada, San Francisco."

"You been looking after yourself? You been eating well?"

"Sure."

"You been attending a church, worshipping regular?"

"Sure, Mama, on and off. And how you been keeping yourself?"

"So-so. We had our ups and downs. You got yourself a livelihood, Lee?"

"Photographer," I say.

"Families and weddings?" she asks.

"Politicians, actors, and musicians, for newspapers and magazines."

"Maybe it's less than I hoped for," she clucks, "but if you're happy . . ."

Then Celeste sounds off in my head, after a long time away, and clear as a bell:

Yeah, so what you ever do with your life, chile, except get knocked up by some Iceland sailor, marry a fool, and wear your knees down on the church-house floor?

"Happy, I am."

"So how you fixed *personal?*"

"Personal," I say, "I'm fixed real good."

"Excuse me for being old-fashioned and asking, Lee, but is this with a girl or a boy?"

"A woman."

"You don't say . . ." Mama lapses into silence. But sideways, I can see a metronome twitch to her cheek. Sometimes, with a mother, whatever you say turns out to be wrong.

Oh, yeah, Corinne Arminta. You all respectable now, now you all dried up, and butter wouldn't melt, not anywhere

"Is she one of us?"

"How do you mean, Ma?"

"Black, son."

"She's white."

"But she's a Baptist, right?"

"Jewish, Mama."

"She's awful beautiful, then, or something?"

"She's got *inner* beauty."

"She's a *pleasant* person, then?"

"Acid and feisty. But she truly loves me. With a vengeance."

"That's something . . . at least."

"Sure is," I agree.

"About your inheritance from Celeste . . ." She screws up her face.

"Yes?"

"I'd better tell you now . . . to avoid unpleasantness later with Scott."

"What?"

"We had you buried. So the money passed to us . . . The upshot is, it's spent."

"Christ, Mama. What the hell? I've already inherited the best that Celeste got to offer. Often it feels like she's very close. The money doesn't mean jack-shit."

"Mind your mouth, Lee. This is sanctified ground."

"Sorry, Ma," I say. I reach out for her hand and feel her racing pulse.

You going to warn her, cher, about the angina, or what?

"Mama," I ask, "have you ever had a doctor check out your heart?"

It takes a licking and keeps on ticking

26

Redemption Lite

So there was no home to return to. Nat is dead. Our old house is sold. Mama and Scott are moved to Atlanta. They'd tried Chicago, Detroit, and Cleveland, but these places weren't all they were cracked up to be, morally questionable and grudging of opportunity. So gravity started to draw them southward again, through Cincinnati and Nashville.

Scott opened his own insurance business but hit a bad run of claims. He bought a dry-cleaning franchise in Cleveland. But the crook he bought from opened a competing store across the street and undercut with newer machinery. So Scott eventual sells back at a loss.

The Clackers and Mood Ring outlet started real busy, but fizzled out like they were just some craze. The Pet Rock and Baby Alive looked surefire replacements and, in the right hands, gave hours of innocent enjoyment, but in the end, they never truly took off, not in any financial sense.

Now he's got a newsstand outside a station, which did real well till the commuter line closed down.

"That's the way business works," Scott tells me. "You win some, you lose some."

"If you got any money left," I advise, "you could invest long term in computers. Time's coming when we'll all have one at home. The thing to look out for is *software*."

"Nah," he says. "Have you seen the size of a mainframe? That stuff's just science fiction."

"Or bet on Cincinnati to take the World Series."

"They can't win two years running," he warns. "The wise money's on the Yankees."

"Or if Mama needs money, just ask me."

"Anyone told you look real foxy as a lady, Lee?" he advises. He likes to look. He likes to touch—pat, stroke, and graze—mostly butt, back, and legs.

"Thanks," I say. "But, hey, Daddy," I warn, "ain't that your hand, strayed onto my rump?"

Mama hasn't taken to her newfound daughter so straight-forward. I don't doubt she loves me the same as ever; it's just she finds me hard to explain. She doesn't feel happy calling me *son* or *daughter*, so she's taken to calling me *offspring*, until she settles on *issue*.

I tell her I'm earning. I promise I'll send money regular. I tell her I'll come visit next year for the whole month of August and bring provisions to pay my way. I'm going to make up for lost time. I intend to get to know the twins. I'm particular taken by Amelia. She got the sensitivity for both.

Back at the Briar Holiday Hut, sprawled on the bed, I sense this niggly itch between the shoulder blades.

They unsightly, chile. Ain't nobody told? A lady got to pluck hers regular . . .

Fay asks if I want to go up to Louisville, May first, to see Bold Forbes run the Derby live.

"All right. For sure. Can you give me a back massage?" Fay's kind of fussy clingy. You got to give her personal jobs to do, so she doesn't feel excluded.

"If you packed a bottle, Fay, I'd sure welcome a drink. And you get me any of those little smokes? While you're at it, honey, better rub me down all over, never forgetting the sensitive out-a-sight bits."

"What did your last sex slave die of?"

"I'm thinking after Louisville, we could duck down to New Orleans. Try the restaurants, clubs, bars. Maybe run into some guys . . ."

sossidge, Tujagues, po-boy, couche-couche, muffulletta, suck some crawfish heads, laissez les bons temps rouler. Jig-a-jig, cher. The whole Schwegmann's

"Guys?" asks Fay. Her hands, which were doing swell work on my inner thighs, have suddenly stalled.

"Figure of speech, honey. I meant *people*."

I've been a leaf in the fall. I been snapped from my stem, severed from my roots, blown high and low, gusted far.

This gives me an ardent wish list. I want to keep all the body parts I still got, God willing. I want to nourish the brains I retain. I want to stay the same sex and color awhile, so all sides of me can come full acquainted. I want to live among ugly and beautiful, young and old, black and white, man and woman, with beast, fish, and fowl. I want friends, kin, and strangers. I want American and foreign. I want my own roof, nearby water. I want to be grounded and I want to float. I want tranquillity and Mardi Gras, football and baseball, absinthe and milk, cocaine and grits, cheroots and fresh air, Cajun and zydeco, voodoo and Baptist, jazz and hymnary.

I've learned plenty along the way. You never know what's coming. The Almighty got himself a sense of humor. Gravity doesn't always behave herself. Skin got a mind of its own. The dice can roll thirteen.

Seems to me, everyone got the chance to be a jumbo shrimp. We're all small in the scheme of things. But each of us got the capacity to be big. We just got to find the grace.

I don't know what it is that keeps you feeling the same whatever the personal changes. For me it hasn't been race or gender, face or mind, circumstance or situation.

Celeste reckoned it was your two personal souls—big soul and little soul—*gros bon ange* and *ti bon ange*. But I don't know. I reckon they tempered along the way with the rest of me—so maybe your *self* is some deep, soft, hidden organ.

My spirit has toughened up with time and knocks. It's got less patience or reflex kindness. More often than not, I speak my mind. I ain't afraid to be rude when the opportunity presents. But I don't take myself so seriously. I sure enjoy acting cranky. I rejoice in loving someone. And I try not to hate too severely.

I can't abide two-tone talk like *Men do this and women do that* or *Well, you say that because you're black* or *What the kids don't realize is* . . . or *Am I right or am I wrong?* or *Are you Republican or Democrat?* or *Are you with us or against us?* or *Is that smoking or nonsmoking?* I always demand a third option.

My taste's are changing too. I've taken to cheroots. *Chacun à son goût,* I got a partiality for absinthe too. I partake of herbal energy powders, in moderation, derived from the coca plant. Those Indians knew a thing or two. I travel with my Lufa, my snake. Some of Celeste must have rubbed off on me. The genes always catch you out in the end.

As soon as we reach N'awlins, I know I come home. It's all fresh, familiar. Some folks hold their eyes, half smiling, as we pass on the banquette, say, *Where y'at*, like they know me already. This is where Mama and Daddy conjured me out of their hasty snatched pleasure. This is where Celeste knew her prime. I'm bent to N'awlins, which is twisted my way.

The gambling scam has given us capital. It just snowballs. The more you win, the more you can stake next time, the more you win the time after. Guys have started refusing our bets and asking questions. They're worried in case Fay has gone fixed the World Series. Anyway, enough's enough. You need a roof over your head and some capital in the bank for your indulgence. More is greedy. Once you start getting money-fixated, your life doesn't belong to you.

The time's come for Fay and I. She has to go back to her job in San Francisco. While I need to stay South awhile.

"This it?" She clings sniffy at the airport. "You ditching me, or something?"

"Hey, hon," I comfort. I nuzzle her neck. I pat her back. "It's just some time apart. There's things I need to explore. We can still see each other weekends . . . You fly down, or I'll come up."

"Yeah?"

"Sure." I release her hand.

The truth is, I need to loosen the knot a touch. At root, I'm shallow, emotionally speaking. I need to meet new folks. I need a break from monogamy. I need some new routines. And Fay's made real progress. I reckon she's got herself a real positive outlook now. She's off the sauce and pills. I feel she's most parts cured.

I'm renting a house off Esplanade and looking to get myself some new wheels, maybe a Mustang.

Or maybe a charmante Mercedes

Many people have gone the extra mile for me. You try to give back where you can. The way I see it, you don't turn away from someone needy. A few words of advice, an insight, five hundred dollars can turn a life around, pitched the precise, proper time.

As soon as you settle, you get grounded and start spreading roots. I get to know folks at the corner grocery, stallholders at the French Market, regulars at the rummage stores on Decatur, priests from St. Louis Cathedral, herbalists, peddlers of coca powder, staff at the Lafayette Cemetery and the Historic Voodoo Museum on Dumaine Street, musicians from Lafitte's and Donna's, barmen from all over.

Folks are warm. Sure, guys are an acquired taste, particular between the sheets, but they ain't so bad as they're written up. Fay flies in most weekends. Maybe I can get her fixed up with some nice bright boy who values integrity and brains, and doesn't just read from plain appearance.

It's been a bumpy ride from white boy to black woman. But every life got its reasons. There's always a Purpose to things, whatever. There's always someone bigger, more knowing, than you. You got to cede to the will of the Spirit, for sure.

It was Matt who first points things out. You know what it's like to have to pluck between your shoulders twice a week? And always entertain with the lights on?

Matt is my personal waiter at Peristyle. He's wide receiver on a football scholarship, yet majoring in philosophy. He's got talents scattered all over his corpus, like other folk got freckles. So I sense he'll go far. I've just borrowed him awhile. I'm helping him financial while broadening his CV. As beautiful young men go, he's adept, managing the high-wire act of balancing his passion and serenity, arrogance and attentiveness, promiscuity and fidelity, ath-

leticism and delicacy, demand and supply. On his days off, he sometimes calls to serve me at home. Often he stays over to give me a
rubdown and workout, with a relaxation class thrown in. Sometimes
he explains me Leibniz, or Descartes, or the mind-body problem,
Zeno's paradox, or crazy shit like that. He has strong firm hands and
is working my spine how I like it, when he stops of a sudden at the
resolute itchy spot between my shoulder blades.

"Lee, baby," he asks, "what's that?"

"That?"

"These . . . ," he explains, flicking the skin. "Tiny fluffy things
like . . ."

itsy-bitsy feathers

"Shit," I say, *"Merde."*

"And I'll tell you another strange thing, Lee."

"Yeah?"

"The curtains are drawn and the lights are off, but there's a radiance off your skin."

"It's called beauty, Matt."

"No, it's more than that."

"Charisma, honey?"

"More than that even. The plain truth is . . ."

"Yeah?"

"You glow in the dark, Lee."

"Glow?"

"You shine pale, phosphorescent. Luminous, like moonlight."

that nothing to worry over, cher, that just your Aurora Bleu

Is nothing simple? You think you're sorted, with all the bases
covered. You think you got yourself settled at last. Then something
always comes up to disturb.

I ring my personal dermatologist in San Francisco. He says, "Hi, Miss Cotton. Yeah, thanks for the advice. I owe you one. Leonie and I got married . . ."

When I finally stall his discourse on love and get round to explain him my personal problem, he sound real put out and surprised. He confirms I'm suffering a real bad run of luck in the derma department. He says I've got real restless skin. He says—the way the textbooks see it—bioluminescence is not unknown. But feathers are not an option.

"Don't wish to alarm you, Miss Cotton . . ."

"But?"

"There's a rational scientific explanation for everything."

"So?"

"It's off-the-wall, but go to an army and navy store and buy an old Geiger counter. Just to check yourself out . . ."

"Check out what?"

"That you aren't radioactive."

"Sure, Doc. Thanks."

Scientists, huh! And rationalists! What do they know? Life's stranger than they ever guess. They're listening to Mozart with earplugs in, complaining they don't hear nothing.

27

The Featherback Club

I take myself to Jackson Square and into the cathedral; I blink at the radiance from the stained glass of St. Louis; I sink to my knees on the cold stone floor; I ask the Almighty for guidance. Just give me a sign. Every soul got its purpose. I just need to know mine.

You're never alone in a church, child

Off to the side, I am aware of folks drifting in and out of the confessional boxes. They come all nervy and wired, and they leave contented, calm. I don't know what they're hawking there, besides kind words, but it sure delivers.

then, when I wake up I'm in a closet, Father, and I find my face stinks and my dick hurts

So I decide to duck in, to go try it myself.
It's marginal gloomy and chilly. I sense a pretense—that you're

not meant to make out the looming soul, God-side of the grille, twisting his rheumatic back, squirming his butt, flicking smears of breakfast off his teeth with a curled finger, waiting for the kidney pain to kick in.

Suffer them to come unto me. The wife beaters, the child molesters, the drunks, the perverts, the harlots, the lazy liars, the mirror watchers, the self-dramatists, the self-deluders, moral morons, the sheer fucking time-wasters

"I'm not a signed-up member," I start off. "But . . ."

"A member?"

"I mean I'm not a Catholic, sir. More a lapsed Baptist, but I was wondering if you got an open-door policy . . ."

"Christ embraces every last sinner. Do you want to confess?"

"Hell," I say, "I'll try anything once. And there's some serious shit to get off my chest . . . But, the way I see things, my priority is gaining *understanding*, not *forgiveness*."

"You have a dilemma, child?"

"Restless skin." I cut to the quick.

"Sins of the flesh?"

"Well, sure. Those as well. I'm no angel. I've tried most things once, both sexes. But it's not what I do with skin. It's more what skin does with me . . ."

"Tell me, then . . . ," he allows. Call me intuitive, but I sense he's growing testy.

"Medicine wasn't any help. So I thought I'd ask around—likely authorities, never forgetting the church . . . It's a surface condition, but progressive. You keep changing skins—sex and skin color— and it gets to feel like you're fated or something. Have you heard of it?"

"I have not."

"How about *personal plumage*? You had experience of that?"

"Plumage?"

"Well, look," I explain him, "in your line of work, do you ever run into any shiny folk, with back feathers?"

"Folk?"

"John Doe. Real ordinary. Girl next door."

"Feathers?"

"Real tiny, fluffy, gray white, like miniature duck down."

"Shiny?"

"Kind of glow very soft, bluish in the dark . . ."

"Are you asking about spiritual manifestations, child?"

"I don't believe I am," I explain. "Because, it just so happened, I met a manifestation once, when I was a kid. But he came across real ordinary-looking, if natty dressed. So the only physical give-away was his yellow goat eyes and the way he could *see*, despite being blind . . ."

"Are you on drugs, lady? Or medication, child?"

"Only the usual recreational stuff."

"Usual?"

"Alcohol, nicotine, cocaine, coffee, weed. That kind of thing."

"Look . . . ," he says, "I can take a joke as well as the next person. But do you know it's a sin to mock the church? Have you come here to waste my time, or what?"

"Sorry." I rise to go. "I know y'all do real good work with poor folk, the needy, and such. And I know there's a deal of sin to sweep up off the streets. So no disrespect intended. And I sure hope you get your faith back quick."

"My faith?"

"Well . . . Sometimes the flames die down to embers, don't they? And the rheumatism sure don't help. So we end up popping too many pills. We all get cranky sometimes, when we look back and regret."

"Look, lady, these small, sporadic, occasional *uncertainties*," he asks, "that don't quite amount to doubts, do they show in my voice?"

"Hell, no, sir. That's just my lucky guesswork. No, you come across real firm convinced as a rock. That's why so many folks rely on you. They come to you weak and go away strong. If anything were to happen to you—they'd be lost without . . ."

"Good to meet you, young lady," he says, with firmer voice and renewed conviction. "If you have any more problems to discuss, be sure to bring them to me. I'll see what I can do to help."

"Well, bless you, Father," I say. "And bless your suffering kidneys."

"Wait a moment . . ." I see his hands and lips pressed to the grille. "Have you been *sent?*"

"Shit, sir," I observe, "the way my life's turning out, that's a real possibility."

What do you do? You feel half normal, half charmed, and half persecuted. You just got to take life's blows on the chin. When you got a restless skin condition, you got to struggle on, best you can, and hope to grasp a helping hand along the way, because sometimes it feels like you can help everyone but yourself, for we're all joined up, in this riddle of life, together.

Two days later, on the sidewalk, down Decatur Street, behind Jackson Brewery, my nostrils twitch from an overstrong scent of a gentleman's cologne—musk, sandalwood, and lime. There's the tap of a twitchety stick on the paving, and I sense someone's keeping pace on my shoulder. I turn to find a distant-remembered face.

And the relentless loop of time, and the ear-throbbing Muzak of the spheres . . .

Yeah, but it truly is. It's James Jones VII, Interventionist and fellow traveler. I only met him once before, on a bus trip as a kid.

But he gave me advice and a glimpse of my future. And he sure left
a lasting impression.

He's wearing a three-piece silk lavender zoot suit and an egg-
yolk cravat with a single pearl tiepin. He's staring out blankly
through opaque sulfur-yellow eyes, sweeping the pavement clear of
fellow pedestrians with his long tappety white cane.

on call, all hours, as doctor, confessor, and call girl, rolled into
one, for the rude and the lewd, to lay down with them in their
mean stretch of gutter . . .

"Jeez, Louise," I say, "Mr. Jones . . . I been praying for you, or
something similar."

"Celeste's bleached-up grandson, Lee?" he asks, cocking an ear.

"Too right," I agree. "Good memory, sir."

"I sensed another presence. I see you've been working my turf,
son. I thought I'd come pay my regards."

"It's real nice to see you, sir. It's been a long while. You been
keeping busy, sir?"

"New Orleans, kid . . ."—he raises his blind eyes to the heavens—
"it's always been a busy station. A lot of work with the Big Seven.
Plenty of worst-case scenario stuff. There's a deal of Crisis Manage-
ment. At root, there's a lot of Rebranding. But you get to realize your
limitations. And you find gratitude is thin on the ground . . ."

"That so?"

"So what you've been doing yourself, son?"

"This and that," I explain. "Here and there. I've been round the
block. I've seen most sides. I caught a glimpse of the future."

"I heard about your promotion, but I kind of lost touch with
your career path, son. Have you got a CV or résumé on hand?"

"I don't believe I have, sir." But I pat my pockets, to look, to
show willing. "I believe I'm clean out today."

"You were always a really promising kid. How did you play it? Did you pick up a law degree along the way?"

I shrug and shake my head.

"Ivy League scholarship, I bet?"

"Nah," I explain him. "Some other kid got that."

"Master's in business administration?"

"No."

"Medicine?"

"Nope."

"Philosophy training?"

"Only homespun, from my uncle Nat."

"A doctorate in anything useful? I'm scraping the barrel here. And I'm excluding the social sciences, so don't give me any sociology or psychology crap . . ."

"Doctorate?" I confess. "No such luck."

"You've got languages though?"

"Only the obvious."

"Spanish, phatic, demotic, French, German, emotive, Latin, poetic?"

"No, only this one I'm speaking."

"Foul-mouth Delta farm boy?" He scowls and scratches an ear. "With San Francisco smart-ass overlay and some Nevada trucker sideswipe?"

"That's the one," I agree. "It says most everything that needs saying. It's rarely let me down."

"But you finished high school, right?"

"I got sidetracked, sir. But I did army basic training."

"Not much call for a *shootist*, is there? Not in our line of work. But I guess self-defense comes in handy. And you can't go far wrong with well-polished shoes."

"Right, sir."

"Well," he winces. "You've been *heart-hunted*, son. You've got to have something. You realize how much senior-partner time has been spent on progressing you?"

"Progressing?"

"Through the junior ranks and middle-management grades. You don't get chosen for nothing."

"Chosen?" I say.

"Sure. Few enough senior executive colleagues around. So I thought we ought to meet up. Maybe have lunch—exchange experiences, swap stories, talk technique."

"With me?"

"Who else?"

"*Colleague* to *colleague?*"

"Are you slow on the uptake, kid, or what?"

"Well, Jesus, sir. I guess I am."

I smile real broad. It all slots into place. So that's it. I see the pattern. I always guessed I was fashioned odd for some purpose. You don't get afflicted with voices for nothing. And ever since I died and came back, I sensed I was headed some way special. When you change color and sex, gain a glow and grow feathers, you're steered toward a suspicion that someone or something senior is playing some serious tricks on you.

So I'd had the signs in flashing neon. But I always need to have things underlined, with all the t's dotted and the i's crossed. Maybe it's army training. I don't like to take the initiative before I got the superior nod.

I guess it all comes as a weight off my mind, and a hefty load onto my shoulders. Still, as jobs go, being an *Interventionist,* with a capital I, ain't bad. Not if you like traveling and meeting new faces, getting acquainted with their feeling, rooting around in their private life, peering under their beds, and helping out where you can.

I guess it would help to get some business cards printed up.

LEE COTTON McCOY

INTERVENTIONIST AND PHOTOGRAPHER

· · · · ·

No job too big or small

RITA'S, 945 CHARTRES STREET, NEW ORLEANS

"Well," says Mr. Jones, "I guess what you lack in formal education, you make up in savvy, grit, and wit. You're a young soul, kid. And a profound slow developer. It means you've got a steep learning curve. You'd better start catching up quick."

"Guess so."

"It's not like we're hawking cola here."

"Understood."

"We're shorthanded as it is. If anyone slouches on the job, son, things fall apart. The center cannot hold. Then it's work down the line for everyone else."

"Sure. Understood. We featherbacks got to stick together."

"*Feathers?*" His face crinkles tight as a walnut. "You telling me you got *feathers* now?"

"Haven't you?"

"Son," he says, "each to his own. Some souls can't grasp the job until you stick them in a uniform. Others cotton on quicker."

Well, aren't I the bozo, half-wit, slow learner? We walk on in silence.

"Just tell me you haven't got *winglets*, kid."

"Winglets, sir? No, not me."

Sure, Bianca, I say, you got lovely wings, with real sweet curves, and an iridescent sheen, but in the sack they can really snag the action

"No offense, son." He softens as we turn the corner, onto Bien-
ville Street. "I guess you're here to help. N'awlins has always been
a test posting. Think of this as Sin Central. I didn't mean to ruffle
you any. Plumage can look real handsome, distinguished. On a
gentleman. In discreet moderation, under wraps. If you haven't got
a feather allergy."

He sneezes, then dabs his nostrils with a yellow silk handkerchief.
"Sure."

"So, do you want to take lunch?" He claps a forgiving, comforting hand on my shoulder, his long twitchy fingers reaching down toward the slope of my tit. "Maybe I can give you some pointers . . ."
He skims a hand down the small of my back.

*Well, doesn't eternity lag? Yet doesn't time fly? It seems like only
yesterday. But it's thirty-seven years since I last got laid*

Well, there's info I need from him. My head's buzzing with curious questions. How does this *Intervention* business work, anyhow?
I mean, I know we're working for God and Truth and Goodness and
Human Dignity. But even Republicans, Hollywood actors, and
lawyers claim as much. So what's our unique selling point? What's
the career path and prospects? How long do people stay in the job?
Are there set working hours, or do you slip in and out as you
choose? Is there some code of practice, like they got in law or medicine? Are we affiliated to anyone else? Or stand-alone? Are we
unionized? Is there anyone central, keeping a watching, overall
brief? Do we have some leadership structure? Or do we all just go
our own sweet ways? Or what?

I eye him sideways. This brittle-bone, scrawny old guy has sure
served his time. He must know all the ins and outs, gimmicks and
wrinkles.

He means well, I reckon. It's just he comes across awful cranky and painful lonesome, edging burned out. And all this senior-partner status play speaks real insecurity.

And I think he's hankering for some lady time, frisky between the sheets. And yet he seems to have got his genders confused, which means he's digging a dry hole, because I noticed the way he keeps calling me *son,* despite his wide roaming hands, which have touched on my hips and chest.

I guess I'll have to help him out, the very best I can. Because, the way I see it, he's a burnt-out case and *lunch* is a cry for help.

"Lunch. Sure thing," I agree.

"You tried the fried catfish in Mama Smith's?"

"It's good?"

"Kid"—he purses his lips and smiles his ecstasy—"it's pure angel food."